SCENT AND SHADOW

SCENT AND SHADOW

MERCY LOOMIS

ROOKERY CREEK MEDIA

For R—, always and forever.

There are still no words.

ACKNOWLEDGMENTS

Many people have contributed to this book over the years. There are some that need specific thanks.

The 2011 Write By The Lake Novel Masterclass: Christine DeSmet (instructor), Teria Robens, EK Schnabel, Karla Kroeplin, Jessica Vitalis, and Jennifer Bal. You all had tons of wonderful input and this novel would not be nearly as good as it is without you!

Toni Rakestraw (unbridlededitor.com) for the copyediting. Any mistakes are probably from where I decided not to listen to her.

The original E-Writers, remnants of the UW-Stevens Point writing group (1995-96): Erik Carlson, Victoria Grundle, and Laura Melvin. You guys have been putting up with this idea of mine nearly as long as I have, and your feedback (and patience!) have always meant a lot.

Heather Cook Peart, the only person besides me who has read the original, crappy, handwritten first pages of what became *Scent and Shadow*. And somehow you continue to be enthusiastic about my writing. It still trips me out that you and Jim named one of your kids Gabriel. Just sayin'.

James Peart, for being a cheerleader when I really needed one, and supporting me when I cut out of tae kwon do class for a few months to finish the first draft. Thanks, Coach!

My current writing group: Jesi Lea Ryan, "Zombie Joe" Alfano, R. Scott Steele, and Jennifer Lowe. We keep each other honest. And Victoria Flynn, who was instrumental in getting the group started without actually attending. Thanks!

My parents, for always encouraging me, even when what I wanted to do was too artsy to make money.

And most of all, my husband, for reading more drafts than anyone should ever have to, and for always, always being supportive of my writing, even when it was just a hobby, and especially when I was under deadlines. You're the bestest ever. (Mine!)

CHAPTER ONE

Madison, Wisconsin
Friday, May 14th, 1999

The itch burned in the base of his skull, dangerously strong, as Gabriel Chapel watched his prey through the haze of cigarette smoke.

She sat at the bar with her back to him, her face in shadowed profile as she talked to her two friends. Gabriel had no trouble finding her scent amidst the smells of smoke and sweat and beer that permeated the place; the absence of his scent-mark on her was a provocation he found increasingly difficult to ignore. He stifled the need to get up, to go to her. It had been hard to wait, but he wanted her undivided attention when the time came, needed to keep the disruption to her schedule as unobtrusive as possible.

She wasn't smiling tonight. She was jittery, playing with her drink, shifting in her seat, sensing his scrutiny as she'd begun to do over the last couple of weeks. Gabriel reached out with a psychic caress, the thought brushing over her defenses like a breath of wind against closed shutters, and noted with satisfaction the shiver she couldn't quite suppress.

Her searching gaze slid harmlessly past him, foiled by the low-level psychic broadcast he was projecting. *Look elsewhere,* that insidious mental whisper said. *You never even saw me.* His prey was just as susceptible as any other human, and yet, as she passed over him there was a hesitation that hadn't been there before.

He leaned forward, watching her, his lips curling upward just at the corners.

She was learning him already and he hadn't even started.

* * * *

Amanda Bairns found herself scanning the faces around her—again—and wondered who she was looking for.

The bar was packed with University of Wisconsin-Madison students celebrating the end of finals, just as she and Brandy and James were doing. Normally, Amanda liked the press of people, the odd mix of camaraderie and anonymity that was part and parcel of State Street on a Friday evening, but tonight she couldn't shake the itching between her shoulder blades, the hint of a breath on the back of her neck.

"You know, I thought once the Business Law exam was out of the way I'd stop feeling so paranoid," she commented to Brandy.

"I told you your professor wasn't out to get you specifically." Brandy poked at the sunken cherry of her brandy old-fashioned, the tiny black straw too small to be used for much besides fishing out muddled fruit. "Have another drink, you'll feel better."

Amanda shook her head, the very thought making her shoulders hunch defensively. Her gut said she needed her wits about her, and she trusted her instincts. *Even if my instincts* have *been saying the same damn thing for the last week or more.* "I have to work tomorrow."

"At noon." James leaned over the bar so he could see her around Brandy, just to make sure Amanda couldn't miss the eyeroll. "It's not like you have to drive home."

"Drunk on the bus has never appealed to me." Amanda toyed with her half-empty gin and tonic, spinning the tumbler in idle circles, and unapologetically changed the subject. "Are your parents doing another cruise this summer?" she asked James.

"Yeah, Alaska again. They're leaving Memorial Day weekend." He grinned devilishly. "I'm already making plans."

As she and Brandy made their usual pledges to help with the cleaning up, Amanda forced her paranoia to the back of her mind. Brainstorming ideas for the party James wanted to hold at his parents' house was just the distraction she needed.

Amanda girl, the only premonition you need to be worrying about is how many pizzas we're going to need to order.

* * * *

Gabriel stopped probing his prey's defenses and let her relax for a little while. Her psychic shields were crude but strong: much stronger than the natural defenses of her friends, or most of the humans in the bar, for that matter. All humans had some rudimentary mental barriers to buffer them from outside thoughts and emotions, but most never developed their gifts enough to need the sturdy—if piecemeal—shields his prey had. Not that he couldn't get through her shields; he just couldn't do it from here without her noticing. When she was looking at him, though, with her hazel-brown eyes fixed on his, her guarded expression slowly melting in response to a joke or a smile…then it was almost disappointingly easy.

Once she was his, her shields wouldn't matter. Gabriel watched her nervous fiddling slow and then stop altogether as she fell into animated conversation with her two cohorts, leaning forward and talking with her hands as she tended to do when she was excited. In no time at all she was dominating the discussion, taking over as if she had every right to do so. Though the bar was loud, Gabriel's sensitive ears filtered out the excess noise, just as the dim lighting and the shadows could not hide her features from his gaze. Her reddish-brown curls were pulled back from her face but fell in careless waves to cover the nape of her neck, the perfect offset to the long, graceful exposed throat.

His head throbbed in time with her pulse, each beat a thundering chorus of *Mine! Mine! Mine!* Anticipation made his fangs tremble in their sockets, but he forced the muscles to relax. *Not yet. Soon, tonight, but not yet.* Despite his efforts he tasted venom on his tongue, bitter as briars, and felt it weeping down the backs of his fangs.

"Fancy seeing you here."

The other chair at his table scraped against the floor. Few creatures would be able to notice him under that look-away aura Gabriel was hiding behind, but Paul Galati was definitely one of those few. Gabriel kept his gaze on his prey and said nothing as his son sat down. He felt the movement of Paul's head more than saw it, but even so his teeth clenched and his lips started to curl back. *Mine.* Gabriel stifled the protective urge, but couldn't make himself relax until Paul turned to face the other direction.

"So that's the way of it." Paul's voice and scent were both carefully calm, but that meant nothing. He stroked his dark beard. "Isn't it a bit soon? Cian was, what, 1848?"

"Forty-nine," Gabriel corrected absently. Cian had left Madison hardly a century ago. Paul was right, it was too soon, but two hundred years was only an average. Gabriel shrugged and dismissed Paul's concern. The itch came when it came, as inevitable as morning.

Paul refused to be put off. "You're making the natives restless."

With a snort, Gabriel finally glanced away from his prey, his eyes finding the growing knot of skinshifters that was gathering in the far corner. Immune as they were to any kind of psychic influence, the shape-shifting fae were, of course, also among the few. While it was true that Gabriel usually left the campus and the Square to the rest of Madison's unseen communities, it was only tradition. A politeness. Without moving his head, he met his son's worried gaze.

"Nothing bars me from the isthmus." Gabriel's mild, even tone betrayed no hint of the eagerness slowly consuming him. "If someone takes exception to my unusual excursion here, they can take it up with me, not hide behind a proxy." His ears caught the grumbles from the group in the corner, just as he knew perfectly well that they could hear every word he said. Isolde's hearing had always been better than his, and she had taught him well the abilities and limitations of her original people.

"Stop teasing them," Paul chided. "The state you're in, *I* hardly wanted to talk to you."

Gabriel smiled, but his attention was already being drawn back to his prey. "They won't have to put up with my presence much longer."

It was time. While he enjoyed pushing the boundaries of his self-control, he knew his own limits. The itch built over several months to give him time to find a suitable candidate, though often enough he didn't recognize it until it was too late. He would find himself already fixated on his prey, his subconscious having chosen for him.

This was one of those times.

He knew from long centuries of experience that the itch would drive him to take her eventually, regardless of whether he wanted a fledgling. Not that he didn't relish each contest, but occasionally it could be damned inconvenient.

Gabriel closed his eyes and let the need sweep through him, gave himself to it, savored the rush of expectation. The itch grew until his whole body ached with it, his vision growing hazy at the edges, but just like with the hunger, once he stopped fighting it he could channel it, could use all that demanding, shrieking energy in pursuit of his prey.

The ache evened out into a buzz that made every line and shadow jump into sharp focus, every sound resonate with extra clarity, every scent burst with complex nuances of emotion and health, environment and habit. His skin all but quivered under the stirring air. *Yes. Now.*

Gabriel wrapped himself in an aura of harmless amiability, checking one last time to make sure no hint of his true nature peeked through before dropping the aura that hid him from the humans. *Look away* slid into *you like me* with hardly a ripple. He touched the thoughts of the boy sitting next to his prey and told the boy's subconscious it was time to go home. As the oblivious student rose to his feet, Gabriel shot Paul a mischievous grin. "Besides, I wouldn't want to show up to your latest wedding without a date. The last time I was fairly mobbed with female relatives, if you recall."

Paul sighed and pinched the bridge of his nose. "By all means, bring her to the wedding." *If she survives,* he added, his voice a whisper in Gabriel's mind.

Already moving to claim the vacated bar stool, Gabriel didn't bother looking back. The hunting grin was all in his thoughts anyway, not on his face.

* * * *

Amanda was only dimly aware of the guy next to her leaving, but a moment later a new voice stopped her mid-sentence.

"Well, that's a bit of luck, isn't it?"

Turning away from Brandy and James, she watched Gabriel Chapel settle in on the seat next to her. She smiled at him, her heart speeding up just a little. *Relax, you,* she scolded herself. *You hardly know the guy.* "Hey," she said by way of greeting, her friends echoing her. Brandy giggled. Amanda kicked her. "How are you?"

"Not too bad. Feel like I've been through a wringer, but at least that's done with for another semester." He rested both elbows on the bar and faced her with his chin on his shoulder.

If he wasn't so supremely relaxed Amanda would've assumed he was posing, because the position showed off not only his muscular arms, but also his strong, chiseled features and finely sculpted lips. Not to mention his eyes, which changed color from blue to gray to green, depending on the light. Amanda felt her stomach begin to knot and quickly turned away.

"We were just talking about...um..." Shit, she'd totally forgotten. She stared at Brandy with wide, panicked eyes. *Why does my brain turn to mush around the pretty ones?* Although it wasn't so much Gabriel's looks as his *looks*; the blatant, unflappable self-confidence and good humor she saw in his face the few times they'd talked had made a bigger impression on her than his features had. He wasn't exactly handsome by conventional standards—his nose was a little too strong, his hair a muddy brown-gold that could barely be called blond—but striking, yes, definitely striking. *Sexy with a capital S, you mean.*

"Finals," Brandy supplied with a knowing grin. "Amanda has also been through the wringer, as you might've noticed."

"Thanks, Brandy," Amanda muttered, spinning her tumbler on the polished wood.

"Happens to the best of us." Gabriel squinted at her as if trying to remember something. "Marketing, right? You said this is your third year in Madison?"

"Yep." The tumbler spun faster, the remnants of her drink sloshing dangerously close to the rim. Out of the corner of her eye she saw him smile.

"So what do you think of my fair city?"

She glanced over at him, furrowing her brow a little. *My city? Arrogant much?* With a mental shrug, she said, "You mean other than being the biggest small town in the country?"

He cocked his head to one side. "How so?"

Amanda spoke more to the tumbler than to him. "Everyone knows everyone here. It's like, if the rest of the country needs six degrees of separation, in Madison you only need three. I mean, I'm not even from here and I can't go anywhere without running into someone who knows someone else I know. It's not a bad thing, but I swear it's beyond all normal probability."

Brandy and James were natives to the area and had never understood why she found Madison such an odd city. Gabriel turned in his seat to face her a little more squarely, leaving one elbow on the bar so he could still lean against it, cool and casual, but when Amanda looked up she thought that his eyes were too bright, too interested, to quite fit with his relaxed posture. Her heart gave another little lurch and her cheeks heated under that not-so-casual regard, and to her own mortification, she started to babble.

"And it's not a very impressive city, visually. From the Beltline or the Interstate it just looks like suburbia, and there's no skyline because of that goofy law about not blocking the view of the Capitol, and the streets are a freaking mess downtown. It reminds me a lot of Point, er, Stevens Point, you know, up north? But bigger. Except Point has a river instead of these stupid lakes. I mean, why build a big city on an isthmus where there's limited square footage and then make it illegal to build up?"

She managed to cut herself off and started stirring her drink with the stupid black straw, because if she kept spinning the glass she was going to tip the thing over. With her luck, all over Gabriel. *Nice one, Amanda girl. He tries to start a conversation and all you do is bash his hometown. Assuming it is his hometown. Hell.*

But he didn't appear annoyed, only curious. "Why didn't you go to school in Point then, if you don't like Madison?"

"I never said I didn't like it." The words nearly tripped over each other in her hurry to get them out. "I just said it was weird. I like weird. The vibe here, it's not quite like anywhere else I've ever been." She wasn't sure how to put it into words. Gabriel and James were both watching her with interest, but Brandy was already bored and looking around for cute guys to gawk at. "Besides, two hours is the minimum distance I want to live from my folks. Since Point is right in the middle of the state, it makes it hard to get too far away from them. I'd have gone out of state if I could've afforded tuition." *The last thing I need is Mom trying to run my life for me like she did at home.*

"How is the vibe here different from up north?" Gabriel asked. "I've never been up that way."

"Not much reason to go there unless you have family," Amanda replied with a sour half-smile. "It's sort of muted and desperate and hopeless and oppressive." *Or maybe that's just me not wanting to get trapped there.* "It's friendly here. You don't get that whole townies attitude, and there's just so much energy. Like there are big things going on, you know?" *You sound like an idiot.* "It's really…really *alive* here, I guess."

James said something about how she should've seen State Street five or six years ago, but Amanda wasn't listening. Gabriel continued to watch her from under half-closed lids, his gaze holding hers, ignoring James just as she was. Maybe it was the light, or those color-shifting irises, but his eyes glittered in a way that was beginning to make the hairs on the back of her neck rise.

A finger of unease crept up her spine, and she looked down at her glass. An image flashed before her mind's eye: a snake coiled and motionless, staring at a mouse.

You're imagining things, she told herself. She'd talked to Gabriel several times before now and never had the slightest cause for concern. She reviewed each meeting briefly. *A few times on the bus, once or twice at the bookstore, down at the Inferno the one time...*

That had been the first, and when Brandy and James had met him, too. They'd been out for Leather and Lace, a monthly techno night at the club, all dolled up and decked out, but Gabriel had just been in black, jeans and a t-shirt, nothing fancy, his gray eyes like bits of old green glass against the pallor of his face. He'd looked almost dangerous, stark and cold, until he'd smiled at her.

I haven't seen him all in black since then, she mused with a speculative look at his dark attire. *Hell, could be the same outfit for all I know. Maybe it's just not his color.*

I really am getting paranoid. I should get some sleep.

"Sorry, guys, but I'm dead on my feet. I think I'm gonna catch the bus home." Amanda gave a short wave and hopped off the bar stool.

Brandy pouted at her until Gabriel said, "Yeah, me too." At which point Brandy grinned at her and James gave her a surreptitious thumbs-up.

Damned matchmakers, the both of you. Amanda rolled her eyes at them as she walked past, and Gabriel followed her out the door, falling in beside her as they headed up State Street to the Capitol Square.

"I hate the new transfer point system, don't you?" she said to him as they navigated the busy sidewalk. "I mean, used to be you could hop any bus and you'd get to State Street, and any bus you wanted would be there eventually. Now, God knows where you'll end up if you get on the wrong bus."

"Why don't you drive, then?"

He actually sounded interested in her banal attempt at conversation. She wasn't sure she believed him, but she appreciated it anyway.

"And pay for parking downtown? At least the bus is free with the student pass." She glanced at him and accidently caught his eye, and hurriedly glanced away again as she felt her cheeks flush. She'd had guys look at her speculatively before, like they might be imagining her naked, but his look had been...not cold, far from it, but *dispassionate* almost. *That makes no sense. How can you be dispassionate and heated at the same time?* She fought down the urge to look again until they got to the bus stop, but by then whatever expression she'd seen was gone.

The wait for the bus wasn't long, which was just as well since Amanda couldn't think of anything to talk about and Gabriel had given up asking her questions. After climbing aboard, Amanda took an aisle seat and Gabriel took the one across the aisle from her, close, but not too close.

Poor guy's probably just trying to see if I'm interested and I'm being a total basket case. And she *was* interested. *I mean, we haven't had any long conversations, but I'll give him points for persistence. And cuteness. Assuming I haven't made him think I'm a complete fluff-brain. I wish I was better at talking to people.*

Oh, hell with it.

They were coming up on St. Mary's Hospital, which was where he'd always gotten off the bus before. Amanda turned in her seat as the bus began to slow. "Hey, I'm sorry I had to bug out right away. I'm just totally scattered tonight, you know?" She meant to go on, say something about maybe getting together on purpose some time, but Gabriel was already smiling and shaking his head.

"No worries," he said as he stood up. "You've just got good instincts, and I'm not trying as hard tonight."

Before she could think of a reply, he turned and walked off the bus.

What the hell does that mean?

She mulled it over as the bus lumbered south to the transfer point, and mulled it over some more as she waited under the brightly lit awnings for her transfer, and was still turning it over in her mind as she rode the second bus to the stop near her apartment. The longer she thought about it, the less she liked it.

Maybe it's just as well I didn't get that second part out. She shivered a little in the cool night air as she trudged up the steeply sloping driveway. *Confident is good, but creepy is definitely a turn-off.*

She let herself into the building, grabbed her mail from the lock box, and trotted downstairs to her half-buried one-bedroom. Already thinking ahead to a long, hot shower and some serious zzz's, Amanda unlocked the door to her apartment, stepped inside, and turned to lock the door again.

A hand reached around from behind her and clamped down over her mouth.

Something thin and cold pressed into her throat.

Adrenaline shot through her like electricity, ready to be channeled into movement. Amanda was dimly aware of her keys dropping to the floor as her hands shot upward, closing around the hand that held the blade. Her thoughts raced madly as she realized her attacker was effectively pinning her in the corner. There wasn't a lot of room to maneuver, and that blade felt very sharp...

"Yes, you should wait until I move you away from the door," Gabriel whispered in her ear. "You'll have much better odds."

CHAPTER TWO

Gabriel?!

Confusion splintered Amanda's focus. How could he have known what she was thinking? How could Gabriel even be here so quickly? And *why*, of course, but that almost didn't matter.

Through pure effort of will, Amanda pulled herself together, forced her thoughts into order and shoved aside the churning of her stomach and the cold shock of gooseflesh shooting down her spine. *Focus! This is why you take those self-defense classes every semester!*

"Good." Gabriel's voice was a low rumble. "Very good. Calculating and analytical under pressure. A little slow to improvise, but I think we can work on that."

The metal edge pressed harder against her skin until she was afraid to swallow.

His breath tickled her ear. "Just now you're running through it in your mind: how you'll twist my wrist out and away, stepping forward, pivoting, one hand swinging free to collapse my elbow as you step into me, driving my own weapon back toward...but you stop there."

Bile rose in the back of Amanda's throat, and she leaned back so she could swallow against it without cutting herself. Her hands trembled where they gripped his wrist. *He can't know that.*

"But I do." He pulled her tight to him, his chest pressing into her back, the blade pricking at the soft spot under her jaw until her head bumped up against his shoulder and she could go no farther. Even though his voice was so soft and low that it sounded like something out of a dream, she could still hear him clearly over the thundering of her pulse and the soft, high-pitched gasps of her breathing. She wished she couldn't. "You're thinking so loudly just now. You turn the blade, drive it up and in… Where, Amanda? Stomach? Liver? Lung? No, you know better than to chance hitting a rib, don't you?"

She couldn't help but picture it, just like when she was a child and someone told her not to think of a purple cow. She saw herself performing the move drill-perfect, only instead of ending with the rubber knife flat against her opponent's belly, she drove metal into soft flesh with all her weight behind it, so hard she swore she could actually feel the blade glance off Gabriel's spine, both of her hands tight on his hand and the handle now, still moving, stepping behind him with the near foot, tripping him as she shoved him back but not letting go, no, let the metal tear its way free of him as he falls, the bones of his arm snapping, the vibration dancing under her fingers even as the blood fountains up, scalding her skin, the rush of pure power filling her, making the adrenaline seem like a caffeine buzz in comparison as his eyes widen in shock and disbelief, her snarl turning up at the corners into a hideous, rictus grin as she reverses the knife and plunges it down…

No!

Control gone, focus gone, it was all Amanda could do to tear herself out of that macabre vision.

Revulsion morphed into rage.

She shrieked against Gabriel's muffling hand, pulling at his wrist and kicking at his legs, but he ignored her attacks so completely that she wondered if she was imagining them, too, until he bent backward a little farther so her feet no longer reached the ground. Only when she started kicking the wall and the door did he finally step back into the middle of the room, the blade vanishing from her throat as he wrapped an arm around her waist.

He was *laughing*, God damn him, a delighted, condescending laugh that only increased when she reached up to claw at his face.

The sound filled her with impotent fury and a vicious hate that made her forget the horror she'd felt only seconds before. She would've torn his eyes out if she could've reached him, but he hid his face in her shoulder and just kept laughing.

"I am not helpless, you sonofabitch!" The words came out as a garbled mess, but she didn't care if he could understand her.

Amanda drove her elbows into him, but it was like trying to hurt an armchair; the soft parts gave and the hard parts held and neither seemed any worse for the wear. She screamed again in wordless frustration and tried to bite the hand covering her mouth.

"Ah, the mouse remembers she has teeth." His jovial tone dropped into a growl that made her chest seize. "But so do I."

The movement was so fast that she never felt him raise his head, only felt the searing pain as something ripped into her neck. It wasn't the blade; it didn't slice across her exposed throat but tore savage and hard, digging through the muscle. Her vision faded out, her senses overwhelmed by the pain, but that lack only heightened her awareness of another threat.

Spectral fingers burrowed under her skull and behind her useless eyes, ghosting over walls she hadn't even known she had, seeking purchase in cracks and rough spots and sending in tendrils like roots to rip them apart.

She was choking on her screams now, gurgling, trying to breathe past the hurt and the shock, desperate to stop those invasive whatever-the-hell-they-were but she didn't know how, she couldn't think, and then the agony shifted. It was like someone turned a dial and everything changed frequency, sliding from torment to a wave of pleasure that took her completely by surprise.

The last of her defenses shattered under the onslaught.

A wordless croon filled her mind, a thick, velvet purr that stroked her insides in ways that shouldn't have been possible. It soothed her, cradled her, lifted her out of herself. Every muscle she had vibrated with the ecstasy that raced through her, but there was something just out of reach, some threshold she absolutely had to cross that called her. She strained toward it, the voice—*Gabriel*—urging her on, and while some tiny part of her realized she was squeezing herself dry for him, most of her didn't care. It was so close, so very close…

She passed out long before she got there.

* * * *

Gabriel lowered Amanda carefully to the carpet, his fingers tight against the wound he'd made, every instinct but one begging him to finish her, to keep drinking until her soul seared him with its nearness as it fled. The itch was stronger, though, and he sent up a brief prayer of gratitude to whatever had guided him to her, or brought her to him.

Devouring you would be such a waste.

His scent-mark spread through her body with each slow beat of her heart. He traced her cheek with one hand while he raised the other to his mouth, slicing open the flesh of his wrist with his teeth. His hands trembled in anticipation, but he made no effort to still them.

I knew you'd be a fighter, he whispered to her as he gently lifted her head, tipping it back so that her mouth opened. He pressed his wrist to her lips, and with a deft mental touch, forced her slack muscles to swallow. *Drink, Amanda. You aren't meant to die just yet.*

The first mouthful hit her stomach. He felt it in the pit of his belly, felt it moving, working, his blood invading her, claiming her, tying them together. The hum in his veins turned up another notch, his heart beating in time to hers, a claxon that drowned out all other sound.

Her lips stirred against his skin.

Gabriel bowed his head, tried to gather himself, but the growing roar of the itch made him dizzy. With an almost pleading cry he repeated, *Drink.*

Still unconscious, Amanda's brow furrowed. Then her mouth clamped down around the wound, and she began to suck.

He felt that pull in every cell of his body, as if she were draining away all other sensation and leaving only pleasure behind. When she swallowed again, the brief lull made his head spin. As she fell into a rhythm, he gritted his teeth and fought to stay in control as she drew the itch from him, stealing it with his blood.

Gods below me, he begged, *yes, drink!*

She needed no encouragement, demanding back every drop he had just taken from her and more, hooking her fingers into the very fabric of him and trying to rip him away from himself, to make him hers every bit as much as he was making her his, his energy infusing her until her very flesh exhaled his scent...

The itch melted abruptly into a flood of rapture. He wanted so badly at that moment to give into it, to let Amanda consume him down to the dregs. Theodore nearly had, over four hundred years ago—a lesson Gabriel could never quite take to heart, since the itch and its subsequent release had been noticeably stronger ever since.

He allowed himself one heartbeat to wallow in it before gathering his resolve—more, and he wasn't sure even he would have the strength. "That's enough," he murmured, his voice sounding guttural even to him.

The moment he tried to pull away, Amanda reacted on instinct. Her hands flew up to hold him tight against her mouth, but the movement made her wake with a start. He waited while her confused gaze cleared, waited for the revulsion, the fear, the knowledge of what he was and what he had done to her.

It was there, for a split second. Then her eyes narrowed, hot and angry, and she swallowed again.

His whole being thrummed, his breath hissing through his teeth, the gratification only intensifying as he watched her expression grow distant as the blood slid down her throat, her fluttering eyelids not quite hiding the gleam of hunger that was taking root. The satisfaction must have shown on his face, because when she refocused on him she abruptly shoved his arm away.

He pressed down hard on the wound in his wrist, feeling it knitting together under his fingers just as the bite in her neck was healing, slowly now but gaining speed as his blood spread through her. The euphoria was fading, but the image before him still made his breath catch. Amanda glared up at him, eyes hard and blazing with fury, her expression fierce and fearless, his blood running freely down her chin.

"Yes," he told her softly. "That is how you should look."

Confusion cut across her features. She tried to prop herself up on her elbows, but the movement was too much and she collapsed back onto the floor with her hands clutching her head. "What do you mean? What have you done?" Her voice broke, and she coughed.

"I've made you mine. My blood is moving through you even now. Healing you. Changing you." He smiled, enjoying the dawning horror on her face. "But I haven't turned you, not yet. That choice will be yours alone, if you're strong enough."

She shook her head, more in denial than anything else. "I don't understand."

"I know." Gabriel felt her trying to rebuild her mental walls and caught her gaze before she could finish. The bond was growing—already her presence was a siren's song in the back of his mind—but it would be days before he could use it fully. "I'll explain it all tomorrow, I promise. But for now, you need to sleep."

Amanda struggled to look away, wriggling feebly in his mental grip. "But—"

"Shh." He touched a finger to her lips. "Go to sleep."

She did. She had no choice.

* * * *

The North Carolina sun had been up for just over an hour—not that it could be seen through the clouds—when Enrique Morales and his two apprentices broke into the vampire's lair.

The house was one of a score of nearly-identical suburbanite homes that lined the wide street, with a brick façade and siding everywhere else, purely decorative black shutters, and more gables than a Hawthorne novel. The other houses were full of middle-income families, mostly, which meant that Mom and Dad would still likely be a-snooze in their beds, recovering from the weekly grind of commuting to nearby Charlotte. Kids would be up, of course, but most of them would be glued to Saturday morning cartoons.

Morales stood blocking Tawny Briggs from casual view as she assessed the lock on the back door. His junior apprentice, John Travis, watched Briggs closely as she tested the door. It was always best to stagger the newbies. Two newbies could get even a seasoned hunter killed pretty easily, but one was usually manageable. For him, anyway.

Most vampire hunters his age had retired long ago, aside from providing basic training to raw recruits before sending them on to do fieldwork with a more experienced hunter. Not that there were many hunters his age, retired or otherwise. At forty-nine, Morales was ancient by hunter standards.

We generally don't retire so much as reach our expiration date.

"Three locks," Briggs announced quietly. "The knob, a bolt above, and a bolt into the foundation."

Typical. "Well, we didn't expect she'd make it too easy for us." Morales gestured for the other two to move over to the patio door.

Felicia Night—Morales bit back a grimace; seemed like half the vamps in America used "Night" as their surname—was a young but up-and-coming leech. Barely over seventy years old, and she'd already set herself up in a choice little enclave. Like most of her kind, Felicia liked her thralls young and smart, using them to keep up on society and technology, culture and language.

And, apparently, home security systems.

"All right, then." Morales shifted the tank on his back and tightened one of the shoulder straps. The canister was decorated with bug spray warnings and stylized pictures of cockroaches. They were dressed as pest exterminators—which they were, in a way—but the disguises wouldn't fool any but the most gullible of observers.

Morales unzipped the duffel bag he was carrying. "The windows we checked have break sensors, and there're probably motion detectors, too. We're going to have to act fast. No time to sweep the whole house. You both remember the layout?"

His apprentices nodded. That was one nice thing about these modern-day-Levittown subdivisions: it was a piece of cake to get ahold of the floor plans. Since they couldn't case the house ahead of time—you never knew who the leeches had watching, even during the day—the floor plans were a definite bonus.

"Travis, you've got the tranks. Briggs, you've got our backs. I'll take point."

Briggs's lips thinned, but she made no protest. This was a training run, for the most part, and she could've handled point nearly as well as he could. Hell, he probably should've cut her loose by now, but Travis was still too green. This was Travis's first hot run, first time getting his hands dirty. If Walker hadn't zigged when he should've zagged, Briggs would be long gone and Walker would be watching Travis.

Just as well—it saved him the trouble of tracking her down for the next run.

"Eyes on the prize," Morales murmured to Briggs as he passed her a shotgun.

Morales hadn't told her about the message that had been left with his answering service a few hours earlier.

He's chosen. Gather as many of the others as you can.

Briggs was still passionate enough to lose her edge at news like that, and Morales needed her to be sharp. This run had to go smooth so Travis could get a kill under his belt before they went after the *big* prize.

Besides, after all the preparations they'd made for Felicia, Morales was not about to leave the leech alive, even if he now had bigger fish to fry.

The biggest fish.

Gabriel Chapel.

Eyes on the prize yourself, old man.

The actual breaking and entering was pretty standard. Morales held the now-empty duffel over the glass door near the handle, and Briggs swung a weighted rope at it. The heavy lead ball punched through the glass and the bag muffled some of the sound. Morales reached through, thick leather gloves protecting his hands from the sharp glass, and unlocked the door.

Glass shards crunched under their boots and skidded across the linoleum, making footing uncertain. With quick but measured steps, Morales led them toward the basement.

Something thumped on the second floor.

"Be ready, Travis." Morales didn't spare a glance for either of his apprentices, his gaze fixed on the cheap-looking wood door ahead of them. The "gun" in his hands was connected to the tank on his back by a thick hose, and he kept his finger just touching the trigger. The tiny flame at the end of the barrel made an eerie blue glow on the varnish.

No sounds from below. Morales kept his gaze at roughly chest height, using his peripheral vision to watch for movement. *Watch the chest, never the eyes.* Stepping up to the handle side of the basement door, Morales shifted so he was just out of the direct line of fire. He signaled Briggs with a quick up-and-down movement of the flamethrower.

Briggs rested the barrel of the shotgun against her shoulder, the business end pointing straight up, and stood near the hinges with her back to the wall. Travis stood next to her, his eyes scanning the room with nervous little flicks. His knuckles were white where he gripped the tranquilizer gun.

Crouching down, Briggs reached across the door. Her hand hovered near the knob, fingers counting down.

Three…two…one…

Briggs grabbed the knob and twisted it violently, yanking the door toward her. Morales leaned around the frame, sweeping the nozzle across the stairwell.

Nothing. Just stairs descending onto a dark landing.

"Clear," Morales murmured. He hated stairs. Easiest place to set up an ambush or a booby trap. Not that you saw as many booby traps these days, at least with the younger vamps. Too reliant on their tech and their thralls for that.

Briggs scrambled to her feet, running one hand over the door's surface. "Metal. It's a fire door."

"Sprinkler system, too." Morales gestured at a nozzle protruding from the ceiling. "Briggs, you take the trank gun and watch the door. I don't want to get locked down there. Travis, bring the shotgun."

Travis looked nervous as he switched weapons. *Time to pop that cherry, son. It doesn't get much easier than this.*

Morales went down the stairs first, placing his feet close to the wall and moving quickly. As he approached the landing, he swung the flamethrower around to cover the basement, but nothing moved. Travis waited two seconds and came after, his nervous breathing echoing in the closed space.

The basement was mostly unfinished. Concrete floor, drywall that was taped but not mudded or painted, bare bulbs in the fixtures overhead. There were no windows, and the only light came from the stairwell and the little jet of blue fire at the end of the flamethrower. Morales descended from the landing, his feet moving in small, sliding steps once he reached the concrete.

Sensing no immediate threat, Morales took a moment to pull on a pair of night vision goggles. The dark corners jumped into focus, everything washed in shades of green. The room looked tight. No entrances or exits other than the stairs. A few support poles broke up the monotony of the bare floor. The furnace and water heater sat lonely and naked against the far wall.

It was one, big, empty room.

When nothing jumped out at Morales, Travis scurried down the rest of the stairs. "Where is it?" he asked in a harsh whisper.

Morales walked along the closest wall. The builders hadn't even closed in the area under the stairs, as if they wanted to make it absolutely clear that there was nothing down here. He ran his hand over the drywall, moving from panel to panel. "Where are the windows?"

Travis's eyes were too wide. You'd think he'd never been in a vampire's lair before. "What windows?"

"There were basement windows from the outside," Morales explained patiently as he moved along the walls. "Where are they?"

Travis looked around. "They must have dry-walled over them."

"Right."

It took a moment to sink in. "And if they walled over the windows, they might have walled over something else."

It didn't take them long to find the panel where the tape was only attached on one side. Travis set down the shotgun and got a good hold on the loose side of the tape while Morales stood back, flamethrower ready.

Travis pulled, and the panel swung back.

Another metal fire door was set into the concrete behind the drywall.

This one didn't have a knob.

Travis ran his fingers over the edge but couldn't get a grip. "Is this when we use the C4?"

"You got it."

Morales continued to cover Travis as the young man rolled out long strands of the explosive and wedged them into the cracks surrounding the door. His was quick and sure with this part, fingers flying like a Rubik's cube champion. If killing vampires only involved demolitions, Travis would be the best in the country.

Once the detonator was in place, Travis retrieved the shotgun and the two hunters retreated up the stairs. When they got to the top, they found Briggs still standing guard, but now there was a young woman lying unconscious on the floor nearby.

Travis started to go to her, but Morales put a restraining hand on Travis's shoulders. "Leave her there, son. Thralls are tougher than they look; it's hard to tell when they'll shake off the tranquilizer."

"She was trying to sneak up on me with a butcher knife," Briggs added, as if that wasn't anything unusual.

Travis hunched his shoulders, but nodded. Morales could practically see the thoughts running through the kid's mind: he hadn't been able to save his girlfriend, Carrie, but maybe there would be time to save this girl.

After the vampire was dead.

"Fire in the hole," Travis muttered, and activated the detonator.

The fire door at the top of the stairs muffled some of the sound, but the explosion still shook the whole house. That might well wake up the mommies and daddies next door, and the broken glass of the patio door was not particularly subtle.

"We might get some nosy neighbors," Morales warned as Travis pulled the basement door back open.

Briggs nodded, unconcerned. "Just hurry it up so we can leave, Boss."

The two men hustled down the stairs.

The once-hidden door was still standing, but the surrounding concrete had been pulverized. It only took a few seconds for the hunters to figure out where the bolts were on the other side of the door, and a few more moments to knock out enough concrete that they were able to push the door inward, frame and all, to land with a resounding *bang* on the floor of the room beyond.

It was a small room, probably meant originally to house the washer and dryer. The edge of the fallen door landed only a few inches from the foot of an occupied bed.

Travis raised the shotgun to his shoulder, but Morales signaled for him to wait. "Know your target, Travis. You can't even see who it is from here. Look around first."

True to his advice, Morales was looking neither at the bed nor at Travis, but was casing the room. He flicked the light switch. It was set up like a normal bedroom, with a half-open closet on one wall, a bureau shoved up against another. An antique vanity sat near the bed, loaded with bottles and containers and girly clutter. The walls were papered, red on red with some gold thrown in.

"Cover the closet." Morales stepped over the fallen door, his back to the wall, and approached the foot of the bed. Keeping his flamethrower trained on the unmoving figure, he reached down and yanked the blanket back.

The woman he uncovered didn't move. She wore a simple, black sheath nightgown and her hair was up in curlers.

She wasn't breathing, which was all that mattered to Morales.

They made a quick check of the closet—nothing unusual, aside from a few "costumes" from decades earlier that were very likely originals—and returned to the bed.

"Okay, Travis. Blow her heart out so we can go."

Travis placed the end of the shotgun between the woman's breasts, but he hesitated, his eyes searching her face. "My mom used to wear curlers like those," he murmured, his brow furrowed. He looked confused.

"Don't let yourself be fooled by appearances. This bitch has killed hundreds of people. Thousands. They're monsters, Travis, just like Quinn was."

The boy's face grew hard. Quinn was the leech that had taken Travis's girlfriend.

Travis studied the vampire for another couple of seconds. Then he pulled the trigger.

CHAPTER THREE

Saturday, May 15th, 1999

"Wake up, sleepyhead."

Amanda moaned, rolling onto her side and burying her head in the pillow, hardly aware of what she'd heard. She'd been sound asleep, more so than she could ever remember being, and she wasn't much inclined to do anything but sink back into that comfortable blackness.

A masculine chuckle made the bottom drop out of her stomach.

Why is there a guy in my bedroom?

The thought snapped her awake just as Gabriel pulled the pillow out from under her. "You've slept long enough," he said. "It's tomorrow."

Everything rushed back at once. With a strangled yelp, Amanda sat up and scrambled away until her back was pressed painfully against her wrought-iron headboard. Her head throbbed and spun with the sudden movement, and she grabbed onto the headboard to keep from falling over. She wasn't sure if she was going to pass out or throw up.

Gabriel sat on the edge of the bed, watching her with one eyebrow raised in amusement. "Don't move too fast yet, you aren't ready for it. You lost a lot of blood last night."

The hell with that. Despite the way the bed seemed to tilt under her when she moved, Amanda tried to bolt for the door.

She wasn't even sure where the impact happened, but the next thing she knew, she was flat on her back with the breath knocked out of her and Gabriel had her pinned to the bed under him. His lips were drawn back in a fierce snarl, exposing long, glinting fangs where his eyeteeth should've been.

Oh God, oh God, it's happening again, God, please, I can't move, get off me get OFF...

Gabriel shook himself, the snarl fading. His lips moved but all Amanda could hear was a loud ringing and the harsh rasp of her own breathing. He tried sitting up very slowly, but as soon as his weight was gone she was struggling to get past him again. Just like before, the movement was too fast to see; between one blink and the next he had his hands around her wrists, and no amount of twisting and tearing made any difference. She couldn't even make him shift his weight.

Her darting, panicked eyes met his almost by accident. The world shrank down to two little points of light the color of Lake Mendota on a stormy day.

Don't scream. His voice came from everywhere and nowhere all at once.

Her throat closed up. She couldn't breathe. She started struggling again and wondered when she'd stopped.

Dammit, I said don't scream, not choke yourself to death. He sounded distinctly annoyed. *Relax. Breathe.*

Air rushed into her lungs, and the tunnel vision receded. Closing her eyes just to see if she could, she sucked in another greedy breath and tried to stop shaking.

"That's better," Gabriel murmured. "Don't ever run from me, Amanda. That could end very badly for you."

"Let go of me," she growled from between clenched teeth.

He released her wrists and she squirmed away until her back was to the wall. Her movements were slow and jerky, but she managed to sit up without wanting to hurl this time. Carefully keeping her gaze fixed on his chest instead of his face, she swallowed hard. *This can't be happening.* "What the hell are you?"

In her peripheral vision she saw his mouth quirk up at one corner. "Do you really need to ask?"

God, her throat was dry. She swallowed again. "What...what do you call yourself?"

He laughed. "I call myself Gabriel Chapel, but the word you're looking for is vampire. It's a fairly modern term, but it will do."

Her head started to spin and she caught herself against the headboard. It was worse, hearing him say it out loud so casually. "How...why—?"

Gabriel cut her off with a soothing noise. "We'll get to that soon enough. I thought you might want to get a shower first, and some clean clothes. Do you need help getting there? I could carry you?"

A shower was not anywhere on her list of immediate needs, but some time alone to get her shit together would probably be a good idea. She eyed the bathroom door, not more than ten feet away. Her vision swam just thinking about it. "I can get there. I'll crawl if I have to."

Gabriel's smile had a distinct edge of pride that Amanda didn't care for, but all he said was, "As you will."

She managed to stand and sort of tipped herself toward the door, trusting her feet to keep up long enough to stop her from falling flat on her face. It worked, although by the time she caught hold of the doorframe she thought she might be sick from the headrush. She hung on until the dizziness passed, then pulled herself into the bathroom with one hand on the counter and one on the towel bar.

As she turned to close the door, Gabriel stood. He moved slowly and deliberately, as if concerned that any sudden movement on his part would set her panicking again. The worst part was that she was afraid he was right, and if she lost her footing in here, she'd probably crack her skull on something.

"Don't stand in the shower," he said. "And don't turn the water on too hot, either."

She didn't know whether to be annoyed or flabbergasted. *I know perfectly well how to avoid passing out in the shower. Where the hell was all this concern last night when he ripped my throat out?* But all she said out loud was, "I know," and shut the door behind her.

Whatever sense of calm he'd imposed on her vanished as soon as she was alone. Amanda slid to the floor, her legs refusing to hold her upright. She held her breath to stifle the sobs that threatened to bubble up and crawled to the shower, hoping that the sound of the water would mask the hysterics she was about to have.

Oh, God, she wailed silently, curled into a little ball on the tiles, her forehead pressed awkwardly against the side of the tub. With trembling fingers she searched her throat, but there was no healing wound, no pain, no scar. *Oh, God, he's real. He can't be real, but he is.*

She wanted so badly to believe that she was hallucinating somehow, but the memory of last night was too vivid. She shuddered. There was no way she could have imagined sensations like that just out of fever dreams. Amanda pressed her lips together, biting back what might have been a whimper or might have been a moan. She didn't want to find out which.

Don't think about that! You wanted to get yourself together, didn't you? Then you better damn well do it before he wonders what's taking so long.

That was enough to get her moving. She stripped off the clothes she'd been wearing since yesterday and clambered into the tub, trying not to accidently pull the shower curtain down around her ears. Despite her intentions, it was a long time before she could do more than huddle under the hot spray. She wasn't cold, but she felt like she should be.

When she finally turned the water off and shoved the curtain aside, she found her pajamas folded on the counter. She shivered, glancing at the door uneasily. She hadn't heard the door open, and didn't like the idea that he'd been in the room with her without her knowing it.

Amanda's stomach growled as she climbed to her feet. She got dressed without bothering to dry her hair more than rubbing the towel over the tangled mess. Her bedroom was empty when she left the bathroom. Odd sizzling sounds drifted in through the open bedroom door. She gulped. *Just get it over with. He must want something from you or you'd be dead already.* With one hand on the wall to keep her balance, Amanda edged out into the living room.

Gabriel looked up from the stove and gave her the same friendly smile he had at the bar last night. "Dinner's almost done. Why don't you have a seat?"

Irritation flashed through her at his presumption. Unfortunately her knees were not quite ready to hold her upright for long periods, so she shuffled over to the battered recliner she'd rescued from her parents' basement the last time she'd been home. It creaked with comfortable familiarity as she curled up on the cushioned seat, and she could still keep an eye on Gabriel over the back of the couch and the half-wall that separated the tiny galley kitchen from the living room.

The vampire ignored her, his attention focused on whatever he was cooking. Amanda gave the room a nervous once-over, but there was nothing out of place, and no bloodstains on the carpet.

With a small shake of her head she passed a hand over her face. *I did not imagine it, or hallucinate the freaking fangs.*

Gabriel brought her a plate of food. She studied him as he approached, but nothing in his appearance or movements hinted that he was anything other than the attractive twenty-something she'd always taken him for. The plate held a sirloin steak and green beans and mashed potatoes. She stared at it while he went back into the kitchen, wondering if she dared eat it.

"Here you go," he said as he returned, holding out a knife and fork in one hand and a glass of milk in the other. Amanda gave an involuntary shudder. Milk was for cereal. "Tuck in. You'll feel a lot better once you've eaten."

Amanda balanced the plate on her knees and took the glass, setting it on the end table next to her before reaching for the utensils. He handed her the knife handle-first, and as her hand closed around it, the remembered image of burying it in his stomach flashed before her eyes. She glanced up and found him smiling at her as if they were sharing a private joke.

Her lips tightened. "What the hell is going on?" She was proud of how calm she sounded.

"Maybe you should eat first." Gabriel sat down on the couch, at the end farthest away from her.

Amanda was grateful for that, and then irritated for being grateful. "I'm not eating until you start talking."

"If you insist."

He *still* didn't look any different than he had all those other times she'd talked to him. *It's not fair. There should be some mark, some warning sign, something.* Amanda readied her utensils and tried not to be distracted by how good everything smelled. Her stomach growled again.

"It's quite straightforward," he said, watching her hands. She speared a couple of green beans to keep up her end of the bargain. "Every couple hundred years, we get the urge to take a fledgling. Survival of the species and all that, perfectly natural."

His gaze flicked over her, but she couldn't read his expression. "You are my chosen candidate."

Amanda shivered. She had to force the words out, and they fell like lead into the conversation, heavy and irrevocable. "You want me to become a vampire?"

Gabriel tipped his head to the side, his lips pursing as he hedged, "You are my candidate. I take pride in the success of my...offspring, I suppose." He tipped his head to the other side as if he were a hawk, considering her from every angle. "I think you have it in you. You have to understand, a fledgling is a huge time investment. Not just anyone will do."

This is ridiculous. It's like a bad movie. "Why me?"

"You're not eating," Gabriel pointed out. "Truly, there is nothing wrong with the food. It will make you stronger."

She looked down at her plate reluctantly. *He could've killed you already,* she reminded herself again, and shoved the forkful of beans in her mouth. They were buttery, lightly salted and just crunchy enough that she knew they hadn't been frozen. Amanda made a surprised *"mmm"* noise in spite of herself.

Gabriel chuckled. "I don't have to be able to eat in order to know how to cook."

Amanda swallowed her mouthful. "You can't eat? No, wait, answer that later. Why me, Gabriel?"

"Some of it I can put into words and some of it I can't." He shrugged. "I hadn't even realized I was looking until I found you a couple months ago. The more I watched you, the more suited you seemed to be. Confident without being reckless, stubborn without being hide-bound, motivated but patient. These are all good traits, but there are other factors that are more important.

"You are cautious in letting others get too close; you have a few close friends rather than many acquaintances. That makes things easier, later. You prefer to take charge rather than follow, but you follow when it seems prudent to you. And most of all, you're self-centered and ruthless when you know what you want."

Amanda's head jerked up, but before she could spit out an angry retort, Gabriel raised a finger to his lips. "You did ask. That's only my opinion, of course, but your behavior for the last two months has been remarkably consistent."

"But we only met two weeks ago, not two months," she protested.

"I've been watching you two months," he explained patiently. "I only let you see me two weeks ago. I know your work schedule, your school schedule, the bars you like, your favorite places to shop. I even stole your keys once and had copies made, and returned them to you before you realized they were gone." He spoke pleasantly, as if discussing the weather. "I would've taken you before now, but someone would've noticed if you'd missed your finals."

Amanda's fork hit her plate with a clatter.

"Don't look so shocked. You've known, Amanda." His mild tone made his words even more sinister. "You could tell something was hunting you. You felt me watching."

That stuff's all nonsense. She couldn't deny that *something* had had her on edge for weeks, but to put it down to being watched? How could you know someone was watching you? That sounded like something her crazy aunt would say.

Gabriel gestured at her plate, the movement bringing her out of her reverie. His eyes caught hers before she could think better of it. The room began to dim around the edges. "Finish your dinner. You need to be strong enough to fight me."

She was eating again before she was aware of him looking away. *Damn, how the hell did I forget about that?* It was so hard to have a conversation with someone and not look them in the eye. "You want me to fight you?"

"Yes." Gabriel steepled his fingers, leaning back against the arm of the couch. "You see, a vampire needs to be strong-willed to survive the transition. No former human could bear to take so many lives if they were weak."

Suddenly the food tasted like cardboard. "You have to kill?"

"You'll kill at least one person a night for the first ten or twenty years. It tapers off a little after that, and most learn to feed without killing after about fifty years." He cocked his head. "It varies, depending on how strong you are and how motivated to get out from under your master's thumb."

Amanda nearly gagged. *One person a night for ten or more years, and he says it as if it were nothing.* She couldn't help doing the math. "No! That's, like, four thousand people at a minimum! I won't let you do that to me."

"Good." Again came that proud, anticipatory smile. "I want your eyes open and your guard up. I want you to be very aware of the consequences of everything that you do. No mistakes, no accidents. That's why you need me close to you: to help you understand what's happening to you, and what it means. To teach you to control it. I need you to be strong, Amanda, because I want you to *choose* to become a vampire. That's very important to me."

He leaned forward for emphasis. "You see, if you don't truly want it, after you turn you'll probably find a way to off yourself sooner or later, and that's just a waste of my time. Even the ones who think they want it from the get-go usually don't understand what that kind of killing really entails. Most people don't have the fortitude to look their prey in the eyes and watch as the life goes out of them night after night. And the sociopaths who truly wouldn't care, well, they tend to be flawed. Either they're overconfident, or they never learn to blend in, or they have poor impulse control. They usually end up with a fatal case of hubris, and I'm still out all that time and effort."

"And if I don't choose to become a vampire?" She tried to stiffen her spine, to at least look like she wasn't cringing in horror at the idea.

"If you are strong enough to never drink directly from the prey, then you get to stay mortal." His mouth quirked up at one corner, and suddenly she wondered how she could ever have thought him human. "Unless you choose otherwise. If you are weak and can't control your hunger, well…I'm afraid I can't let a weak vampire survive. It's nothing personal. So it's in your best interest to keep your strength up."

"All I have to do is not drink anybody's blood?" That didn't sound too hard.

Gabriel glanced away with a silent laugh, and she wondered if he'd heard that thought. "My blood is spreading through you. Soon you'll begin to notice changes; you'll be stronger and faster, and your senses will become sharper. Other abilities vary from individual to individual. But those changes are fueled by energy and blood, more than a human body can produce on its own. Your body will begin to consume itself; that's where the hunger comes from. A mature vampire can feed without killing for weeks, even months, but true hunger is simply too powerful for a fledgling to control."

He spread his hands. "Right now you're still producing new blood, so your hunger will not be quite so great. If you're as strong as I believe, you'll be able to keep it reined in. Eventually my blood will be too diluted, and the changes will fade, and you'll become a normal human again."

Amanda swallowed hard. "How long is 'eventually?'"

"The worst of it will start to subside after about a month. If you haven't turned at the end of four weeks and you still wish to be human, then I'll concede defeat."

"Which means what?"

"As long as you never try to hunt me down, you will never see me again unless you wish it. You will be absolutely safe from me, and I will not allow any hurt to come to you if I can prevent it. I give you my word."

He said *I give you my word* as if it ended all doubt, as if it bound him utterly to his promise, but she refused to accept that weighty reassurance. *Words. Worth less than the paper they aren't written on.* She almost didn't ask, but she'd always preferred to know the worst up front, and now was not the time for squeamishness. "By your own admission you must've killed tens of thousands of people." She shook her head. "Why would you let me live?"

"You're mine." He said it as if it should have been obvious. "I'm very protective of what is mine, vampire or otherwise."

Amanda scowled at him. "I'm not yours."

Gabriel smiled patiently. "Finish your dinner."

CHAPTER FOUR

Sunday, May 16th, 1999

The lights came on in the parking lot, shining through the windows at Amanda's back as she worked her register. She glanced over her shoulder nervously. Gabriel had promised to stay away from the bookstore, but she couldn't help the feeling that he must be just behind her, now that the sun was setting.

He'd confirmed the legend about sunlight, warning her that she'd want to take some time off work. "It's sunlight specifically, by the way, not full spectrum light or ultraviolet light or any of that. It won't harm you as it would me, but you won't much like it. And no more working at night, after this week. The schedule was already posted or I would've had it changed. It might raise questions, changing it now."

"Whoa, wait a minute." Amanda glared at him. "Why should I change my hours?" *What right do you have to try and reorganize my life? No one tells me when I can come or go but me.*

His gentle, patient expression had melted, like wax running over steel, and her indignation had shriveled back into fear. "From sunset to dawn, your time belongs to me. I only have a limited time to convince you, and I expect, with your stubborn streak, that I'll need every moment of it."

Amanda shivered and looked again through the darkening windows, wishing she could put the sun in her pocket and carry it with her always. He hadn't stayed long last night after she'd eaten, wanting her to get more rest. When he'd locked the door behind him with his own set of keys, Amanda had thought she'd never sleep again.

For the first time in my life, I don't feel safe in my home. She shuddered. *I don't want to go there, knowing he'll be waiting for me. Knowing he can waltz in whenever he pleases.*

"You okay, Amanda?" Lily came by, her hands full of till slips from the registers.

Amanda jumped and turned away from the window. "I'm fine. A little under the weather, I guess."

Lily passed an appraising eye over her. "You look a little pale. Why don't you head home? We'll finish up here."

Great, just what I wanted. She forced a smile. "Thanks, Lil."

After punching out, Amanda gathered her courage and walked outside. It had been hard to go to work and pretend that everything was normal; now, she found that walking out to her car was one of the hardest things she'd ever done. Even with the comfort of the lights, her neck prickled like it was expecting a hand to grab it at any moment, and she had to make sure there was no one in the backseat twice before she felt secure enough to start driving. *It's not paranoia if they're really out to get you,* Amanda thought to herself humorlessly.

It was a miracle she made it home in one piece, given how distracted she was. Every shift of lighting or movement half-glimpsed from the corner of her eye made her jump. By the time she pulled into her parking spot in front of her apartment building, Amanda was so tense her teeth were chattering. Her hands shook so badly it took her three tries to unlock the front door.

She forced herself to take a few deep, slow breaths as she descended the stairs to her door. *No fear. Just like with an animal. Back straight, shoulders back, chin up, and...go!*

The apartment was empty.

She could hardly believe it, even after checking under the bed and in all the closets. Giddy with relief, Amanda stood in the walkway between the back of the couch and the kitchen island and wondered what she should do with herself.

Footsteps sounded on the stairs, so loud and slow Amanda expected to hear someone boom "Fee fi fo fum!" It was so overdone that between his theatrics and the giddiness, she couldn't quite work up the proper level of dread again before Gabriel knocked.

He didn't wait for an invitation, but opened the door and came in as if he had every right to. "How was work?"

"It was fine." She leaned against the back of the couch, arms crossed, watching him warily.

He locked the door. "And how are you feeling tonight?"

"Better." She shrugged. "Fine."

"Good." He came over to the couch, mimicking her posture, and it took Amanda a great deal of effort not to sidle away from him. "Are you hungry?"

Now that her stomach was done tying itself into knots... "Yeah, starving."

"Then let's—"

All he did was gesture to the door with one hand and place the other lightly, casually, at the small of her back.

Before Amanda could stop herself, she knocked his hand away with a strangled shriek. She retreated a few steps until the corner of the couch was between them.

Gabriel ceased to move, his hands still spread wide as he watched her.

"I'm sorry," Amanda stammered, and then wondered why she was apologizing. "You startled me."

Like a man trying to corner a frightened horse, Gabriel walked slowly around the couch, keeping his hands wide. "I didn't make it clear, last night. You're mine now, Amanda, under my protection. By my own rules, I can't harm you." His gaze flicked over her, hesitating over her throat. His eyes, when he met hers again, were as serious and solemn as she'd ever seen them, and a deep, luminous blue. "I can't take anything you do not freely give."

Her breath caught, the weight of his gaze making it hard to speak. "Really?"

"I give you my word." Then he smiled at her, the charming I'm-just-a-harmless-human smile she was beginning to recognize as his way of breaking tension. "Shall we go get you something to eat?"

She hesitated, still a little creeped out by the abrupt switching of gears. *But then, intense scary vampire Gabriel is a bit too much for me, right now. I can pretend if he can.* "Do I get to define harm?"

Gabriel laughed. "No." But he said it with a good-natured grin that Amanda found obscurely comforting.

"Damn." Her feet dragging, she followed him back outside.

He led her over to a compact black coupe, unlocking her door before walking around to the driver's side. Taking a deep breath, Amanda opened the door and sat down. The seat molded itself to her shape, the scent of the leather surrounding her as she shut the door. "Nice," she murmured, grateful to have something to say.

"Thanks." The engine purred to life. "This is my baby. I do all the work on her myself." He rubbed the steering wheel affectionately.

A giggle broke loose. "A vampire gearhead?"

"Cars beat the hell out of horses." His tone was just a little on the defensive side. "Where are we going?"

"Taco Bell? I'm not sure what else is open at this hour."

"Taco Bell it is." He put the car in motion.

Amanda ran a hand over the upholstery. "Horses," she mused. "Just how old are you, anyway?"

"I forget the exact date. I can never remember how it converts to the Christian calendar." He spoke without looking at her, his eyes on the road. "I was born about a hundred years before the fall of the Roman Republic, if that helps you."

Amanda's jaw dropped. "You're more than two thousand years old?"

"You know something about history, anyway. Refreshing."

The idea that someone who looked her own age could be so vastly ancient made Amanda's head swim. "Um, you hide it well."

Gabriel chuckled.

"How did you become a vampire? If you don't mind my asking," she added. Amanda wasn't sure how much she could trust his "protection" if she offended him.

"I don't mind. I was living on a farm in Gaul, and I was coming home from town late. I'd left later than I should, but I had a new toy for my eldest, can't even remember what it was, and I couldn't wait to see his face."

Gabriel's expression was mild, as if he were talking about a trip to grocery store. Amanda, on the other hand, was having a hard time wrapping her head around the idea that Gabriel had had children.

"My mare stepped in a hole, though. I was leading her home on foot when I was attacked. Of course, she took off well enough then. Can't say I blame her, but that was no help to me. I was face first on the road with some *barbarus* on my back."

Gabriel pulled into the parking lot of the Taco Bell and got in line at the drive-thru. "He took me like a two-bit whore," he said disgustedly.

"He bit you?"

He gave her an amused glance. "It's not the bite, it's the blood. Yes, he bit me. I don't know why he decided to turn me, not for sure. Without feeding me his blood, I would've just died. But he did. I was so weak from blood loss by then that I turned immediately. And then passed out. I woke up in a cave the next night."

Gabriel pulled up to the menu board, then added a little too casually, "The townsfolk killed him two days later." He powered down his window. "What do you want to eat?"

* * * *

In a small clearing deep in a northern Minnesota forest, Isolde Constantinus finished building up the fire and turned to face her prisoner. Toby Cartwright's wrists and ankles were cuffed together behind the trunk of a small maple. The firelight cast flickering shadows across his face and made the rest of the surrounding woods even darker than before. There was no other light, no sounds save the distant call of an owl and the impersonal calls of insects.

No one would hear Cartwright's screams.

Cartwright had been easy to find; the fool still used credit cards when he traveled. Isolde had several contacts in the credit industry—some tied to her by blood, and some merely bought with large monthly bribes—so when she had returned to the States, she had simply called three of her contacts and chosen the most likely candidate from the few known hunters that were still on the radar. Morales had stopped using plastic years ago, and he was teaching the others.

Enrique Morales was the one she was truly after, not small fry like Cartwright. Kim Hyo had been the most dangerous vampire hunter in the world, and Fury Lee Bae had nearly killed the hunter several times until Kim fled to Colombia, out of Lee's reach. Isolde had caught and killed Kim in Bogotá, which left Morales as the next most dangerous hunter in the world.

The Fury Isolde always hunted the best.

Cartwright glared defiance from where he knelt on the uneven ground, his back as straight and stiff as the tree trunk he was bound to, but his scent was lined with fear. Isolde smiled at him. The ones who were too self-righteous for fear were hard to break—at least, hard to break in such a way as to leave anything useful at the end. Isolde needed information, not blubbering. She had chosen her target well.

Cartwright was a formidable hunter with a long kill record. He had watched her kind die by blade and fire. She doubted he would make this easy on himself.

The vampire hunter clenched his jaw and drew himself up to as much height as he could manage as Isolde knelt in front of him. He did not speak.

She started simply, her tone conversational. "Tell me where Morales is and I'll give you a quick, clean death."

He spat at her.

Isolde dodged, sliding to the side faster than he could see. She sighed. "Hunter, you know what I can do to you."

"Go to hell."

His voice was deep and rough. Isolde liked the sound of it.

"Do you know who I am?" she asked, taking a slim knife from one of her wrist sheaths.

"Isolde Constantinus." He made a brave mockery of her name.

She would change that tone soon enough.

"Very good," she purred, leaning in close. Cartwright eyed her, but did not shrink back. "Then you know my reputation. I assure you, it is not unearned."

The slim blade flashed in the firelight, and a hair-thin line of red seeped from a tiny wound just below Cartwright's left eye. His flinch came far too late; Isolde was already holding up the knife, its tip stained red. She sniffed at it, then made a show of licking the blade clean, exposing her lengthening fangs.

"Your blood is still pure," she said as she lowered the blade. "But I will bleed you all night. Bleed you and heal you, bleed you and heal you, until your voice is gone from screaming and your blood runs thick with vampire taint."

She leaned in and licked the tiny trickle of blood from his cheek.

When Cartwright tried to turn away she seized his chin and held him steady. His refusal to look her in the eye was just a bittersweet reminder of why she had to do this the hard way. It was good training on his part, but she was still skinshifter enough that he had nothing to fear from her gaze.

"Then, just before dawn, I will turn you. I will turn you and not feed you and I will put you in a metal box to cook in the sun all day while you sleep. I will leave you there to suffer from the heat of the sun and the fire in your veins until I know that you are nothing but a ravening killing machine.

"Then I will take your box and drop it in the middle of one of these delightful little hamlets, and I will open it, and I will leave."

His gaze darted to hers despite his training.

"Oh, don't worry," she whispered. "I'll be nearby, making sure none of them manages to elude you. It might take you a little while to kill them all. But you will. And when their deaths are heavy on your soul and their lives fill you to bursting, you might even regain your wits, and remember what it was to be a man like they were. Then you will either help me track down your hunter brethren, or I'll send you on your way to hell personally."

Sweat had broken out on Cartwright's face, and his lips were white and bloodless, but it would take more than threats to break his spirit. "You're bluffing. You'd hunt down a rogue like that yourself."

The tiny cut had stopped bleeding. She kissed his cheek. "Who better than me to clean up after your massacre? Once you're dead no one will ever guess I created you. The Fury Isolde is a hero to her people." *A hero to be feared, a boogeyman to frighten fledglings. And their masters.* Even among the Furies, the vampire paladins, she was an outsider. "Isolde Huntersbane. Isolde Rogueslayer. So few people use my real name." Not her true name; at least, not all of it. Her father and brother would die before revealing that, as she would die before revealing theirs. "Say it again, hunter."

He whispered it, and Isolde shivered. He did have a wonderful voice. Such a pity.

"Morales told it to you, didn't he?" she asked.

Cartwright barked a derisive laugh. "You are a legend to us. It's been known for hundreds of years."

Isolde could smell the lie. She clicked her tongue in mock reproach. "And we've been getting on so well. Tell me true now, hunter."

Instead of answering, Cartwright closed his eyes and braced himself.

Sighing, Isolde went to work.

* * * *

"Whoa, what do you mean, go hunting with you?" Amanda was already regretting dinner, her stomach twisting at the idea of the vampire feeding. Her hand started to creep up to cover her neck, but she forced it back down.

"I'm not planning on killing anyone tonight," Gabriel replied as he drove, his tone conveying his amusement. "A swallow here and there keeps me going between kills, and I usually only kill once a month or so. Most of my regular prey don't even realize what I am."

"Your regular prey?"

"Blood fetishists, mostly, although a lot of them didn't start out that way." He tapped the corner of his eye with one finger. "Warping someone's desires is an investment of power, but considering how long I've been here it pays off handsomely. If I don't actually bite them I don't have to make them forget about it later."

Amanda stared, appalled. "You mean you brainwash people into enjoying having their blood drunk?"

"Yes."

35

Swallowing hard to keep her tacos down, Amanda turned away. "Ugh! That's awful! Can't you just find people who are willing to let you bite them? I would think, given what it feels like..." Her cheeks were burning, and she didn't finish.

"And what did it feel like?"

She couldn't sort out his tone, whether he meant the question tauntingly or teasingly or—doubtful—honestly. "I think being forced to enjoy something doesn't mean it's not still rape," she snapped.

"Agreed. And I do have pets, people who are willing, but they're few. It's an even bigger power investment to make sure someone can't betray me. Vampire hunters are just as real as vampires."

Amanda looked back at him, but she couldn't read his expression. "Vampire hunters. Like, stake and holy water vampire hunters?"

Gabriel grimaced. "Sometimes. Those are the easy ones, too stupid to live past their first encounter. But there are enough of the ones who know, who've learned how best to kill us, that I don't take chances by being sloppy with my prey."

"I see." She bit her lip. "And what is the best way to kill you?"

He gave a silent laugh. "Oh, daylight, fire, removing the head or heart, that kind of thing. Spells and charms—religious or otherwise—can be effective deterrents, but the only liquid I've ever seen harm a vampire is acid." He paused, then added thoughtfully, "And fire would've been a much better choice."

"I'm surprised you answered that."

"You have a right to know."

He pulled into a parking spot in front of what looked like a barn, and Amanda did a double-take. *He's going hunting at Branch Street Retreat?* She hadn't been to the bar in a while, but mostly she remembered pool players and people watching sports on TV.

Gabriel parked and killed the engine. "Besides, there is a certain amount of risk inherent in vetting a fledgling, and a certain amount of trust required as well. I don't think you're the type to go tale-bearing, even if it wouldn't get you killed."

Amanda definitely didn't like it when put her and "killed" in the same sentence. "Why does your bite have that effect, anyway?" she asked before he could say anything else. "I mean, it makes no sense. Fangs in my neck shouldn't feel good, it should just hurt like hell."

"I think you'll recall that it does hurt, until the venom kicks in." He shrugged. "The venom gets produced by glands right behind the fangs when I bite down hard, but it takes a few seconds to get circulated enough to be effective."

Amanda shook her head. "Your teeth look totally normal. That's so not fair."

"Camouflage. They're retractable, like a cat's claws. Watch."

Gabriel closed his eyes, and Amanda was startled by a sudden, inexplicable feeling of movement from him, almost like breath against her skin, that rose up through him from his gut. His lips parted with a silent exhalation, and his fangs extended.

Amanda leaned forward in spite of herself. She could see the difference now; not just the length, but the angle of the bottom edges was more acute, tapering to point that was sharp like a dagger, not rounded and worn as human teeth were. She started to reach up to touch, but caught herself.

Gabriel chuckled, his eyes glittering under half-closed lids. "Have a look," he said, gesturing her on. His smile was an amused dare and a promise all at once. "Just watch out for the ridge on the back. It's sharp."

That smile goaded her, combining with her natural curiosity to tip the scales against her better judgment. She pressed one fingertip against the front of one of his canines, half expecting it to feel loose, and nearly jumped out of her skin when she felt pressure back as muscles in his gums flexed.

She laughed at herself, feeling like she'd just shrieked after glimpsing a spider. *Spiders bite too, you know.* "I'd love to see an x-ray of your teeth."

Gabriel snorted, keeping perfectly still as Amanda slid her fingertip around to the back. The ridge made the tooth feel more triangular than round. Delicately she tested the sharpness just as she would a knife's edge, and wondered how he kept from slicing his tongue open on it. Before she could ask, she felt a little divot next to ridge. *No, more like a groove.* She followed it up along the ridge, all the way from the tip to his gums, and there against his hard palate was the small, soft bulge of the venom gland.

Gabriel sucked in a startled breath. Amanda looked up to find him watching her warily. Raising one speculative eyebrow, she traced over that bump with gentle pressure. The vampire started to shake—a very fine, light tremor—and a look of desperation flitted past those odd irises. That feeling of movement, the wave of energy she had felt, roiled in the air between them.

Finally Gabriel reached up and moved her hand until he could close his mouth. With a sigh he relaxed, his head drooping as the wave of his hunger retreated, vanishing under the general cloak of his presence. He looked down at her hand rather than at her face, rubbing the skin of her finger as if to make sure it was still whole.

"Nothing that you do not give," he said. "Damn, but I have the munchies now. Let's go."

* * * *

The clearing was every bit as isolated as Isolde had thought. No one came to investigate Cartwright's screams, which was just as well. She didn't think making him watch while she killed an innocent bystander would do anything but bolster his resolve, and truthfully she avoided it whenever possible. Her threat about the massacre was not entirely idle, but most hunters broke long before she had to start considering whether or not to go through with it.

This time was no exception.

It was well past three a.m. when she finally blinded him. Isolde was not a sadist. She took no pleasure in giving pain, but his voice held out surprisingly well, and she truly did enjoy the sound of it. Even so, eventually she needed to move on. Blinding and amputation went a long way in breaking someone. They both drove home the message of, "You are not going to live through this. I'm going to kill you, and I don't care what I do to you beforehand." Amputations were such a waste of blood, though.

She was careful to hold his head hard against the tree trunk both times. When she took his first eye, he struggled to get away as the knife drew closer.

One short, precise stab.

After he stopped screaming, she asked her questions again, but he still refused to answer. This time when she held him she felt him struggling to throw himself onto the blade. Isolde scolded him gently as she pierced his other eye.

"You'll not get out of this so easy, Cartwright. You haven't answered my questions yet. I decide when you die, not you."

His screams turned into harsh sobs.

There he goes. She'd learned long ago that you couldn't start with blinding; you had to work up to it. You had to make them *want* to die first. Then you took even that away from them.

"Please kill me," he begged, sagging bonelessly against the tree. "Please, just kill me."

"I can't do that yet," she replied, voice thick with regret. She leaned hard against him, chest to chest, and whispered softly into his ear. "I can't yet. You're too stubborn. You're making me keep going."

38

His whole body shook as her mouth moved down to his neck. "No, no, please no. Please, not again."

"I'm sorry," she breathed, and bit deep.

He cried out, despair turning into a wail of pleasure as the endorphins hit him, washing away the pain.

His blood burned all the way down to her stomach. She took only a little, and then sliced her wrist open and held the wound to his lips. He was limp in his bonds. She held him up, tipped his head back, and let the blood run down his throat. He'd tried to drown himself in it once, but his gag reflex betrayed him. Now he was too broken to fight.

She'd only given him a few swallows at a time before—now she let him drink, and drink.

She'd made new vampires before, centuries ago, but the Furies were sworn to create no fledglings. Since joining their ranks five hundred years ago, Isolde had found that she needed this release more often than she used to. She needed to feel the blood drawn from her veins, needed to pit herself against the seduction of a hungry mouth.

More than the ceaseless hunt, more than the constant migration of following target after target, the most dangerous part of Isolde's existence were those fleeting moments when she forced her blood on a human and chose whether or not that would be the night she finally died.

Not tonight. I want Morales. He's eluded us for too long.

With her free hand, Isolde picked up two extra pairs of handcuffs from the pile she'd left next to the tree and cuffed Cartwright's wrists and ankles again, just in case.

She took her wrist away from his mouth.

Cartwright sucked in a long, startled breath, and then he screamed. It was a deep, full-throated sound that rose and fell along the scale, ringing through the clearing and echoing back in odd ways. Isolde shivered delightedly. The hunter tried to bash his head against the trunk of the tree but Isolde put her hand in between. Cartwright didn't seem to notice. He just kept thrashing and screaming while her blood seized him. The handcuffs bit into him, his skin tearing and knitting back together by turns. The metal protested, digging furrows into the tree bark, but held firm.

When the screaming stopped, Cartwright blinked and looked up at Isolde with two whole but haunted eyes.

"You can feel it inside you now, can't you?"

He nodded wordlessly.

"If I kill you now, you'll turn."

His gaze flicked toward the fire. He stared at it as a starving man stares at a feast. "You can still kill me," he whispered.

"Yes." She turned his face back toward her. "Give me a reason to."

When he hesitated, she laid the tip of the blade against the corner of his eye. "They might grow back on their own this time."

Cartwright began to speak.

CHAPTER FIVE

Monday, May 17th, 1999

Paul absently stirred his lemon soup and listened to Cecelia with half an ear. It was his turn to pick, so they were having lunch on the campus end of State Street. Mediterranean Café was much closer to Paul's office than it was to Cecelia's. Tomorrow they'd be eating somewhere closer to the Square.

He wondered how his father's hunt was going. The skinshifters and the mages were all on edge; none of them were old enough to remember Gabriel's last protégé, who had already been a vampire for twenty years when Gabriel and Cian moved to Madison.

Paul remembered. He remembered all of them.

The other communities are right to be worried. They're used to Father being cold and calculating. They've never seen him be reckless.

Paul suppressed a sigh. For all the times his father had played this game, Paul still didn't fully understand it, or the need that drove it. He glanced out the café's window at the sunlit street. *In between worlds in so many ways.*

Something Cecelia said caught his attention. "What, love?"

She pouted at him. She was particularly good at pouting, but only did it to tease. "You *have* been preoccupied, haven't you?"

He reached across the little table and took her hand. "Yes, I'm sorry."

Her playful expression faded. "Is it about your book?"

That was their code, their way of talking about impossible things in public. "Yes. Sort of a subplot tangle." He squeezed her hand. "It's not important."

She let it go. "Well, I was saying, I had thought to have Randall give me away at the wedding, since Dad passed on, but I wondered if maybe your father would want the honor."

Paul gave a startled jerk. "No, let your brother do it." Gently touching her thoughts, he added, *You can't mention to anyone that he's my father.*

Her brows drew down, and Paul suppressed another sigh. He doubted Cecelia would ever get the hang of having two conversations at once without letting her face show it. *Why not?* he heard her think. She couldn't project much, but Paul spent energy trying *not* to hear people; picking up his fiancée's responses was as easy as breathing.

"If you think Randall wants to, that is," Paul said out loud, reminding her to keep up both halves of the discussion. *I look older than he does.*

"I'm sure he will." Cecelia looked down at her bowl to hide her surprise. *How can you be older than your own father?*

"Good. Then that's settled." *I age, he doesn't. He was twenty-three when he was turned, so that's how old he looks.* Paul himself looked close to forty, and wanted to keep it that way. As it was, he'd need to start putting gray in his beard in a few years or Cecelia would catch up to him.

"I *am* going to get to meet your father before the wedding, right?" She cocked her head to the side. "I mean, it might be a bit awkward otherwise."

Paul looked down at his soup. "That would probably be best," he agreed reluctantly. "But he's pretty busy right now. Maybe in a couple months."

Cecelia didn't press him, but Paul could practically feel her curiosity ratcheting up another notch. She'd wanted to meet Gabriel ever since she found out he was still alive, which had been disappointingly soon after Paul had told her about his own nature. Most of his wives had known enough to be afraid of a vampire, but Cecelia was too much a child of the TV era. He was pretty sure she didn't believe him that Gabriel was a monster in the classic sense of the word.

And you aren't, Paulus?

The thought was in his father's voice, but it came from inside his own head. He'd heard the lecture often enough that Gabriel didn't even have to give it anymore; Paul gave it to himself out of pure reflex. *You can't be the hero with the dark secret if the secret is too strong for you. The hero is always able to overcome his inner demons in the end.*

"You don't think he'd want to have some part in the ceremony? Groomsman, maybe?" Cecelia took a bite of bread and a sip of tea, watching him with intense interest as she chewed.

Paul sighed and reminded himself that her tenacity was one of the things he loved about her. "I don't think so, Cici. He's...not fond of being up in front of large groups." *He may very well just slip in and slip back out again,* Paul told her. *He really dislikes being documented.* Of course, so did Paul, but it was far easier for him to change his appearance than it was for his father.

Even that oblique thought made his stomach clench hard. Damn, but it was getting close to the surface again.

The bell above the door chimed softly, but the gust of spring air that kissed his cheek told Paul who it was before he even turned to look. The scent of the mage's fiery blood made Paul's mouth go dry, but he throttled the response as he usually did. Mostly.

"Gil!" Cecelia grinned, waving at the lean, grizzled man as he entered. "How are you?"

"Well, if it isn't the lovely Cecelia. You certainly are a welcome sight for these tired old eyes." Professor Gil Spielmann dropped a fatherly kiss on the cheek Cecelia offered up to him. "I was just down to Paul's office but he wasn't there, so I thought I'd get a bite of lunch, and here you are!"

Bullshit, Paul thought to himself with a silent groan. "What can I do for you?"

"Oh, it's just a bit of research I'm having trouble with," Gil said, "nothing that can't wait. I wouldn't want to interrupt your lunch date..."

Gil let the words trail off, and Cecelia leapt into the breach just as both men knew she would. "I have to get back to the office soon anyway. Why don't I leave you two to your translations?" She stood, gulping down the last of her tea while Gil murmured weak and insincere protests. Cecelia waved him off. "No, no, I'm probably going to be late as it is." *Try not to fall asleep, dear. You'll hurt Gil's feelings.* She gave Paul a quick kiss and a mischievous wink, and vanished out the door.

Paul pursed his lips and raised an eyebrow at Gil. "You couldn't have waited?"

"I'm afraid there's been a bit of a wrinkle. Perhaps we could go back to my office?"

With a mournful look at his half-full bowl, Paul reached for his wallet.

They hardly had to dodge anyone as they crossed Library Mall and started up Bascom Hill. The walk across campus wasn't long, and faster now that most of the students had gone for the summer. Gil kept pace with Paul's longer strides easily enough, showing no sign of his age now outside of his silver hair and steel mustache, for all that he liked to put on a show for Cecelia.

Paul hadn't told her about Gil being a mage; he tried his best to keep her shielded from dangerous knowledge. As far as she knew, Gil was just a professor at the University like Paul was. Gil taught Latin, among other things, and since Paul had grown up speaking Latin, it made perfect sense to her that the two men would collaborate on occasion. Not that Paul advertised where he'd learned the language, of course.

The scent of the power stored in Gil's veins flared slightly each time they crossed one of the many ley lines that crowded under Bascom Hill. Paul couldn't tell what kind of magic Gil carried; that had been Isolde's specialty, not his. Her nose had always been more discriminating, but his served well enough. *I don't need to know if he's a sorcerer or a witch or a cleric to some god. He smells like mage, and all mages are dangerous.*

Van Hise was a rather boring rectangle of glass and concrete compared to the older, more ornate buildings they passed to get there, but Paul had to admit that the view of Lake Mendota was a damn sight nicer than any view at Humanities, where Paul's office was. Once the two men were safely behind Gil's office door—and, Paul assumed, a bevy of privacy spells—Gil got to the point.

"Did you know Gabriel was on the cusp of taking the child?"

Paul shook his head. "Not before Martin called me on Friday."

Gil frowned with patrician disapproval. "I thought you were supposed to be keeping tabs on him."

Paul allowed himself a small smile. "Just how close do you expect anyone to get? The vampire can be a mite prickly, even with me."

That was an evasion, but true enough in its own way. As far as Paul knew, none of the mages could sense a lie, but the skinshifters could, so he kept in good practice.

Gil shifted in his chair. He was seated behind his great desk and used to the emotional advantages it usually granted, but Paul had dealt with far more imposing personages than Gil Spielmann.

Including real patricians.

Paul's inexhaustible composure under scrutiny always put Gil off-balance. The mages thought Paul was a human, a mage like themselves most likely, though speculation ran rife as to whether he was a necromancer or a blood mage, or perhaps just a thrall of the vampire. They probably would've shunned him if his relationship with Gabriel hadn't made him so useful. The mages weren't sure just what that relationship was, of course, but that didn't stop them from taking advantage of it. Gil, at least, remembered what dealing with Gabriel had been like before Paul had come to Madison.

It's hard to intimidate someone who is used to defeating his rivals by outliving them.

"Well, it looks like he's not just making a pet of *this* one." Gil's tone was suggestive, and he watched Paul to see if his words elicited any response, but beneath his posturing, Gil's distress was great enough that it turned the scent of his blood sour.

Paul shrugged, refusing to rise to the bait. "I hear that happens, every now and again. He's quite mindful of our situation here; you needn't be concerned. I'm sure if she turns they'll do most of her hunting in Milwaukee or Chicago…"

He'd been certain that was what Gil had been worried about, but to his surprise the old man was shaking his head.

"I went by her place of work a short time ago to have a look at her myself." Gil's lips were set in a thin, hard line. "I don't think our resident vampire quite realizes what he's done."

* * * *

Still dressed in her work clothes, Amanda collapsed on her couch and kicked off her shoes. *I can't wait until the new schedule starts,* she thought, too exhausted to resent why she was so tired. The bookstore didn't open until ten a.m., so even a late shift the night before didn't normally present much of a hardship. Being out until four a.m. made getting up in time for work just a bit more of a struggle than usual. She could function all right on six hours of sleep, but with less than five she was prone to biting people's heads off. *Although, not literally. Yet.*

That was supposed to be a joke, but she wasn't laughing. *I don't know if I'm just too tired or if that just wasn't funny.*

The phone rang. *Probably Brandy.* Amanda had left a message on Brandy's machine that morning before work, returning a message Brandy had left on Amanda's machine the night before, which Amanda had apparently slept through. This sort of phone tag wasn't unusual, but she didn't want Brandy worrying. *She hasn't talked to me since I left the bar with Gabriel on Friday. She's more right to be worried than even she realizes.*

Amanda grabbed the phone from the end table and brought the receiver to her ear. "Hey."

"Is that how you answer the phone now?" Her mother's voice dripped disapproval.

I so do not have the energy for this. "Hi, Mom. I thought you were Brandy."

There was a sniff so loud Amanda could see her mother's nose wrinkling. "That's a terrible habit, Mandy. What if I'd been someone important?"

But you aren't someone important. Amanda gritted her teeth. "Stop calling me Mandy."

"You've always been Mandy, dear, don't be silly."

"No, you've always called me Mandy. Everyone else stopped in the fourth grade when I asked them to." Amanda counted to three and tried to stop growling. "What can I do for you, Mom?"

"Can't a mother just call to say hello?"

Someone else's mother, maybe. You, on the other hand, always want something. Amanda didn't say it, though. She just waited, rolling onto her side and wedging the receiver under her head so she didn't have to hold it. There was no chance of her falling asleep on the line, not with her mother on the other end, but she wished she could.

Penny Bairns never could stand a silence. "Well, I know you said you had to work Memorial Day weekend, but Robbie is going to be in town."

Amanda's breath caught. "He is?" God, she hadn't seen her brother in over a year. He'd sworn he couldn't get leave last Christmas, but Amanda wasn't sure she believed it.

"Yes, and it would be so wonderful to have both of you in the house again…"

Her mother's wistful tone made Amanda wince. There was no way any of them would live up to the image Penny was already building in her mind of what the visit would be like. There was going to be at least one shouting match, guaranteed. It always went that way. *So it'll probably be at least another year until Robbie comes home again. I'd better see him while I can.* "I'm sure I can swap shifts with someone, at least for an afternoon. What time is he getting in?"

"Couldn't you stay the weekend? We never get to see you."

Hell, no. "I can't, I already agreed to work the hours and swapping out's going to be bad enough."

Penny gave a long-suffering sigh. "Well, I suppose. Although you'd think you could be a little more considerate of your poor parents; it's not like we ask all that much…"

Amanda closed her eyes and stopped listening. She didn't even bother with "mm-hmm" or "uh-huh" to pretend she was paying attention. Amanda had been doing this since she moved out and Penny had yet to notice.

Finally she heard, "…and he said he should be here around noon on Sunday."

"Great," Amanda broke in. "I'll see you at noon then."

Her thoughts whirled in sluggish circles as she disengaged with her mother; ending a phone call with Penny could be a lengthy process unless you didn't mind being absolutely rude. *If Robbie's there at noon, things should explode in plenty of time for me to get home before it gets dark, even with a two-hour drive. Gabriel doesn't even have to know I'm going.*

Even if they are annoying, I'm not letting him get anywhere near my family. Dad and Robbie are both he-men enough to want to try and save me, and probably get us all killed in the process. If there's any protecting anyone to be done here, I'm the one who's gonna be doing it.

Finally, she was able to hang up the phone. Amanda forced her eyes open with a groan and blinked blearily at the VCR clock. *I have a few hours yet before sundown. I should get a shower, have some dinner. Change clothes.* She'd been exhausted *before* talking to her mother; now, the bedroom seemed miles away from her spot on the couch. *A nice hot shower would do you wonders. You've just got to get back up.*

By the time she'd talked herself into it, she was already asleep.

* * * *

The dream started out as a memory. She was following Gabriel through a sparsely crowded bar just as she had last night, the low lighting and smoky atmosphere and neon signs blending together into an archetypal caricature of Wisconsin bars, not any one specific bar but all bars at once. The vampire ignored her, stopping here and there to talk to a faceless patron, smiling, laughing, before making his choice and using light, causal touches to draw his victim away from the others. Amanda sat on a stool at the endlessly long bar and watched Gabriel and his dinner disappear into the shadows, save for a stray gleam of light that caught the edge of the straight razor he carried with him.

It was that razor she'd felt pressed to her throat in the darkness of her apartment, its blade every bit as sharp as she'd feared. She'd watched him press it to other throats last night, but those people had all welcomed it.

He's twisted them. She shuddered. *He's made them want it.*

The act itself had been remarkably discrete; if she hadn't been looking for the blade, mostly hidden by his hand, she probably wouldn't have seen it, and the necking that followed had just looked like, well, necking. He took so little from any one person that no one had shown the least suspicion or concern, but that also meant he had to nuzzle quite a few necks. By the third venue Amanda's nervousness had given way to boredom, and she'd spent most of the night at the bar nursing one drink after another.

Trying to read the shifting labels on the bottles that lined the wall, Amanda started to spin her glass out of habit and nearly knocked it over. A tall bloody mary sat in front of her instead of her usual short gin and tonic. She wrinkled her nose. *I hate tomato juice.* She lifted her head to call the bartender so she could get the right drink, but she was startled to see that he had an oozing red wound on the side of his neck. Blood ran down under his shirt in little pulsing rivulets.

Amanda frowned. *That's not very like Gabriel.*

She turned to look for the vampire but only found more bleeding patrons, all of them laughing and chatting while their clothes turned red and started to drip onto the floor. *He won't like this. Someone's bound to notice this mess, and he told me no one is supposed to notice.*

She didn't see Gabriel anywhere, but the room was huge and dark and full of moving shadows, so she hopped off her stool and went to look for him. Her shoes made a sticky, squelching noise as she walked.

They have to see what's happening eventually. Amanda tried to walk a little faster. The floor was slick now, the blood almost half an inch deep and rising. *I don't want to be the only one not bleeding when they realize they're all dying slowly. Where the hell is he?*

The lights around the bar were fading behind her, the shadows growing deeper the farther she went until she couldn't see at all, and she walked with her hands stretched out in front of her, feeling the currents of the patrons' breaths against her skin. *Too warm,* she thought, edging to one side to avoid bumping into someone, reaching, searching. *Too warm. Too warm. Gabriel, dammit, where are you?*

A tendril of cold air brushed past her fingers, and Amanda grabbed at it. The dream shifted.

After the absolute dark she'd been searching through, the dim light here was almost blinding. Even so, the scene was pretty hazy—more so than cigarette smoke could account for. She would've blinked if she had eyes.

Gabriel sat at the bar at the Union House, the eyes of his image in the big mirror drifting from the door to the patrons and back in a lazy circuit, occasionally glancing at the man next to him as they chatted amiably about the weather. Amanda was sort of between them and behind them and in front of them by turns, unable to settle into one perspective. When she was in front of him, Gabriel looked straight through her; when she was behind, she could find no hint of her presence in the mirror. There was a buzzing sound, not quite in her ears since she didn't have any, that had nothing to do with the hum of conversation.

Or does it? The sound sort of had that cadence, the rhythm of two people talking. Amanda tried to tune out the crowd around her, focusing so hard on listening to the buzzing that her vision dimmed and nearly went out altogether.

I don't see what he's so upset about. I know what I'm doing. Gabriel's voice echoed, as if he were talking through a heating duct.

Do you really? The response came from the man beside Gabriel, but it was even fainter and more echoey and harder for Amanda to make out. *She's a natural adept. Gil nearly blacked out when he did the sounding.*

I trained you, didn't I? Gabriel was beginning to sound peevish.

The other man sighed. *You know psionics are not your strong suit, Father.*

Amanda gave a start. *Father?*

Both men raised their heads at once, suddenly tense. And then the one she didn't know looked right at her.

CHAPTER SIX

Amanda's field of view narrowed down to the shifting gray eyes of the stranger, the rest of the Union House fading from her awareness. His eyes looked just like Gabriel's, but his hair was darker, mustache and beard just as black as the hair on his head. He was leaner as well, and while there were certainly similarities in chin and cheekbones and mouth, the rest was different enough that she wondered if maybe "Father" was some sort of honorific instead of a familial relationship. She wished she could blink. The haze made it hard for her to guess at his age; she'd thought him older than the vampire, but he *felt* younger. And warmer, too.

Well, well, aren't you a quick learner. The man's words were suddenly clear and loud in her mind, and there was a good-natured glint in his eye. The stranger stared at Amanda just long enough for her to be sure he saw her, then went back to his perusal of the bar. She could feel his gaze on her even when he was facing the other direction. *I think this makes Gil's point quite nicely.*

The last comment was as clear as the first, but it wasn't aimed at her. It was an odd sensation, a vague feeling of movement, like an arrow shooting past her toward the vampire.

Gabriel had his eyes half closed, but when he focused his attention on her a jolting pull shook Amanda that would've made her teeth rattle. He was still talking out loud, something about the flood of '93, but the words faded into the background babble of bar noise. *I see,* he thought at the other man, and this time there was no tinny echo.

I'll leave you to it, the stranger thought back with a distinct edge of amusement.

Amanda. Gabriel's grip on her tightened, and she had a sense of impending movement, water gathering behind a dam. *Wake up. Now.*

Gabriel shoved her somehow, and the dam let go, and then Amanda was tumbling through the darkness like a piece of flotsam in a storm-swollen river, hurtling through nothing at what felt like breakneck speed, and she was just thinking that she was glad she apparently didn't have a neck to break when everything slammed to an abrupt, jarring halt.

Amanda sat up, arms and legs flailing so wildly she fell right off the couch.

When Gabriel arrived about twenty minutes later, Amanda was just coming out of the bathroom. His footsteps were light and even as he came down the hall. She ignored him, toweling her wet hair furiously, glad for the excuse not to look at him right away.

Was that just a messed up dream? The more time that passed, the more foolish it felt to think otherwise…but she was still afraid to look. She didn't want to see that same cold, considering look on his face now as she'd seen right before he'd told her to wake up. *It wasn't a look, exactly, it was…like he was weighing me against something else, something valuable.*

Gabriel stopped in the doorway but said nothing. Swallowing hard once, Amanda threw the towel at the hamper and turned to face him.

He was leaning against the doorframe, arms crossed loosely, one leg bent, his head cocked to one side. The pose emphasized the breadth of his shoulders and the way his snug jeans hugged his hips, but he was still wearing that calculating expression, and she couldn't repress the shudder fast enough.

"It wasn't a dream, was it?" The words came out as a mortifying squeak.

His steel-gray eyes followed her every movement. "Tell me."

She sat down on the bed and drew her knees up to her chest, hugging them as she recounted the dream. Or whatever it was. She wanted to look at the floor, or the ceiling, or anywhere except at him, but she forced herself to watch his face, his posture. Nothing changed, even after she was done.

A human would move. A human would shift his weight, or scratch his face, or do something that might give away what he's thinking.

Gabriel did none of these things, not even when he finally spoke. "The part in the Union House was real. The rest was a dream."

Her stomach was so tight it was hard to breathe. She waited for the other shoe to drop.

"You're afraid." When she made no reply he added, "I gave you my word."

"Things are different now, aren't they?" This sudden, uncharacteristic coldness made her realize just how much she relied on his pretense of humanity to keep her courage up.

He tipped his head to the other side in a roll that seemed more avian than mammal. "Are you afraid of the man I was talking to?"

Amanda blinked. "No. I don't think..." She bit her lip, remembering the sound of his... could you call it a voice, when no vocal chords were involved? "No."

Gabriel smiled at that. The expression didn't make him look any friendlier. "He would regret having to kill you, but that wouldn't stop him from doing it if you ever, ever repeated any of that to anyone, in any form. Understood?"

Amanda nodded. Her mouth felt like it was full of sawdust.

"Good." His expression thawed a little, and his eyes looked a little more blue than gray. "He's been under my protection a lot longer than you have."

"He's not..." She frowned, and started over. "Are there any vampires in Madison besides you?"

"No." Gabriel walked over to the bed and sat down on the corner of the mattress. Close, but not too close. "We don't like to share territory. Big cities can support more than one of us, if we aren't hunting the same demographic, but it can be contentious." His smile quirked higher at one corner. "Madison could probably support another mature vampire, but I don't share."

"Right." She hoped he would keep going without her having to ask. She didn't think asking would be healthy, no matter what he said about giving his word.

Gabriel had other plans. "You don't think of yourself as psychic, do you?"

It was barely a question, and the insult made her forget her fear. "Of course not. That stuff's all nonsense."

He leaned back on one elbow, lounging on her bed like an insolent rake. Presumptuous bastard. "Would you've said vampires were nonsense, before Friday night?"

Amanda's jaw was clenched so tight her teeth hurt. "That's different."

"You just had a conversation with me from half the city away." The words came out as a patronizing laugh.

"That's different," she insisted, her voice getting louder. "That was something you did. Some weird vampire thing." *I am not a nutjob, or some sideshow freak.* She bounced to her feet and stalked into the kitchen. *I am not monster like you.*

"*You* found *me*, Amanda. You went looking for me in the dark, and you found me. After only three days." He followed her out of the bedroom, laughing softly. "But you're not psychic. Did you meet anyone interesting today?"

"What?" She shot him a confused scowl and yanked the fridge door open.

"Perhaps at work?"

She grimaced as she scanned the nearly empty shelves. She'd been hungry even before she'd fallen asleep on the couch. Now that Gabriel wasn't threatening some unmentionable doom, she was ravenous. "There was one creepy old guy, but other than that, no."

Gabriel leaned against the island, watching as she slammed the fridge shut and started pawing through the cupboards. "What made him so creepy?"

Was he mocking her? "I dunno. He was a little too interested, I guess. Too intense." The memory made her hand ache all over again and she rubbed it, trying to suppress a shiver.

Gabriel's eyes fixed on her hand. Suddenly all softness went out of him, as if he were carved from vibrating stone. "Did he hurt you?"

Even his voice was sharp and edgy. Amanda hid her hands behind her back as if they'd done something wrong. "No, it was just static. Helluva zinger though."

She'd been working her register, and the old man was just another face in a long line of customers. He meant the touch to be gentle, she was sure, just a grandfatherly pat on the back of the hand, even if his expression had a slightly predatory edge to it. She'd started to pull away but was too slow, and when his skin made contact with hers she got such a shock that her knees had gone wobbly and she'd had to catch herself against the counter. He hadn't looked too good, either.

Gabriel shook himself, visibly forcing his muscles to relax. "That man was a mage, the head of one of the larger cadres in the city. He was testing you to see how much of a threat you might pose."

Her eyes widened. "A threat? Me? I haven't done anything!"

"Yet. He's afraid your…elevation…will upset the balance we've all been working to maintain here."

Amanda snatched a packet of Pop-Tarts out of the box and slammed the cupboard door closed. "I didn't ask for this," she snapped as she ripped open the foil. "This isn't my fault."

"He knows that, but it's beside the point." Gabriel made an impatient gesture. "The mages and the fae know me, even if they have no love for me. I'm old and I'm strong, and I like my city to stay quiet. It benefits all of us to keep a low profile, and we all do our parts to keep things stable here because it's in our own best interests." He ran a hand through his hair. "Do you remember how you said it felt alive here?"

Amanda's mouth was full of Pop-Tart, so she nodded.

"That's because of all the ley lines. There's a huge confluence of ley lines that run through the isthmus, and it attracts people and creatures sensitive to such things. Mostly mages and skinshifters, and a few other fae who can bear to be out in our world. Metal messes with the fae and the lines' aethereal tides, that's why they don't let anyone build up. Too much iron and steel."

She swallowed. "What does all that have to do with me?"

The way he watched her throat move was almost as discomfiting as his words. "They see you as a threat to the peace. It's bad enough when a normal human is thrust into their world; it's exponentially worse when the human is gifted and of uncertain disposition. You might endanger them without even knowing it, save for my influence, and I can't be with you during the day. They know how many lives a fledgling needs, and a strong psychic grows in power very quickly when exposed to things like vampire blood."

"But they're fine with you?" She didn't try to hide the disgust in her voice. "Knowing what you are, how many people you've killed, they're okay with that as long as you do it somewhere else?"

"Yes. Strange as it may seem to you, they'd rather have a powerful vampire here than a weak one. It keeps migrating vampires out of the city."

"Right. They'd rather have one scary-big vampire that they can't control. Sure." She took a bite from the second Pop-Tart.

"Do you have any idea what would happen to Madison if I were suddenly gone? This is a highly desirable city. Another vampire would move in, probably a young one from Milwaukee or Chicago. And then yet another vampire would come to challenge him.

"Vampires mark their territory with people. The people we bite carry our scent and warn off interlopers. When a vampire wants to move in on a weaker vampire's territory, he kills off the signposts and marks new ones. Then the first vampire kills those off, and so on until one flees or they fight it out. For a city this size, with such a large migrating student population, it'll probably take twenty years before someone powerful enough to hold the city permanently comes out on top."

Amanda's mouth went dry and her stomach twisted, but she forced herself to swallow the last mouthful. *He can't be serious. He just can't.*

Gabriel sure didn't look like he was joking. If anything, he was more grim than he'd been before. "A city where five murders in a year is a travesty will suddenly be looking at dozens, maybe hundreds of deaths and missing persons. Do you know how hard it is for the other supernaturals to operate under that kind of scrutiny? Of course they want me here."

Frustration had crept into his voice, and he took a deep breath. "Look, most of this stuff doesn't come up until later. After you turn. You don't need to know the politics involved; just stay away from the mages and the non-humans. They won't harm you if you aren't doing anything stupid. They don't want to deal with what I'd do to them."

Amanda still felt queasy at the thought of people getting slaughtered in what amounted to a vampire pissing match, but she pushed the images from her mind. *She* was certainly no threat to Gabriel. "If I can't tell a vampire from a human, how am I supposed to tell a mage from a human? And I don't even know what a skinshifter *is*."

"It's a shape-changing faerie, and no, not the kind with wings or a wand. They call them pookhas back across the pond, among other things. And mages *are* humans, most of the time." He pushed away from the counter and headed for the door. "Come on."

"Where?"

"You want to know what they all look like?" He held out one hand to her. "I'll show you."

She gingerly put her hand in his, almost more to see if he was cold like in her dream. His palm was cool, but no worse than some human hands she'd touched.

Unless they weren't human, and I just didn't know it.

* * * *

The motel room reeked of gun oil. Morales was out hitting the pay phones, trying to get in touch with more of his diverse network of hunters. Once he got back, they'd blow this town before anyone tracing the calls could figure out where to trap them.

In the meantime, it was maintenance duty for the apprentices.

Travis looked up from the shotgun he was cleaning. "Briggs?"

"Yeah?" She was cross-legged on one of the motel beds, stripping apart the tranquilizer gun. She didn't lift her gaze from the metal pieces in front of her.

It was hard to get the words out. Briggs was such an intimidating, ball-busting bitch of a woman. Travis admired her greatly. "D'you think that girl's gonna be okay?"

Briggs held the barrel up, sans the rest of the pieces, and looked through it. "Don't know. Don't know how long the leech had her." She picked up the cloth and rod next to her and started swabbing out the barrel. "Not our problem, anyway."

Morales had made a few calls, and they'd delivered the girl—still unconscious, so Travis didn't even know her name—to a mental hospital somewhere in Kentucky. "But they know how to take care of her, right?"

Briggs sighed, and stopped cleaning the gun. "They'll do the best they can. Some thralls are just too broken to be saved."

She'd said it gently—for her, anyway—but Travis still winced. He wondered how long the girl had been the vampire's slave. Travis's girlfriend Carrie had run off with the vampire Quinn only a few days before the hunters, with Travis's unwanted assistance, had tracked the leech to his lair. And when Quinn died, Carrie killed herself within minutes.

"It just seems like we should be more organized than this." Travis picked up the gun oil, and a moment later he heard the soft sound of Briggs's cleaning cloth. "Instead of individual free agents scattered all over."

"That's how we keep them from finding us. A friendly abbot here, a curious psychologist there, a sympathetic chop shop owner someplace else. Lots of little pieces, and the only ones big enough for the leeches to care about are the ones actively doing the hunting. Like us." She sighted down the barrel again. "Europe is more organized, and they still haven't recovered from the last time Armin attacked their supply lines."

Travis shuddered at the name. The Furies were fearsome enough; their leader and founder was, to Travis, something akin to the Devil himself.

"The Furies operate just like we do," Briggs went on. Whether or not she was aware of Travis's discomfort was up for debate. She wouldn't have shown it either way. "Free agents like us. No lairs for us to raid, no obvious support network, no thralls or other liabilities for us to exploit. Thank God there aren't that many of them."

Travis reminded himself that Armin hadn't been seen outside of Europe in more than two centuries. "And that they don't leave their territories much."

"Right. Except for Isolde."

The shape-changing vampire was the only Fury with no set territory. As Morales had put it, she went wherever the hunting was best.

Next to Armin, Isolde was the scariest thing Travis had ever heard of.

"Right." He swallowed hard and bent his head over his gun. "Except Isolde."

* * * *

Isolde flew east, surrounded by the murder of crows that guarded her by day. Though she had never been able to make use of the mind tricks her father and brother specialized in, she didn't need them to communicate with her crows. Her wings rowed the air, one bird among many. The crow was her second skin, almost as familiar as her human shape, and she'd been speaking the birds' language long before she'd learned Latin, much less English. She had been Isolde Corvus for centuries before she had pledged herself to Constantine's service.

Cartwright had known much, and little. He had worked with Morales for several years before striking out on his own, and had scoffed at the older man's caution. What Cartwright had apparently never understood is that Morales trained to fight elder vampires. Cartwright had mostly encountered the young and the stupid.

Arrogant and foolhardy as Cartwright had been, Morales had either been impressed enough or desperate enough to reach out to him. Cartwright had been on his way to meet up with Morales and a number of others in Milwaukee.

"I don't know why he is gathering us," Cartwright had told her, "but he said it would be the biggest hunt in our lifetime."

Below her she could feel the faint pulse of ley lines, the call of the Ways and the Underground, but those paths were forever closed to her. The ache of that loss festered in her heart, the wound torn open anew every time she traveled, a pain that had become as familiar as her blades. Isolde altered her course a little, slowed by her companions. They were all bound to her and so were more powerful than normal crows, but they could only go so fast. It would take nearly ten hours of flight time to reach Milwaukee. She would be in plenty of time for Morales's rendezvous, but the delay galled her.

It was unfortunate that crows had no concept of directions, but even if she could have told them to meet her in the big city and flown ahead, she wouldn't have. Too many times they had protected her as she slept for her to forego their company now, as she stalked this most dangerous prey.

She had a sinking feeling she knew who Morales was hunting.

CHAPTER SEVEN

Tuesday, May 18th, 1999

The phone rang, the sound shooting through her aching head. *I really need to stop drinking at all the bars.* Amanda cursed and fumbled for the handset on her nightstand without opening her eyes.

She'd crawled into bed in the wee hours of the morning, having already left a message on Lily's voicemail at work and intending to sleep until well past noon. Gabriel had warned her off sleeping after dark, and she'd needed little prompting.

"There is a bond between us, between every master and novice. You just found it a little sooner than usual." His eyes had teased her, daring her to deny it.

She refused to rise to the bait. "And just how long does that effect last? How long am I going to have you lurking in the back of my head?"

"It's permanent, I'm afraid, but you'll learn to block it out. It's stronger with my blood in you; if you do go back to being human, I imagine you'll be able to ignore me without too much difficulty." He cocked his head. "In the meantime, best for you to be awake after dark. If you sleep while I'm awake you have a good chance of finding me again, and I don't think your sanity would quite survive echoes of, say, me feeding. At least, not yet."

Amanda had no doubts on that score, even though their long hours of pub-crawling had reminded her uneasily of that first dream. She found herself looking for the tiny scars his razor left, wondering if every person she saw might be one of his donors. They'd hit a different set of bars and clubs and taverns than they had the night before. She half wondered if he had a schedule.

The worst had been their one stop downtown early on, when Gabriel had taken her to Wando's. He didn't feed there, only pointed out perfectly human-looking people with a murmured, "Fae" or "Mage."

Amanda had shaken her head, not sure if she should despair at ever figuring this out or if she should be glad she couldn't see some weird colors around them or something, to let her know she was truly losing her shit. As far as she was concerned, the only thing that had marked out those people as different were the sharp, pointed looks they gave the vampire before stiffly ignoring him.

Amanda finally got her hands on the phone and dragged it to her ear. "'Lo?"

"Hey, just calling to remind you about the movie tomorrow." Brandy sounded far too chipper for whatever ungodly hour it must be.

Amanda squinted at her alarm clock. 1:28 p.m. Well, it was after noon, at least. She sighed. "Movie?"

"Um, hello, Episode One? Star Wars? Midnight premiere? Only just the biggest movie event of the decade?" Brandy's voice dropped conspiratorially, the last words coming out in a sing-song. "Do you need an extra ticket? Someone's been pretty scarce lately, ever since she ran off with broad, dark, and handsome."

Amanda groaned. *Crap, that's tomorrow already.* "I didn't run off with anyone."

"Whatever. Do you need another ticket?"

"Yeah. I mean, no. I don't think I can go." *That is just what I don't need.*

"Aw, c'mon Amanda, you promised! We already got your ticket, and I bribed Kayla to stand in line for us so we can get good seats."

And Brandy was off, whining and cajoling until Amanda held the phone away from her ear and yelled, "Ok, fine, yes, get me another ticket." *It's not like they haven't met him before, after all.*

"Ha! I knew it!" Brandy's triumphant squeal made Amanda's head throb. "You're totally seeing Gabriel, aren't you! Didn't I tell you he was into you? Tell me everything!"

"Not now," Amanda gasped, clutching her head. "I have to go. I'll call you tomorrow, okay?"

"Sleep it off, girlfriend. Laters!"

Amanda hung up the phone on the second try. *What did I just agree to?* She pulled the pillow back over her head. *At least it won't be another bar. I don't know which will kill me first, the alcohol or the lung cancer.*

She hadn't meant to drink so much the night before, but she'd desperately wanted something to calm her nerves. *Mom always said that psychic stuff was a load of bull, that Dad just used it as an excuse for all mental problems in his family.* That had been a hard nut to crack. *If it is real, are my aunt and my cousins not really nuts? Did they get locked up because they couldn't hide it well enough? Or am I just crazy, too?*

Or maybe it's just easier to think you're insane than deal with a world full of vampires and faeries and mages and God knows what else.

She'd wanted to ask about the other man, the one who'd called Gabriel "Father," but every time she'd screwed up enough courage to do so he'd sidetracked her with another non sequitur. It was obvious he didn't want to talk about it, but when it also became clear he wasn't going to go all cold and scary again, she started taking a perverse pleasure in trying to bring it up just to make him ask another question.

He'd won that game, though. They'd just gotten back in his car after the last bar had closed, and Amanda's head was starting to swim a little. She'd tried to pace herself, but she'd lost count after the sixth drink, and there'd been several after the sixth.

"So," she'd begun, grinning, as Gabriel buckled his seatbelt.

"I've been meaning to ask you," he responded immediately. Amanda should have known by the tiny smile that this time was different, but she'd only laughed and gestured for him to go on.

He'd turned in his seat to face her. "Why did you keep drinking my blood, when you woke up after I bit you?"

The bottom dropped out of her stomach, and the memory of that moment swept over her. The wash of emotions had been brutal, fear and loathing and anger and determination, but those had paled beside the taste in her mouth, blood but more than blood, and the raw feeling of power that surged through her when she swallowed.

Something stirred low in her body, a sharp, sleepy twisting like jealousy gone wrong.

"Your blood was the only thing keeping me from dying," she managed to croak, "and you were going to take that from me, too."

After a moment he nodded, but Amanda had the sickening feeling he'd seen the desire underlying her words, the knowledge that even if it hadn't already been too late, she would've wanted one more taste.

Still wanted one more taste.

"Fair enough," was all he'd said, and she hadn't tried to broach the forbidden subject again.

As much as she wanted to go back to sleep, now that she was thinking, her brain refused to turn back off. Grumbling under her breath, Amanda crawled out of bed in search of some Gatorade.

Sunset found her in the Arboretum, watching the birds settle into the bull rushes and cattails that cloaked the shore of Lake Wingra. The Arboretum cut a swath through Madison from the south side nearly to campus, a preserve of woods and prairie and cultivated gardens owned by the University. Ostensibly it served the same purpose as the Schmeeckle preserve back home in Stevens Point, an outdoor classroom for students and researchers, but unlike Schmeeckle, there were houses in the Arboretum, and a golf course that bordered one side buffered it from the affluent neighborhood to the northwest. *And the zoo. Can't forget the zoo.*

Amanda had spent more time in Schmeeckle than she cared to think about, growing up. Her mother could barely be coaxed past the backyard, much less into the "wilds" of the University forest. Penny had always sent Robbie or Dad in after her, on the nights when Amanda had decided not to mind her curfew. Not that you were supposed to be in Schmeeckle past certain hours; you also weren't supposed to go off the trails, but that had never stopped her.

It didn't stop her in the Arboretum, either. Amanda's apartment building was right across the Beltline from the trees, but the actual entrance to the Arboretum was close to a mile away. After her first exploratory visit, whenever she wanted some peace she'd just cut under the highway at Todd Drive, slip around a couple of buildings, and hop the pathetic chain-link fence.

Now she stood in one of her favorite spots, not too far off the trails, and looked out over the small lake. *At least when Gabriel's here I don't have to sit around wondering what's going to happen.* She supposed he would expect her to be at home, but screw that. She hadn't promised him anything. *He can come find me, if he wants.*

She watched the slivered moon chase the wake of the setting sun. It had been nice enough out when she started walking, but the temperature had dropped off and she wished she'd thought to bring a windbreaker. The robins chirped their evening songs and the red-wings trilled and the cranes hollered. From across the lake came the distant roaring of one of the zoo's big cats. Amanda had to grin. The sound was primal, but not frightening;

that cat wasn't angry, he was just doing his cat thing. *Saying hello to the moon, maybe. Wanting to be part of whatever's going on.*

The fleeing clouds were a fierce red-gold and the sun had disappeared behind the trees across the lake before Amanda left the shore and started heading back. The Arboretum was safe enough most of the time, but the area around her apartment wasn't the best place to go walking after dark.

The sky still held an edge of gold, though the east was a deepening sapphire blue, and she was back on the main road through the Arboretum when Gabriel stepped out from behind a tree and fell in beside her. She hid a smile at his predictability.

"Not running from me, I trust?" His voice was as light as his silent footfalls.

"Do you see me sweating?" She shoved her hands in her pockets and didn't change her pace.

"Not afraid to be out in the woods with the monster after dark?"

"Should I be?" *Yes, you idiot. You should.* But she wasn't; or at least, not much. That wasn't what he wanted from her, and besides, she couldn't stop him if it was. Not that she wouldn't try, but it took some of the pressure off, knowing that she couldn't stop him from killing her. *See, that just proves you* are *insane.*

"Thank you," he said, matching his strides to hers.

"What for?"

"For your trust."

Amanda laughed, and if there was a bitter edge to it she felt that she'd earned it. "I don't trust you. I just don't have much of a choice, and I'm tired of being afraid."

She felt the weight of his gaze but didn't look at him until he stopped walking. Even then she was tempted to keep going, but her curiosity got the better of her.

He was watching her quizzically, as if she were an interesting insect he'd never seen before. "You're harder to read tonight, when you should be easier. You've found your feet again. What changed?"

She fidgeted under his impersonal scrutiny. "I don't..." Hesitating, she bit her lip, then held one hand out. "Stay there," she said, and closed her eyes.

What breeze there'd been down by the lake couldn't find her among the tall trees. The air was moist with the breath of late spring, but it wasn't the heavy, humid air that would be smothering the state in another month or two. She spread her fingers, trying to remember how it had felt in her dream. There were no warm bodies here, just the empty night air.

Letting out a long, slow breath, Amanda reached out, searching.

She felt him almost immediately, his presence a cold pressure against her fingertips. A gasp escaped her throat, and then the cold moved. Her arm followed it, and her eyes flew open as she turned. Her outstretched fingers still pointed right at him, though he was ten feet away from where he'd started.

"Fuck." Her hand trembled, and she snatched it back as if the cold had burned her. *"Fuck."*

Gabriel's eyes were brighter than they had been. "You really never believed you were psychic, did you? I thought you must've had some training—even when I took you I couldn't get through your shields until the venom kicked in—but you haven't."

Amanda looked away into the trees, wracked with sudden shivers.

"Or have you?"

His tone was sharp, and Amanda flinched, closing her eyes and shaking her head. "My mother always said there was no such thing. She used to browbeat my dad about it sometimes—"

She choked on the words because suddenly that cool pressure was back against her skin, a movement that she felt on her shoulders and her spine and the backs of her arms.

Amanda whirled around. Gabriel was so close behind her that her arm brushed his chest as she spun, the heat of his body a shock in contrast to the cold miasma that surrounded him.

His gaze caught hers and held it fast.

His irises were a light, shining green, almost silvery, like aspen leaves in the wind. The pupils were deep pits by comparison, so much so that she felt a wave of vertigo staring into them. She tried to look away, balanced there on the edge, but simply could not shift her gaze. Her body swayed as if she were standing at a precipice, ready to fall.

"Stop it," she whispered even as she reached out to him to steady herself.

Gabriel took her hands and tipped her right off the edge. *Show me,* he whispered as the darkness engulfed her.

She wasn't even waist-high to Uncle Stu. He sat cross-legged on the kitchen floor, and was still taller than Amanda was, standing. "Like a soap bubble," he was saying, "all around your head, and thoughts bounce off of it."

"Like this?" She squeezed her eyes shut and pretended as hard as she could.

"That's good, baby." He mussed her hair, which made the soap bubble go away. He laughed at her disgruntled expression. "You just keep practicing that, and it'll stay quieter in here." He tapped her forehead with one finger.

"Okay."

Suddenly the memory was gone, and she was staring at Gabriel again.

"That explains a lot," he said as she tore her hands away from his. He didn't try to hold on.

Amanda rubbed her face. "I was three when he died," she said softly. Then she rounded on the vampire. "Don't *do* that!"

His expression said he'd do as he damn well pleased. "So stop me."

Amanda opened her mouth, but the angry retort cut off before it began. She glared at him, tried to start again, hesitated.

Gabriel laughed. "Yes, if you learn how to block me you'll have to admit to yourself that you're gifted. And no, you're not insane and you're not just imagining all of this."

Her cheeks heated, and she growled at him through clenched teeth. "Stop that."

"Stop thinking so loudly," he countered. "Your shields go to pieces when you're angry."

Amanda felt herself check for the bubble, and realized doing so was so second nature she'd never been conscious of it before. The anger drained out of her as if she were a balloon with a slow leak.

"Is that what this is?" She gestured at her head. "Shields?"

"Yes. Crude ones, but fairly effective at keeping your thoughts in your head and other people's out of it."

Just having this conversation made her nauseous with dread, as if men in white coats were going to jump out of the bushes any second. "And that thing you do, where I can't look away. Is that a vampire thing, or a human thing?"

"A bit of both. It's a vampire twist on a human ability." He grinned. "I have a feeling you're going to be very good at it, and probably sooner than later."

Amanda shuddered. "And you can teach me how to stop you from doing it?"

"Yes."

She waited, but he didn't say anything else, just watched her. Of course he was going to make her ask. "Would you please teach me?"

"Just that bit or all of it?"

She sighed. "All of it."

CHAPTER EIGHT

Did I really just ask him to teach me how to be psychic?

She must have, because Gabriel was already answering her.

"As you will."

Amanda wished the night were darker, so she couldn't see the eager anticipation on his face. Unfortunately, they were coming up on the ornamental gardens and the Arboretum's well-lit visitor center, and beyond that was the open expanse of restored prairie before the line of pines that bordered the preserve. The moon was too low to be seen now, but the stars and the glow of the surrounding city provided more than enough light for her to have no doubts about his expression.

To her relief, Gabriel turned away from the open spaces, leading her deeper into the shadows until he found a cluster of trees close to the road.

"Better than nothing," Gabriel murmured as he led her into the under-brush. The trees gave them some cover from the road, and the leaves of the maples made a soft clatter in the evening breeze. He sat on a broad root and gestured for her to join him.

"Why here?" Amanda asked nervously as she sat down. The scent of the lilacs and crabapples was thick even this far from the gardens.

"If I wait until we get back to your place, you might change your mind."

Amanda had to admit he wasn't wrong. "Okay. What do I do?"

Gabriel rubbed his face, choosing his words with care. "A shield is sort of a psychic wall, built with energy and will, not bricks and mortar. Most humans have weak shields, as if made from rice paper and bamboo if you want to stick with the wall analogy. In order to fascinate, a vampire first has to be able to touch her prey's thoughts. Eye contact helps because people tend to open up when they make that connection, and it's also very distracting, but it's not truly necessary. Usually it's not too difficult to find a hole in the wall. Worst case, you can create one, but that's not subtle and you risk damaging the prey."

Amanda remembered the rooting tendrils that had invaded her own shields, and shuddered.

Gabriel ignored her reaction. "We'll work on strengthening your defenses overall, of course, but for now we'll deal specifically with fascination. This is one of those cases where you just don't want to risk that your passive defenses will be strong enough. The best way to fight it is to not let my power touch you, regardless of whether I have eye contact or not."

Amanda frowned. "How do I do that?"

"Shields, and keeping your head. First, don't panic, and don't let yourself be afraid if you can help it. I can use your fear against you. Emotion is energy, and you want it to be energy you can use. What you need to do is get angry, as angry as you can. Imagine that my will is like a wave of water about to crash down on you, and if it touches you, you're mine. Make your anger like a fire surrounding you that boils off the water before it can touch you."

"Do you have any idea how cheesy this sounds?" she asked skeptically.

"Yes, but it works with some practice."

"Okay." Amanda took a deep breath and let it out. "Let's give it a try."

Gabriel's eyes locked onto hers. She felt herself trying to pull away and stopped, but the wave came before she could gather her strength. Cold crashed past her shields. Her vision started to blur.

Gabriel released her with a shake of his head, and reached out to steady her as she swayed. "Too slow," he said. She nodded, gathering her resolve to try again. "It's got to be right away, as soon as I catch your eyes."

She squeezed one of his hands as she sat back up. "I'm okay," she breathed. "Let's try again."

Damn, but his eyes were distracting. What was it about meeting someone's gaze that made her hesitate? The precipice was there under her feet and she started to fall, only to have Gabriel pull her back. He held her upright until the dizziness passed. She cursed.

"Don't be too hard on yourself," he counseled. "This isn't easy. Just remember to be angry. I haven't felt any anger from you yet."

"Sorry. Again?"

After the fourth failure, Amanda was lying flat on her back, waiting for the branches of the tree above her to stop spinning. "I don't think this imagery is working for me." Her voice wavered.

"Anger's usually easiest to start with. Is there something else you have in mind?"

"Yeah, actually. Gimme a minute to recover from the last time." She lay still for a few minutes more before sitting up again. "Boy, that takes a lot out of you."

"Tell me about it." Gabriel stretched his arms above his head. "Ready?"

"Yep." Amanda stared into his eyes.

He took hold of her easily, as if planting hooks in her shields that kept her from looking away, but when he tried to swamp her she leaned forward ever so slightly, her lips tight in concentration. His power slid around her.

Gabriel clapped his hands in quiet applause. "What did you do differently?"

Her cheeks flushed with embarrassment and pride. "I, uh, made my determination like a wedge in front of me, so your power went around it."

He considered her for a moment, his gaze distant. Amanda felt that cold pressure again, not quite on her skin; sort of outside her head and inside her head at the same time. "Deflection is a slightly more advanced technique, one most candidates don't master until much closer to the end. I wonder if you haven't been doing a little of that unconsciously already."

His eyes slipped half-closed, and his fingers twitched. She felt that same sort of probing, rooting sensation that she had right after he'd bitten her, invisible fingers running over invisible walls.

"You are quite the prodigy. Auras should be easy for you, I think. But we'll work on that later. Shield work first. And we'll have to work—" He caught her gaze, the sudden shift of attention stabbing through her, "—on surprising you, too."

Distracted by the uncomfortable poking around in her head and completely off her guard, Amanda tried to throw up her defenses but was only partially successful. She managed to keep him from grabbing her but the jolt sent her consciousness spinning. She felt herself start to fall, felt Gabriel's hands catch her shoulders, holding her upright. At least, she assumed that was upright; she couldn't tell through the vertigo.

She blinked hard, her eyes jerking from left to right, unable to focus.

Easy. His voice whispered inside her head, drawing her thoughts to him just as he pulled her body close. *You almost had that one.*

Amanda struggled, trying to right herself, but he crooned softly at her, the sound a lilting vibration that buoyed her up and cradled her against the dizziness. She let herself be soothed, relaxing into that strong, sure grip. His thoughts were warm, and she floated on them like they were bathwater.

His chuckle was a ripple on the water's surface. *Although, I think you would've recovered faster if you'd just let yourself fall.*

Oh, be quiet. Held and surrounded by Gabriel's power, she was hardly aware of her physical body at all. She wasn't even sure if she was in his mind or if he was in hers. The longer she floated, the more artificial that distinction became. Not good. *I'm gonna have one nasty headache when you let go of me, aren't I?* she asked.

Probably.

She sighed. *Better get it over with.* She wiggled free of the buffer his thoughts had created, and gave a strangled shriek as the pain hit her.

She found herself cuddled against Gabriel's chest, her head resting on his shoulder. The starlight reflecting off the road lanced through her brain, and she buried her face against his collarbone to get away from it. She started to curse but the sound grated against her headache, and the words dwindled sharply into a whimper.

What she had taken for some sort of ringing in her ears suddenly ceased. She belatedly recognized it as tires on pavement only when it was followed by the slam of a car door, which made her whole head throb.

He would've missed us if you hadn't cried out, Gabriel said, his mental voice distant and emotionless.

"Who's there?" a man called. A flashlight clicked on, the beam glaring between the tree trunks and making Amanda moan.

"Here," Gabriel called, poking his head out into the light. "My friend has a migraine, and it's darker back here. Would you mind turning off the light?"

"Friend, huh?" The man stomped around the tree, raking the light over both of them. Amanda convulsed, pressing the heels of her hands against her eyes.

The light clicked off, and she heard the man kneel down next to her. "Are you all right? Do you need a hospital?"

Cautiously, Amanda peeked out at him. The badge was the first thing she saw. "It'll go away in a minute," she lied, covering her eyes again. "They usually do. I'll be fine. Thank you, officer."

"Well, the Arboretum's closed now," he said, suspicion thick in his voice. "Let me drop you off somewhere. Are you sure you don't need a doctor?"

Gabriel broke in. "That won't be necessary."

His voice was too calm, too confident. Amanda peeked out again to see that the officer's face had gone slack, his gaze locked to the vampire's. Gabriel lifted her and set her to one side without once looking away from the entranced cop.

That roiling motion she'd felt before, the wave of hunger that he'd called up to show her his fangs, felt different now that her defenses were at low ebb. If it had a sound it would've been a shrieking, gibbering wind, the kind that howled around corners and windows and tried to claw its way into the house on stormy nights. But it wasn't a sound, it was…

Amanda shook herself free of it, pulled her ragged shields together. She grabbed his arm. "No! Don't even think about it."

Gabriel had been leaning toward the man, but he stopped and half turned toward her. The officer didn't even blink, only stared blindly ahead. Gabriel's fangs were already out, glinting from between parted lips. "Too late," he said.

Amanda recoiled, snatching her hand back before she could think better of it. "He's a cop," she protested, struggling to sit up. "You don't do stuff like that to cops! He was just doing his job."

"A human's a human," Gabriel said, his voice devoid of emotion, "and I'm hungry. Unless you have a better idea?" His gaze was cold, empty. Waiting.

"We can go out to the bars again," she offered desperately.

He shook his head. "Too much work when this one's already here."

Amanda managed to lever herself upright, half hauling herself up one of the tree trunks until she was in a sitting position. She leaned against the tree wearily, her head pounding. God, she couldn't think through this pain. "What do you want from me?" she whispered, anger sharpening her voice.

His lips tightened ever so slightly, just curling at the corners, though the smile never touched his eyes. "I want blood, Amanda. Are you offering?"

The sudden chill of fear actually made her headache lessen, but she took no comfort in that fact. "What?"

His gaze flicked down to her neck. "Are you offering your blood in exchange for his, since you don't want me to feed from him?" He licked his lips. "Just a taste. A mouthful. Not enough to make you weak."

She felt like she was pinned to the tree by that look, covetous and calculating. His hands came up to brush her forehead, his cool skin a welcome balm against her fevered brow, his eyes icy like snowmelt, and when his hands slipped down her cheeks to her chin they seemed to take most of her headache with them. Any clarity of thought she might've gained from the sudden lack of pain was lost when he gently turned her head and leaned in. Amanda swallowed hard as his breath, then his lips, brushed her throat.

"One swallow," he whispered against her skin. "From here." His lips caressed the skin above the artery.

She stared at the frozen cop and tried to think, but all she could remember was the earth-shattering, mind-blowing ecstasy she'd felt when Gabriel had bitten her before. *And this time would be different*, a tiny, treasonous corner of her mind pointed out. *He wouldn't be taking it from you with fear and pain. You'd be giving it to him.*

A tear escaped one eye and trickled down her cheek, because she did want to give in, to surrender, to feel the venom running through her veins again. The strength of that want terrified her. *Am I so weak, to feel this way? If I agree now, am I strong enough to say no the next time? Because there will be a next time, count on it.*

She studied the man's face. *But if I give him to Gabriel, am I any better off? It's my fault he's in danger. He's not one of those idiots at the bars...*

Her whole body went still at the idea, and it was as if she'd had a bucket of cold water thrown over her. She reached up and pulled Gabriel's hand away from her chin, and when his slightly glassy eyes looked up to meet hers she jerked her head at the officer. "Get him out of here."

He blinked at her. It was hard to tell, but she thought he looked surprised. Or was it disappointment?

"As you will." His eyes unfocused for a moment, but that was all, and then the officer smoothly stood and walked back to his car without ever looking at either of them. The slam of the car door came a moment later, and then the sound of tires on pavement growing fainter and fainter until it was gone.

Amanda stood, her back pressed against the tree. She wasn't entirely sure her legs would support her, but being curled up together on the ground like they were was too intimate. *Here goes.*

"One swallow, from here," she repeated, touching her neck, "but no teeth."

Gabriel sat back on his haunches and looked up at her with narrowed eyes. "What?"

"No teeth. You have a razor on you somewhere." She tried not to show her nervousness, but her hands clenched into fists. It didn't help that some part of her wanted this to fail.

He didn't move, but something in his expression shifted, a gleam of... Ire? Humor? Respect? She hated how opaque his face could be. "That was not the agreement."

"You never said fangs," Amanda replied with forced sweetness.

Gabriel barked a laugh, and Amanda let out a relieved breath.

"No, I never did," he said. He rose to his feet, and with one smooth flicking motion drew the razor from his pocket and opened it. The edge glimmered in the wan light. "Are you sure this is what you want? It's going to sting."

She closed her eyes again so he couldn't see how thin her resolve was. "I'm sure."

The blade was so sharp she almost didn't feel it. It was only after Gabriel pressed his face to her neck that she felt the small pain. She winced as his tongue probed the wound, widening it so the blood could flow freely.

I told you so. His voice whispered through her thoughts with more than a hint of smugness.

"Oh, hush."

His hands slipped behind her back, one of them at her waist and the other holding her head in place. She dug her fingernails into the bark of the tree to keep from returning his embrace, to keep herself from pressing against him out of pure instinct. He held himself a few inches away from her, and yet the weight of his presence kept her pinned as surely as his hands did. The scent of him was warm and male, with a sort of spicy-musky-leather undertone that damn near made her mouth water.

Amanda focused on the pain of the cut, which was beginning to burn. Thinking about it made it hurt more, but that was better than thinking about what the vampire was doing, or about how good his fingers felt as they tightened against her flesh, or how much she still wanted things she shouldn't.

Eventually she felt him swallow. He held onto her, his exhaled breath a soft protest and a purr all at once. Then his tongue made one last swipe against the cut, and he pushed away from her.

As he turned, Amanda saw the tips of his fangs between parted lips that glistened red, and then his back was to her. He was shaking.

"Gabriel?" she asked, reaching out one hand in spite of her better judgment.

He gestured for her to stay where she was. "A moment." He sounded breathless, but without the panting or wheezing that came with exertion.

Then he went perfectly still, the trembling ceasing abruptly. "My apologies. It was more difficult to stop than I expected."

Amanda stared at his back, wanting to ask why but dreading the answer.

Gabriel gave a quiet laugh. "Shields, little mouse. You can shield even against me if you think about it. Right now you are shouting at me."

Amanda's cheeks reddened, and she slammed her defenses into place.

"Better." Gabriel turned to face her. His fangs were hidden again but the pupils of his eyes were still blown wide. "To answer your question," he continued lightly, "fascination takes a good deal of energy—more than I was planning on when I fed last evening." His gaze dropped briefly to her throat. "Your blood tastes of your own power, but it also tastes of mine. That combination is...heady."

Amanda gulped. *He's saying I taste good. Great.* Unconsciously she reached up to touch the cut, and was surprised to find the skin whole. "It's gone," she blurted.

"I healed it." Gabriel's gaze dropped to her throat again, and this time it lingered wistfully. "A vampire's blood can heal quite a bit of damage. You heal faster than a human now because of the vampire blood you carry, but there's an anticoagulant in my saliva. That's the burn you were feeling." He licked his lips. "A drop of my blood in the wound was enough to overcome that and let it heal over."

"Oh." She wished he would stop looking at her like he was trying to figure out how to un-heal that skin. She shifted from foot to foot. "That's, um, handy."

His nostrils flared, and he gave himself a shake. "You weren't afraid while I was feeding. Why are you now?"

"Who says I'm afraid?"

I do. His voice whispered in her mind. She hadn't even felt him reach for her. He stepped closer, invading her personal space. *I can smell it.*

She lifted her chin and stood straighter, refusing to back away.

"That's better," he murmured. "Fear smells like prey." He put his face close to hers and inhaled, closing his eyes as if savoring the scent.

"That's really creepy, Gabriel," she growled through gritted teeth.

Anger tastes better on you.

The thought drifted through her inner ear, light and warm as a caress, and for the life of her Amanda could not figure out where he was getting past her defenses.

"Tastes?" She put a hand on his chest, trying to preserve some personal space. "And get out of my head."

He caught her hand and brought it to his lips, turning her wrist up at the last moment. He sucked in a sharp breath just over the skin. *Yes, tastes. From arms-length I could smell your emotion. From this close, I can feed from it.* His expression turned wicked, lascivious, his lips twisting up into a half-grin. *The pain from the cut was delicious.*

"Get out of my head!" She tried to pull her hand back, but this time he did not oblige her.

There was something else there, he mused, teasing her. Mocking her. He tasted the air again. *Something else under the pain. Not fear. What could it have been?*

If she hadn't already been so furious at him, she'd have been mortified that he'd sensed that tiny impulse of desire. *I said stop it!*

She shrieked the thought as loud as she could, focusing it right between his eyes and shoving hard.

Energy left her in a rush.

Gabriel grabbed his head and dropped like a stone. His pained cry hung in the air between them.

"G-Gabriel?" Amanda whispered in shock.

He groaned, but not in reply. She hesitated, then knelt at his side. His palms were pressed to his eyes, his mouth a grimace of pain.

"Gabriel?"

"Ow."

"Are you okay?"

He held up one finger, then went back to clutching his head.

After a moment he said, more to himself than to her, "I deserved that." He lifted his hands from his eyes, groaned, and covered them again. "Do you have any idea how long it's been since I had a headache?"

She breathed a sigh of relief. "Just a headache then?"

"Just a headache?" he repeated scathingly. "You see how much fun your first splitting headache in half a century is. Gods of Night, it *hurts.*"

"I told you to knock it off. Did I really do this?" The sight of the vampire knocked flat on his back made her feel immeasurably better.

"Yes, you did this." He tried opening his eyes again. He winced, then blinked a few times before focusing on her. "That strategy is not going to be viable, I see."

She sat down next to him. "Why were you being such an ass, anyway?"

He gave her an irritated glance. "You were afraid. I don't want you to be afraid of me."

"I was not afraid," Amanda retorted. "It's just, you were looking at me like I was food, and it made me nervous."

"Nervous is afraid. It's just a matter of degree. I don't want you nervous, either. And for the record, if a vampire is looking at you like you're food, then don't act like food unless you want to *be* food." He closed his eyes.

73

"When I told you not to run from me, it's not because I don't want to chase you. It's because I do."

"Oh." She considered this. "So you don't want me to be afraid because it will trigger your instincts?"

With a sigh and a groan he sat up, resting his elbows on his knees and his head in his hands. "I want you to trust me, and you don't trust me when you're afraid of me."

She frowned. "I don't trust you any time," she said, but her voice sounded uncertain even to her.

His eyes glinted green in the dim light. "It never once occurred to you that I would not stop at one swallow, did it." It was more of a statement than a question.

After a moment's thought, she shook her head. Damn him, he was right.

One hand reached out to brush her cheek. "You don't have to agree with me, or believe what I believe in, but you can always trust me. I keep my word. I will not take anything you do not give, and I will do my best to protect you."

It made no sense that she believed him so utterly, but there it was. Maybe it was because she'd been in his head and felt the shape of his character. Or maybe she was just losing it. Whatever the reason, she nodded.

His smile, relieved and rather disarmingly pleased, made him look almost human.

"Come on," he said, climbing to his feet. "I need to feed something fierce."

CHAPTER NINE

Wednesday, May 19th, 1999

"Hey. Bloodboy."

That was not a form of address Paul expected to hear at any time, much less on the way from his office to his parking spot. He stopped and turned around.

Five young skinshifters blocked the sidewalk behind him. Males in their mid-twenties by their looks, barely out of adolescence by shifter standards. Paul raised an eyebrow at them but didn't answer.

The one in the front bounced on his toes, stinking of nervous sweat and testosterone. He was puffed up and posturing, apparently the mouth for the group. "This thing that your boss has going down, you gotta tell him to watch himself. Messin' with the cops, man, that ain't cool."

"I may be psychic, but you're shifters. You're going to have to make sense when you speak." Paul stared the boy down until the shifter reddened and looked away.

"Big G," one piped up from the back, displaying the shifters' superstitious dislike of saying Gabriel's name. "He was gonna snack on a cop last night. We saw him."

Paul felt his face go blank. "Oh?"

"Yeah." The mouth jumped back in, trying to salvage some face in front of his little pack. "He was in the Arboretum with his new bloodgirl."

"Ah." Paul shifted his attention to the one in the back. "You. You're one of Martin's nephews, aren't you?"

The boy exchanged nervous looks with his fellows. "Yeah."

"Tell your uncle to call me if there's some concern. He has my number. You all don't need to be talking to me again."

Paul was about to leave, but the sudden whiff of unease from all of them made him pause. They were all looking at each other and shuffling their feet. Silent and untouchable as their thoughts were, Paul didn't need to be able to read their minds. "Some little shifters snuck out last night, didn't they? Took a shortcut through the Underground they weren't supposed to."

The tinny, sweaty, leaf-mould smell of them increased exponentially. *Gods, they're young.* The mouth started to say something but Paul cut him off. "No more talking. Let your elders deal with this. Stay away from Gabriel if you see him. I'll look into things." He caught the nephew's eye. "I won't mention this to Martin, but I'd better not hear about you sneaking out again." He turned back to the mouth and gave him his best lofty and enigmatic stare. "You. You call me 'bloodboy' again and I'll have your newest skin for a rug. Got it?"

Without waiting for a reply, Paul stalked off.

What the hell am I, Father's parole officer? He grimaced, and was surprised to feel his fangs pressing into his lip. They weren't out much, but it was a bad sign. He needed to calm down.

The skinshifters tended to be more straightforward than the mages, but handling them took more self-control. Paul's shields were strong enough that he didn't worry about what the humans might pick up off of him, but the shifters had noses that were as good as his own, maybe better. It was a lot harder to control emotion and the body's reaction to it.

Martin would never have given away as much as those pups.

Of course, Martin wouldn't have insulted him, either. Martin Conant wasn't the oldest or the strongest or the bravest shifter in Madison, but he was an Elder, and the others listened to him.

Hell, even I listen to him. Martin Conant had more of Faerie in him than most skinshifters did, and enough old courtesy that Paul sometimes wondered just how much the shifter had guessed about Paul's nature.

The shifters' noses told them that Paul smelled like human and like vampire. Having never smelled a cambion they assumed, and not unreasonably, that he was a tainted human like Amanda. *A pet, a proxy, a daytime errand runner.* Not that Paul hadn't been the daylight hands of his father before, much less the years he spent with Isolde…

Don't think about that.

…but it was rather galling to have it thrown in his face. If not for Cecelia it would be high time he moved, except that Cecelia was what made his current position so irritating.

The thought of her made him smile, made his heart twist with that sick, hopeful joy that meant he was screwed, well and truly head-over-heels. Being in love always made life so complicated.

If not for her, I'd still enjoy tweaking all their noses and keeping them dancing. But now they're just a distraction. Worse, they're a reminder.

He wanted to pretend, just for a little while, that he was human, that he was the man Cecelia deserved and not just a bastard half-breed. *If I could get away from Father's scent and shadow, if I could leave the mages and the skinshifters and their badgering and squabbling behind, could I hold out a little longer?* It'd been almost three decades, and the most he'd ever managed was four. *And the repercussions of that were rather unfortunate.*

The older his body got, the harder it was hold the need at bay. His body wanted healing, wanted life and youth, and the longer he put it off, the more likely he was to lose himself in the killing, to take more lives than he needed.

He suddenly realized that he'd stopped walking. He'd tucked himself into a doorway, little more than a shadow himself, and was watching the passers-by. His teeth were out again, and need stirred in his gut like lazy indigestion.

It was all he could do not to scream in frustration.

* * * *

Gabriel watched Amanda as she scanned the packed movie theater. They'd gone out for dinner and drinks beforehand with James and Brandy and a few more humans Gabriel hadn't paid much attention to. Not that he'd eaten, of course, but he'd gotten quite proficient over the years at making it look like he did. Amanda had made the mistake of ordering pasta, and only picked at her food after the first few bites.

The banal conversation had been easy enough to keep up with, even when Paul had tapped him from the other side of town. The skinshifters getting their hackles up was nothing new, even if they'd all more or less agreed that the police force was off limits while they were on duty. *I had to do something with the guy, after all, and it's not like I actually bit him.* Not that he wouldn't have, of course, but the shifters didn't need to know that.

No, the bothersome part of that conversation had been the obvious strain in Paul's voice. *He needs to stop tormenting himself like this. It doesn't do anyone any good, and just puts off the inevitable.* Of course,

Paul never appreciated that advice. *How did he end up so damn sentimental? Must be Lucretia's influence.* Paul's mother had been a spitfire, of course, but she'd also had a surprisingly tender heart.

Speaking of spitfires... Gabriel put an arm around Amanda's shoulders and stifled a grin when she stiffened. *You're the one who wanted me to pretend I was your boyfriend,* he reminded her.

Her lips thinned, but she tried to relax. *It seemed like the explanation that would draw the least attention.*

And it is. That doesn't mean I can't enjoy myself.

She refused to rise to the bait, ignoring him and continuing to watch the crowd as people streamed in.

"What are you looking for?" he asked her.

"Brandy. She went to get snacks and she's been gone forever. I hope she didn't forget her ticket stub." There were ushers at every theater entrance, regardless of the fact that Episode One was the only thing showing on any screen.

"Why don't you look for her then?"

Amanda frowned. "It'd be just my luck that I'd go out one door just as she's coming in the other."

No, silly. You can find her the same way you found me at the Union House.

He felt her freeze. *I can?*

Yes.

Amanda hesitated only briefly. *How?*

Think of Brandy. Picture her in your mind. Feel her aura, smell her scent. Concentrate everything on her. Don't push, he added as she tried to reach out. *Just make her as real in your mind as you can. Be passive.*

Amanda let out a deep, slow breath and relaxed into him. Gabriel lowered his voice, murmuring. *Good. Now feel around, slowly, until you find her mind. No rush. Just reach out and find her aura.*

He closed his eyes, trying to watch through her as she let her mental fingers drift. She nearly jumped out of her seat when they finally caught on something.

I think I found her. Amanda's voice buzzed with repressed excitement.

Good. Now focus down that link. There is no distance between you. You are there.

Her essence stretched away from him, a graceful, glittering line of power that he itched to touch, to mold to his will. *Patience,* he whispered to himself.

After a moment she returned, sitting up a little and putting one hand to her forehead.

Ow. You could've warned me about the headache this time.

Headaches aren't unusual when you're first learning, he told her with a silent laugh, *but I can't do that without a true link, so I couldn't know for sure.*

Amanda's jaw dropped. *Really?*

Shut your mouth, little mouse. You have no external reason to look surprised. You'll have to learn to hide your feelings better than that. Where is Brandy?

Amanda closed her mouth with an audible click of teeth. *She's coming. She ran into someone from her Chem class.*

Ah. He kept his arm around her even after she tried to sidle out from under it, knowing that the contact would help waken her sluggish, hungry blood. Like called to like. Her scent was a pungent mix of human and *daemon*, her flesh nearly saturated with the contagion.

Soon the true contest would begin.

* * * *

Amanda was sad to wave goodbye to her friends after the movie was over. *That's the most normal I've felt in almost a week.* But there'd been a certain amount of tension, too, waiting to see if Gabriel would do something awful. She wasn't quite sure what she'd expected—or feared—but he'd been a perfect gentleman all night.

And that made her more nervous than ever.

"So, are you hungry?" he asked as they headed out into the parking lot.

The thought of the sweet snacks and soda had made her stomach turn, and she'd passed on the overpriced popcorn. And dinner had been awful. *That was the blandest fettuccine alfredo I've ever had.* "I'm famished." She felt like she was always hungry anymore, still trying to recover from the blood loss.

"I can cook you up some dinner, if you like. The stuff's at my place, though."

That was a baited hook if ever Amanda heard one, but she couldn't help the surge of curiosity. "Your place? Where do you live?"

"I'll show you. It's just off East Wash."

Gabriel drove them downtown, skirting the ever-present construction on East Washington Avenue. The apartment building he pulled up to was near an industrial park, and obviously had been a warehouse once upon a time.

Now it had retail shops on the ground floor and living spaces above. Gabriel drove around the back to an underground parking garage and hit the opener. Inside the dim garage he stopped in front of what looked like a storage unit door. He touched a button on the steering column and the door swung inward with a barely audible rumble. Gabriel drove the car inside, and the door swung shut again.

Amanda stared over her shoulder at it. "How thick is that door?"

The vampire waited until it was shut all the way before turning off the car. "About two feet. Solid steel."

Recessed lights around the ceiling glowed softly, revealing the monstrous mechanical apparatus that was responsible for moving that formidable hunk of metal. Amanda looked around her in awe as she got out. If she hadn't known better, she would have thought it was a professional garage. There were tools everywhere.

"You really *do* do all the work on her yourself," she murmured as Gabriel walked around the car.

"It's hard to find a mechanic that will work on armored cars, much less one that works at night," he replied.

She started, staring at the car as if she'd never seen it before. "Armored?"

"Someone tried to blow me up once." He said it matter-of-factly as he typed something into a keypad on the wall, then bent close for the retina scan. A smaller door in the wall that Amanda would have assumed led to another storage unit unlocked with an audible thunk. Another tap on the keypad caused thick bolts in the door that led to the public garage to shoot into the floor. "I take my security very seriously."

"I see that." With one last look at the mechanic's wet dream, she followed him through the second door.

She stopped just across the threshold. There was no light except what flooded in behind her.

She felt Gabriel move off to her right, and two halogen lamps lit up on the far wall. Gabriel took his hand off the light switch and closed the door behind her. More bolts slid into place.

"Welcome to my humble abode," he said, walking past her into the kitchen.

The apartment was an efficiency, only one room and a bathroom. The wall on the right was mostly taken up by a large closet. There was a queen-sized bed in the far right corner, covered with a simple maroon spread. Two halogen lamps divided the far wall into thirds, with an entertainment center standing between them. Two black beanbags sat on the floor in front of the TV. To the left, an island with a black marble countertop separated the kitchen from the living room. The floor was a dark, wood-patterned linoleum, and the walls appeared off-white in the dim light.

Across from the bed, on the same wall as the door, stood a partially folded silk screen. To her left, on the wall shared with the bathroom, was a silver-on-black Oriental triptych depicting wild horses. The screen and the triptych were the only real attempts at decoration. There were, not surprisingly, no windows.

"Nice place," she commented. "Cozy."

"It's all I need." He set a frying pan on the stove. "I helped finance the renovation on the building. Not that you'd be able to find that on paper anywhere, of course."

"Of course," she echoed. She wandered up to the island and leaned over it, the black stone cool against the skin of her arms.

"I'll have this done for you in a few minutes." Gabriel opened the fridge and took out an apple and a package wrapped in white paper. "There's this or the rolls on the counter if you want something now." He set the apple in front of her.

Amanda picked it up. It felt odd in her hand, as if she wasn't sure what to do with it. *Like it's a piece of wax fruit.* She watched Gabriel unwrap a sirloin steak, and her stomach nearly cramped it made her so hungry. Without thinking, she took a bite out of the apple.

Sweet exploded across her tongue, so potent it was almost sour. "Ugh!" She spit the piece out before she could stop herself, and wiped her mouth with the back of her hand. The taste lingered, foul and pungent, as if she'd bitten squarely into a lemon that'd gone bad.

Gabriel glanced at her as he drizzled a little olive oil into the pan. "Fruit tends to be the first to go. Try the rolls."

She chucked the apple at the wastebasket. "Maybe I'll just wait for the steak," she muttered, but reached for the bag of rolls. *Just how bad is this?*

The steak hit the frying pan with a hiss.

The bread didn't smell any different than usual, but then, neither had the apple. Amanda nibbled cautiously. "It doesn't taste like anything," she said after a moment, and tried a larger bite. "It's like eating paper."

Gabriel only nodded and flipped the steak.

It was hard to think about bread with that rich, heavy scent filling the room. "So what gives?" she asked, continuing to eat the roll without much enthusiasm. *Please tell me the Spicy Cheese Bread from Stella's Bakery isn't going to start tasting like this.*

"Your taste buds are changing, that's all." Gabriel lifted the pan and slid the steak onto a plate. He set it down in front of her, then handed her some silverware. "I'm afraid I'm not set up for entertaining."

"If you put a table or something in here it'd be too cluttered. You might consider barstools, though." Amanda tossed the roll at the wastebasket. She wanted to be angry about the fruit and the bread, but the scent of the meat was literally making her mouth water, driving all other thoughts from her head. She cut off a piece of steak. It was still bloody in the middle, which normally would've made her send it back, but she didn't care. She was *starving*. She took a bite.

"Something wrong?" Gabriel asked as she grimaced.

"It's still cold in the middle." She was already cutting off another piece.

"Do you want me to cook it some more?"

Amanda stared at the hunk of bloody meat on her fork. The thought of cooking it more was about as appealing as the dinner roll. *This is only temporary,* she reminded herself. *One week down, three to go.* She raised her eyes to his, and her lips twitched into a wry grin. *God, that's good steak.*

"Not really," she answered, popping it into her mouth. The flavor was even better the second time.

CHAPTER TEN

Thursday, May 27th, 1999
One week later

Amanda sat in a quiet corner of the bar, practicing her shields and trying to figure out Gabriel's look-away aura. The latter was proving harder than she expected, but the former she had down pat—except for the vampire himself, that is. The cool wind of his presence licked at her awareness, a beacon she could choose to ignore but not entirely shut out. She wasn't sure if it was because she was getting stronger or if it was just from working with him so much, but she couldn't be in the same building with him anymore without being aware of exactly where he was.

I guess that means he can't sneak up on me.

As much as she didn't like to admit it, so far this whole psychic thing was pretty freaking cool.

They'd spent most of the last week—when not in the bars of course—working on Amanda's shields. She could reliably block his "fascination" four times out of five now, and she was starting to learn about other people's shields too.

She sent out the lightest, most delicate of mental probes so she could check out the other patrons. Most were just normal humans. Their shields were weak, full of gaps and holes and soft spots where stray thoughts came arrowing out with annoying frequency. Other psychics, with their thicker, cobbled-together shields, were often not much better than the normal humans; most seemed to be more concerned with keeping thoughts out rather than in. Part of Amanda's improvements came from her increasing need to guard against these broadcasts. The more she used her abilities, the better she got. The better she got, the more she could hear, whether she wanted to or not.

There were also two skinshifters at the rail, easy for her to spot now because as far as her probe was concerned, they weren't even there. Visually she still couldn't tell them from humans, but if she closed her eyes, she'd never know those seats were occupied.

"Skinshifters are untouchable, completely immune to any form of telepathy or thought control," Gabriel had advised her when she first could tell the difference. "Their thoughts are literally on another plane, or at least that's what the mages say."

Mages were also easy to identify. Their minds were like fortresses, and the fortress walls pulsed with power. It was hard even to probe one without them noticing, but as long as she didn't linger, the mages didn't seem to pay it any heed. She herself had felt the passing touch of another mind on occasion, but it was always brief, sort of like accidently making eye contact with a stranger when looking around for a friend. She supposed there was some form of telepathy etiquette, but if so, Gabriel hadn't bothered to share it.

Amanda sipped at her water. The ice cubes left a slightly bitter aftertaste, but all in all, it was about the only thing left she could stand to drink. *Besides the obvious, of course, which I'm not touching.* Any food that wasn't meat dripping in its own juices had become nearly inedible, though she still tried to eat something else every day, just to make herself feel better.

She felt Gabriel approaching and pulled in her probes, settling herself comfortably behind her shields. He appeared a moment later. Trailing in his wake was a thin, blond boy who didn't even look like he was out of high school. They both sat down at Amanda's table.

"Amanda, this is Nicholas," Gabriel said, nodding at the boy. His voice had a slight sing-song to it that Amanda recognized all too well. She wasn't going to like this.

"Nice to meet you," she murmured.

Nicholas never took his eyes off the vampire.

"He's one of my pets. I thought you could use him for practice."

Amanda blinked at Gabriel. "Practice?"

"Defensively, you're coming along nicely, but there are other skills yet that you need to learn, and I'm afraid practicing on me is out of the question." The expression on his face was pleasant enough, but his eyes had a hard edge to them. *Mages hide behind their walls,* he told her. *Vampires hunt, and we have many ways of bringing prey to us.*

I'm not a vampire, she snapped, her gaze flicking between Gabriel and Nicholas. The boy had hardly moved since they'd sat down, and either he didn't realize they were talking about him, or he didn't care. *Is he, you know, okay?*

Of course not. I told you, he's a pet. Gabriel brushed a finger along Nicholas's jawbone and Amanda thought the boy was going to melt. *Pet, thrall, slave, take your pick. I broke him months ago.*

Amanda remembered what he'd said about forcing people to enjoy it when he drank from them, but this was leaps and bounds beyond even that corruption. She barely kept the revulsion from her face. *Why?*

Because it's fun. Now, I know you've wanted to try fascination yourself. Give it a shot. He pushed the boy's chin until Nicholas was facing her and raised his eyes to hers.

Amanda stared at Nicholas in shock. She could feel the boy's shields without even trying, but she had no idea where to start. Not that she had any intention of doing so. This was nothing like her usual lessons with Gabriel, which were half lecture and half psychic sparring session. She'd come to enjoy those hours spent pitting her strength against his, discovering the ins and outs of her new abilities, but somehow she'd forgotten that there was more to this than learning to control long-dormant gifts.

"No." She wrenched her gaze away from Nicholas's with only a tiny pang of regret. "It's not right. He's not…" She shook her head.

"Don't be so squeamish. He's perfectly willing, aren't you?"

"Of course, *Dominus,*" Nicholas murmured.

Amanda thought she might be sick. *Dominus* meant "master" in Latin. *He really has made a slave of him.* The idea of having her will stripped away, of becoming little more than a puppet, made cold sweat break out along her back and shoulders. *I'd rather die.*

Relax. I would never do this to you. Gabriel's words wove through her brain even though she tried to block them out, and she remembered what Gabriel'd said about not needing eye contact. The vampire continued. *He is nothing. A tool to be used and discarded when no longer useful. You are something else entirely.* Self-satisfied pride echoed in his voice.

He's not a tool, he's a person, she snapped back. *I know you're a Roman and all, but we don't hold with slavery anymore.*

In Rome, a slave could be freed, becoming a citizen with most of the same rights as any other Roman. Nicholas will never be free of me. His life is mine.

Her hands curled into fists. *He's a human being, not an object.*

He's a human, I'll grant you that. Then Gabriel grinned. *But I'm not.*

Amanda crossed her arms over her chest and turned away from them. *You can't make me roll him,* she said, though she knew it sounded petulant and childish. As much as she did want to learn more, to learn *everything*, she wouldn't give Gabriel the satisfaction.

I probably could *make you, but that would be rather counterproductive.*

She bristled, but was distracted when Gabriel threw his camouflage over them, a combination of look-away and an air-shifting *something* that made their corner even darker. As she tried to study it, Gabriel put an arm around Nicholas and pulled him close. "If you don't want to play, I guess I'll just eat and run."

Amanda's stomach seized up as the vampire leaned forward and sank his fangs into the boy's neck. When he'd bitten her, he'd moved too fast to see; this was damn near leisurely by comparison. Nicholas sucked in a hard breath, arching into Gabriel's embrace with a look of rapture that bordered on obscene, that was worshipful and joyous in a way Amanda had only seen on the faces of religious devotees.

Gabriel changed his angle, the tension in his body making the air almost vibrate around him. A tiny trickle of red escaped his mouth to leave a shining trail that ran along Nicholas's collarbone and disappeared under his shirt. It reminded Amanda too much of her dream. She shut her eyes, but she couldn't shut out her awareness of Gabriel's presence. His aura was a cold, swirling breeze against her shields, and it pulsed in a ragged, thundering rhythm that Amanda could only assume was dictated by the beat of the boy's heart.

The bar was far from silent, but all she could hear was Nicholas, his panting breaths accented by the tiniest, faintest mewling moans. The boy's reactions made everything far more intimate than Gabriel's usual feedings. Amanda felt dirty just being there. Her lip started to curl but she fought to keep her expression neutral, taking a slow, deep breath to calm her own fluttering heart.

She tasted the scent as much as smelled it, weighty and cloying, coating her tongue and the back of her mouth as if droplets of blood coalesced out of thin air. Her mouth went dry, and it was hard to swallow. The scent was blood, that much was unmistakable, but it was so much more than that—vibrant and lively and savory and sweet all at once. The tangle of sensation drew her, made her pulse race and her gums tingle.

Amanda shot out of her chair, but as she started away from the table, a hand grabbed her wrist, hauling her up short. She looked back. Nicholas's fingers were wrapped around her forearm, but his eyes were closed. Just past his chin she saw Gabriel staring at her, mouth still locked to the boy's throat.

Did you think this was all going to be mind games and midnight movies?

She tore her gaze away from Gabriel's, attacking Nicholas's pathetic shields until she found a way through. *Let go of me,* she hissed, pushing the thought at the boy.

The grip on her fell away. Amanda stalked out of the bar without looking back again, Gabriel's laughter ringing through her head.

* * * *

Isolde crouched behind the decorative stone balustrade that crowned the roof of the hospital, scanning the windows of the apartment complex across the street. Her crows had followed Morales to this remote Wisconsin town, and watched him and his crew enter the apartment just before sundown. He hadn't left. The gentle evening breeze carried a thousand scents to her, but none of them were his. She knew his scent all too well—few of her marks had managed to elude her for this long.

Her long black hair was braided and coiled attractively—and practically—around her head, but tiny short wisps stuck out around her face and stirred in the restless breeze. She blinked as one touched her eye—blinked, but did not move.

The wind was shifting.

Cursing silently, Isolde weighed her options. She counted on her sense of smell to tell her if Morales left the building by the back. From her perch across the street, she could see the front and side entrances, the doors glowing under the light of the building's many lamps. If she moved downwind, she would only be able to see one entrance, and in moving at all she would risk being seen. Morales knew she was after him—he couldn't not know and still be alive.

It had been a most frustrating week.

Morales and his group of hunters moved strictly as a unit. She'd found them easily enough—Cartwright had described the building perfectly—but she'd immediately run into a serious setback. The entire building had been magically warded. Not only had the wards prevented her from entering the building in her gaseous, nearly-invisible aethereal form, but her attempt had set off alarms that had the whole place in an uproar in seconds. Worse, she knew so little about sorcery that she had no idea whether the spell had been protecting against vampires, or skinshifters, or the supernatural in general.

Now the group was on the move, changing locations by day and holing up at night.

The unceasing hunt wearied her, always another target no matter how many they killed, but it kept her sharp, kept her going even if it didn't provide the thrill it once had. Isolde could think of five men without even trying that would've given a year's earnings for a target as tough as Morales, and that wasn't counting her fellow Furies. Though only the youngest Furies cared whether their targets were difficult. *Fools,* she murmured to herself, and even that thought held no emotion.

Mechanically, she glanced from window to window, searching for Morales's silhouette and not finding it. *Possibly on the other side, might be worth moving, then.* Her eyes flicked over the surrounding landscape, considering the best path to take. Killing gave no satisfaction either, apart from a little pride in another assignment completed. She did not especially enjoy killing, but she was good at it. She'd been doing it for centuries.

When you stop hunting, you become prey.

That thought was in another voice, from another time. Isolde's lips pressed together. She had to stay focused.

Below her, inside the hospital, a stair creaked.

Isolde noted it without alarm. It was late, but a hospital was never silent. Still, most nurses used the elevators. Perhaps it *was* time to move... Spreading imaginary wings, she felt gravity's hold on her lessen, and she raised her head two inches above the balustrade.

The gun was silenced, but she heard the shot clearly. It came from the building directly behind the apartment, a business center that should have been empty at this time of night.

In an eye-blink she was gone, hurtling up from her prone position, twisting through space to land behind an air-conditioning unit near the center of the hospital roof.

The door to the roof crashed open. Isolde launched herself into the air again, not toward the hunter emerging through the door, but back, directly away from the sniper who had already shot.

Directly toward the one who hadn't.

The second sniper had been waiting patiently downwind for the trap to spring, for her to move either toward the bait at the door, or to the "safe" side of the roof, farthest from the apartment where Morales waited. If the sniper hadn't been human, hadn't needed to breathe out soft and slow to steady his aim, he might actually have had a chance.

Fools, she thought again as she writhed in midair, successfully dodging the one shot this sniper was going to get off. *Who do you think you're dealing with?*

The second sniper tried to duck, but he didn't have enough time. Isolde sailed past him, kicking the gun from his hands, grabbing the back of his jacket and pulling him down with her.

A bullet brushed past her head. She landed like an acrobat on one hand, pushing off again, dragging her prize with her. *Never stop moving.*

Her prisoner, to his credit, reached for a blade. Impatiently she slapped him, knocking him out.

Back on her feet, a split second to gather her prize to her, more bullets coming, she could hear them—*got to move!*

She was nearly to the far edge of the roof when she heard the high-pitched sound of a radio signal. Instantly she hurled her prize over the roof edge and dove sideways, rolling along behind the balustrade until she heard the *whoosh* of the detonation. *I wonder if he knew he was carrying? Are you all such dedicated hunters that you'll become suicide bombers, or is Morales just that ruthless?*

The bullets were getting closer. It was past time to go. *Shoulder, back, feet, PUSH.* Isolde propelled herself out of the roll and over the balustrade. The remains of the sniper had almost reached the ground. Heads would be poking out of the blown-out windows at any moment. Isolde took a few running steps down the side of the building and launched herself into the air.

She breathed out as she fell, though it wasn't exactly breathing. The aethereal essence of her escaped through her lips, pouring through that opening in a rush of roiling air, pulling her human skin through behind her until it vanished and she was free. No weight, no sight, no longer falling but still moving, Isolde took hold of her crow skin and dove into it, pushing the skin out ahead of her until she settled in with a snap like shaking the wrinkles from a shirt. A simple thought pulled the shadows close—Paul called it bending the light, but Isolde privately thought her own way of looking at it to be more accurate—and she vanished into the sleeping town.

When Morales and his crew left the apartment building a few minutes later, they didn't appear to notice the crow flying high above their vehicle, a bird whose body temperature so perfectly matched the night air that it didn't show up on thermal imaging.

Years went by, names and faces changed, but no new technology would outwit Isolde Constantinus.

Sorcery, on the other hand, was a threat she had not faced in some time. Isolde bitterly regretted the loss of her prisoner, and whatever charm he had borne that had kept her from scenting him when the wind shifted.

She had no facility for such things, and hated the practice of it with what little passion was left in her.

Morales is unconventional as well as clever.

Of course, he would try to set another trap for her. He was a hunter of the old guard; he knew what a victory her death would be for his brethren. For as long as she was willing to chase him, he'd keep leading her on, hoping that his paltry half-century of experience could stand up to her eighteen hundred years of practice.

It would be laughable, if Morales didn't have daylight on his side.

Intent on her quarry, Isolde suddenly realized she was toying with the idea of contacting Paul, of enlisting his help. Her brother's talents were many and perfectly complemented her own weaknesses. As soon as she recognized the path her mind was wandering down, she shoved the idea from her head.

I will never forgive Paul. Never.

CHAPTER ELEVEN

Friday, May 28th, 1999

The Inferno's multitude of lights blinked and flickered and pulsed across the dark stretch of the dance floor, limning the other dancers in weird hues and colorful shadows. Amanda hid in the midst of the crowd, studiously ignoring Gabriel where he sat at a small table with some of his regulars.

It felt good to be among humans. She and Gabriel had gone out with James and Brandy and Sammi and Kayla and a few of Amanda's other friends a couple times since going to see Episode One, but she'd never been able to relax, too worried that Gabriel might take a fancy to one of them. And then last night, Gabriel had kept Nicholas with them for several hours, but you could hardly call his company "human."

It's not his fault. But fair or unfair, Amanda couldn't help but be repulsed by the boy's fawning behavior. Sure, he probably hadn't asked to be the vampire's slave, but did he have to be so disgustingly happy about it?

Amanda pushed the thought away. Here she was just another body, another face in the faceless mob. The auras and shields and energies of the people around her buoyed her up, warm and lively and familiar even though she didn't know anyone here tonight. It was that same feeling she'd had the night this whole mess started, the anonymous camaraderie of being part of a crowd. Amanda wrapped herself up in that energy, hugged it close like it was her favorite afghan on a cold night, and tried to forget.

During the day it wasn't so bad; maybe she felt the sun a little more than she had before, but not enough that she couldn't still write it off to paranoia. It was like she had two different lives, was two different people: one who stubbornly refused to admit that anything had changed, who had a day job and bills to pay and friends who wanted to borrow her clothes, and another who could hardly stand to eat solid food, who had to consciously block out the rogue thoughts of the people around her, who'd been so intrigued by Nicholas's blood that she hadn't been able to stop thinking about it since.

Her stomach tightened up, and she danced harder. It was tough to argue with the monster when you felt the same urges he did, manipulated people as easily as he did. That Gabriel had been using the boy as a puppet made little difference; she'd still made Nicholas let her go. She'd broken into his mind and forced him to do what she told him.

God, his blood had smelled good. She could still almost taste it.

As if called by her reaction, she felt the slight ripple in the crowd's energy as Gabriel slipped in among the sheep. *Guess he's done with dinner.* Amanda danced away from him, unwilling to leave the comfort of the crowd just yet.

He cut sharply toward the stage, heading her off. She turned and went back the way she'd come, like a child pretending not to hear her parents calling. Gabriel's presence followed at a leisurely pace.

She looked back, both of them moving with the music to avoid attracting attention. He stood out so starkly to her, as if everyone else was out of focus, but no one else gave him a second glance. The lights made his skin and hair change color from moment to moment, casting weird shadows across his face that emphasized and hid his otherness by turns. *Human. Not human. Human. Not human.* There was a hunting gleam in his eye and a predatory twist to his tiny smile as he slid through the press, herding her toward the bar as if she were one of the sheep.

Hunt me, will he?

Suddenly it was a game, another test, just another sparring session. Amanda dove back into the crowd, always one or two people ahead of him but no more, slipping between dancers and dodging around the support posts, leading him on. *Let's see what you can do when your quarry isn't some mindless drone.*

He almost caught her as she came to the end of the floor, moving left, then right as she tried to dodge around him. His lips were parted, tasting the air. His chin was tucked a little closer to his chest than normal, and she knew she was grinning like an idiot, laughter almost choking her as she darted past him, pivoting on one foot at the last second. His fingers slid down her arm, his power crawling over her skin, fierce and lethal, cool and biting, and completely unlike that of the humans around them.

Her breath caught at the sensation, but she spun away again. *Is that the best he can do?*

Amanda danced backwards away from him, just out of reach, all but daring him to try harder. The crowd parted around her seamlessly, never faltering, oblivious to their contest. Gabriel followed, openly stalking her now, the grace of his movements giving him the illusion of dancing even though he'd left that charade behind. This was sparring at its best, where the rules were in her favor and the presence of the crowd meant the consequences would have to be subtle.

Subtle doesn't mean you'll like it any better, you idiot. Part of her was screaming that this was stupid, that he had warned her about running from him for a reason, that pushing him like this could have consequences she wouldn't like at all.

I don't care, she thought in a rush of adrenaline. *He still can't take what I don't give.*

But even as she thought it her better sense made her turn away, trying to break the tension between them.

His arms wrapped around her the moment her back was to him. He pulled her tight against him, curling around her, fitting together as if they were two pieces of the same puzzle, his chest and abdomen warm and solid against her spine.

"Giving up so soon?" he whispered, his lips brushing her ear.

A whiff of bloodsmell on his breath made her close her eyes with sudden longing. "Who says I'm giving up?" she answered, breathless. "Maybe I have you right where I wanted you."

"Do you?" His reply was somewhere between a purr and a growl.

She shivered, unable to answer, unsure exactly just what she truly wanted.

"Were you hunting me, little mouse? Or was it that you wanted me to catch you?" His arms tightened, his words low and rumbling. Her breath caught as he nuzzled her neck. "Hiding among the humans like a wolf in sheep's clothing. Covering yourself with their scent." He nipped at her reproachfully. "You are not one of them anymore, Amanda. Look at them."

Drowning under the weight of his presence, she stared at the oblivious crowd. Bodies writhed en masse before her.

"No," he breathed. *"Look."*

A man directly in front of her caught her eye. He was a little older than she was, or so she assumed, with a muscular physique was partly good genetics, and partly hours spent in the gym. The rest of the crowd fell away as she watched him, the music fading into the background.

She could've counted the tiny black hairs curling over the low neck of his shirt. His skin glistened under the lights, drawing her in even closer. Skin slid over muscle, muscle bulged and flexed, sweat dotted skin where pores marred the flawlessness of the surface. And just under that surface…spidery lines of red and blue, gently pulsing even from here and unbelievably *alive*.

Gabriel's arms still pinned her to him. Amanda felt him looking through her eyes, wondered when he had hidden his face in her hair. Forehead, nose, and cheekbone were hard lines against her scalp. Her gaze drifted, distracted.

Look.

Gabriel's power reached past her to touch the dancer's mind. The man threw his head back, muscles straining, throwing everything into that one motion at the climax of the music. His heartbeat was so clear against the taut skin, so strong, beating against the skin like it wanted to get out…

No, something is wrong, something…this isn't…

Amanda realized her chest was heaving, her breath coming in uneven gasps. She shook her head a little, trying to stop whatever was happening.

The vampire clawed his way deeper into the man's psyche, and forced the dancer to raise a hand to his own throat.

Torn between eagerness and horror, Amanda watched.

With slow deliberation, the dancer dragged his fingernails down his neck, leaving four long furrows that ran from jaw nearly to collarbone. The blood welled up, ran over the gouges, trickling down neck and chest.

The smell of it made her whole body ache…she found herself straining against Gabriel's embrace, trying to lean forward, to get closer to the source of that fascinating scent.

It calls you, the vampire whispered, his face still buried in her hair. His breath on her scalp was ragged, as ragged as her own breaths as they fought through her tight throat.

The bloodsmell grew as the man danced a little closer, seemingly unaware of the damage he'd inflicted on himself. The blood shone under the lights, so inviting…

Her hands clenched at her sides.

You want it. You want to touch, feel the warmth, the wetness.

She was shaking all over, and she didn't answer. She didn't think she could lie to him mind-to-mind.

He will come to you, if you want him.

The dancer swiveled to face her, his eyes fixing on her. Amanda strained to control her vision, to meet his gaze, to look away from the blood. The cold wind of the vampire's power had enveloped the dancer completely.

Feel how eager he is, Amanda. How much he wants you to take him.

And it was true. She could feel the man's desire as if the air around him were burning.

The dancer had made a present of himself and was only waiting on her to accept it.

Yes...no. No, this isn't real, this is like...like... She struggled to remember, but it was so hard to think straight. The blood was so very distracting.

Gabriel's hunger gnawed at Amanda's back, resonating through her as if the vampire blood in her veins recognized its master's need and ached in sympathy, growing sharper as more of his power poured into the man in front of them.

The dancer desperately wanted her to take him. Needed her to. The only reason for his existence was to satisfy her.

Just like...Nicholas. That's right.

The memory gave her a little breathing room. Amanda reached out to touch Gabriel's power, the bite of it cooling the raw heat of this new hunger, and she looked up to meet the man's eyes.

Utterly empty.

Like a puppet, the dancer dropped to his knees before her, his expression imploring but his gaze blind.

Almost before she could register it, a thought bubbled up—*Perfect.* Amanda reached out to tip his head back, to expose this gift, Gabriel's gift to her, her hand trembling at the warmth of the man's skin under her fingers. Her jaw ached so sweetly...

"*No!*"

Amanda hardly realized she'd shrieked it out loud. Behind her, Gabriel sagged, and she spun away from him. She only caught a glimpse of him as she took flight, but the image burned itself into her mind: the vampire on his knees next to the dancer, both hands clutching his head, and the dancer blinking at the staring crowd in confusion. The bouncer put out a hand to stop her, but she ducked under it with a snarl that made him pause, and then she was out.

She tore down the sidewalk blindly, dodging across the street without looking. The squeal of tires couldn't break her panic; without thinking, she put out a hand and vaulted the hood of the car. The shouts of the driver faded as she cut between two buildings, turning a hard right and pounding down the empty street. She didn't know where she was going. She couldn't think that far.

I've got to get away, I've got to get away, I've got—

Amanda.

She sobbed and put on a new burst of speed, turning down an alley that ran between the buildings.

The voice was weak, unsteady, but it persisted. *You cannot hide from me.*

"Leave me alone!" she screamed. The alley dead-ended but she leapt at the wall, scrabbling over it and coming down into a parking lot on the other side. She hit the ground running.

You are mine. I will find you.

"I'm not yours!"

She came to the edge of the lot and crossed the street, not slowing. This time there were no cars to distract her and she cut between two houses across the way.

The shadows behind the house on her right suddenly grew arms as she passed, wrapping around her and jerking her back into the gloom before she could draw breath to scream. A delicately boned hand clapped over her mouth.

"Don't move, and don't make a sound," a feminine voice with a slight accent hissed in her ear.

Amanda froze, her heart racing.

The arms loosened enough for her to look at the figure holding her. A woman with short, very straight black hair looked back at her. Deep brown eyes regarded her with caution. The hand over her mouth lifted slightly, and the woman raised her eyebrows.

Amanda nodded. The hand came away. Amanda kept her mouth shut and tried to wheeze quietly.

"Good." The woman's aura swirled against Amanda's mental senses, sharp and cold as the dark brown eyes searched the night.

"You're a vampire, too," Amanda whispered.

"And you're his new toy." Hard eyes left off their scan and drilled into her.

A week ago that gaze would've sent her staggering, but now, even after her panic, she snapped her shields in place. The woman arched an eyebrow as the power slid around the shields without effect.

"I am," Amanda admitted. "But you're one of his old ones."

"And what makes you say that, mortal girl?" Amanda couldn't place the woman's accent, the words rolling off her tongue as if they had extra vowels.

"I can feel your link to him. Faint, closed away, but his presence rides within you." Amanda leaned in nose-to-nose with the startled vampire. "You're bound to him forever, just like I am."

The woman nodded once, her mouth a firm line. "Bound until death. Nothing is forever."

"Is that why you're here?"

The woman shook her head. "Even were he the Devil incarnate I often curse him to be, I could not kill him. I…cannot bring myself to do it." She sounded rueful, and more than a little bitter. "Nor, do I think, would I be the one to survive even if I could."

"What do you want with me?"

The woman took a step back, examining Amanda with a critical eye. "You are strong, young one. But he is stronger. I would not see another succumb to him as I did. I wish to help you defeat him."

Amanda's jaw dropped. "How?"

The vampire shook her head. "There's no time now. I can hide you from his thoughts but not forever, and it won't take him long to follow your scent in any case." She grimaced. "This opportunity was unexpected, and I am not prepared. I will try to resist morning's oblivion. When you feel him sleep for the day, call me. We'll talk more then." The woman pressed a business card into Amanda's hand. "Go now. Be hopeful he doesn't smell me on you. Run! We will talk later. Run!"

Amanda thrust the card into her pocket and fled. When she glanced back as she rounded the house, the woman was gone.

He might smell her on me? What is he, a bloodhound? No, not funny.

She crossed another street into another backyard. She didn't want to consider whether she might be able to smell another person on Gabriel. *Scent, scent. I don't think rolling in the grass will be enough.* She smacked her forehead and put on a new burst of speed. *Duh! The lake!*

Lake Mendota wasn't too far, maybe half a mile, but now it was down to whether she could get there before Gabriel found her. She didn't know what the woman had done to hide her from Gabriel's power, but it was starting to slip the further she ran. Bursts of him, his presence, flickered through her mind like static on a radio.

He was hunting her. Hunting her for real this time and not as part of some game.

Rage sizzled like lightning through her skull. She bit back a scream that would've wasted breath she desperately needed to keep running.

Oh, my God, he's angry. I've never felt him angry before. He's going to catch me. I know he's going to catch me. Just let me get to the lake first!

Another burst of him washed over her, frustration and pain, targeting her before he was thrust away again.

Amanda vaulted a chain link fence, her lungs burning with the effort. She tried to ignore the stitch in her side. *Just a little farther!*

She burst into the last street, dodged a car, and crossed into the park on the other side. The scents of water and algae welcomed her as she lurched across the beach. Unable to keep back a triumphant cry, she dove into the dark waters.

Surfacing, she scanned the shoreline for him, but there was no sign. Hugging her thoughts close in the hopes that it would help, she started swimming for the nearest boat dock. *Maybe I can hide there.*

She ducked under the water again to make sure she was as scent-free as possible, swimming below the surface for as long as her tired lungs would let her. She came up for a breath, reoriented, and dove under again.

Her hand brushed the slime-covered wood of the dock, and she came up gasping. She had time for a single breath before the weight of Gabriel's rage broke through her barriers, and a hand seized her by the collar of her shirt and lifted her out of the water.

The vampire held her close to his face, her feet dangling over the lake's surface. "How did you do that?" he hissed.

She stared at him blankly, spluttering in surprise.

"How did you hide yourself from me?"

Her mouth opened and closed, but no words came. Distressed whimperings were all she could manage. She shook her head, eyes wide.

The vampire grumbled to himself and set her down on the aged wood.

As soon as he let go of her, Amanda stumbled back to the end of the pier. Gabriel rounded on her, his movements smooth and fluid, not even pretending to be human. "Why did you come here?" he asked, suspicion thick in his voice.

Amanda swallowed hard and tried to stop shaking. "Running water," she managed at last. She looked down at the lake below them. "I guess that isn't true, either."

"Vampires can cross running water just fine." Slowly he pulled himself into a more normal posture, as if he had to remind each muscle how a human might stand. "You got all soaked for nothing."

The wind from the lake whispered against her back, reminding her of just how soaked she was. It cut straight through her wet clothing; hell, it felt like it was cutting straight through *her*. She shivered harder.

"How did you hide yourself from me?" His voice was calm now, but his eyes still burned.

"I j-just tried to p-pull everything ins-side." She hugged herself and rubbed her arms.

He frowned, but let it pass. "Come, I'll take you home."

He reached out to her, but she jerked away.

"D-don't touch me!" The memory came rushing back—the scent of the hot blood, Gabriel's face buried in her hair, his icy aura surrounding her. The dancer's forced surrender. And that one moment, when she'd touched his soft skin with the blood pulsing just beneath. How dearly she wanted to blame Gabriel for that one moment when everything had seemed *right*.

"You don't want me to touch you?" Gabriel was stalking her again, scenting the breeze. He reached toward her.

"No." Her fingers dug into her arms, trying to block out the sensory memory.

He brushed her cheek, cool skin sliding against the wetness of lake water. Amanda forced her heart to go as cold as the rest of her, though it made her dizzy.

"I'm c-cold, Gabriel. And w-warmth is something you c-can't give me."

His hand dropped back to his side. "Come then." He turned and walked away.

With a relieved sigh, Amanda followed.

"You shouldn't have run like that," he said over his shoulder.

"I d-don't want to t-talk about it."

She heard him snicker, and gave a quick prayer of thanks that his anger was as mercurial as his other moods.

"We'll have to go out again once you're dry. You hit me with another headache, if you didn't notice at the time."

"No, I hadn't n-noticed." Her mouth twisted in a grimace. "You d-deserved it, th-though."

"Did I?" His disdain echoed through their bond. "I did nothing to you to make you give me pain."

"I s-said I d-didn't want to t-talk about it."

Her shivering was getting worse. It wasn't that cold out... She stopped as the world suddenly started to sway. Or maybe she did. "G-gabriel?"

She saw him turn and start toward her before she blacked out.

CHAPTER TWELVE

Motion. Someone was shaking her. Her head felt like it was about to split open, and the shaking was only making it worse. She groaned, and the way the sound reverberated made her immediately wish she hadn't.

"Come on, Amanda. Wake up."

Gabriel. Damn him. Feebly she batted at his hands. "Stop it."

The mattress creaked as he sat back. "Hurts, doesn't it," he said, sounding peevishly pleased.

Very carefully, she nodded. That wasn't so bad.

The mattress creaked again as he got up. "I'll be right back."

She felt him leave the room. Hesitantly, she cracked her eyelids. The lights were all off, but there was enough ambient light through the curtains for her to recognize her bedroom. Even that small light—which wouldn't have been enough for her to see anything two weeks ago—sent searing pain through her head. Biting back a moan, she put her hands over her eyes.

The movement of the sheets over her bare skin made her freeze. She was totally naked.

Gabriel returned with a glass of water and a mug of something that steamed and smelled like meat. "Here." He handed her the water along with a couple of aspirin. She tucked the sheets close around her chest before accepting his offerings. She swallowed the aspirin and lay back, exhausted.

"Why am I naked?"

He sat back down, making the bed jump. Amanda's head throbbed harder. "You were going into drain shock. I stuck you in the bathtub until your core temperature evened out again." He growled low in his throat.

"Normally, I would've enjoyed that quite a bit, but right now I'm too tired, hungry, and hurting." He handed her the mug. "Drink this."

She glanced warily at the contents, but it was only beef broth. She wasn't hungry in the slightest, but she drank it anyway.

"Good." His face was stony. "As soon as you can walk, we're going hunting."

"What happened? What's drain shock?" The broth warmed her but it was heavy, sitting in her stomach like a ball of lead.

"You used up too much of your power. You hit me with one hell of a psibolt, then ran over two miles in less than three minutes while trying to hide yourself from me, all without having had any blood since the first night, and with only that little bit of extra energy you took off the crowd at the club." He shook his head reproachfully. "I'm not surprised you hurt. I hurt, too. Maybe next time you'll be a little more careful?"

"Fuck off, Gabriel. I'd hit you again if I didn't think I'd pass out."

"I did nothing to you." His anger battered at her raw mind, and she couldn't block it out. A harsh cry of pain escaped her throat. He ignored it. "I did nothing to bring you pain. You did that all yourself. You punish me for your own desires." Contempt dripped like acid through her mind.

"Stop, please!" she whimpered, her knuckles white where she clutched the sheet.

He sighed in disgust. "You're not even going to let me yell at you. Just as well, I suppose. It's not helping my head any, either."

The burst of pain subsided to an aching throb. Her gut ached, her mouth was like sand, and she craved red meat—or at least, red meat was as far as she'd let that thought go. Biting her lip, she closed her eyes, trying to fight the need down.

She heard Gabriel crouch down next to her, but didn't look. His hands were like ice when they cupped her burning face, numbing the pain a little.

"I can feel your hunger, Amanda. Your need. You have used up too much of yourself tonight, and that demands its price." His voice was soothing, full of understanding. So easy to be lulled by it, and the cool balm of his touch. "What strength I can give you, I will, but you must come with me. We both need what the hunt has to offer."

The words were insistent, inviting, echoing the pulse of her hunger. His anticipation crept into her through their bond like a stain under her skin. It was so tempting...

She tried to turn away, but he wouldn't let her. Startled, she opened her eyes at last.

"I won't let you make yourself ill because of this. You're coming with me if I have to carry you wrapped in that sheet."

Despite her aching head, Amanda giggled. Gabriel's brow knitted in confusion, which only made her giggle harder.

"What's so funny?" he asked.

"When the seductive, otherworldly vampire schtick doesn't work, try brute force, huh?" She shook her head, her hands coming up to hold Gabriel's in place. The ache receded to where she was pretty sure she could walk unaided. She didn't know how Gabriel was doing it, and she didn't care. "You are amusing, sometimes."

The hard edge left his face. "And you are a stubborn mule sometimes. You *are* coming with me."

"I am not drinking any blood."

"I give you the last of my strength, and this is all I get," he growled, but she saw a good-natured glint in his eyes. "Perhaps you won't need the blood, yet, but I do, especially if you want me to be able to do anything about that headache of yours."

She smiled at him. "Okay. I'll come with you."

He took hold of her hands as if to help her up. Then suddenly his nostrils flared. He dropped her hands as if they burned him, gritting his teeth and bowing his head.

"Are you all right?" Amanda started to sit up, to reach for him.

His gaze snapped to hers, but he made no other motion. She froze. Pupils like black holes hid most of his irises, no longer cold and empty, but burning with hunger. His fangs accentuated his snarling lips, distorting the line of his mouth into a curving, bestial leer. His whole body trembled. As if he were afraid any sudden movement would break his concentration, he slowly shook his head.

"No. I'm not all right." He stared at her unblinking, devouring her with his eyes.

Amanda swallowed hard. That intense animal gaze made her heart skip—she imagined this was how a mouse felt under the snake's gaze. *If the mouse were extremely attracted to the snake.* That dangerous mouth was so inviting... *This is not the time to be thinking this way, Amanda girl. You smell enough like food as it is, apparently.*

"Maybe you should go wait in the living room," she suggested.

"Maybe." His eyes never left her, and he didn't move.

It was hard to form the words with those black pools trying to suck her in. It wasn't some vampire mind trick, it was pure, raw attraction. When had the sight of him hunting her become such an incredible turn-on? "Gabriel, go into the living room."

To her relief, he flowed to his feet and headed for the hall. He paused at the door and spoke without looking back at her. "Hurry," he said, his voice a strained, guttural snarl. He shut the door behind him.

Amanda let out the breath she'd been holding, and got up as fast as she dared. She stumbled to her dresser, her head feeling not quite aligned with the rest of her. *Maybe I was being optimistic about walking by myself,* she thought as she threw on the first things that came to hand. Her temples throbbing every time she moved, Amanda shoved her feet into a pair of sandals and staggered to the door.

The vampire did not look up as she left the bedroom, but kept his vigil next to the window. Even the indirect light from the streetlamp seared Amanda's eyes, but she bravely made her way to the couch, where she stopped to lean against it.

"Are you gonna be okay to drive?" she asked.

The vampire turned, and though his eyes fixed on her, he didn't seem to see her. "Come," was all he said as he strode to the door. She struggled to keep up.

Amanda didn't recognize which little hole-in-the-wall bar Gabriel drove them to; in Madison, there were too many to count. She followed him inside. The pounding heavy metal made her legs want to buckle, and she dropped into the first empty booth she found.

The vampire ignored her, singling out a robust girl in black leather pants and a motorcycle jacket. The girl greeted Gabriel warmly—it was obvious he'd fed from her before.

Gabriel's attempts at conversation were stilted and rushed for once, and the girl grew concerned. Amanda heard him plead exhaustion. Would the girl mind sitting down for a bit?

He led his prey back to the table.

"Sarah, I'd like you to meet my sister, Amanda."

The girl's face lifted at the lie, and she beamed at Amanda as she scooted into the booth. "Nice to meet you," she gushed. "I can't imagine growing up with this rascal."

"It was an experience, all right," Amanda returned wryly.

Across the booth, she heard Gabriel murmur something in a language she didn't recognize. He caressed Sarah's neck, and the girl's eyes went dull. With a grateful sigh the vampire pulled her to him.

What the hell was that? Amanda asked.

Something akin to a post-hypnotic suggestion. Sarah's one of my emergency rations. I have a few around the city. Heedless of the bond which was still wide open between them, Gabriel bit deep into Sarah's neck. Amanda's headache vanished as a rush of power hammered into her. The icy river of energy rolled her under, drowning her even as the hunger in her belly gleefully and greedily begged for more. She could feel Gabriel devouring Sarah, stealing her heat and life for himself, but it was *his* power that was filling Amanda—sharp, cold, and inhuman, sweet as spring water in a desert. Her skin tingled and her muscles clenched and her breath caught hard and fast in her throat.

When Gabriel cut Amanda off, the sudden cessation of the energy rush actually hurt. She slumped back in her seat with a sob of loss, shuddering with reaction. Her hunger, a tiny thing compared to the raging chasm she'd felt in Gabriel, curled up purring in her chest and disappeared. Looking up, she saw the vampire was still feeding, and before she could stop herself— not that she wanted to, or could bring herself to try—she reached for him again with mental powers so refreshed and energized Amanda expected to see them shimmering like heat lightning. The vampire shrugged her away.

No more freebies. I need the rest of what she can give me.

Acute disappointment stabbed through her, startling her with its intensity. *Too good by far,* Amanda whispered to herself as she built her shields back up. The energy the vampire had funneled into her sang under her skin, enough to fix the damage she'd done to herself, but nowhere near how much she wanted. She wedged herself into the corner of the booth, hugging her knees to her chest. The cool wind of the vampire's power swirled inside her, finding all the empty corners of herself, slowly warming as she made it her own. Only now she felt like there was more of her somehow, more to fill, and Gabriel's gift grew thin. Amanda resisted the urge to reach for him again.

Across the table, Gabriel lifted his head and whispered a few words in Sarah's ear. She blinked a few times before focusing on Amanda.

"It was so nice to meet you," Sarah said, her words a little slurred. "I'm afraid I have to run, though."

"We need to get going, too," Gabriel assured her, back to his usual charming self. "Just thought I'd stop by since we were in the area."

"You two have fun now." Sarah slid from the booth and walked away, a little wobbly but not appearing much worse for the wear.

"Let's go." Gabriel's voice was smooth and languid. He stood, waiting as Amanda uncurled herself and got up.

"How do you feel?" he asked as they headed to the car.

"Better," Amanda returned cautiously. "A little hyper."

He snickered. "I'll bet." He unlocked her door, and paused, considering her. "Smile for me?"

"What?" His incongruous request caught her off guard.

"You know. Smile. Looks like this." He grinned. Despite her confusion, she couldn't help smiling in response. Gabriel opened the door for her. "That wasn't so hard, was it?"

"What is wrong with you?" She sat down, shaking her head.

He came around to the driver's side. "You looked a little shaken."

"I can't imagine why," she muttered.

He sat down and started the car. His expression was mild, but there was a little self-satisfied quirk to his lips, another nuance she wouldn't have caught even a few days ago.

Amanda sighed. "What gives, Gabriel?"

"What do you mean?" His tone was as bland as his face.

"What are you so smug about?"

"What makes you think I'm smug?"

"Stop ducking the question and answer me."

A quiet, sinister twist to his lips warned her she wasn't going to like this. He reached over and flipped down the sunshade. Her own eyes stared at her in confusion from the mirror on the back of it.

Smile for the mirror, Amanda.

"Wha—?" As soon as she opened her mouth, she understood. She leaned forward in dismay, poking at her eyeteeth. "Shit! How long have they been that way?"

Though not really noticeable unless you knew what to look for, her canines looked exactly like Gabriel's. The points were narrower now, and sharp. She felt for the ridge and nearly cut herself.

"I noticed it yesterday, but they weren't that advanced. They had just started to change. Now they've already finished the cosmetic part of the change. That should've taken most of a week."

Her head whipped around to look at him. "How is that possible?"

"These things are supposed to happen slowly. Physical changes and mental ones. But the more you flex a new muscle, the more it grows. When you pushed yourself like you did, and then used my power to heal yourself, you advanced your change."

"Wonderful. Just wonderful." She sat back with a scowl. "Did you know this was going to happen when you took me with you tonight?"

"I suspected it might," he admitted shamelessly. "But there was little choice. We were both too weakened to be able to keep out of each other's heads. You would have started siphoning off me as soon as I started feeding anyway. You needed it too badly."

"Then why drag me along?"

He was silent for so long she thought he wasn't going to answer. Finally, he said very quietly, "You're stronger than I am over a distance. I might not have been able to cut you off, if you'd stayed behind."

Amanda's eyes widened. "Oh! My. Really?"

"Really."

"Huh." She stared at the outline of her mouth in the mirror.

"So will you try not to do anything like that again, please?" He sounded tired.

She looked over at him incredulously. "You make it sound like I started the whole thing! It was your fault to begin with!"

"My fault? That you can't handle your own desires? You give me too much credit."

"If you hadn't—"

"If you had just taken my gift, instead of shoving a psibolt between my eyes, this would never have happened."

"Your gift." Saying it left such a bad taste in her mouth that she wanted to spit. "You can't give me someone. You didn't own that guy."

"I beg to differ. I owned him completely, just then. He was quite willing, if that's what's bothering you. You felt it."

"I felt you making him be willing, which is not the same thing."

"It's even better, because he can't change his mind." Gabriel chuckled. "He was mine, one hundred percent mine, and I offered him to you. And you threw it back in my face."

"Will you stop talking about him like he was a Valentine's present?" she demanded. "He was just an innocent bystander."

"And you wanted him. Sure, it didn't have to be him, necessarily, but he's the one you picked."

"I didn't pick him for anything! I was just looking at him!"

"You chose him. You felt me touch his mind, but you never objected. Did the sight of his bared throat not please you?"

They had reached his apartment building. Amanda grimaced. This was not high on her places-to-hang-out list.

"No, it didn't please me," she said as he drove into his garage. "It pleased you."

"I was watching through your eyes, Amanda. I saw how you could not look away, especially once the blood was freed." He parked the car and got out, leaving Amanda to follow him into the apartment.

She locked the door to his haven behind her. "You wouldn't let me get my equilibrium! As soon as I started trying to back off, you made him…" She hesitated, her hand rising to her throat unconsciously. "…do that."

Gabriel had opened the fridge and was unwrapping a package in white paper. "You knew what I was going to do."

She approached the kitchen area and was surprised to see two barstools next to the island. Even more surprising, she found she was pleased he had taken her suggestion. "These are new," she said, sitting down on the nearer one and hoping to change the subject.

"I had Nicholas pick up a few things for me." He hefted the white package, which proved to contain a large sirloin steak. He began slicing it into thin strips.

Just looking at the raw, red meat reminded her that she hadn't eaten tonight except for that cup of broth. The clock on the stove said it was nearly three in the morning. It seemed like days since sunset.

"You knew what I was going to do, though, didn't you?" Gabriel was not going to let the conversation drop.

"Yes," she sighed. "At first I thought you were going to make him tear his own throat out, but you weren't…" She frowned, trying to find the right words. "Weren't commanding him hard enough, I guess, for that."

"Very good." Possessive pride flavored his tone as he set a plate in front of her.

Irritation at his proprietary manner flashed through her, but vanished as the thin strips of meat hit the pan with a sizzle. Each piece spent only a few moments in the pan before he ferried it over to her plate, nearly as red when it came out as when it went in.

The little bloody pile made her gums ache, especially around her new fangs. She popped one strip in her mouth, sucking all the juices out. The taste was intense—warm, salty-sweet, with an undertone of something heady and rich. She hardly bothered to chew the meat before swallowing it so she could take the next one.

Finally the sizzling stopped, and he handed her the last one. She pouted and ate it like she had all the others. He watched her with a tiny smile that she found curiously endearing.

"So are you quite recovered from our little mishap?" She pushed her plate away.

"Somewhat. I am healed, but still weakened. As are you." He put the dishes in the sink. "But sleep should suffice to restore your strength."

"And your strength must be stolen from others? Seems a bad trade."

"My true strengths are far beyond what even you are capable of, my dear," he replied, a hint of warning in his eyes. "They merely lie in a different direction."

She held his gaze, but her hands itched to fiddle with something. Her fingers found a seam in the black marble and traced its path. "You said I'm stronger than you over a distance. How can that be?"

"You were already gifted before you tasted my blood, and the change amplifies your mortal capabilities. When I was still mortal, I had no great potential in that area. It's only my centuries of experience that have given me the abilities I do have. Were you to become a vampire, you would completely outstrip me psychically in perhaps only a hundred years."

That was a heady thought. "So what are your talents, then?"

In an eye-blink, Gabriel was behind her. "I have many talents."

She whirled in surprise, nearly falling off her stool. Breathless, she looked up at him.

Gabriel was utterly still, not even breathing, only his eyes moving as he watched her. Yet for all that stillness, his body radiated potential energy like a coiled spring waiting for release. All of that power so tightly contained, so carefully controlled…she wanted to touch him, to loose all of that wonderful, deadly energy.

"What *is* this?" she demanded in a harsh whisper. "I don't even *like* you."

His lips curved into a knowing grin that gave her shivers down to her toes. "Funny, I'm rather fond of you."

She shook her head at him, fighting the nearness of his body. "You don't care about anyone. I'm not even sure you care about yourself."

He clicked his tongue. "Now, that's not true at all. I care intensely for a number of people, including myself. It's just not the kind of caring you're used to."

"Tell me one person that you actually love," she challenged.

He shook his head. "I can't love, Amanda. I feel affection, protectiveness, loyalty, duty." He traced her cheek with a finger. "Desire."

"But not love?"

"No. Nor compassion or empathy. I sacrificed those emotions millennia ago."

"Why?"

"Because my survival was more important to me than my humanity.

There is power in sacrifice, and self-sacrifice. Above all, I wanted to live."

"But if you don't have to kill all the time—"

"I like killing. I enjoy it. That is what vampires are made to do. Don't make the mistake of thinking you can redeem me. I like it just fine here on the dark side. I don't want to come back." That knowing smile reappeared. "And that is exactly what you find so attractive. Even if you don't like me." His tone said he didn't believe her.

Amanda stared at him in dismay. *Damn it, I hate it when he's right.* "Don't you need to feed again?" she said, changing the subject. His hunger pricked at her through his skin, nothing like the raging need from earlier, but enough that it would need to be addressed before too much longer.

"There are, possibly, alternatives that would suit us both," he offered, brushing her hair back from one side of her neck.

She shook her head at him. "After everything that's happened tonight, you still have to try, don't you?"

"Can you fault me for it?" He traced a line down her neck with his fingers, a fond quirk to his lips.

"I could." She refused to shiver, or lean into that touch, but she couldn't keep her pulse from stepping up a notch. "But I don't. I'm sure I make quite a convenient snack just now."

"So much more than that," he whispered. His façade of humanity slipped away, his otherworldly aura flaring around him like a cobra's hood. She couldn't put a finger on exactly what it was that changed—only that he radiated the same sort of impersonal menace as a hungry tiger. "You are not to be compared with mere prey, my dear."

His fangs were out. Her stomach tightened, and not with fear. "I've moved up in the world, then."

"Indeed."

"You might as well put those away," she chided him, tracing a finger over his swollen upper lip. "I need to keep all the strength I have, remember?"

He caught her hand as it pulled away. "I would not hurt you, Amanda. I would never take enough to bring you harm." Reverently, he brought her wrist to his lips, laying a most chaste kiss on the skin above where her pulse hammered.

"I know that," she answered softly. "I suppose it's not really the point, anyway."

His scent filled her lungs, all warm male and cold lethality, mixed with leather from the car seats and the musky, mouth-watering *something* that was uniquely his. *I shouldn't want this. God help me, I shouldn't want this.*

Her eyes unfocused for a moment as she reached for a distraction. "I can feel the sun," she whispered. "I can feel the day coming, like a weight hovering over me. It's worse than it was yesterday." She shook herself. "It would be best if you went hunting."

"Perhaps." The word purred against her skin. "But is that what you want?" The hand on her neck slipped down to trace the artery. She could feel it throb beneath his fingers.

"I want you to kiss me." She stared into his eyes, using their mutual attraction to hold him as tightly as he had ever held her with his tricks. "I want to feel your teeth pierce my skin."

She took hold of his hand, brought it up from her throat to her lips. Without looking away she bit gently at one of his knuckles, not enough to break the skin, but enough to feel the sharp edge of her canines scrape against his flesh.

He shivered, longing burning in his eyes.

Ah, that's what you really want. How often does the vampire get bitten, I wonder? The thought made her heart flutter for an entirely new reason, but she did her best not to show it. *Men are men are men. Why didn't I think of this before?*

"I want a lot of things, Gabriel." She kissed the knuckle she'd been teasing, then let go of his hand. "But not having to give in to every little desire I have is part of what makes me human, and right now we are going out. There's got to be some place where you can find a snack that isn't me, right?"

CHAPTER THIRTEEN

Saturday, May 29th, 1999

Amanda stood in her bathroom, running the hairbrush through her tangled mess of hair, counting the strokes long past the point where she would normally have stopped. Gabriel had dropped her off a short time ago. The sun was a burning in the back of her brain, but day had not yet broken.

Finally she felt Gabriel grow quiet in her mind. Moments later her sense of him vanished as the sun rose over the horizon. Amanda dropped her hairbrush and raced into her bedroom, sweeping up her still-damp jeans from the floor.

I hope her card's still legible. I didn't even think of that when I dunked myself, she thought as she reached into the pocket, allowing herself to think of the strange female vampire for the first time since they had parted. Holding her breath, she drew out the wet paper. The numbers leapt out at her from its surface. With a triumphant cry she flung the jeans at the hamper and snatched up her phone from the nightstand.

She punched the buttons even as her stomach began to churn. Who was this woman? How did Amanda know she could trust her? The sun's weight in the back of her mind kept her fingers moving. She had no idea how long a vampire could stay awake after dawn. Her mouth tasted like tin. *It's only a phone call, for Christ's sake. Nothing to be so nervous about.*

The phone only rang once, but there was no greeting. Amanda waited two heartbeats before giving a breathless, "Hello?"

"It is you." The female vampire's words were slurred with the effort of remaining awake. "What is your name, girl?"

"I'm Amanda."

"Elizabeth," the vampire said. "We have barely more time now than we did earlier this night. You must answer my questions so I can see where you stand now, yes?"

Amanda hesitated. Just how much should she tell Elizabeth anyway? Then again, what harm was there? Elizabeth must have gone through all this herself. "All right."

"When did he give you his blood?" Elizabeth asked.

"Friday, the fourteenth."

"Have you drunk of him since that night?"

Amanda shuddered. "No."

"And has he drunk of you?"

"Just once, but I wouldn't let him use teeth."

Elizabeth made a surprised squeak. "You wouldn't let him use teeth?"

"No, I made him use the razor he's carrying now. He uses it to bleed the kids at the bars."

"I see. Have you slept with him?"

"No."

"Has he killed anyone in your presence yet?"

Amanda found that "yet" rather ominous. "No."

"Describe for me your bond. You seem rather strong for being so new."

"Gabriel says...I mean, I'm psychic anyway..."

"Yes, yes, obviously."

Amanda frowned. "I dreamed him on my fourth night. I could track him by feeling his presence my fifth night, although I had to be looking for him then. By the eighth night, I think, I was having to shut him out, not look for him."

"Well! Impressive indeed!" Elizabeth was cheerful now under the fatigue. "Maybe he has bitten off more than he can chew with you. I believe you've set a record."

"I've given him nasty headaches twice. He called the second one a psibolt," Amanda offered.

"Do you think you could do this at will?"

"I know I can."

Elizabeth chuckled with delight. She had a throaty voice to begin with, and exhaustion only made it deeper. "What about other things? Are you stronger? Have you found yourself feeling weightless?"

"My senses are all sharper."

"Can you smell blood under the skin?"

"Not yet."

"And the rest?" Elizabeth's voice cracked with weariness.

"I can run farther and faster," Amanda said, thinking of her earlier flight, "but none of the other things. Except my teeth look like fangs."

"Already? Do they extend, retract?"

Amanda tugged on one of her eyeeteeth, but it was as firm as all the others. "No," she replied in relief.

"That would have been truly fantastic, but just as well for your sake that they do not yet. Have you yet tasted blood?"

"No, but I'm eating raw meat like it's candy."

"No blood yet? Extraordinary. Why not?"

"Why not?" Amanda repeated in disbelief. "Why would I?"

"The only harm in drinking human blood is in how you get it. Being dependant on Gabriel for it would be unfortunate. I may be able to help you in this respect. We shall have to discuss that at another time. As long as you remember not to drink directly from the prey you will be fine."

Amanda's eyes narrowed. "Won't that make me change more?"

"My dear," Elizabeth said, "there is very little change left for you to do, outside of the true change. You have most of the muscles; now they will just get bigger as you use them. If you continue to fight the blood, you will eventually lose, and you will lose hard. The hunger is too strong. Besides, human blood will dilute the vampire blood."

"So it'll make me weaker?"

"No. Human blood will only make you stronger. The hunger comes because you don't have enough human blood in your system to fuel what your changed body is doing. When you have more human than vampire, the negative effects of your condition will be reduced, because your body has the resources it needs to cope." Elizabeth swallowed, as if her mouth were dry. "Given what you've been doing to yourself, you'll need to start feeding soon."

Amanda bit her lip, then asked, "And what about vampire blood?"

"Dangerous," was the immediate response. "Heady. Our blood holds more power than a human's does. The thicker his blood is in your veins, the more you will want to fill that capacity. And the more you will be bound by our nature. Yes, his blood will feed you, but it will also make the craving stronger."

"But will it keep me from becoming human again?" That longing she'd seen in his eyes was the only weakness she'd seen in him so far. Her only hope of controlling him.

"I cannot say for certain. To my knowledge, only one of his novices ever returned to humanity, and she was long before...my time." Elizabeth was fading now. "Think on this though...what have you not been fighting...while you fought the lures of blood?"

The line went dead.

Amanda set the phone back on the cradle with numb hands. The day was like sandbags on her eyes, and yet her mind was abuzz with unasked questions. She stripped mechanically, not even bothering with her pajamas but crawling naked between the sheets. The exhaustion she'd been pushing off now had the sun on its side. She repeated Elizabeth's question to herself as her head hit the pillow.

What have I not been fighting?

* * * *

Paul sat at the kitchen table patiently waiting for Cecelia to find the address book she was searching for. The wedding wasn't until December, but she insisted on getting the invitations out now.

"There won't be any hotel rooms left if we don't reserve them now," she'd said when he'd pointed out that six months was rather too much warning. "Everything will be booked for Christmas."

Everyone will have forgotten by then. Still, there were worse ways to spend a Saturday morning, and Paul knew better than to argue with a woman about her wedding. He'd been married often enough. He also knew better than to bring up that point; even when they knew he'd been born in Imperial Roman times, only one of his wives, Georgette, had ever liked hearing about her predecessors. He missed all of his wives, of course—they'd all been very different women—but he missed Georgette the most often. She used to sit by the fire and listen to him tell stories of past battles, past loves, past lives. Of all his wives, he always felt she'd understood him best.

"I love to hear how you talk about them, the ones who came before me," she'd said once. "I can hear in your voice what they meant to you. I hope you'll want to talk that way about me, after I'm gone."

He wanted to, Night knew he wanted to, but none of the others had wanted to listen. Paul gave a mental shrug. Women were strange, and he was used to keeping his own counsel.

Speaking of which...

The mages were finally leaving him alone, off chasing some chimera of their own that he didn't bother to ask about because he already knew they wouldn't tell him. Martin and he had speculated over glasses of whiskey, but the mages didn't talk much to the shifters either, and all Martin knew was that there was some unidentified activity going on in the vicinity. They'd agreed it was probably just another splinter group, or a newbie moving into the area, before Martin had launched into his latest round of complaints. Mostly about his own family, fortunately, but he'd had plenty to say about Gabriel as well.

"She's not exactly subtle, your friend's new girl." Martin had frowned at his empty glass until Paul signaled the bartender for another round. "I've told the kin to keep a low profile, but it's hard, not knowin' where those two're like to end up of a night. Most've decided to avoid goin' through town at all, but the kids, well, they don't listen. My brother's eldest, now; a week ago you couldna keep him out of the Ways, but now, eh, try to tell him to cut through and he gets as snippy as a redcap."

Paul genuinely liked Martin, perhaps because of all of Madison's skinshifters, Martin was most like the pookhas Paul had known back in Britain, but Paul didn't particularly want to hear the gossip about his father. Unfortunately, he couldn't say so without looking like he was jealous of the attention Amanda was getting, so there was little he could do besides listen sympathetically to how inconvenient all this was for the skinshifters, and assure Martin that things should settle down in a few weeks.

A stack of finished invitations sat on one side of the table, neatly labeled in Paul's precise Italianate hand. He doodled idly on the blank one in front of him while Cecelia dug through her desk.

"It's too bad you don't have more family you could invite," she muttered, not really thinking about what she was saying. He was used to that. "Your half of the church is going to be awfully empty."

Paul grinned, imagining his father sitting through the Catholic ceremony. It wasn't the length of the wedding that was the problem—the priest's terrible Latin would have Gabriel in fits. Paul had insisted on a Latin mass mostly for his own amusement, but also because it felt more real, having the ceremony in what passed for his native tongue.

"Father said he'd stop by the reception," Paul reminded her. "And there'll be my friends, and some of the other professors."

"Right, but that's it? I mean, I don't know, no long-lost cousins or something?"

Paul's smile drooped. He remembered the look on his sister's face when they'd watched Constantine throw aside his regalia, draw his sword, and run into the horde of oncoming Turks. Paul would've admired the man, if

Isolde had not tried to follow his suicide charge.

Afterwards, when Isolde woke on the ship and realized Paul'd knocked her out, realized her emperor was dead, and the last vestiges of her beloved Roman Empire lay shattered under the Turkish onslaught, the fury and hate that filled her eyes had all been for him.

The doodle-marked invitation bore a name now, just one, as if he couldn't decide which surname to give her. He knew damn well which one she'd choose, just as he knew that even if he had an address to send the invitation to, Isolde would not come.

Paul made great swirling, crisscrossing loops over his sister's name until it was illegible. "Nope. Just my father."

* * * *

Enrique Morales rubbed his face and stared up at the sun as he pumped gas into his van. The sun comforted him, but he couldn't let his guard down. Isolde Constantinus had been known to hire human assassins before. Hell, he was pretty sure he'd been tailed when he and the others started out this morning, but they'd split up and Briggs had managed to lose the bastard somewhere around Chicago.

Morales rubbed his weathered face again.

He'd left Travis up in Madison with Wayne Jefferson. Morales preferred to season the newbies in the field—cut 'em loose too soon, and it just meant you had to find more recruits—but Travis would learn more from Jefferson and his team than from driving around the Midwest with Morales. And Travis was a lot more likely to keep living by working on the trap than by playing catch-me-if-you-can with a Fury.

Not that there weren't always new potential recruits out there. But finding them before they did something fatally stupid was a bitch.

By their very nature, vampires created the vampire hunters. Vengeance was the driving factor behind ninety percent of recruits. The other ten percent were just crazy, but as long as they were good with a weapon, Morales didn't care.

The pump clicked off, and Morales went inside to pay. Cash, of course.

Briggs was finishing a cheap breakfast sandwich from the gas station's heat-lamp offerings when he returned to the van. She licked her fingers and stuck the key in the ignition. "Where to, Boss?"

Morales buckled his seatbelt, then reclined the seat and pulled his battered cowboy hat down over his eyes. "East St. Louis."

"Good God, why there? That place is a pit."

"It's contested right now. No established vampire for the Fury to go to even if she wanted to. And it's away from Madison." He shifted a little, trying to ease the ache in his back. He was getting too old to hunt all night and drive around all day. Let the kids do the driving. "Things are getting too close. Get on the CB. Have Tyson and Dunsan split off and head back north when they're sure they're not being followed. We've got to lure the Fury away from Gabriel, but I'm not leaving Jefferson's team in the lurch. They need backup."

Briggs was quiet for a moment, then he heard her start talking into the mic, long strings of code words hidden in banal gibberish.

Morales let himself drift off to sleep. Isolde's hired humans were a bad sign. He'd been circling too long, hoping they could get the trap set; the Fury had to be getting suspicious by now. Running might buy some time. He'd find a way to keep Isolde from warning Gabriel even if it killed him.

CHAPTER FOURTEEN

Amanda sulked in her corner of the booth, trying to ignore the flirting going on next to her. Gabriel had insisted she stay close from now on—*have to keep you out of trouble somehow*—and tonight's plaything was none too pleased. The booth had benches on three sides, and goth-girl Melanie had wormed her way into the middle and now sat with her back to Amanda, ignoring her completely and cooing at the vampire like a lovesick mourning dove.

This was not exactly what Amanda'd had in mind.

Patience, she counseled herself. *Let him feed. He'll get rid of the prey soon enough, and then you can start wrapping him around your finger.*

Amanda adjusted the neckline of her off-the-shoulder knit top a little self-consciously. Not that she'd ever *tried* to wrap a guy around her finger, but then, she did tend to have terrible taste in men. *See current attraction to Mr. Fangs in the corner there.* None of her exes seemed like the easily-wrapable type. But it couldn't be that hard, right? Women had been doing this for millennia. *And you did pretty much have Leon whipped. And Justin, come to think of it...*

Amanda wished she'd worn a watch. *How long have those two been going at it?* Melanie was kissing the vampire so passionately it was as if she would devour him. *You'd think she was the one with the unnatural hunger.* The girl's perfume wafted over, thick and cloying and vaguely familiar. Amanda shifted, restless and uneasy, and tried to focus on watching the crowd. All humans tonight, save her and Gabriel, but she kept herself from reaching out to them. Their energy was too distracting. *Stay focused. If you don't die of boredom, that is.*

After what seemed an eternity, Gabriel pulled out his razor. Amanda's stomach turned over with a sudden burst of excitement. She frowned at herself and forced her muscles to relax. *We are not the ones getting fed this time,* she told her tummy.

Amanda's stomach continued to churn. The musky-sweet scent of perfume grew stronger. Gabriel laid the flat of the blade against Melanie's cheek and she groaned, tipping her head back with an almost drunken grin. The vampire trailed the blunt edge down her face, then her neck, following the cool metal with equally cool kisses. The girl shivered, whispering "yes" in a hiss that was almost drowned out by the music. Amanda didn't see Gabriel make the cut, but saw Melanie twitch, then smelled the overpowering scent of blood. Rich and metallic, it mingled with the perfume to make an intoxicating cloud. *Trust one of his regulars to find a perfume that compliments blood perfectly.* Amanda drew in a shuddering breath as Gabriel pressed his lips to Melanie's throat.

The sound of him swallowing was louder than the bass beat that rattled the walls. Her tongue felt thick and dry, as if she'd been sucking on unbuffered aspirin. Pressing her lips together against the clenching of her stomach, Amanda took another deep breath, and her muscles convulsed as she drew in something other than air. A cloudy tendril of what felt like the girl's aura slipped between her lips, rubbing past her teeth and over her tongue, a heady incense that tasted of sweat and sex and rubies.

Oh hell, that's not perfume... Heedless of the vampire's feeding and the euphoric overflow it usually caused, Amanda reached out to him. *Um, Gabriel?*

Hmmm? The thought was edged with a rosy glow that tried to make her head swim.

Is this what you meant when you said you could taste my fear?

Yes. He opened his eyes and looked at her over Melanie's shoulder. *Of course, lust tastes rather different. I think you'll find it more...stimulating... than what the crowd had to offer last night.*

Amanda started. *What?*

The vampire's chuckle rumbled through her. *High emotion gives off energy, Amanda, that's all. Normally it settles back into the aether, but you've already shown you can harvest it. Drink deep, little mouse. You're still weakened from yesterday. It won't hurt her, and the energy will do you good.*

Is that what I was doing? She remembered the way she had surrounded herself with the crowd's auras, how their collective enthusiasm had lifted her up. Was it really that simple? Warm, lively, human energy, and not the chilling gale of Gabriel's power…she closed her eyes and took a deep, slow breath through her mouth.

It was like trying to drink moonlight on a humid summer night. Energy rolled off the girl in waves, but it was elusive, teasing, slipping away just when Amanda thought she had it. She didn't realize she was chasing it until she felt the warmth of Melanie's body against her skin. Amanda opened her eyes in surprise to find herself hovering just inches away from the girl. She had the craziest urge to wrap her arms around Melanie and bury her face against the back of Melanie's neck.

Gabriel wove the fingers of one hand into Melanie's hair, his other hand reaching past the girl to cup Amanda's cheek, bringing Amanda the mingled scent of vampire and prey. *Oh God, I can smell her on him!* A chemical smell, dusty and used, and underneath that the skin-and-sweat scent of human. Amanda turned her face toward that scent, tasting not only Melanie's lust, but also Gabriel's, beginning to waft from under his skin. Before she could think better of it, she nipped at his fingers, chasing his lust just as she'd chased the girl's.

Shuddering, the vampire closed his eyes and bit down, hard.

A wave of emotion slammed into Amanda, drowning her in Melanie's venom-induced ecstasy. The girl's psyche lay stripped bare, utterly defenseless and yielding, waiting to be molded by a stronger will. Amanda itched to explore, to experiment and analyze, but the surfeit of energy was far too distracting. Before anything else, she needed more of that psychic feast.

Amanda opened her shields like a funnel, channeling the girl's pleasure so that it roared into the core of her, silk-smooth lava to soothe her empty insides. Melanie's surrender screamed through Amanda's mind with wild abandon and a strange, joyful freedom that made Amanda feel unaccountably protective. Possessive.

Mine.

Amanda shook herself and tried to refocus. Her hands gripped the bench so hard that her fingernails had torn the vinyl. Her lips hovered just above Melanie's skin, savoring the taste of her aura. The scent of blood was so strong that Amanda's whole upper jaw ached. Stubbornly, she pushed that hunger aside even as Melanie's heartbeat thundered in time to it.

No. Not thunder. Amanda held her breath, listening. The girl's pulse was growing fainter.

Amanda turned her head toward Gabriel and found his eyes already on her, devouring her as he devoured Melanie.

You're draining her, aren't you? All of her. Part of Amanda wanted to make it accusing, but it came out as more of a statement than a question. Nothing seemed real from this high up.

The vampire raised one eyebrow. *Do you care?*

Amanda gazed down at the fragile life sandwiched between her and Gabriel. For all the lust and pleasure she was drinking in, she felt curiously detached. *Maybe this is what drug addicts feel like.* If so, she understood why they'd destroy themselves to feel this way. She was beyond buzzed and nothing could touch her. Not a goddamn thing.

She lifted her gaze back to the vampire's. Did she care? *Not really,* she replied with a shrug. *But you aren't going to kill her, not here.*

Not here. His eyes glinted. *Shall we take her home with us, then?*

Amanda shook her head, feeling her detachment wilting as her conscience fought to make itself heard. She pushed it back down. This felt too good to stop so soon. *None of that. You're ruining my mood. Don't make me go back just yet.*

She could feel him struggling not to argue, to not say that she didn't have to go back at all. His eagerness reminded her that she had an agenda. He wanted to herd her, and she wanted to put a ring in his nose. Chuckling to herself, half-drunk on power, she caressed his cheek with the back of her hand and put her plan into action. *Tonight just let me enjoy myself, Gabriel. Indulge me.*

Frustration from him, almost anger, but he stopped feeding and that was all that mattered. Snarling, he lifted his head from an unblemished neck. Melanie sagged in his arms, his blood mingling with hers in red rivulets over her healed skin. *I indulge you too much. I need—*

You need to shut up. Refusing to lose the upper hand, she reached through their bond, caressing him with her words, seeking a particular place inside him, the same place in her own chest that twisted up every time she met his cold, yet burning eyes. A sharp thrust of stolen energy made Gabriel gasp, his eyes darkening with sudden desire.

This is a dangerous new toy, she thought to herself, biting her lip so that one fang-tip showed. *But the best toys are dangerous.* She leaned in close, amused at how his desire flared brighter when she did, loving that for once *she* was the one controlling *him.*

I don't want to argue with you, she purred to him. The smell of blood was making her stomach clench up all over again. *I'm so tired of it. So tired of fighting...* She traced his jaw with one finger, and his lips parted with a look that was close to pain.

Then stop fighting, he hissed, his eyes fierce. *You know what you want.* He drew her nearer, both pressed tight against the more-or-less unconscious Melanie, until they were hardly a breath apart. This close, his eyes seemed to fill her whole world, the pupils sprung wide, the irises a gray that bordered on ice blue.

"Amanda." Her name was a murmur more felt than heard, his lips just barely touching hers. He held himself poised there, not breathing, waiting, and Amanda made him wait, knowing he would not continue if she did not give him leave.

Her heartbeat sounded in her ears; once, twice, three times, his pulse echoing hers so closely it was hard to tell which was which... She laughed with elation at the power she had over him, but the laugh turned into a moan, and then the taste of hot copper was filling her mouth, and all thought fled. There was no room for breath, only the bruising intensity of the kiss and the violence of their need and the raw, screaming taste of blood.

The vampire shoved Melanie out of the way, crushing Amanda to him and half-pulling her across the girl's legs. Amanda scrabbled the rest of the way over, pressing Gabriel hard into the corner of the booth. He twined one hand in her hair, twisting the strands around his fingers, his mouth fierce and demanding on hers. She opened her shields to him so she could feel the burn of his passion inside as well as out, enjoying the way their energies wrapped around each other, pulling them closer.

The vampire reached over to touch the Melanie's bloody neck, then raised two blood-coated fingers to Amanda's lips.

The taste of the girl's blood lingered from his kisses, like sun-scorched metal and summer skies, and Amanda didn't hesitate. She nibbled at his fingers, trying to savor it, but it was gone too quickly. She reached over herself, the smeared blood hot and slick against textured skin. The pulse fluttering just under her fingers sent tremors up her whole arm. Laughing, Amanda painted Gabriel's parted lips an infernal, gleaming red.

He grinned, showing his fangs as he met her for another kiss.

She lost herself in the flavor for a moment. Inside her mind, she could feel the vampire's desire, a hunger unlike the blood need she was familiar with but equally greedy. She wondered what that focused fire would feel like in his haven, his safe place, where he didn't have to keep some part of him in reserve to watch and guard against enemies...

With a shudder, Amanda broke off the kiss. Shoving that glorious and terrifying thought aside, she took one of his hands in one of hers and tilted her head down to taste the pulse of Gabriel's wrist.

The gentle prickle of her teeth against his skin made him purr. *You horrible tease,* he murmured with a smile.

She sat back far enough to meet his gaze, her fingers tracing over the skin of his neck. *It's nothing more than what you've done.*

Ah, but I would follow through.

Hmph. She leaned forward and nibbled at his chin. *Some of us like making out just for itself,* she replied, amused. *But I could stop if you want.*

I most certainly do not want. The heat of his desire burned brighter in their minds, her own lust almost making her tremble. His hands caressed her bare shoulders, fingers toying with the low neckline of her tight off-the-shoulder top. *What do you want, my protégé?*

Amanda leaned back into the touch. She couldn't separate *want* and *should* in her mind—thinking of the first invariably called up the second, sparking off gut-wrenching battles between desire and conscience. *How about this,* she replied. *I want you not to ask me that again tonight.*

Very well. His eyes glimmered. *But that means I'm going to have to try and figure out what you really want by feel.*

A sly tendril of thought brushed sensuously through her mind and her whole body tingled.

That could be interesting, she mused. She intentionally became aware of the skin of her back, just between her shoulder blades. She made a point of feeling the way her knit shirt clung close to her, just slightly coarse and warmed from her body heat.

Gabriel's fingers ran down her back from her shoulders, and then the sensation of skin on skin as he slipped his hands under her shirt, gently massaging between her shoulder blades.

The vampire's mind was open, his own desires plain—Amanda leaned hard against him, delivering a searing kiss. His fingers flexed against her flesh, working their way around to her sides, tantalizingly close to touching her breasts. The skin under his chin called to her and she obeyed, nibbling delicately with her almost-fangs, her hands stroking his jawbone.

A fine tremor ran through Gabriel's body, his desires urging her a little lower.

She paused just above the carotid artery, teasing him, her breath stirring the fine hairs on his skin. She couldn't tell if the urge to bite was hers or his, but it didn't much matter.

On the bench beside them, Melanie shifted and opened her eyes. Gabriel and Amanda looked at her as if they'd both forgotten she was there.

Melanie's skin had achieved the bloodless pallor so many goths seemed to crave, but Amanda thought it didn't look like the girl would live long enough to enjoy it.

Gabriel dipped a napkin in Melanie's drink and wiped away the drying blood from her neck. "You don't look too good," he said. "Better go have the bartender call you a cab."

Melanie nodded dumbly. It took her three tries to get to her feet. She shuffled off toward the bar looking a lot more like Hollywood's idea of the living dead than the vampire did.

Is she gonna make it? Amanda wondered, almost worried for her.

Depends on if the cabbie takes her home or to the hospital when she passes out. A waste of a good death, though, if she dies now. With a gentle touch he turned Amanda's face back to him. *I thought you didn't care,* he chided her.

I said I didn't care that you were draining her, she corrected. *I didn't then, but it comes and goes.*

Is it better if I drain her than if she just dies from blood loss?

Not better. She frowned. *Just different. She's still dead.*

Ahh, but to have her death on my tongue, her heart's blood inside me, her life... His lips twitched. She felt the effort it took him to turn his thoughts away. He considered her, brushing her lips with his fingertips. *Another night perhaps. Some place a little less public.*

Speaking of... Amanda offered slowly, tracing the neckline of his shirt. *I trust your thirst is sated?*

For tonight. He gave a little shiver at her touch.

Then let's go find some place a little less public.

CHAPTER FIFTEEN

The parking lot was blessedly quiet in comparison as they left the bar. A brisk wind from the nearby lake blew Amanda's hair back and she paused, lifting her face and closing her eyes.

Beside her she felt Gabriel stiffen. *What is it?*

He scented the wind, then shook his head. *It's nothing. What do you wish to do now? Are you hungry?*

She shook her head. "I'm not hungry. Quite the opposite, really." She sighed, pondering. "I suppose I *should* eat something solid." The thought was unappetizing. The wind kissed her cheek again, and she gazed up into the dark sky. "Fuck it," she whispered. "I'll eat tomorrow. When it's light out. Now is for other things."

"Yes." The vampire's voice was distant but his eyes shone with reflected light. "Tonight is for you, little mouse. How can I indulge you?"

"I thought you said you indulged me too much."

"Perhaps I think you take well to being indulged." He brushed her hair back from her face. "My own needs can wait."

"You've already fed enough for two nights, at least," she admonished him, teasing.

"There are times when I require more." He scanned the parking lot, and then fixed his gaze on hers. "But that is not for tonight."

Death seethed behind his beautiful eyes. She shuddered. *No, not tonight.* "Let's go. Somewhere."

"It will be my pleasure."

They drove out of town, south through Fitchburg and out past Oregon and Verona, slipping into the countryside. Gabriel took every back road, every lonely, seldom-used turn, until the glow of the city faded behind them and the few houses they passed huddled fearfully around their lights.

Amanda was still too hyper, bursting with energy. When she couldn't hold still any longer, she told Gabriel to pull over. The field that stretched away from the road had been left fallow, long grasses rustling in the breeze.

"Race you," she called with a grin, vaulting the fence. Without looking back, she sprinted toward the other side of the field, glad to be moving. The cool balm of Gabriel's presence wrapped around her as he appeared beside her, loping easily.

She pushed herself harder, trying to work off some of that excess energy. *Not like that,* the vampire said. *You'll burn yourself out again if you force it like that.* Mental hands steadied her. *You try too hard. Your strength, your speed, doesn't happen because you make it happen. It's part of you now. Don't try to run. Just run.*

She nodded, trying to let go of trying. The night goaded her on, Gabriel running at her side, the sheer speed making her laugh with delight. She surrendered to it, and found she could go faster.

That's it. Gabriel's voice echoed her exhilaration.

The field whipped by in a blur, the fence that marked the end approaching unbelievably fast. Gabriel darted ahead. Amanda tried to slow down, but she had too much speed. She leapt to avoid smacking into the fence and the vampire jumped with her, almost running up one of the fence posts, his arms encircling her and pulling her tight. He pushed off from the post, pivoting and using Amanda's momentum to spin them around so that they landed back on the same side of the fence they'd started on.

Amanda grinned wildly as Gabriel steadied her on her feet. "That was great!" Looking back the way they'd come, she could barely make out the car. She was only slightly out of breath.

Gabriel's hands still held her at the waist. He wasn't winded at all.

She laughed and draped her arms around his neck. "That wasn't anything for you, was it? A mild stroll?"

He smiled. "You're young yet."

For the first time she felt a pinch of envy for his years. She pushed the thought away. "Race you back!"

This time Gabriel didn't wait for her. Amanda had hardly started running when a gust of wind made her blink, and then the vampire was at the other end of the field, leaning up against the car.

"I am both the quick and the dead," he said with a laugh when she caught up to him a few seconds later. "But you will never be fast enough to outrun yourself, little mouse."

She leaned against him, resting her head on his shoulder. "I know, but it's nice to pretend I can, at least for a little while."

He stroked her hair. "Know also that the night will always welcome you."

She looked up at the bright clusters of stars. "The night cares little to whom—or what—she gives shelter," Amanda mused.

"True. I find Her much more tolerant. Day is too picky in His favor."

Amanda's gaze swept over his face. She brushed his wind-tousled hair off his forehead, drunk on the power she had at her command. She was filled with an icy emptiness, but she also burned with desire, and it seemed quite incongruous until she realized that lust by itself was an empty thing. The emptiness was comforting. It made her reckless teasing almost make sense.

"Day has no taste," she replied. "But will you always welcome me?"

"For as long as you welcome me," was his careful answer, "my haven shall be open to you."

She chuckled. "So cautious, Gabriel. Even now, when my scent makes your head swim and your teeth ache to be in my flesh."

He only nodded. "It is my way."

"Good." She kissed him.

Gabriel kissed her back, slow and languid and without the frenzy of before. His hands traced meaningless patterns on the skin of her arms, her shoulders, her neck, and it was as if he were leaving tracks of moonlight behind, as if no touch but his had ever been real. She broke off the kiss to toss her hair back with a shake of her head, and his soft lips sought her throat. With a sigh she melted into his arms, and he guided her to the ground.

She wanted more. She ran her hands over his back, and then tugged at his shirt, pulling it free. The vampire sat back on his heels, and with one quick movement, the shirt landed on the ground. His pale skin gleamed in the light of the nearly-full moon, the muscles of his arms and shoulders standing out in shadows and highlights that she itched to explore.

Amanda came to him, running her fingers through the fine hairs on his chest, her hands tasting the warm sleekness of his bare skin. The tips of his fangs showed through parted lips as he watched her, and that wicked, animal intensity in his eyes made her shiver. That look made her feel valuable, desirable. *A prize worth pursuing.*

His hands slipped around her waist, sliding up her back, working up under her shirt again. She needed to feel his flesh against hers, more than just his hands and his lips. With a glint in her eye she moved just out of reach. Amanda removed her shirt, first slipping one arm out of its sleeve, then the other, leaving her breasts hidden for as long as possible before exposing them to the moonlight.

His gaze devoured her, drank her in as if she were a priceless work of art. He'd left his humanity behind somewhere, hawk-like as he watched, waiting for that perfect moment to swoop down on her. Anticipation of the impact made her tremble. His scent permeated the air around them, full of desire and patience and vows that were more threat than promise.

Amanda held out a hand toward him, inviting the danger closer. It was important that he come to her, and not the other way around, though she didn't know why. He approached her slowly, not a hawk now but a tame tiger—something you know could kill you, easily, but you trust won't. Not this time, anyway.

He took her hand in one of his, kneeling before her. His expression was questioning—not uncertain, but expecting uncertainty. When she didn't object, Gabriel's gaze left hers to drop to their joined hands. His lips parted as he followed the line of her outstretched arm to her shoulder, then her shoulder to her neck, somehow undressing her with his eyes despite her nakedness. His gaze moved down her body, and the heat of that look caressed her breasts like a physical touch.

Her skin pebbled in goose bumps, and the vampire licked his lips. Slowly, so slowly, he raised his gaze to hers. The sharp, intense focus in his eyes stabbed through her, and heat pooled between her thighs.

Eyes locked, he brought her hand to his lips, brushing a kiss across her knuckles. One fang rubbed harmlessly over her skin, and he sucked in a quick breath, rolling her scent over his tongue. The alien, animal ease with which he tasted her on the air made Amanda's stomach clench and her heart flutter somewhere in her throat.

Her nipples were so hard and tight they actually hurt. *God, he's barely even touched me.* Swallowing hard, she hissed, "No teeth, Gabriel. No blood. And the pants stay on."

"Yours or mine?" he asked, his voice a low rumble.

Amanda was so distracted she almost missed his question. "Both!"

He clicked his tongue, tilting his head to study her out of one eye. He turned her hand palm up and kissed her fingertips one by one. "You call this indulging yourself?"

"All things in moderation."

He drew her index finger into his mouth, his tongue pressing the pad of her finger against his hard palate. He rolled his head to one side, then the other, so that her finger traced the softer bumps of his venom glands. He shuddered, and Amanda was glad they were kneeling because the covetous longing on his face made her knees go weak.

If it is as you say, then there will be no release for either of us, his voice whispered in her mind. Reproachful, teasing, but nothing more. *How much control do you think I have?*

"If you can't handle it, then stop." But God, she didn't want to stop. Her whole body ached at the thought of his mouth on her.

As if he had heard her, he released her finger and instead pressed his lips to her wrist. Her hand cupped his cheek as he breathed her in.

"You're not afraid," he said.

Amanda shook her head.

He pulled her closer, wrapping her arm around his waist as he pressed into her, his muscled chest so firm against her soft breasts, his fingers kneading the curve of her lower back just above her hips. Their noses brushed, his breath warm on her lips when he spoke.

"I can give you so much, Amanda," he whispered.

He teased her lips with his, not letting her kiss him when she tried. She gave a little mew of protest before she could stop herself.

His hands rose higher, skimming over her flesh. This time his thumbs caressed the swell of her breasts, up and over, just barely brushing her nipples, and the sensation zinged through her in a wave of tingling heat. Gabriel kissed the corner of her mouth, then her jawbone; then his thumbs made another circle and he nudged her head back, kissing down her throat.

"I could be so gentle." The words were almost lost against her skin. "You have no idea what heights I can take you to." His tongue traced her collarbone as his hands slid around to her back, then down until he gripped her ass. She gasped as he sat on his heels and pulled her onto his lap. Straddling him, his erection pressing into her through their clothes, she threw back her head as his hot mouth covered one of her nipples.

Amanda tried to speak, but no words would come. She just knew she wanted him to keep going.

He made his way back up to her neck, sucking at the skin over the artery until Amanda moaned aloud. His arms wrapped her up, supporting her as she melted. So strong. So safe.

Safe? How could she ever think this was safe?

"Please," he implored her. "Let me show you. Just one night. Please, Amanda." He kissed her mouth, tracing her lower lip with his tongue. "Give me this night. Just this once, stop fighting and do what you want to do. Let me do what you want me to do."

His power cocooned them. Amanda knew there was a world out there, with wind and moon and grass and little stones that dug into her shins where she knelt straddling the vampire's legs, but she couldn't feel any of it. There was nothing but Gabriel—his arms around her, his erection hard against her pubic bone, his scent making her head swim, his desire so much more potent than Melanie's had been. His lips as insistent as his words, begging, teasing, coaxing her to respond, to say yes, God yes. She wanted to so badly.

"No."

She wasn't even aware that she'd spoken aloud until Gabriel froze, almost literally. All motion ceased, and his skin—still flushed with stolen heat—suddenly cooled. Panting with frustrated need, Amanda met Gabriel's gaze and saw, for just a split second, pure, furious rage. Then even that shut down, and the night rushed back into her awareness.

"No," he repeated, his voice absolutely devoid of emotion.

"No blood. No sex." Amanda realized she was still embracing him and let go self-consciously. He let her slip through his arms with no resistance. "If you can't..."

"I can't. Not right now." He stood and walked stiffly to the car. He leaned on the hood, his head hanging as he took a deep breath, and then another. Left sitting alone on the stony ground, Amanda still couldn't help but admire the way his posture emphasized the line of his hip, the firmness of his—

"Stop it." The vampire's voice was cold, edged with anger. He spoke without looking at her. "You said no, and I'm respecting that, but don't push me, Amanda. I have limits."

Her cheeks burned. "Sorry." Embarrassed, she turned her back to him and busied herself with struggling back into her tight shirt.

By the time she was properly clothed, Gabriel had recovered. He leaned against the car, watching her with a thoughtful expression, his arms crossed over his chest. Shirtless as he was, he looked like something out of a jeans commercial. Trying not to stare, Amanda scooped up his discarded shirt and handed it to him. He took it with a distracted nod and pulled it over his head.

"What?" she asked. If he'd been staring at her like any other man would, or even as if she were prey, she would've understood. But this pensive examination, cold and calculating, was starting to creep her out.

He shook his head. "I must be losing my touch," was all he said.

"Just because I said no?" She put her hands on her hips and raised her chin.

With a shrug, he pushed away from the car and turned to open the door. Amanda huffed and stalked over to the passenger side.

Gabriel was quiet for the first few minutes of their trip back into town. Finally he said, glancing at her quizzically, "I hadn't expected you to give in about the blood so quickly."

"Oh?" Amanda kept her thoughts carefully blank.

"What made you change your mind?"

She shifted uncomfortably. "Well, I mean, you already had it on your lips, and, well… I wanted to kiss you, damn it. So I did."

He laughed, low and deep. "What did you think of it?"

"The kiss or the blood?"

He gave her an amused glance. "The blood."

She raised a hand to her lips. "Too brief," she said at last.

"That I can fix."

"Gabriel…"

"Hush, I'm not suggesting you drink directly."

"Then what are you suggesting?"

He grinned.

CHAPTER SIXTEEN

The strip club was dark and noisy, which Amanda had rather expected. She looked around curiously, blushing a little, while Gabriel had a quiet word with the manager. A moment later the man led them to a little room, more a booth really, with a curtain for a door.

Gabriel sat on the cushioned bench and motioned Amanda to sit next to him. "You've never been to a strip club before?"

"Never. What are we doing here?"

"Getting a lap dance."

Just then the curtain moved, and a buxom blond stepped into the booth with them. She was carrying a bottle of wine and two glasses.

"Hi, I'm Sunny." The stripper plunked herself down on Gabriel's knee, facing Amanda. "I love it when we get couples. Is it a special occasion?" She wriggled.

Amanda gaped at her, but Gabriel chuckled. "You could say that," he murmured.

Sunny turned toward him eagerly enough. He caught her gaze, taking the bottle and the glasses from her as she swayed and then collapsed against his chest.

"Here, hold this," he said, handing Amanda one of the wine glasses.

Bemused, she did as he asked. "You have got to be kidding me."

The vampire held the sleeping stripper's wrist over the glass and made a single cut with his razor. "Never cut the artery unless you want a mess," he advised, licking the blade clean.

Blood pooled in the glass, the scent filling the tiny space until Amanda was certain that anyone passing by would surely have to smell it. Need shot through her. Gabriel's bloody thumb entered her field of view, pressing tight against the wound, but Amanda could not take her eyes off the deep red of the liquid she held. The bowl of the glass was so warm against her hands.

"If you keep admiring it, it'll get cold," Gabriel teased.

Letting out a shaky breath, Amanda raised the glass to her lips.

That same taste of molten copper, but this time it poured over her tongue and down her throat the way it was supposed to. The full flavor was indescribable, vibrant, as if the liquid itself was alive and moving. She swallowed, feeling the heat of it roll all the way down into her belly. It was so very different from the cold wind of Gabriel's power, but it filled her in the same way, only with heat—blessed, necessary heat, seeping into the cracks and crevices of her psyche. The energy swam through her veins until her whole body hummed, singing to her of what she could be, what she *should* be. Her inner geography shifted, reshaping itself. A great chasm opened, bottomless, aching, screaming to be awash in blood, to be filled with that sweet, resonant power.

Amanda gasped, nearly doubling over with the strength of that need.

The glass was empty. She stared at it as if it were a viper.

"Still too brief?" Gabriel asked, startling her. She'd completely forgotten him. "Another glassful won't do any lasting damage to her."

Amanda shook her head. She didn't dare. It took all her concentration just to set the glass down. She wasn't sure if she wanted to lick it clean or dash it against the wall.

"No?" He *tsk*ed at her. "Well, I'm sure you won't mind if I have a nibble then."

She shook her head again, unable to speak, and Gabriel sank his fangs into Sunny's throat. Amanda felt it deep in her gut, a sharp twisting pain of pure want. She gritted her teeth and looked down at the grimy floor. *Get ahold of yourself!* Wrapping her arms around her middle, she squeezed her eyes tight shut and fought the bloodlust down.

Amanda opened her eyes a moment later. She was half afraid the bloodlust would come storming back as soon as she saw the vampire feeding, but he was already done. He sat watching her, an amused quirk to his lips, one hand idly toying with Sunny's hair.

"So that's it, then? Blood and power trips, that's your schtick?" she asked, breathless.

"If you want to boil it down so far, as well to say that a human's schtick is eating and sleeping." Gabriel leaned toward her, eyes bright with memory. "I have lived so much, Amanda. I have seen battles, and colonization, and more wonders of nature and man than I could ever count. I have met men and women that you've only read about."

"And killed them," she snapped.

"Not so many of the ones that were important enough to get into the history books. But yes, I have killed. I do kill. So does every vampire. It is our nature." He stroked Sunny's face and she started to stir. "Why don't you give the lady a dance," he murmured to the groggy stripper. "I've had all the teasing I can take for one evening."

Sunny wobbled to her feet with a drunk-sounding giggle, but by the time she had crossed the small space she was completely awake.

"I really don't—" Amanda began, but Sunny dropped onto her lap anyway, shoving her breasts in Amanda's face and grinding her hips. She still smelled of blood and Gabriel's scent, and Amanda's hunger flared.

You bastard, she thought at him, raising her hands to try and ward off the stripper. "Really, I—"

"Ah-ah, no touching," Sunny scolded, grinning at her. Sunny grabbed Amanda's hands, pinning them against the wall of the booth, and jiggled her breasts in Amanda's face again.

"Gah!" Amanda turned her head, intensely uncomfortable with the whole situation.

Sunny laughed, and across the booth Gabriel's cruel, delighted grin was wider than she'd ever seen it. Amanda's cheeks heated in humiliation. With an angry hiss, she forced her hands away from the wall, moving Sunny back even when the stripper tried, playfully, to use her body weight to keep Amanda pinned.

"You must work out," Sunny said appreciatively.

Amanda locked eyes with her...and her frustration and anger abruptly died. Staring into Sunny's eyes, Amanda could feel the other girl's defenses, could sense every crack in her psyche. It was so damn easy. Between one breath and the next she had slipped past the outer walls and hooked her fingers in the girl's mind.

Sunny's eyes widened, and she began to struggle to look away.

"Shh," Amanda whispered. The world narrowed down to the two big blue eyes in front of her, and the rising panic in Sunny's pulse. Amanda's heartbeat was rock steady, all emotion left behind her somewhere. "Shh. Let go of me, Sunny."

Sunny's hands sprang open.

Amanda took hold of them, putting Sunny's hands behind the girl's back and lacing the fingers together. "There. That's better."

Sliding her hands up Sunny's arms, Amanda cupped one hand around the back of the girl's head and stroked her face with the other. Blood pulsed through all the little vessels, dancing under Amanda's fingertips.

Tears pooled in the blue eyes, spilling down the soft cheeks to wet Amanda's fingers. The scents of hot tin and cold sweat drifted past, growing stronger by the second. Fear. Amanda didn't want fear. She wanted to feel surrender again, but she wasn't sure how to find the fear so she could change it. Frowning, she riffled through the girl's emotions.

"What are you trying to do?" Gabriel asked, his voice a quiet murmur.

"She's afraid," Amanda replied distractedly, not taking her attention off her target.

"Ah." Gabriel's power slipped past her. "Observe."

Gabriel's mental touch was feather-light, caressing certain spots here and there, moving deeper through paths Amanda hadn't even known existed. In moments Sunny was half-asleep, swaying in Amanda's arms.

As Gabriel withdrew, Amanda started stoking the girl's desire, feeding it until Sunny's skin was flushed and her breath came in gasps. Leaning forward, Amanda kissed Sunny's lips before tipping the girl's head back and leaving a trail of kisses down her neck. Sunny sagged against her, moaning.

Amanda's ears rang with the sound of Sunny's frantic heartbeat, and the sickly-sweet scent of surrender filled her nose, but the hunger was quiet. It waited in patient anticipation for her next move, savoring the rush of the moment before feeding, the seductive thrill of ownership. She dragged her lips across Sunny's skin, not so much kissing her as laying claim. *Mine.*

Yes, that felt right. So very right. She tried out the word again, her mental grip on the girl tightening as if to brand Sunny's brain with Amanda's signature.

Mine.

No.

Amanda pushed the girl at Gabriel and walked out of the booth.

She kept her head down, walking purposefully but without undue speed. If she went too fast, she would fall. *Mustn't draw attention.* Distances were deceptive, and Amanda could barely hear the music through the ringing in her ears. Concentrating on each step as she took it got her out the door and into the parking lot.

The car was locked, and she'd run out of steps.

Amanda dropped to her knees.

The wind of Gabriel's aura swirled closer until it was just behind her, but she couldn't seem to stop dry heaving. There was only one thing in her stomach, and apparently that wasn't going to come back up.

The vampire knelt beside her, wrapping his power around her. Safe. The last retch turned into a sob, and she buried her face against his chest. He held her silently, his cheek pressed against the top of her head, stroking her hair, rubbing her back. Amanda clung to his shirt, his calm presence the only solid thing in her world. Her emotional detachment had burst like a pricked bubble and now she was drowning in fear, disgust, and longing.

"You're hyperventilating," Gabriel murmured. "Take a deep breath for me."

He coached her until the hysteria passed and she lay limp and wrung out in his arms. Then he picked her up and put her in the car.

Amanda moaned and turned her face away as he got in.

"There's nothing wrong with you," Gabriel said as they pulled out of the parking lot, answering the first coherent thought she'd managed.

"Yes there is. Oh, God, I wanted her, and not even the blood. Just...her." She thought her chest was going to split open, the self-loathing hurt so much.

"You wanted power. You took power. She was weaker than you, so you took her. Not because you needed her, but because you could." The bastard smiled. "That's what we do, Amanda, and you did it splendidly."

"I don't want this!"

His smile turned cruel. "Yes, you do, or at least part of you does. My blood doesn't affect your personality, it just gives you new tools. You wanted to try them out now that you're strong enough to use them. You'd just fed, so it was unlikely that your hunger would take control. She was completely alone with us, though with people nearby to keep you in check, and I was there to help you. It was the perfect situation, and you took full advantage of it."

"You set me up!"

"Of course. Everything I do is with one ultimate purpose. You know that. You forget it at your own peril. Besides, that was hot as hell."

Amanda closed her eyes with a grimace.

"I see now my mistake from the other night," Gabriel continued. "I wrapped that guy up and handed him to you. Nicholas, as well. You don't want that. You want to do your own hunting. You want to feel the power of seduction, convincing them to give themselves up to you, the rush of their submission. And all of that without even a drop of venom."

Amanda groaned and covered her face with her hands. A hint of desire had crept into his scent, and between that and his words her gut tightened with longing. "God, shut up!" she hissed.

He laughed. "My silence won't make it any less true."

She pinched the bridge of her nose. "I swear I didn't used to be like this. What the hell is happening to me?"

"A new path opened up, one that was not accessible to you before, one that is wholly different than the path you were on." The satisfaction in his voice sent chills down her spine. "You are walking the new path."

Her heart sank. *He means I'm losing.*

* * * *

Paul wandered slowly down State Street, too restless for sleep. He needed less sleep than a normal human did, and certainly much less than Cecelia, who could barely function with less than a full eight hours. She complained that it was middle age creeping up on her, but thirty-five seemed like nothing to Paul. It was hard to keep perspective, sometimes.

Especially times like this.

He liked wandering the city at night, liked watching the people moving about, intent on lives that had nothing to do with him, each the hero in his own little three-act play.

You can't be the hero...

There were precious few *others* out tonight, with the mages investigating their own mysteries and the skinshifters keeping themselves scarce. If not for his father's scent-marks, Paul could've pretended it was his own city. He let his shields down a little, reached out to the minds around him and the ley lines underfoot, felt the energies sweep through him without touching him, intent on other destinations. He practiced little sorcery himself, but enough to appreciate the strength and clarity of Madison's lines, the complex beauty of the confluences as the lines wove and twined about each other, spilling into nodes as deep as lakes before diverging, each flowing away in a different direction.

A magnificent trap, but no less dangerous for all its beauty.

London had been a bit like this, when he was a boy. It had made it hard to leave; a trap that had nearly proved fatal. High-aether environments tended to set hooks in you after a while. He knew that, and so did his father, but Gabriel had made this city his own in spite of it, and when Paul last needed to reinvent himself, he'd come here knowing the danger, confident that forewarned was forearmed, with the bitter memory of their burning villa forever etched in his mind.

As he let his psychic fingers trail through the energies around him, Isolde's screams still rang in his ears, the light of the fires as bright in his memory as ever, but he felt the hooks digging in as well.

He'd been here too long. He needed to leave, but he wouldn't go without Cecelia, and Cecelia was sensitive enough that she'd never want to move. Most Madisonians didn't, unless it was to go to Denver or Portland or Seattle, or another place with similar conjunctions. Even if he could convince her of the necessity, she'd never leave before the wedding.

He'd never make it that long.

Paul ghosted through the thoughts that surrounded him, tasting, testing. Searching. *You wanted to hold on,* he reminded himself, but he didn't stop what he was doing. The need was rising strong and hard, as if there were another him under his skin. He could feel it stretching like a cat, slowly waking, settling into his veins like he would settle a coat on his shoulders.

Cecelia won't like this.

That other Paul shifted lazily. *You warned her,* it said. *You told her what you are.*

The minds around him blurred, the voices fading, until they were nothing but points of light against the background of the street, little shining bits of life floating like flotsam on a perilous, hungry sea. Any one of those lives would fill him, ease the ache before it rose too close to the surface. He knew. He'd done this so many times before.

Paul bent the light around him, drifting invisibly through the dark sea, his senses caressing each pulsing light as he passed. Hopes and fears, loves and hatreds, dreams and petty inconsequentials passed through him like tiny ley lines until the empty place where the other Paul lived throbbed with the beat of a thousand different hearts.

You can pretend all you want, that rhythm seemed to say. *You are cambion. Now and forever.*

You will never be other than what you were born to be.

Paul stared upward, past the so-called toxic orange glow of the city lights, up into the deepest dark of the night sky, a wordless plea trapped behind his lips. He left it there. Night had refused him, and if he was not Hers, then he was no one's.

I'm half Yours, whether You claim me or not.

The vast, starry sky filled his vision, as huge and calm as it had been for all of his eighteen-hundred-odd years. He breathed it in as his father had taught him, and felt his need grow quiet under Night's soothing touch.

Soon, he promised himself as he exhaled long and slow, pulling back into himself until he was just another man on the sidewalk and not a thirsty, ronin half-*daemon. Not yet, but soon.*

He'd been telling himself that for months. One of these nights, he knew, his vampire half would stop believing him.

CHAPTER SEVENTEEN

Sunday, May 29th, 1999

Amanda sat on the ground under her favorite tree, staring up at the leaves and listening to the soft muttering of the stream that ran a few feet away, and wondered just what the fuck was wrong with her.

It was a little after noon, and she should've been at her parents' by now, but she rarely came to Stevens Point without stopping at Schmeeckle first to brace herself for the visit. The University's nature preserve had been her refuge as a child, the place she could go and hide from her mother. For all her mother's lectures about how something terrible would happen to Amanda if she kept running off alone around all those college kids, Penny had never been troubled enough to come looking for her daughter herself. She would send Robbie at first, but Robbie commiserated and just walked the trails calling for Amanda until it got dark, at which point Penny would send their father out after both of them.

Amanda's favorite spot was nowhere near any of the trails, of course. You couldn't make things too easy for people coming to punish you, right?

The leaves danced in the light breeze, sunlight glimmering off them in sudden bursts of brilliance that vanished as soon as they appeared. Bark pressed into her back, rough and strong. If any place in the world could center her, this would be it; but instead of feeling like part of the forest, a wild child among the wildlife, she felt isolated. There was no connection here. Even Schmeeckle couldn't recognize her.

What am I doing to myself?

She'd asked herself that same question the entire drive north, but her mind just spun in useless, despairing circles. *I think I would've come here even if I wasn't already planning to visit the folks.* This was her place. There was nowhere in the world that held less of Gabriel than here. Surely here she'd be able to think more clearly.

But here she was, and her thoughts still spun.

Dammit, focus!

Amanda closed her eyes, forced her breathing to slow, made each individual muscle relax one by one. Then she imagined herself sending out roots deep into the ground, imagined growing into the tree behind her, her fingers sending out runners until they found the stream. She could almost feel the cool water on her skin.

She couldn't remember if someone had taught her the visualization, or if it was something she'd made up, but it had gotten her through a lot of angry times. Normally she pushed all her anger and frustration down those imaginary roots, into the ground and the tree and the water, and it left her feeling calm and in control. Now she tried to rid herself of the confusion and despair and recrimination, but it was hard. There was a lot of it, and her roots didn't seem as well-connected as they used to. But eventually she felt, if not at peace, at least neutral enough that she could think in a straight line.

Sunny.

It had been so *easy*, that was the worst part. It shouldn't be easy to own someone, to control their emotions to the point that they'd let you do anything you wanted to them. Melanie was different; that had been the venom, and the venom made sense to Amanda. You couldn't fight your body chemistry. But emotions? Those you could control. Had to control.

Look at me, for example. I didn't eat her. I didn't even make her do something stupid for my own amusement.

She'd wanted to, though. She'd wanted proof of her power, to see just how deeply she controlled the girl. The sense of ownership almost demanded it, because it wasn't real until you'd proved it, and proved it in a way that was lasting and public and completely against what the prey would've wanted.

Amanda's fingers curled into a fist, but she uncurled them and ran through the visualization until she felt relaxed and buoyant again.

Sunny. Amanda hadn't taken things that far. She'd recognized the desire and she'd walked away. That should count for something. *But why did I feel it in the first place? Am I really so much of a control freak that I want to control other people?*

God, it had felt good, though. Better than a rollercoaster, but with that same sort of euphoric rush. Like a rollercoaster that went where you told it to instead of following someone else's tracks. Who wouldn't like that?

Just because I want something doesn't mean I need to do it. God knows I wanted Gabriel bad enough last night.

Gabriel. She shifted uncomfortably against the tree trunk. Seducing him was heady stuff, but she needed to level their playing field somehow. There had been a new respect in his eyes, even after her panic attack. Of course, it was a calculating new respect, but she'd take what she could get. *Step, sidestep, and distract. Make him dance to your tune, and maybe you'll get through this without killing anybody. That's the important thing. Just hold on for a couple more weeks and you're home free.*

There was a tiny rustle in the undergrowth nearby. Amanda reached out a thought, figuring it was a bird or a squirrel, but her probe encountered empty air.

"What the..?" Amanda opened her eyes.

A small black and brown calico cat was peeking at her from under some leaves. It froze when she looked at it.

Amanda cocked her head to one side. "Skinshifter?"

The cat licked its nose, eyes darting in all directions. Then it took a step forward and opened its mouth…and seemed to melt into the air. Not all at once—it sort of shimmered, almost like heat rising from blacktop, but the shimmer moved from tail to head, obscuring it in a brief sweep that left nothing but a bit of unsettled air that rose up a few feet from the ground. And then, much faster this time, the shimmer swept back down, and a little girl stood in the spot where the cat had been three seconds before. She was wearing cutoffs and flip-flops and a Hello Kitty t-shirt.

Amanda wondered where the clothes came from. Maybe they turned into the cat's fur?

"You're not supposed to be here," the girl said with a stubborn set to her chin, glaring at Amanda with distrust in her eyes.

Me specifically? Here as in right here, or Schmeeckle, or Point, or what? "It's a free country."

The girl scowled. "You're not supposed to be *off the trail*."

"Then neither are you." Amanda raised one eyebrow and smiled.

The smile didn't seem to help. The girl just crossed her arms and raised her chin. "Cats can go wherever they want."

"Unless they're hunting songbirds. You wouldn't be hunting songbirds in the nature preserve, would you?"

The girl ducked her head and shuffled her feet, and Amanda knew she'd guessed right. "You leechkin aren't supposed to be in here at all," the girl muttered.

"Leechkin? What's a leechkin?"

"You know. Leechkin. Fang-bait. Bloodgirl. Duh." The girl wrinkled her nose as if she smelled something bad. "The Elders aren't going to like you breaking the rules."

Amanda's jaw dropped. "Whoa, wait a minute. You mean there's a vampire living in Stevens Point?"

The girl went still and eyed her sidelong. "Yeah..."

I guess it makes sense, but here? Really? "And I suppose there's one in Wausau, too?"

"Duh." The girl took a step away, watching Amanda distrustfully.

"I'm not from here," Amanda explained. *At least, not since I found out about Bizarro World.* "I'm just passing through. I didn't know we...uh, I...wasn't welcome here."

"Well, you better not be here after dark," the girl said, her eyes widening. "Leechboy won't like it, and the Elders don't like when he kills people. Then they have to smack him around and somebody always gets hurt."

Smack him around? He must be pretty young. Or else there are a lot of skinshifters. "Thanks. I'll keep that in mind."

The girl nodded, looking Amanda up and down once as if wondering why she wasn't taking this more seriously. Amanda wished there was more of a breeze down here; she missed being able to sense the emotions of those she was talking to. Scenting them would definitely help.

Amanda started to get to her feet, and just like that the girl vanished. A few seconds later came the sound of an animal scampering away at high speed.

Even here, I can't get away from them. She brushed herself off and headed back toward Maria Drive. Why couldn't she unsee this stupid secret underworld, even when she wanted to? *What's next? Werewolf gas station attendants? Zombies working the drive-thru?*

She emerged from Schmeeckle near the baseball diamond and walked past the campus dorms to the Kmart, where she'd left her car. The sun shone down on her full force, no trees to block it out, but aside from some mild prickling discomfort, it wasn't bothering her today. *I guess Elizabeth was right about that, at least. I drank human blood last night, and today I'm stronger.*

She'd chickened out of calling Elizabeth that morning, emotionally exhausted and still shaken by her experience at the strip club. The last thing she'd needed was *another* vampire to try and manage. Amanda got in the car and headed into downtown. She still wasn't sure if she could trust Elizabeth, and telling her about everything that had gone on last night was out of the question, at least for now.

Reluctantly, Amanda made her way to her old neighborhood. *Dealing with Mom will be stressful enough.*

She didn't hate her mother, but Amanda was pretty sure that was only due to the distance that separated them. If nothing Amanda ever did was good enough, might as well keep out of her mother's sight and give her less ammunition. That was what her father and brother did; Daniel Bairns went fishing, and Robbie'd played football and worked out with his buddies. When things at home got uncomfortable, they'd both find an excuse to get out of the house. Not Amanda. She'd never been able to *not* give Penny a piece of her mind.

Of course, when she'd been stuck living at home, she'd always felt she was defending herself. Distance had shown her that she'd started nearly as many fights as Penny had. Still, hindsight didn't make the years of cutting remarks vanish, or change all the times her father had never stood up for her. *Dad is so whipped.* He'd carried out Penny's punishments even when Amanda knew for a fact that he didn't agree with his wife. "I know it doesn't seem fair, honey," he'd told her once as he put her favorite stuffed dog on a high shelf in the pantry, "but it'll make your mom calm down, and you can have him back tomorrow."

The memory was sour on her tongue, but she'd never been able to stay mad at her father for long. And Robbie had waited until their parents were asleep, and had carefully climbed the pantry shelves and gotten Pinkie down for her. Dad hadn't mentioned that to Penny, either.

Robbie's rebellions were much sneakier than mine. He always was the smart one. She'd missed him so much when he left home, and not just because he wasn't there to distract Penny with his academic and physical prowess. Robbie had been her rock. He was the one who'd drilled the importance of school into her head, when so many of her friends were sneaking joints out in the woods. "School is how you get out of here. School is how you get away from Mom. You fuck this up, and you'll be stuck here forever." After he'd enlisted, the shouting matches had gotten worse and more frequent, but Amanda still showed up for class every day.

And for all that, she'd seen Robbie twice since she graduated.

But I got out. She laughed bitterly as she stared through the windshield at her parents' house. *I got out, and just look at me now. Halfway to being a vampire. Not exactly what you had in mind, is it, bro?*

Robbie, if you stand me up, I will hunt you down and...

She swallowed hard. That wasn't exactly a phrase she could use lightly anymore.

The houses that lined the street she'd grown up on looked more or less the same as they always had. The landscaping changed more than the buildings did. The stately Foursquares and Victorians stared down their porches at the street, as if their hauteur alone could disguise the faded paint, or how weathered the gingerbread decorations were, or the dingy shingles on the steeply-sloping roofs, or the vanished caulking that threatened to spill the old, wavery glass of the windows onto the neatly-trimmed lawns below. The grass might be meticulously watered and fertilized and sprayed for weeds, but the houses rarely received that sort of attention.

These old houses, eh, there's always something. Amanda could hear Mr. Gorinski next door as if he'd just spoken to her yesterday. *Never can keep up with everything that needs to be done.*

She wondered if he was dead yet.

Amanda parked along the curb across the street from her parents' house, but her fingers hesitated as they closed around the keys. *There aren't any extra cars in the driveway. Robbie might not be here yet. I could drive around a little, maybe...*

With a decisive flick of her wrist, she turned off the engine. Better to get it over with.

It was hard not to hunch her shoulders as she walked up the driveway to the front porch. She'd grown up here, but she felt like a stranger and it had nothing to do with the vampire blood in her veins; when she'd moved out, she'd really moved out. This wasn't her home anymore. She half wondered if she should ring the doorbell.

Fortunately, her father saved her the trouble. Daniel Bairns pushed open the screen door and held his arms out wide. "There's my little girl! How are ya, baby?"

The sour feeling in her stomach melted, and the tension went out of her shoulders. Amanda stepped onto the porch and into her father's comforting embrace. "Hey, Daddy."

The smell of *Dad* drowned out the scent of living human, and the sound of his heartbeat was reassuring, not arousing. It felt so good to relax, to let her guard down. She always thought of her dad as a big bear of a man, even though she was almost taller now than he was. He'd been the one she ran to as a child, not her mother. Even though she'd known it wasn't true, it felt like nothing could hurt her as long as he was holding her.

He makes me feel safe, like Gabriel does.

The thought startled her. She pulled back, but Penny was already coming out the door behind her husband.

"There you are!" Penny's smile was thin. "I wondered what was keeping you."

The feeling of safety shifted, grew hard at the edges even as it went soothing in the middle. "Now, Penn, it's barely past noon," Daniel said, turning to face his wife.

Amanda gaped at him. *That was an aura. Son of a bitch, Dad was throwing a fucking aura!*

CHAPTER EIGHTEEN

Amanda's thoughts raced as she stared at her father's back. *He's psychic, too, he must be. No wonder I could never stay mad at him.* She'd grown familiar with the auras Gabriel used, broadband psychic projections that subtly affected the subconscious minds of those around him. Hell, Amanda herself had learned the one that made people ignore you, even if she couldn't figure out how Gabriel did the part that made him physically hard to see.

Only she'd just learned about auras recently, and here her father had been doing them all along.

"Punctuality was never one of her strong suits." Penny gave a dismissive sniff, then frowned at her daughter. "What are you staring at? Close your mouth, you look like a fish."

Amanda's jaw snapped shut with a click. "I...sorry, I..." She shook her head, trying to focus, and leaned forward for a lecture-distracting hug. "How are you, Mom?"

Hugging her father was a full-body affair, warm and genuine. Penny always bent forward from the waist, barely allowing her shoulders to touch the other person, her arms giving a loose, light squeeze before disengaging, her face turned to the side as if she expected a kiss on the cheek. Amanda could count on one hand the number of times she'd seen her parents kiss on the lips.

"Oh, I get by," Penny said as they separated.

Daniel muttered something about the grill and went back inside, and the two women followed after. *Was he doing that on purpose? Does he even know he's psychic?* Amanda let her eyes unfocus, making her way through the house to the kitchen more by memory than by sight, and sent tentative probes toward her father.

He had shields all right, but they were a patchwork, cobbled together with layers stacked on layers stacked on layers. The mages' shields were strong but thin, well-crafted; these were rough and uneven, and so thick they made Amanda's head feel heavy.

Daniel glanced back over his shoulder, his brow furrowed just a little. "Did you say something?"

"Nope. Must've been my stomach growling," Amanda replied with forced cheerfulness.

He shrugged and continued on, sliding open the screen door that led onto the deck.

Either he doesn't know, or he's just totally untrained, Amanda decided as she followed him out into the sun. *Those shields are a mess.* She hated to think what her own must've looked like, before Gabriel started teaching her. But she couldn't help wondering now just how much of the affection she'd always felt for her father was manufactured. Just how long had he been holding their family together with those subtle emotional tricks?

And I always thought Mom was the manipulative one. But that rang false, and she instantly felt guilty for her suspicion. *No; he had no idea what happened when I touched his shields. He must be doing this unconsciously.*

Daniel slipped on a pair of oven mitts and pulled the steaming pot off the open charcoal grill. Penny hated the smell of beer and onions and wouldn't let her husband boil the bratwurst in the kitchen. He set the pot on the prep stand and started pulling the brats out with tongs, setting them on the grill with a hiss. Amanda's stomach went queasy as the casings began to sear.

Not even Dad's brats? she thought in miserable supplication to whatever gods might be listening. *Just one? They're mostly meat, right? Please?* But her stomach ignored her, twisting even harder as the fat began to drip onto the coals.

She hadn't thought about the food when she'd agreed to come. She hadn't thought about any of it. Was it only two weeks ago? Amanda plopped down onto one of the wooden deck chairs. It seemed like months since that short phone conversation.

"How were your finals?" Daniel asked as he worked the grill.

It was hard to think back that far. "Fine, I guess. They haven't kicked me out yet."

Penny, fussing with the arrangement of plates and napkins and bags of chips on the table, made an exasperated noise. "You 'guess.' You could take your education a little more seriously, Mandy. That's a lot of money you're spending for that marketing degree."

There was a distinct edge of condescension on the word "marketing." Penny had been pushing hard for her children to go into computers. *That's the future. That's the way the world is going. You can live anywhere if you're in computers.* Never mind that neither Robbie nor Amanda had the slightest interest.

A car pulled into the driveway, but her parents didn't appear to hear it over the popping and hissing of the grill, so Amanda pretended not to notice even though her chest got tight and her pulse picked up. "How's the fishing been, Dad?"

"Good, good. Caught a nice bunch of bluegills this morning. I could fry some up, if you—"

They all heard the car door slam. And then a second slam. Penny jumped up and hurried back into the house. Amanda rose to her feet, but didn't follow her mother. She didn't want the first sight of her brother in over a year to be marred by Penny's obvious favoritism.

Daniel cleared his throat in the way that meant he was about to say something Amanda didn't want to hear.

"Did Robbie say he was bringing a friend?" Amanda asked before he could speak.

Her father frowned. "No. Why?"

Amanda cocked her head, listening, but the unfamiliar voice had stopped speaking. There were definitely three sets of feet coming toward them, though. A moment later, Penny reemerged from the house, her "company" smile firmly in place, her perfect family visit already falling apart. Robbie was close on her heels, and for a moment Amanda couldn't see anything else.

She'd forgotten just how tall he was. Amanda was about the same height as her parents, but Robbie was nearly a head taller, and broad like their father. *He really looks like a soldier.* His dark brown hair was buzzed close, and his muscles stood out under the t-shirt he wore. Every one of Amanda's female friends had had a crush on Robbie in high school, but if anything, he looked even bigger and buffer now than he had when he was playing football.

Robbie's eyes met their father's first, and they shared a smile, but her brother quickly scanned the deck until he found her. As their gazes met, Amanda was rocked by an assault of emotion. Relief, nervousness, confusion, fear, hope; she struggled to keep the barrage from battering her shields to pieces, and to keep herself from lashing out in response.

The first impression Amanda had of the stranger was of him touching Robbie's arm, and the emotional projection ceasing abruptly. Amanda blinked and put her hand on the back of her chair to steady herself. Robbie's friend was Asian, with hair just as short and a physique just as well-honed as her brother's, the chain of his dog tags peeking out from the neck of his shirt. He was calm and relaxed, and the gesture he'd used was so slight that Amanda might not have noticed if the effect hadn't been—to her, at least—so obvious. The casual familiarity of that touch surprised her; Robbie was not a particularly touchie-feelie sort of guy.

The stranger's dark eyes fixed on her. The lightest of probes brushed over her shields, and Amanda looked away, forcing her face into a happy, welcoming smile.

Oh, bloody hell.

Robbie seemed oblivious. "Dad, Amanda, this is my buddy Chi. Chi, my father and my sister."

Chi turned to shake Daniel's hand. "Pleased to meet you, Mr. Bairns."

Amanda took the opportunity to do a quick, light probe of her own. Chi's shields were strong but unobtrusive, like a brick wall hiding under ivy. A surge of resentment shot through her. *I can't get away from this supernatural crap. This is my day off, and Robbie brings home a freaking mage.*

Chi was turning toward her, but Amanda had no desire to make physical contact with the man. Instead she gave a slight bow. "Hi. Can I get you guys something to drink?"

Chi bowed back, somewhere between a shifting of weight and a nod of the head, with a wry grin that said they understood one another. "Water would be fine."

Robbie was getting a hug from Daniel, but called back that he'd like a beer. Amanda slipped past them all and into the kitchen with a sigh of relief. The air on the deck had been getting pretty thick with all the forced politeness, and the tension made her twitchy.

Her reprieve was short-lived. There was a soft hush of cloth, a whiff of tinny nervousness, but no hint of aura or energy. If she hadn't felt his mind a moment ago, she would've sworn he was another skinshifter. "You too, eh?" Chi said from behind her as she reached for a glass.

Amanda spun, pretending surprise. "How did you do that? I should've felt you," she blurted, itching to see how it was done and hoping he'd show off.

Chi's shields gave a little ripple. It was almost like…not quite an inversion, but… Amanda frowned, then tucked her shields in tight with a sort of fold-and-twist, and had the satisfaction of seeing his eyes widen briefly.

"I wanted to see how good you are," Chi said with an apologetic half-grin. "You learn fast."

"You a mage?" She said it quietly, glancing at the screen door to make sure no one else was coming in.

"Nope, just a psychic. You?"

"Same." Amanda got a pitcher of water out of the fridge and filled the glass. "Are you teaching my brother?" she asked as she handed it to him. He was close enough that she could smell his blood under his skin, but her hunger was muted while the sun was high and she did her best to ignore it.

Chi took the water with a nod of thanks, carefully not touching her fingers. "Not yet. He's got some other stuff to straighten out first."

Amanda raised an eyebrow, but Chi only shook his head. She grabbed a beer out of the fridge and opened it, and they went back out onto the porch.

She doubled-up her shields as she closed the screen door behind them, and this time when she met Robbie's gaze, the flurry of emotions was more like a light rain. Whatever stability Chi had given was already starting to crack.

Robbie reached for the bottle, but Amanda moved it out of reach. "Where's my hug?"

His laugh had too much emotion in it. As they wrapped their arms around each other Dad-style, Amanda quickly assessed her brother's defenses. What shields he had were splintered, falling apart under whatever was stressing him out. It was easier than breathing to get past them, to find the fear as Gabriel had done last night, to soothe it as she'd watched the vampire do. She was in and out before the hug was half over.

"I've missed you," Amanda said as they parted, handing over the beer. "You could call, you know. Or write. I hear the post office is still in business."

The dry tang was fading from his scent, and he stood straighter than he had before. "I don't recall getting any phone calls from you, either," he teased before taking a long drink from the bottle.

Amanda stuck her tongue out at him and turned to go back to her seat. Behind her, Chi was struggling to control his expression. His eyes were a little too wide, his jaw a little too loose, and he reeked of shock and approbation. She reached out through her shields as she sat down, and with a carefully controlled thought tapped on his defenses. *What?*

An equally controlled thought snaked out to meet her. *You're not supposed to manipulate people like that.* His mental voice was aghast, and she wondered if it was because of what she'd done, or how easily she had done it. Or both.

She gave a mental shrug. *Says who?*

Says everyone. He was openly staring at her now, and she decided that he wasn't as well-trained as she'd first thought. Hell, her emotional control was at least as good as his, and she'd only been doing this for a couple of weeks. *Who trained you?* he asked, appalled.

Amanda tightened up her defenses, just in case. *A friend.*

Chi frowned, but just then Robbie elbowed him and Chi broke off the conversation.

"I can tell you all about what I've been up to, Mom," Robbie said, apparently in response to Penny. Amanda hadn't been paying attention. "But first, I, uh, I have something I want to say."

Daniel looked up from the grill, still turning the brats so they seared evenly. Penny leaned forward in her chair, her attention riveted on her first-born, probably hoping for news of a promotion. Chi was holding his breath.

Amanda's hackles went up.

Robbie's knuckles were white as he gripped the empty beer bottle. "Mom, Dad, Amanda...I'm gay."

There was a moment of absolute silence.

I did not see that coming, Amanda thought faintly. "But, you're in the Army," she heard herself say, as if they couldn't both be true.

Robbie and Chi exchanged a glance. "Don't ask, don't tell," Robbie said. There was an edge of bitterness in his voice. "What they don't know won't hurt 'em."

"Hurt *them*?" Penny was on her feet. Amanda didn't remember her getting up. "Forget the Army; what about you? This is...Robbie, you can't be serious!"

"I am serious." His face was closing down, getting stony.

Penny paid no attention. "No, you're not. This is just a phase. Really, honey, it's not all that glamorous. If you hate being enlisted there are other options—"

"It has nothing to do with the Army," Robbie snapped. "It has to do with the fact I'm attracted to men."

Penny winced as if he'd slapped her, but she was still shaking her head. Amanda's hands clenched into fists. *Just slow down, all of you. Shut up a minute and let me think!* But Penny kept going.

"No! I won't allow it! You're the responsible one, Robbie. You can't do this to me. You're going to be an officer and marry a nice girl and give me lots of well-behaved grandchildren. There's no way Amanda's going to be that successful; it has to be you."

Amanda shot to her feet. "Mother!"

Penny's voice was steadily rising in pitch and volume, the words coming faster, running together. "Don't you see, Robbie? I simply can't allow this!"

"This is not fucking about you, Mom!" Amanda glared at her mother so hard her vision went dark at the edges. Rage flooded through her, energy rising out of her blood and collecting in a growing, swirling storm that roared in her ears like thunder.

"You watch your mouth!" Penny whirled and pointed a finger at her daughter. "You've been nothing but a disappointment, and I won't have your spiteful behavior making this worse! Be quiet!"

Amanda flung a psibolt at her.

Or at least, she meant to. As the energy left her, Chi grabbed it. With no outward sign except a startled and slightly pained grunt, he diverted Amanda's energy into the ground. Amanda was thrown off balance, as if she'd reached out to grab a handhold and missed, or misjudged how many steps were left on a staircase. She stumbled forward.

Chi, the only one who had any idea why Amanda was suddenly weaving like a drunk, reached out to steady her.

Panic cut through her disorientation. The sudden grounding had pulled more energy out of her than she'd meant to use, and her defenses were scrambled. *What if he realizes what I am?* "Don't touch me!" She twisted away from him, lost her footing, and crashed into her mother.

In the instant before they both went sprawling, Penny's thoughts ripped through Amanda's mind. *She's always been too much like me; I never listened, either. She's going to end up married to the guy with the motorcycle and the pompadour and no ambition, she'll be stuck in some dead-end town in a dead-end job, but not Robbie, God, I can't have ruined both of my children, one of them has to get out, one of them has to have the life I was supposed to have...*

And then they tumbled apart. Dazed from the crush of Penny's guilt, Amanda looked up at the men standing around her. Chi was furious, mentally shouting broadband instead of talking just to her. *Were you trying to kill her? That psibolt would've dropped a horse! What the hell is wrong with you?* Robbie looked stung, one hand on Chi's shoulder, and Amanda realized what it must have looked like to him, her rejecting Chi's touch so violently that she tripped and fell. *They're lovers, of course they're lovers. Why didn't I see that before? I just totally dissed my brother's boyfriend and he has no idea why.* She opened her mouth, tried to find something to say, but the words wouldn't come. How could she explain?

Before she could think of anything, Robbie pointedly looked away, lifting his head and addressing Daniel. "Dad?"

Their father was ignoring all of them, studiously turning the brats. He flipped another one or two before looking up, but his gaze was distant, staring out over the grill and the deck rail, past the neighbors' houses and the trees. "S'posed to rain a little tomorrow," he said, taking a swig off his beer. "Nice little breeze. Pressure's supposed to drop through the morning. Good day for fishing." He turned his attention back to the grill.

They all stared at him in silence for a moment. Then Penny burst into tears, scrambled to her feet, and dashed into the house.

Robbie carefully set down his empty beer bottle on the table. Without another word, he walked off the deck onto the lawn and vanished around the side of the house, Chi trailing in his wake. A few seconds later, the car doors slammed. Then the engine started up. And then the sound of them faded until it was lost in the rustling of the leaves.

Amanda's joints creaked and her muscles were stiff and achy as she climbed into one of the deck chairs. She rested her elbows on her knees and her head in her hands. She felt old and tired, and the weight of her mother's guilt and pain was a burden that swam at the outskirts of her consciousness. She shrugged it away, let it fall to the floorboards and pool around her feet. *Not now. I just can't deal with this right now. Christ, vampires and bloodlust seem simple in comparison.*

"A family of psychics, and we still can't communicate," she muttered.

A slight wince was the only sign that her father heard her. Daniel picked up a plate and started piling the brats onto it. "Lunch is ready."

"Thanks, Dad," Amanda replied without looking up. "But I'm not hungry right now."

"Eh, they'll reheat."

She was upwind of him, and he was safe and serene behind his patchwork fortress. As he set the full plate aside and scattered the charcoal briquettes in the bottom of the grill, Amanda was absurdly grateful. Part of her wanted to know what he was thinking, wanted to know what she could do to try and coerce these people into some semblance of a normal family, but the rest of her was too tired, and sick. *What else did you expect, coming here? These people sure as hell are not going to help you get back on the straight and narrow. They can't even help themselves.*

Satisfied that the fire was out, Daniel hung the tongs on the grill's handle. "I'd better go see to your mother." Taking another swallow of beer, he walked into the house.

The sun burned into Amanda's back. From upstairs, the faint sounds of Penny's sobs slipped through the old, warped window sashes and drifted like cottonwood fluff on the breeze. Amanda looked at her watch. It was twelve-fifty p.m. They hadn't even made it until one o'clock.

Wearily, Amanda pushed herself out of the chair, and then followed her brother's scent around the house to the front. She crossed the silent street to her car, got in, and began the long drive home.

CHAPTER NINETEEN

Given the day she'd had already, Amanda almost didn't mind admitting that she felt more real after dark. Once the sun set there was no question as to which world she belonged in, or who she was or what she was fighting. The battle was joined from the moment Gabriel woke up, and it was refreshingly straight-forward in comparison to her family's issues.

And tonight we are playing by my rules, dammit. Step, sidestep, and distract. Keep him dancing, and nobody gets hurt.

"So what is this party for?" Gabriel asked as he drove.

"It's a 'James's parents are out of town again' party," Amanda answered. "He has one every time they go away for a few days. Their house is incredible—huge yard, pool, an insane entertainment center, pool table in the basement, wet bar, it's crazy. I think he just misses not living there anymore. We're his excuse to make merry with the real estate."

"And how many people are you expecting to be there?"

"Usually around twenty. Not so few that it's a real intimate gathering, but not so many that he can't keep the damage down." Enough to keep Gabriel in check, hopefully, and give her some much-needed mundane human contact.

He won't hurt my friends. He wants too much from me to piss me off that badly.

Gabriel nodded to himself, but Amanda couldn't read his expression. "How long?"

"Oh, it'll go all night." She frowned at him. "You almost killed Melanie last night, and fed from Sunny besides. Shouldn't you be good until at least tomorrow?"

"We'll see," he replied with a smile. "And I get to play the besotted boyfriend again?"

"I don't know about besotted, but boyfriend, yes." She considered him doubtfully. "I don't think I could handle it if you went all lovey-dovey on me."

The vampire chuckled. "I don't do lovey-dovey, fortunately for you. But boyfriends do get to kiss, you know."

She cocked her head to the side, and gave his own mocking smile back to him. "We'll see."

The house Amanda directed him to glowed from lights hidden among the shrubs. More lights lined the walkway from the circular drive, leading up to a shallow front porch. The doorbell was a deep booming gong, two slow tones that always reminded Amanda of church bells. James answered it, ushering them into the foyer with an exaggerated bow.

The moment she saw James, Amanda knew this had been a mistake. She'd been ready to relax and unwind with her friends; instead she felt her defenses snap into place automatically, felt a façade just like the one Gabriel used slipping over her, hiding the fact that she was *other*.

No bloodthirsty monsters here, just plain old Amanda.

Amanda had gone to her parents' house with her guard already up. She hadn't been expecting the knee-jerk reaction here, of all places. And yet, she couldn't fault the logic. She couldn't take the chance that someone might realize what she and Gabriel were.

That James didn't seem to notice made it even worse.

Your best friends should be able to tell when you're lying to them.

"Hey, c'mon in. Glad you guys could make it. Food's in the kitchen, and we've got a movie going in the living room. George and the guys are downstairs playing cards." James made vague directional gestures for Gabriel's benefit as he led them both inside.

"What movie?" Amanda asked, covering her dismay.

"Well, they let Sammi pick, so it's probably *Bram Stoker's Dracula*. Again."

"If you would buy something else with Keanu Reeves in it then we wouldn't have to watch it as much." Amanda's face felt like a mask, her responses like lines she had memorized even though they were exactly what she would've said anyway.

James groaned, oblivious to her charade. "I refuse. I only have that one 'cause she gave it to me for my birthday." But in spite of his protests he made a beeline for the living room.

Amanda followed him, eager to not have to pretend to be herself.

The couch and recliners were already taken, except for one spot which James slid into, picking up a can of soda from the end table. Sammi, next to him on the couch, inched marginally closer. James appeared not to notice, but Amanda heard his pulse pick up as she passed by them.

She found a clear spot of floor in view of the TV, stretching out on her side with her head propped up on her hand. The heartbeat was lost in the sound of Gabriel's approach, but she could smell, very, very faintly, the mingling scents of excitement and nervousness.

Maybe James will finally get up the nerve to ask Sammi out. For a second she was tempted to give James a little confidence boost, but then she remembered the look on Chi's face. Her lips pressed together as she fought back a frown. *Sanctimonious prick. Where's he get off acting so high and mighty?* But she kept her thoughts to herself and left James and Sammi alone.

Amanda wasn't surprised when the vampire dropped down behind her, but stiffened when he cuddled up to her back, draping his arm casually over her waist.

I'm pretending to be your boyfriend, remember? he said before she could protest. *Relax.*

I guess I was just distracted, sorry. She leaned into Gabriel's chest, his body making a warm line down her back. There was that feeling of safety again, but after giving her shields a quick check, Amanda decided it wasn't an aura. No, that feeling came from her absolute certainty that he would utterly destroy anything that tried to harm her.

You've been distracted all night. Gabriel curled his body around hers, and the arm around her waist hugged her a little closer. *What's troubling you, little mouse?*

She shook her head. *Nothing.*

Don't lie to me. The thought was sharp, just this side of painful.

Amanda bit back a growl. *It's not a lie. That's polite society's way of saying, "I don't want to talk about it."*

I've never cared much for polite society.

His mulish tone made her even more aware of her emotional weariness.

Gabriel, can't we just watch the movie? She wrapped her arm over his, taking his hand and squeezing it. *Please?*

It's a ridiculous movie.

Amanda took a long, slow breath and reminded herself of her plan. She leaned back into Gabriel, turning to face him over her shoulder. She let her chin tilt up, exposing her throat, and let her lips part, welcoming the flutter of desire that she knew would flavor her scent.

Just keep your thoughts to yourself for one movie. Please, Gabriel? That's all I ask.

He lowered his head, his lips meeting hers softly, so softly.

She swallowed hard, her eyes drifting closed as she surrendered to the kiss, melting against him as his mouth grew more demanding. His tongue slipped between her lips, teasing her teeth, and the roof of her mouth got tight and achy in a way that made her want to press her legs together. She gasped at the strange sensation.

Chuckling, he broke away. *One movie.*

Amanda breathed a sigh of relief and turned back toward the screen. Just for a little while, she wanted to pretend she was still a part of this group, that she belonged here with her friends.

And what are you going to do after the movie, idiot?

She still didn't have an answer when the credits began to roll two hours later.

Amanda stretched, then wiggled out from under Gabriel's arm. "I'll be right back," she said, and headed out to the kitchen.

Bowls of potato chips and plates of finger food lined the counter, but Amanda ignored them. She'd already tried eating once today on the way home from Point, but everything tasted like ashes. Even the coffee shop didn't smell appetizing anymore, just pleasantly bitter-sweet. She poured herself a glass of water and walked back to the living room.

Gabriel was gone.

"Where'd Gabriel go?" she asked James as he riffled through the movies. She was proud that her voice was steady; she had a very bad feeling about this.

"I thought he went to look for you," James replied.

Amanda glanced around the living room. *Gabriel?*

You're a hunter, Amanda. Hunt me.

His presence vanished from her mind.

Gabriel? Dammit, no more stupid games! She thought she heard a chuckle, but wasn't sure. She ground her teeth in frustration. *Answer me, damn you.*

She got no reply—it was almost as if her thoughts were hitting the inside of her skull and just bouncing back. *Kinda like they used to,* she thought with a wry grimace. *It's hard to remember that I couldn't always do this.*

With a barely repressed snarl she left the room and paused in the hall-way outside. Feeling silly, she scented the air. It was easy to distinguish Gabriel from her friends—none of the humans smelled like old blood, or night wind, or sex-on-wheels—but she wasn't sure how old the scent was. *He came in this way, after all.* She looked up and down the hallway. *Back toward the kitchen, the other way just goes to the bathroom...no, I'd better check.*

His scent was strong in the little room, but the one window had been painted shut years ago and showed no signs of disturbance. *He waited here for me to come back from the kitchen, and then snuck past the living room,* she decided, hurrying toward the kitchen.

She paused by the stairs, testing the air in the stairwells before determin-ing he hadn't chanced either the upstairs or the basement. *He doesn't know this house like I do. He'd be better off trying to hide outside.*

Amanda broke into a slow jog as she reentered the kitchen, heading for the patio doors. With a quick look around to make sure the room was empty, she put her face down to the door handle. *Yes, he came this way.* She slipped outside.

Laughter and splashing from the pool made it hard to listen. In the back of her mind she identified the individual voices as she tried to tune them out—*Brandy, Brandy's sister Kayla, Kayla's best friend Rachel, Rachel's boyfriend Brian...* Avoiding the flagstone path for the quiet of the lawn, she crept up to the bushes that partially screened the pool and peered through.

She didn't really expect to find him there, and a brief examination con-firmed his absence. She turned back toward the house, then paused. *No reason to let him know I'm coming,* she decided, tucking her shields close as Chi had done. She scanned the backyard thoughtfully. *Not many places to hide back here...*

Her eyes passed the huge red maple near the back parlor window and came back. *Possible.* She left the lee of the bushes and darted toward it. Pressing close to the trunk in case someone looked out a window, Amanda peered up into the foliage.

The dark leaves could not hide anything Gabriel's size—he wasn't there. She sighed in vexation, then stiffened. She had lost the scent trail when she'd gone down by the pool, but now she could smell him again. Reach-ing up for the lowest branch, she carefully pulled herself up and started to climb. *Quietly, quietly. Can't let the leaves rattle too much,* she thought as she made her way higher. She gained one last foothold before raising her head high enough to see onto the roof.

The vampire was lounging on the gritty black tiles, watching the tree with bored eyes. If she moved higher, he'd see her. Holding her breath, Amanda withdrew a quarter from her pocket and gave it an underhand toss. It clinked into the gutter behind Gabriel, who turned toward the sound. Reaching up to yet another high branch, Amanda got her feet under her and jumped to the roof.

Gabriel had only been distracted for a moment. He reached out to steady Amanda as she landed, although she didn't need it. "Not bad," he murmured with a smile. "I was wondering what was keeping you."

"Are we done with the glorified hide-and-seek now?" She glowered at him to hide how pleased she was with her performance.

"Are you determined to be surly? Sit down, enjoy the view." The vampire patted a patch of shingle next to him.

"Can't you just behave yourself?" she asked as she sat down.

"I did behave myself. The movie is over."

Amanda rolled her eyes. She released the tight grip she had on her powers and was relieved to be able to feel Gabriel's presence once again. "And I suppose it's just a happy coincidence that this little episode has made me feel less human than ever?"

"You say that like it's a bad thing."

Amanda shook her head, unwilling to start the old argument.

"You seemed to like not feeling terribly human last night, running with me out under the stars. Or am I mistaken?"

"You are not mistaken." She watched her friends cavorting in the pool for a moment, then forced herself to look at the tree instead. Her mouth was dry, and her skin felt a little too tight. "I'm thirsty."

"It's not surprising," Gabriel replied. "We can find you something later, if you wish. Or were you thinking about someone here? James was smelling awfully tasty."

"No!" She glared at him until she saw the glint of humor in his eye, and realized he was teasing her. "It would be pretty rude to feed on my friends, don't you think?"

"True. Unless they offered, and that's unlikely."

Amanda propped her chin in her hand, watching the leaves twist and tremble in the breeze. "I thought coming here would make me feel more like my old self, but it didn't. I feel like I'm acting, like I'm lying to them even when I'm not saying anything at all."

"You're trying to behave as if nothing has changed. You *are* lying to them."

Amanda winced, but she had to admit he was right. "All I've managed to do is put them in danger. Maybe I should just leave them alone. They'd be safer if I didn't see them again until this is all over."

"Perhaps. But you would be in greater peril."

Her brow furrowed. "How so?"

The vampire's eyes followed the forms in the water. "It is easy to feed on the nameless, faceless stranger." The lights from below made his eyes glimmer. "But your own descent from grace can best be judged by how you react to those you care about. For example, you still find it revolting to think of James as food. That should give you hope. You are not as far gone as you might be."

"And would you have willingly fed on your wife or your children, when you first turned?"

The affronted look he gave her was answer enough. She laughed mirthlessly and returned to watching Brandy and the others. "You offer me cold comfort, vampire."

He snorted. "That's the only kind of comfort I have, my dear."

"Oh, I don't know," she replied, giving him a sideways glance. "Things seemed pretty hot to me, out under the stars last night."

He traced the artery in her neck with one finger. "I seem to remember you telling me that warmth was something I couldn't give you."

She suppressed a shiver and caught his hand, bringing it to her lips. "And you said I was no longer prey." She nipped at his fingers reproachfully.

Heat flooded his gaze, making her breath catch in her throat. "Do not think," he said, his voice low and rumbling, "that because you are not prey that I do not still hunt you."

Her whole body tightened at those words, her eyes closing with longing and approbation. *Come on, you twit,* she scolded herself. *Who is seducing who here? Get the upper hand back!*

She was still holding his fingers to her lips. She drew one into her mouth, her eyes still closed, mimicking his gesture from the previous night, rubbing her tiny venom glands over the pad of his finger. He sucked in a startled breath even as she throttled down the pleasure his touch caused. She drew his finger back out again, opening her eyes at the very end as she gave the tip one quick flick with her tongue.

His eyes were closed, his jaw clenched hard, but even as she released him he let out a long breath. His eyes opened, locking onto hers with a fierce, focused possessiveness.

When she was sparring with him like this there was no inner conflict, no question of who or what she was. There was only maneuvering for advantage, thrust and parry and riposte. The power play was even more intoxicating than seducing Sunny, and served her own purpose as well. Sunny was no threat to her, but Gabriel was pure predator. Stalking him had far higher stakes. *And higher rewards.*

She curved her lips in a feral smile that showed both of her fangs, and watched him shudder. "*Now* you are hunting me," she purred.

"Fool." His eyes tracked her every movement. "I've been hunting you this entire time."

She clicked her tongue at him. "Perhaps, if you call that hunting. And yet, here I sit. I have played your little stalking game. I've tasted human blood, fed on human emotion. What else is there, vampire? What's left to catch me with?"

She knew as soon as the words left her mouth, even before the wicked grin crept across his face, that it had been a stupid thing to say.

CHAPTER TWENTY

Amanda's last words echoed in the air between them, and she wished she knew how to snatch them back.

What else is there, vampire? What's left to catch me with?

"I'll show you."

Faster than an eye blink, Gabriel seized her and slung her over his back. Amanda clung to him instinctively as he took a running leap and flung himself from the roof, landing lightly on the roof of the next house over, his feet barely touching the shingles before launching them across to the next house, and the next. The speed of it took her breath away, Gabriel's powerful body propelling them faster and faster. His aura covered her, seeming to draw down the night sky, cloaking them in shadow.

He slowed, running on flat ground now, and Amanda had no idea at what point they had left the suburbs behind. When she tried to lift her head from where it was buried against his back, Gabriel pulled her over his shoulder as easily as if she were an empty rucksack. He set her on her feet, but he was still running, trapping her hand in his and pulling her along.

You can do better than that, he hissed. *Run!*

She stumbled once but recovered, and Gabriel picked up his pace, forcing her to follow suit. They were in knee-high grass, no houses in sight and only rolling wooded bluffs to break up the horizon line.

"Where are we?" she yelled.

"Out under the stars," he called back with a laugh.

Ahead of them, near the shadows cast by a wooded hill, a dozen heads jerked erect, a dozen pairs of ears swiveled to the sounds of their voices. The herd of deer broke and ran for the cover of the woods.

Gabriel's excitement echoed through their bond. He zeroed in on one of the fleeing animals, slowing down so as not to catch it too quickly. They followed it under the trees into what should have been nearly pitch darkness, but was as bright to Amanda's eyes as the grassland had been.

She laughed as they bounded up the worn deer trail, leaping over fallen logs, ducking under tree limbs, dancing over the uneven terrain. There was a freedom in this, more so than just in the adrenaline rush of running. Nothing could hold them back, no place so far away or so treacherous that they could not conquer it. There were no final exams here, no work schedules, no family drama—just an ebb and flow as old as time itself, hunter and hunted.

And damn, it felt good to be on the other side of things. She was so tired of being prey.

The deer they were chasing broke into a clearing and Gabriel dropped Amanda's hand. In three quick strides he caught the animal, leaping onto its back and tearing out its throat. They tumbled to the ground together, the vampire clinging to it, mouth and arms and legs locked tight. The deer thrashed once, trying to get back to its feet, but then went still as the venom took effect.

Amanda managed to come to a stop only a few strides into the clearing, trembling with the desire to fall on the animal and feed as Gabriel was doing. Her blood sang with the thrill of the chase, the lure of the hunt urging her forward to finish what she had started. She clenched her fists and fought to keep her shields tight, afraid that if even a fraction of what Gabriel was feeling got through she would lose herself completely. Just the sight of his muscled limbs wrapped around the still body beneath him made her knees weak with desire.

Gabriel raised his head. Blood ran from his mouth, falling in glittering droplets from his chin. He rolled free of the animal in a movement that would've been too fast for her to see only a week ago, kneeling to cup his hands under the vicious wound. He crossed to her with quick, graceful strides, holding his dripping hands before him like an offering.

Hunger woke in her blood like a disease, a dry, burning ache in her veins. Her fangs trembled in their sockets, still not quite able to extend.

"Drink," he whispered, but she was already pulling his hands to her mouth.

Hot and vibrant, the blood cascaded over her tongue. It had a tangy, gamey taste compared to what she'd had from the humans. The heat of it settled in her stomach and began to spread outward, a warm wave of afterglow that only left her wanting more.

"This is how we are meant to be," Gabriel said. "This is what it is to be a hunter. We live to kill, Amanda. We take what we want, when we want it, beholden to nothing save the hunger and the night that shelters us."

Amanda swayed on her feet, drowning in the seductive abandon of Gabriel's words, in the scent of the night wind, in the silence of the deer's heart.

"People!" she gasped, wrapping her mind around the one lifeline she had left. "We live to kill *people*."

Gabriel's expression said that she was stating the obvious. "Yes, of course."

"That," she said, pointing to the deer, "is not a person."

"Nor could you live off of it," he countered. "Other mammals can sustain us for a little while, but their energies don't mesh well with ours. We need human energies. Human lives. That's what we were made for."

Amanda shook her head. "I don't want to kill anyone, Gabriel."

"Why not? What are they to you?"

Amanda opened her mouth, then closed it again, frustrated. He was a sociopath, and hadn't been human in two thousand years. There was nothing she could say that would make him understand her deep-seated, instinctive aversion to killing her own kind. It was just *wrong*. There was no why.

"You aren't one of them anymore," Gabriel continued. "You are a predator, they are your prey. It's that simple."

She *was* a predator now, no denying it, and she couldn't even truthfully say that she didn't want to be. The rush of the chase was still burning in her and she loved every second of it. She hated that his logic was so sound; it made her emotional gut reaction seem childish and silly.

Amanda ground her teeth. "They're my people." It was the only thing she could think of that might possibly make sense to him.

"James is your people," Gabriel corrected. "Brandy is your people. Sunny on the other hand..." He grinned. "Sunny is food."

The mere mention of Sunny's name made Amanda's hunger twist savagely. Sunny's blood had been so much richer than what she'd just tasted, sweeter, bolder, humming with power. But what made Amanda moan was the memory of the stripper's surrender. She'd tried to push it out of her mind, but it was still there. How could she talk of "her people" after what she'd done? It hadn't been some feeling of kinship or empathy for the girl that had given Amanda the strength to walk out of the little room last night. It had been raw stubbornness.

If that's what it takes to get through this, then that's what it takes. I will not let him conquer me. Let him think he's winning. Make him believe I'm about to give in...and just keep not giving in.

Whatever it took to get through this, she could do it.

Something inside her shut down, some small, human piece of her psyche fleeing into hiding.

"And where does that leave me?" She gestured toward the carcass. "I see what happens at the end of your chases."

"Ah, but I'm not trying to kill you, Amanda," Gabriel said, his gaze heating. "This is an entirely different chase, and the change is only the beginning. There is so much to teach you yet, so much you can't understand..."

"Show me." She kissed him.

It wasn't exactly subtle, but it worked. Gabriel's mouth molded to hers, and his arms wrapped around her. Amanda melted against his body, refusing to think about anything but the pleasure of his flesh against hers. She made no protest as he removed her shirt and her bra, her knees going weak as he kissed the newly-exposed skin. The deer's blood left wet tracks behind, cooling in the night air, a sharp contrast to the heat of Gabriel's lips. His mouth closed over one of her nipples, his hands resting on her hips, fingers toying with the waistband of her jeans.

Do you want this? he asked.

Amanda moaned, empty of everything except desire. *God, yes.*

She tugged at his shirt, and with a quiet laugh the vampire released her to pull it over his head. Amanda kicked off her shoes and shimmied out of the rest of her clothing, watching as Gabriel stripped down to the skin. He was so pale, standing there in the starlight, that his hungry eyes looked like chips of ice set in a statue of snow. The blood on his face and hands was even brighter by comparison.

Amanda kissed him again, licking at the blood like a cat grooming its mate. Gabriel stood motionless under her ministrations, his hands cupping her bare ass, the fingers tightening against her flesh as she nudged his head back, his breath leaving him in a soft moan as she began to kiss her way down his neck, sucking at the skin, pricking him with her tiny fangs.

Groaning, skin flushing with heat, Gabriel sent her a wordless, questioning thought.

Amanda pulled back until she could catch his gaze, her expression deadly serious. "Show me," she said again. "Show me everything."

Gabriel pulled her down with him as he collapsed into the grass, rolling her onto her back and kissing her fiercely, pressing so hard that she could feel the outline of his teeth through his lips. She kissed him back, her hands roaming over his shoulders, his arms, his face. He smelled like blood and lust and moonless midnights, and Amanda wanted to breathe him in until she was saturated. Moaning, she wrapped her legs around his hips.

He broke away with a laugh. "What's your rush?" he asked, squirming down the length of her body until he could take her nipple in his mouth again.

Amanda arched her back, pushing her breast against his lips. "If you make me play twenty questions then I may just change my mind."

"Can't have that." His hand slipped lower, dipping between her parted legs, tracing the path of the femoral artery. He began to tease her with his fingertips, then wormed his way lower and started to use his tongue.

It was as if all the tension, all the desire, all the hunger that she had been holding at bay these last few weeks came crashing down on her all at once. Helplessly she writhed against his mouth, her inarticulate cries spurring him on, but even as she felt the pleasure build she was seized by the desire to dig her fingers into his arms and haul him bodily within reach of her fangs. The very thought made her gums tighten and her teeth ache, her mouth going dry but her venom glands watering, the bitterness only adding to her thirst.

Making little pleading mews, she plucked at his shoulders, but Gabriel only tormented her harder, sucking her clit into his mouth, his fingers teasing her opening. She shuddered, her hands clenching in the matted grass.

Not yet, Gabriel whispered. *Not this first time. Come for me, Amanda.*

She did, screaming her release to the night sky. Finally, breathless and spent, she went limp against his body.

"My God," she managed.

Gabriel chuckled, crawling up to lie next to her, his thumb caressing her cheek. "There is such a thing as being too hot to truly appreciate things. That, my sweet, was merely foreplay."

She stared at him in disbelief, panting for air. "You're kidding."

He smiled, tracing her lips, then stroked his finger along one of her retracted fangs. Immediately it flexed, trying to extend, and Amanda shivered.

"Ooo, it should not feel that good to have someone rub my *teeth,*" she gasped.

Gabriel laughed. "Now you know how I felt, when you did that to me."

"It seems like ages ago." Amanda sidled closer. "Are they always going to be this sensitive?"

He felt along her gums, prodding now and again while she tried to hold still. "They're not full grown yet, but then, they don't always fully form before the true change. If anything, they'll get more sensitive, not less. Odd to think of your teeth as your primary erogenous zone, isn't it?"

Very, she answered, nibbling at his fingers. *But it makes sense.* She ran her fingers over his upper lip, pressing gently.

He caught her hand and kissed her fingertips one by one. Kissing his way across her palm, then down her wrist to her elbow, he reeled her in, embracing her. Seeking lips rounded her shoulder, danced along her collarbone. He sat up, pulling her into his lap. Supporting her in his arms, he followed her breastbone down, detouring to take one firm nipple in his mouth.

"Ahhh," she sighed, twining the fingers of one hand in his short hair. "Teeth may be primary, but the rest seem to be working just fine."

If not better, Gabriel said, his mouth too busy to be used for speech.

Amanda traced a delicate line along the length of his erection, and was gratified at the shudder that ran through his body. "I see that."

Growling, the vampire disengaged and tightened his embrace, raising her up and sliding into her in a single fluid movement. His breath hissed between his teeth as she arched against him.

"I thought there wasn't a rush?" she exclaimed, taken by surprise.

"Foreplay," he reminded her. His face contorted as she settled against his hips. "Just...really good foreplay..."

The vampire lavished kisses on every inch of skin he could reach, rocking against her with languid unconcern. "Night, but I've wanted to be in you," he murmured against her neck. "Give yourself up to me, Amanda. Let me show you what we are."

She felt him hovering at the edge of her shields. She hesitated, wondering if that hidden part of herself was hidden enough, but his gentle demand seduced her because it was exactly, unequivocally, what she wanted to do.

Amanda opened her mind and soul to him, let him deeper inside than his body could ever hope to reach.

His pleasure flared through her as their powers melded and meshed. She didn't have to tell him to kiss her—he understood her need as readily as he knew his own. His lips sought hers, ice meeting flame, each devouring the other with growing fervor.

Their bodies moved together, perfectly in unison. Thought fled, instincts older than thought maneuvering them to fulfill each impulse as it surfaced. And yet, desire grew, need grew, until their passion was a roaring in their ears unmatched by any inferno.

Just as Amanda was certain her sanity was about to shatter under the weight of desires no human could bear, she felt her nails rake down Gabriel's back. The scent of his blood scalded her senses. She shrieked like a wild thing and buried her teeth in his throat.

The first gush of blood seemed to tear her as she swallowed, the pain of being metaphysically ripped open lost in the intense satisfaction of her fangs penetrating his flesh. Only distantly did she hear his half-exultant, half-agonized cry.

The second swallow gouged a ragged wound in her consciousness, and into the breach poured the essence of Gabriel. She felt him climaxing from inside his mind, felt it as if she were him, her fangs buried in her own throat, drinking her own blood. His whole body throbbed in time to her sucking mouth, ripping pleasure from every corner of his being, wanting it to never stop.

He wrenched himself free of that thought with an act of sheer will that Amanda knew she couldn't duplicate. Then the feeling of his ecstasy was overridden by her own sweet, searing anguish as Gabriel bit deep, taking back what he had given. Her whole body arched, every muscle staining against the rapture that swept her up, the pain just another sensation in a sensory overload that left her helpless, drowning in his need.

She'd been waiting so long to stop fighting this.

Willfully, Amanda abandoned herself to his demanding mouth, trusting him to know when to stop, because she sure as hell didn't.

When the pleasure finally released her, Amanda found herself cuddled to Gabriel's chest, his arms holding her close, their legs still entangled. Snuggling a little closer, she wallowed in her sated contentment and wished they could stay here, forever under the stars.

"Dawn will come even here," Gabriel murmured with fatalistic good humor, stroking her hair. "Dawn always comes."

* * * *

As sunrise drew near, Isolde broke off her attacks and went to ground for the day. If there was one thing her crows were good at, it was finding her a snug, sun-proof hiding place while she was out harrying her targets. This time it was a series of caves, but she'd spent more days than she could count hiding among bats and it didn't bother her.

No, what bothered her was Morales; he was leading her farther south, away from her father. The group of hunters seemed to shrink as the days passed as well. She'd made several hard attacks tonight, just to be sure there weren't any extra hunters hiding out. Lost two blades, but she'd killed one hunter and wounded a second. Neither hunter was Morales, but she'd take what she could get at this point.

Morales wanted her to chase him, but he wasn't running. The man was no fool. If he was truly trying to escape he'd have gotten on a plane, or at least headed for Mexico.

As much as she wanted to kill the cunning old fox, Isolde's priorities had changed.

If the other hunters had returned to Madison, she had to warn her father.

She'd hit the hunters one more time, right after sunset. And then she was heading north as fast as her wings would take her.

CHAPTER TWENTY-ONE

Monday, May 31st, 1999

Amanda was practically sleepwalking through her shift, the day seeming heavier than ever before. She hadn't meant to drink from Gabriel last night; it was more a heat of the moment sort of thing, but she supposed it lent some veracity to her charade of weakening resistance. The words from her rushed post-daybreak phone call with Elizabeth kept running through Amanda's head, weighing her down as much as the vampire's blood.

"I can't keep fighting with him all the time. I just don't have the strength."

Elizabeth had been weary but insistent. "You have to keep fighting."

Amanda sighed. "I can't, and it doesn't matter anyway. All I have to do is not feed. If I can keep him balanced between chasing me and the 'look, I caught you' sex, I should be able to get through the rest of this no problem."

"And then what?" the vampire hissed. "When you have 'won,' what will you do? Go back to your mortal life?"

"I suppose so," Amanda agreed dully. She hadn't given it much thought, truth be told.

Elizabeth made a disgusted sound. "You'd be content to go back to being human? To being prey?"

It didn't sound very appealing. "I was content enough before," she replied, wincing at her own defensive tone.

"I asked you the last time we talked, but obviously you haven't thought about it. You've spent so much time fighting the lure of blood that you've let him hook his fingers in your very soul!"

"That's a little melodramatic, don't you think?"

"Don't you understand what he is?" Elizabeth was nearly shrieking with rage.

"He's a vampire."

"That's a modern word, girl. He's a demon."

It was a powerful accusation. Standing behind the cash register, Amanda shivered at the memory of it. "I just don't want to hurt anyone," she whispered, staring morosely at the keyboard.

"What?"

Amanda jumped. Lily stood behind her, a concerned frown on her face.

"I said I don't want to hurt anymore," Amanda lied, hardly having to fake the pathetic whine in her voice. "This bug just won't go away. I'm starting to think I have mono or something."

Lily's gaze traveled over her sunken eyes, her pale cheeks, the weight she'd lost since she wasn't eating solid food anymore. "I don't want to see you back here without a doctor's note saying you're fit to work," Lily said. "Your vacation starts tomorrow. Promise me you'll go to the doctor and get some rest?"

"I hate going to the doctor," Amanda muttered. Lily just glared at her until Amanda hung her head. "All right, I promise."

"Good. Now go home."

Amanda didn't argue, wincing as she stepped out into the bright sunny day. *Ugh. Another forty-five minutes at least until the sun goes down.*

She didn't feel like going home, but there wasn't enough time to do much else before Gabriel woke up. Instead, she walked over to a nearby park and sat down on one of the benches. Maybe it wasn't exactly comfortable, but the sun was not her enemy, dammit. She was still human.

Wasn't she?

A demon, she says. But just what does that mean, anyway?

Amanda'd asked Elizabeth as much, but the answer hadn't helped.

"A demon's a demon. An eater of energy. It's why we are so susceptible to magic."

"You mean like my psibolts?"

Elizabeth made a scornful noise. "I mean magic. Sorcery. Demons can be bound and coerced, although the incorporeal ones are more easily affected. Still, my spell worked well enough on him when I was a human, and I didn't even know his true name."

"You put a spell on Gabriel?"

"Yes." There was a world of bitterness in that one word. "I didn't realize what he was, and used magic to summon him to my bed. It worked too well. He was not pleased."

Amanda imagined not. "True name?"

"The less grounded you are in the physical, the more of your identity is bound up in conceptual things, like your name. All demons and fae have a name that they feel in their heart identifies them. What name did he give you?"

Amanda hesitated before answering. *Oh, come on, there is no way he gave you his true name.* "Gabriel Chapel."

"A common pseudonym of his. It amuses him to use holy words in his surname. Humans are not bound by their names; without a true name, physical essence works best. Blood, hair, something they've breathed on, something that holds emotional value, that sort of thing." Elizabeth rattled off the information impatiently. "But you are no mage, and neither is he, so this is all beside the point. It is your humanity, your mortal soul, that should concern you."

Glumly, Amanda watched a handful of teenage boys playing basketball and the gaggle of teenage girls that were hanging around the ball court. The sunlight seared her eyes, the heat of it etching her skin, but she refused to leave.

All of Elizabeth's talk about fighting isn't worth a shiny penny if I can't keep from feeding, she decided. *I can't let the hunger get out of control, or I'll snap and kill someone. That means I need blood. The rest I'll just have to play by ear, demon or no demon.*

Amanda tipped her face up to the sun. It pinned her to the bench, weighing down her eyelids, her blood running sluggish and thick in her veins. Lethargy stole over her, and before she realized it she had drifted into sleep.

She couldn't have dozed for very long, although the basketball game had broken up by the time the sun slipped below the horizon. The descending twilight woke her. Amanda sat up, wincing as the movement stretched her sunburned skin. *Son of a... I can't believe I fell asleep!* Mortified by her own carelessness, she wrapped and tucked her shields like Chi had done and closed her mind to the vampire. *I so do not want a lecture right now.*

I wonder if he can still find me if I don't let him in to talk to me? She bit her lip, forgetting her sunburn, and almost yelped in pain. Her defenses wavered at the distraction, and Gabriel managed to touch her mind for a split second.

Where?!

Amanda shut him out again. *No help for it now, he's coming,* she sighed. *Might as well make him work for it.*

She moved into the wooded area of the park, working hard to hold her shields through the pain of moving. She found a tall maple with a thick canopy and stopped before it. The lowest branch was five or six feet above her head. Gritting her teeth, she took a running leap, caught the branch, and swung herself up. She climbed a few more feet, then settled back against the trunk to wait. Her hands throbbed where the tortured skin had cracked and split. The small wounds hadn't bled, but they weren't healing either.

Amanda frowned. *Is it because they were caused by the sun, or because they're burns, or just because I haven't fed?* The thought of feeding made the hunger twist in her gut. It was always there now, in varying degree. Tonight it was fairly quiet, still content from last night's late feeding. She shuddered at the memory. After they had finally gotten dressed and back to town, Gabriel had found her another one of his drones, one of the people whose will he had twisted and shattered. The woman had slit her own wrist willingly, ready to bleed out her life for the vampire, but he had not required that of her. Not that time, anyway.

Much like Nicholas, that woman had been different from the people Gabriel used his razor on. She'd looked normal; pretty, but not markedly so, dressed in jeans and sandals, and a red short-sleeved blouse with tiny white flowers at the neck. No jewelry other than small golden heart earrings. *She could have been anyone, except that now she's his,* Amanda thought, her lips curling in a moue of distaste. *It's like a taint on her psyche; anyone who has ever met Gabriel enough to know what he is would know that he's marked her.*

Her thoughts were interrupted by movement below. Amanda peered through the leaves as best she could, distressed by not being able to use her psychic senses. She couldn't see anything, so she strained her ears, holding her breath. Wordless murmurs, soft and low. Rustling. Suddenly she heard a girl's high-pitched giggle, which was shushed by an unfamiliar male voice. Amanda relaxed. *Couple of kids making out, that's all.*

Amanda tried to close her ears, concentrating on keeping her shields tight and staying absolutely still. *Why am I irking him like this? Whether he finds me now or an hour from now, I'll still have this blasted sunburn.*

Again the kids below intruded on her thoughts. The wet sounds of frantic kisses, the hushed *shh* of clothing and skin brushing against each other, the happy little moans all stirred her hunger again. A breeze kicked up, rustling the leaves and carrying the scents of the young couple to her.

Both virgins, she thought absently, then started. *How the hell can I tell that from scent?* She sniffed the air, trying to figure out what was different. *Lust, desire, excitement, a little fear, that's all the same.* She breathed in through her mouth, tasting. She rolled the air over her tongue, considering first the girl, then the boy. *Purity. Not something I thought to find in the average American teenager. They both taste only like themselves. I hadn't noticed before, how once you've mixed your energy with someone else's, you carry a hint of that with you. Maybe that legend about the virgins does have some basis in fact. I'll have to ask him.*

Meanwhile, things below were progressing, and Amanda's stomach growled audibly. Already as motionless as living would allow, she held her breath. The kids below her didn't seemed to notice, and there was no outcry, no sudden rush of wind, no "There you are!" from an angry vampire. After a few more heartbeats she exhaled, and tried not to think about the fact that holding her breath was just as easy as breathing.

I wonder...can I feed on their emotions without opening my shields? That might at least assuage the hunger for a bit. *And possibly give me enough energy to heal this damn sunburn. God, but I'm hungry.*

Amanda closed her eyes and tasted the wind again. The spicy tang made her mouth go dry. Her gums tightened, her teeth tingled, her stomach clenched hard, but she could not draw any energy. *Too far,* she hissed in frustration. Now she was in even worse straits, her hunger fully wakened but unable to feed. *Maybe if I climbed down a little lower. I must go slow.*

With tiny, controlled movements, she lifted her right leg from the branch it rested on, then ever-so-carefully swung it over to a lower branch, touching it with her toe, then gently rolling to the ball of her foot, gradually increasing the weight so that the branch wouldn't shake. Then once her right foot was firmly planted, she shifted her weight to her hands, lifting her torso, swinging her left leg over the branch, concentrating both on her movements and on holding her shields. Eventually her left foot touched the lower branch, and she eased her full weight onto it. Then she began again, noiselessly moving from limb to limb. Just above the bottom of the canopy she stopped, mostly still screened by leaves, and stretched herself out cat-like on her chosen branch.

The young couple reclined under a different tree; she could see them now. They were about fifteen feet to her right, and roughly twelve feet down.

Still too far! she fumed. *If only they'd come over here! I can't get to that tree from this one, I'd never be able to keep the branches still.*

Their nearness taunted her. Her tongue felt like sandpaper against the roof of her mouth. A spasm of hunger ripped through her, and she closed her eyes and gripped the branch until bits of bark flaked away and fell. A whimper broke free, and she couldn't stop it.

"What was that?" whispered the girl.

Before Amanda had finished registering the idea, she was already in their minds. *Go and see. Go and see.*

"I don't know," said the boy. He rose to his knees, peering into the gloom. "I don't see anything."

It came from this way. Come and see.

The boy got to his feet, and the girl followed. "C'mon, let's go see," he said.

Here, yes, this way. Come. Closer...stop.

The young couple paused under her tree and looked around.

"I still don't see anything," the girl murmured.

It was nothing.

"Probably a bird or something," the boy replied with a laugh. Amanda soothed their thoughts, and the boy took the girl in his arms again and kissed her.

"Where were we?" he murmured, and she giggled.

Their youthful exuberance broadcast their emotions loud and strong. Amanda leaned down as far as she dared, until the tops of their heads were only a few feet below. *Don't look up,* she whispered to them. *Don't look up.* When she was sure that this suggestion had taken hold, she gave a silent, grateful sigh, and began to feed. Lust and excitement, joy and pleasure, budding new love, all played over Amanda's tongue like some sort of energy fruit punch, so thick and syrupy she could barely stand it. But it filled her up, and that's what mattered.

It seemed a long time later when Amanda finally felt sated enough to pull herself back onto her branch, where she lay in purring contentment. The young couple below her continued in their tryst, oblivious to her presence.

Ahhhh, she sighed to herself, and stretched. The harvested energy warmed her, and she rolled it over her skin until she tingled all over. Through half-lidded eyes she saw the tiny cracks on her hands close together, and the tight dryness of the sunburn faded until she felt as if she fit properly inside herself again. She still wanted blood, but the need was manageable now, much like wanting something salty after eating too many sweets.

Sweet, yes, both very sweet. She gave a lazy smile. *Too bad I can't feed this way all the time. It's so harmless...and it's so much nicer out here than it is in all those stupid bars and clubs, every night the same thing over and over again...not that I can assume I'd find people making out here every night, I suppose. And I still need blood.* She pouted. *But this part's not so bad.*

Gabriel said that he could drink mammalian blood, but human emotions digested better. I wonder...could I get by on human emotions and animal blood? She considered the idea. *Would have to be during the day, I bet he'd never let me get away with it while he's awake...*

She wriggled a little on her branch, pillowing her cheek on one hand, and mulled the problem over. Below her, on the edge of her consciousness, she heard the young couple finally move away. The normal night sounds resumed. Amanda sighed and shifted again, the sound loud to her ears.

Where the hell is Gabriel? she wondered suddenly. She held her breath and listened. Nothing. Frowning, she sniffed the breeze. Nothing. She relaxed her shields, opening to that corner of her mind that was the vampire.

Nothing.

Gabriel? She called into that void, and then again, louder. *Gabriel?*

There was not even a flicker of reply. She could feel the bond, it was still there, but it was almost as if there was nothing at the other end. Closing her eyes, she reached out as hard as she could, searching for the vampire.

Again nothing. Amanda growled in frustration, a knot of worry beginning to twist in her gut. Where was he?

I'm sure nothing's happened to him, she told herself. *He's far too canny. But then why is he shutting me out? Can he be that angry at me?*

"Gabriel?" she called softly, feeling foolish for speaking to the empty night, but not knowing if he were nearby and watching her. "Look, I'm sorry I hid from you. Are you there?"

She waited, but there was no reply. With a sigh, she climbed out of the tree. *Maybe he's at home, waiting for me. Probably about ready to wring my neck.*

The apartment was empty, however, when she finally turned her key in the lock. She kicked off her shoes and wandered into the bedroom. She stripped and took a shower, half expecting Gabriel to pop out of nowhere at any minute, but the minutes kept ticking by, and she was still alone.

"I never thought I'd feel lonely, being the only person in my head again," she muttered, turning off the water and reaching for a towel. "I feel almost, well, lost. I mean, it's not like he's gone for good or anything..." She paused, wondering what it would mean if he never came back. *Can I do this, alone? Can I control these new powers, and my hunger, without him to help me?*

I suppose there's nothing stopping me from trying out that animal idea...

Determined now, Amanda quickly got dressed. Grabbing her pocket-knife and an old thermos, she ran down to her car and was soon heading through the suburbs on her way out of the city. It was well past dark now, and there were fewer and fewer cars on the streets as the glow of the city lights faded behind her. Finally she passed a farm, black and white shapes indistinct behind a wooden fence.

She drove on a little bit before pulling onto the side of the road. She turned off the lights and the engine, got out, and waited. The night was far from silent—a thousand insects chirred and cricked and clicked, and bats and owls ghosted above her, the sounds of their wings hardly distinguishable from the light breeze that stirred the leaves of the trees around her. The car beside her ticked and hissed softly as it cooled.

She waited another moment, and when she was sure there wasn't anyone nearby she walked back toward the cows.

When she got closer, Amanda ran at the fence and cleared it with room to spare, dropping to her hands and knees on the other side. The nearest cows turned to look at her, ears and tails twitching. She reached toward the closest one with her thoughts, just getting a feel at first. It was a simple mind, and the paths she was looking for were surprisingly similar to the ones Gabriel had shown her in Sunny's mind.

Be easy, she told it without words. *There's nothing to fear. You can go back to sleep.*

To her delight the animal responded to her urgings, relaxing, even turning away from her. Amanda approached it slowly, but it ignored her. She continued to soothe it, reaching out to stroke its flank. The cow only sighed and shivered its skin.

Ugh, it's filthy! I should have brought some alcohol wipes or something. She kept her hand pressed against its hide, though, feeling the cow's pulse beating against her fingers. Her mouth went achingly dry. She pulled out her little knife and sent the animal into a deeper sleep. Fastidiously, she parted the hair as best she could—*I should shave the beast next time*—and, keeping a tight hold on the cow's mind, she slit the skin.

Blood scalded her hands, the smell making her knees weak. Amanda fumbled her thermos out from where she'd shoved it under her belt and held it to the wound. Her gums ached in a pleasant, tingling way, and her veins burned with sudden need. A thrill that was half shock and half delight pulsed through her as she realized her fangs were moving, partly extending as the muscles flexed. Her fingers clenched around the thermos.

She could not tear her eyes away from the sight of the blood spilling out against the pale hide, soaking through the fine hairs. Oh, to press her mouth to that wound, to drink from it as she had drunk from Gabriel, to take in that substance she needed so badly her whole body sang with it! She shook herself and brought the thermos to her lips. Gabriel said that to drink from the prey was to lose, and she knew better than to think that a cow would be exempt simply because it wasn't human.

She gulped the blood greedily and then filled the thermos again.

And then a third time. And a fourth.

She had thought she could never have enough, but now she was finally feeling the hunger begin to ebb. She capped the thermos after the fifth refill, touched her knife to her finger, and sealed the cow's wound with her own blood.

Sipping leisurely, Amanda made her way back to the fence. She felt glutted with blood, almost drunk with it. Half of her wanted to just lie down and look at the stars and think about how good she felt. The other half...she felt like she could do anything. Strength flowed through her. She leapt the fence again but missed her landing, rolling onto her side in the grass. She giggled at herself.

This is so much better than the little sips I've been living off of. That was the way it should be—hot blood gushing down my throat in waves, burning me on the inside. Not those careful little trickles and mouthfuls he's been giving me.

Amanda got to her feet and danced to her car, finishing off the last of the blood as she went. It was getting cold and it lost its savor as the body heat left.

"What now?" she mused to herself as she started the car. She held back from making the tires squeal as she turned the car around, and had to work hard to keep near the speed limit. She wanted to fly. Instead, she rolled the windows down and pulled her hair out of its ponytail. It whipped around her face, stinging her eyes and getting in her mouth as she laughed.

"I'm going out," she declared to the wind. "I'm going to go out and dance and not have to worry about vampires or the hunger or mind games or anything."

She took another shower when she got home—to her own nose she smelled strongly of cow—and called Brandy. Brandy liked the idea and soon Amanda had picked her up and parked them near the campus, and they strolled toward the first of the many bars lining State Street.

Amanda was happy to play the designated driver since even the fumes of alcohol made her stomach churn. They danced, and bought each other drinks—Amanda got a few sodas but didn't drink them—and flirted, and laughed, and giggled to each other over James and Sammi, who even now were out at a movie on their first unofficial date. They stayed at one bar for an hour or two, then hopped to the next bar down the street, starting all over again.

Amanda reveled in her freedom, putting the vampire out of her mind with limited success. Gabriel tended to avoid the campus bars, so she didn't have any recent associations to try and forget. The music was so loud she could feel it on her skin, and she threw herself into the crowds with a passion. She pushed power into her movements, cast it around her like a net, pulling the crowd with her into a frenzied dance, then letting her hold ebb as the music changed, only to catch them all up again a moment later. There were a few with minds so tight she could barely touch them, but she ignored those in favor of those with simple unconscious defenses. The longer she held them, the more she could feel their minds and emotions, and find the weak places where her power could slip in.

So many things would be so easy, she thought to herself, *but I will not do them. I will just enjoy the feeling that I could, if I wanted to.* She laughed out loud, and Brandy grinned at her.

"We haven't had a girls' night in weeks!" her friend shouted, unaware that Amanda could hear her perfectly well even over the deafening music.

"Thank God it's finally summer!" Amanda shouted back. "I'm finally getting some free time again!"

"Ha! Only when I can pry you away from that handsome devil." Brandy bumped Amanda with her hip, throwing her off balance for a second. Half the crowd around them faltered, but Brandy didn't notice.

"Hey, I called you, remember?"

"And about time, too!"

They laughed, and skipped out the door a few minutes later to run across the street to another bar. Here there was a live band, a popular local group, and Amanda found it harder to catch hold of the minds of the crowd while they were so focused on the performers. She found this interesting, still learning the limits of her own abilities, and she let her power wander through the press of people. A few heads turned, searching the crowd, and Amanda pulled her probes back in. *Mages, or psychics.* She decided to be a little more careful.

Finally bar time came, and Brandy was dead on her feet. But after dropping Brandy off at her apartment, Amanda was far too wired to go home. She drove around aimlessly for a little while, still wondering where the hell Gabriel was. Finding herself near one of the public beaches, she parked and walked down to the shore. She pulled off her shoes and wandered through the shallows. The water was warm against her skin. Watching the sand billow in clouds around her feet as she walked, Amanda chewed pensively at her lower lip.

What am I going to do if Gabriel doesn't come back? Even if the cow's blood would be enough, I'm afraid to go through the rest of this alone. For all the pain he's been, at least Gabriel's been able to tell me what's happening to me. In a little too much detail, at times...

She sighed, and kicked up a loud splash. *Damn, I wish this were over. Knowing where that damn vampire is would be nice, too.*

The pressure of the water around her feet seemed strange and new to her, and she allowed it to distract her from her vain musings. *I bet I could stay underwater for a really long time now,* she thought, looking out over the rippling surface of the lake.

Little wavelets lapped against her shins. She hesitated, then looked up and down the shoreline. There was no one in sight. With a giggle, she waded back to shore, stripped to her skin, and dashed back into the water.

The water closed around her as she went farther and farther out, the waves slapping against her flesh like hands. As soon as she could, Amanda dove under.

Being underwater had always made her feel weightless before; now she was aware of the great weight of the water surrounding her. It pressed in on her, warm and thick and heavy, caressing her as she swam. *It's like I'm swimming in cream instead of water. And it's so dark down here. With this vampire-vision, I haven't seen proper dark for days!*

Forgetting herself, she laughed at that absurd thought. Not needing to breathe was one thing, but apparently breathing water was something else entirely. Amanda surfaced, coughing. Wiping the water out of her eyes with one hand, she looked back toward shore.

Two figures lay entwined on the beach. They were kissing, their faces partially obscuring each other.

They were doing a lot more than kissing.

The one on top was Gabriel.

CHAPTER TWENTY-TWO

The wind was blowing the wrong way, but Amanda had stopped breathing at the sight of them so it didn't matter. *I think I would know him anywhere now,* she thought, watching in fascination as the woman wrapped her legs more firmly around Gabriel's waist. His nearness tugged at her, and Amanda started swimming toward them without even meaning to.

The woman didn't have that tarnish Gabriel left on his thralls, that tainted psyche Amanda had felt from the others, but the woman had abandoned herself to the vampire all the same. Her hands gripped his ass, her back arching as she rose to meet him. Gabriel rocked against her in perfect time to her pulse, breaking off the kiss so he could nuzzle her neck.

The moans and grunts and soft, wet slaps skipped across the lake's surface like stones, each a blow to Amanda's ears that she felt all through her body.

I've never watched anyone before, not real, live people, much less someone that I've...

Her face heated, and she couldn't even finish the thought in her own head. Just like with the dancer, the more she watched, the more detail she saw, and she couldn't bear to look away even to duck her head under the water and cool her flaming cheeks.

The rhythm of their movements was primal, even beautiful: the way skin slid against skin; the soft, exquisitely formed "o" the woman's mouth made as Gabriel's muscles tightened under her hands; his hips thrusting just a little bit harder, well within his foreplay speed, still easily human; the woman's staccato breaths mixing with her heartbeat, point and counterpoint.

Amanda was still many yards away from shore, hidden in the darkness, the gentle sound of the water against the sand covering whatever noise her swimming made. *She doesn't know I'm here, but he does. He must, or he wouldn't be here. Does he feel my eyes on him? Does he smell my desire on the breeze?*

Gabriel nipped playfully at the woman's chin, and Amanda gave a tiny, mewling sigh, remembering how it had felt.

The vampire paused, his ear cocked toward her just long enough that Amanda knew he'd heard her. Then his tongue traced the line of the woman's carotid artery with a long, sensuous, slow motion, as if he were licking something thick and sweet off her skin.

For that one lingering moment, Amanda felt connected to them both on some deep, visceral level, Gabriel teasing her by teasing his prey, Amanda's reactions spurring him on more than the woman's ever could, the two of them dancing around each other via this conduit that neither of them cared about.

And then it all went to hell.

The woman groaned and raised her hips. "Harder," she begged, her voice rough with passion.

Gabriel left off his teasing, raising himself up a little so he could look down at her face. "You want me to take you hard?"

"Yes, God, yes!"

The woman's eyes were closed, so she didn't see his expression, but Amanda did. The bottom dropped out of her stomach as the vampire smiled, his eyes hard and sharp as glass splinters.

Gabriel, no!

Amanda still couldn't feel him but she flung the thought at him anyway as she dove forward, arms and legs churning in a frantic crawl toward the beach and to hell with whoever heard her. Her thought skimmed across his shields, searching for a way in, and then his shields were suddenly gone. He grabbed hold of her thought, of the bond between them that was now wide open, and his rage flooded down that channel and slammed into her with such force that she shrieked.

Fire scorched her insides until she thought she could smell her flesh crisping in the heat, and underlying the inferno of his anger was the burning, acid-for-blood agony of raw need. It crawled through her veins like an infestation of tiny, biting insects bent on consuming her from the inside out.

MINE!

He roared it, the sound bouncing around in her skull, seeming to pick her up and shake her until she thought she might fly apart.

Flailing, desperate and disoriented, Amanda managed to bring her shields up enough to dull the brunt of Gabriel's wrath. She'd stopped swimming and started to sink, her nose and mouth filling with water. Amanda thrashed until her head broke the surface, coughing and sputtering, the panic and the shock of choking helping to drive Gabriel back. Dashing the water from her eyes, Amanda reoriented herself.

The woman was looking around now, alerted by all the noise Amanda had made. Gabriel glanced up, meeting Amanda's gaze across the water that separated them, and then turned back to his prey.

Amanda started swimming again, but she knew it was too late.

The flesh of the vampire's back rippled. He drove himself against the woman beneath him, moving with muscles a human didn't have. Her head snapped around, eyes wide with surprise and pain. The woman's mouth opened but no sound emerged. She began to claw at Gabriel's arms but he just grabbed her wrists and held them pinned. With a low, rumbling snarl, Gabriel spat into the sand and then bit savagely into the woman's breast.

Amanda swam as fast as she could, but she felt as if she was moving through gelatin. *This is like a bad dream.* Keeping her defenses close, she reached out to him again. *Gabriel! Gabriel, stop it!*

He ignored her, tearing at the woman's shoulders in short, slicing jerks of his head that kept his venom from getting into the wounds. His face was covered in blood. There was a sickening pop as one of the woman's hips came out of the socket. Gabriel laughed—a short, breathless, delighted sound—and simply moved faster.

Amanda's feet touched the lake bottom, and she frantically propelled herself forward. "Damn it, Gabriel, stop it!"

Both of them turned toward her, and the macabre tableau nearly froze her in her tracks.

The woman's eyes were wide and wild, desperate, begging Amanda to help her, but it was the vampire who drew Amanda's gaze. Blood ran in wet, red rivulets down his chest, dripped off his chin in a glittering rain of rubies, his lips skinned back from his teeth like a wolf standing over a kill.

Every instinct Amanda had was screaming at her to flee. She had to force herself to keep moving toward him.

Gabriel's snarl twisted into a feral, derisive leer. "Lost your stomach for voyeurism since you fed on those two children? Or is she just not to your taste?"

His words startled her as much as if she'd accidentally touched a live wire. *For a second there I forgot he isn't just a mindless monster.* She swallowed hard, tried to keep her voice even and steady, but it was hard to breathe when he was looking at her like that. "Stop hurting her, Gabriel. Please. Don't do this."

She was nearly out of the water when the breeze off the lake died. Seconds later the bloodsmell hit her like a physical blow, thick and heavy and stunning, choking her like the lake water had, except this time it filled her lungs until her chest felt like it would split open.

Amanda found herself on her hands and knees, her nose hovering just over the water's surface where the bloodsmell wasn't quite so strong. Her stomach was a hard knot, her muscles trembling with tension, her fangs straining so hard to extend that even the weight of her own lips against them sent expectant zings racing through her. Her hands were buried in the sand, seeking for something to anchor herself to, something that would keep her from raising her head and drawing in that intoxicating scent until her lungs burst.

But I fed! she thought in desperate confusion.

Cattle, Gabriel hissed disdainfully, slipping past her shields with easy familiarity, forcing a rapport that Amanda couldn't fight because he knew the paths of her inner self too well. *You need more than that, Amanda. Always more. We are made for feasting.*

Wordlessly he called to her, and she crawled forward a few more feet before she could stop herself. God, that smell. She wanted to drown in it, to roll in it until it covered her, covered everything, her whole world reduced to a full-sensory exploration of blood. Gabriel's hunger screamed at her through their bond, making her own hunger rise until her head was spinning with it. Amanda dug in, tried to divorce herself from her rapidly growing need, from the chasm that was trying to swallow her from the inside.

Gabriel's power reached out to the woman, wrapped her up and brought her into the link, and Amanda fell twitching onto the sand. The screams Gabriel wouldn't let his prey give voice to shot through Amanda's mind: long, continuous shrieks of pain and terror that made her mouth go dry. The woman's wounds burned like Gabriel's fury, but her fear was cold, the perfect balance to the pain, an icy rain on a hot summer day.

Moaning, Amanda took hold of those emotions and drew them in, reveling in the taste of sun-scorched tin in the back of the throat, and rose petals candied in the essence of their thorns. Bitter and bitter and bitter, the fear and the pain and the sharpness of her own venom, the energy beating at her skin from the underside, and the bloodsmell so heavy in the air she could almost taste it, sweet and spicy and hot and raw. Sweet to slake her dry, bitter thirst.

There was a sound under the screaming, low and repetitive, and Amanda suddenly realized it was her own voice, chanting. *Don't move. Don't move. Don't move.* She opened her eyes and found herself on her knees, just out of reach of Gabriel and his prey. *Don't move. Don't go to them. If you go to them you'll take her, just like you wanted to take the deer.*

Her body shook so hard her teeth rattled as she fought the urge to move. She forced herself to look down at her hands, caked in wet sand, trembling like a junkie's. Her own hands, smallish, on the delicate side, the fingernails short because she tended to cut herself on them if she didn't keep them trimmed.

"Amanda."

His voice made her catch her breath, but she refused to look up. She brushed some of the sand off her fingers, watching the way the skin stretched and flexed and wrinkled. The woman's shrieks still rang in Amanda's head. The air was still full of tantalizing scents, and emotions that weren't her own buffeted her, but she kept her gaze fixed and let it all wash through her. *Breathe. Don't move, just breathe.*

"Take her." Gabriel's voice shook with strain, a plea for mercy and an angry demand all at once. "Night above me, Amanda, take her. You don't even know why you're fighting it anymore. Gods, to watch you kill her..."

The words choked off. Echoes of his need reverberated down their bond like the shocking, gunshot-loud *crack* of a dam breaking, and Amanda felt his control slipping, the hunger that drove him trapped just beneath the surface, fighting to be set free. Bound as tightly as they were, would she be swept away with him if the floodgates burst? *My choice. He promised. My choice.*

She raised her head and met the woman's wide, terrified eyes. The silent screams increased. Mind to mind, nearly soul to soul, Amanda was connected to this woman more closely than she'd ever been to any human, but the gulf that separated them was too vast to bridge.

It was only right that the woman feared her. *She is human, and I am...not.*

Gabriel made a strangled, desperate sound. Amanda swiveled around to look at him. Her thoughts buzzed and swam with feelings that weren't hers, but he still drew her like a lodestone, a beacon in the chaos. It was hard to tell which of them fascinated her more, the succulent prey or the powerful, magnificent monster.

Amanda wanted them both.

Why am *I fighting?*

"She's yours, Amanda. You want her. Take her."

She could have them, both of them, right now. All she had to do…

All she had to do was let him win.

My choice. I am not helpless. She swallowed, her mouth so dry she could barely form the word. "No."

The vampire roared, fury and frustration blasting her until Amanda wasn't sure what was sound and what wasn't. Gabriel ripped the woman open from jaw to collarbone, fastening his mouth over the severed artery. His body jerked as orgasm swept through him, his cries muffled against his prey's torn flesh as he gulped down the blood. Even as Amanda reached out in a futile attempt to pull him away, Gabriel cut the woman out of the link.

With no other emotions to act as a buffer, Gabriel's ecstasy slammed into Amanda. She fought to shove him out of her mind as it rose, and rose, and kept rising. His aura grew and swelled until it was smothering her. She was trapped between his pleasure in her mind and the weight of his presence against her skin. Together they crushed the breath from her body, and when she gasped for air all she got was raw power. It crashed through her, ripped her open, tore shriek after silent, airless shriek from her lips.

In her mind she heard Gabriel scream in pleasure so intense it was like agony. She felt the life beside her flicker and finally go out, like a candle, and it was as if the smoke from that candle passed into the vampire. He sucked it in greedily, desperately—then, as the last ember died and last of the smoke was consumed, there was a flare of gratification so intense that Amanda's still-partly-human system couldn't absorb it.

She passed out.

The next thing she was aware of was Gabriel's voice. *Wake, my sweet. Wake to me.*

She moaned and shook her head, disoriented.

Then Gabriel kissed her, and everything flowed back into focus.

His lips burned her, the blood on them still hot and wet. She felt like she was liquid inside herself, as though her insides had been through a blender and carelessly poured back into her skin. His hands seemed to be molding her back into her proper shape—ribs thusly, abdomen slightly rounded, navel just so, thighs…

Amanda stiffened as he caressed her, gasping. His hands left bloody trails that hugged her skin, warm and heavy. He took advantage of her gasp, slipping his tongue into her mouth, taking the kiss deeper. He teased her throbbing teeth and she quaked. Everything was hypersensitive, even to her newer senses—the weight and heat of his body pressing against her, the slickness of the blood on her skin, the unbearably sweet taste of it on his tongue.

The more sensations she became aware of, the less brainpower she seemed to have.

Don't think, just feel. And kiss me. Gods, Amanda, so much life, so much power! He laughed, a giddy, relieved laugh that bordered on hysteria. *Touch me, kiss me, my sweet protégé.*

His power moved through her like a hand, caressing her soul until she cried out. He stopped kissing her and raised himself up so that he could see her face.

"Oh, yes," he whispered, his fingers tracing her swollen mouth. "You are exquisite, Amanda."

She licked at the blood coating her lips, and wanted more. She reached for his hand, bringing it to her mouth, and Gabriel moaned as she sucked the blood off his skin.

The blood was burning her. His power was burning her. He shone like the sun behind her closed eyelids.

Amanda opened her eyes and was surprised it was dark. Gabriel's pale form rose above her, shadowed and streaked with blood. His flesh was so hot she felt cold in comparison.

"Let me warm you," he breathed, nudging her legs apart with his knee.

"God, Gabriel, yes." Amanda trembled under his touch, her hands on his as he raised her hips onto his thighs. "I don't understand what's happening, but I need you in me."

She wrapped her legs around him as he slid into her, and they cried out in unison.

"Life is power," he hissed, "and I am bursting with it."

Amanda gasped as she felt Gabriel's energy move through her, his voice, his will, touching and stroking and lingering over sensations she had never thought possible. She reached for him, needing to touch him, to taste him, but he held her down.

"Not that," he whispered. "Not yet."

She screamed out loud as she came, and felt him convulse between her legs. As the pleasure began to ebb, he ran his hands down his chest, smearing them with blood, and then caressed her neck, her breasts, her lips, painting them with warm red.

I'm not done with you yet, he told her as she moaned under his seeking mouth.

His hips rocked against hers, his lips traveling from breasts to throat. Then from throat to lips, and he ate at her mouth, kissing her hard, forcing the back of her head down into the sand. His hands ran down her body, fingers digging in hard enough to bruise, finally grasping her buttocks and pulling her sharply against him.

Amanda cried out into his mouth and nearly bit his tongue, but the vampire broke off the kiss, laughing.

"Not yet," he admonished her.

Amanda growled in frustration and tried to raise her head, her teeth throbbing with the need to bite something, anything. Gabriel held her down again and thrust himself between her thighs, flesh slamming against flesh. Harder, and harder, and she arched to meet him, desperate for release.

"Please, Gabriel!" She writhed under him, teeth bared, fighting with all her strength to reach his throat.

"By the moon, I love seeing you like this," he rasped. "And we could do this all night, over and over..." The thought made him lose control, and he drove into her full force, unable to hold back. Amanda shrieked in pleasure as the orgasm ripped through them both.

After a few heaving moments, Gabriel started to roll away. Amanda locked her legs around him and refused to let him move.

"We're not done yet," she hissed.

Gabriel's hands slid down her arms from her shoulders, no longer holding her down, but the sensation was so magnified on her overly-sensitized skin that Amanda convulsed.

"I would like nothing better," murmured the vampire, "than to remain on this beach and pleasure you until sunrise, but water carries sound, my sweet, and someone will have heard that last one. And I still have to get rid of the corpse."

CHAPTER TWENTY-THREE

The word didn't even register at first, she was so overwhelmed by blood-lust. But Gabriel waited until it did, watched her glazed eyes clear. Reluctantly, Amanda turned her head to the side. The dead woman's eyes filled her vision. Amanda spun back over, shoving the vampire away, and retched.

Gabriel sighed, then seized Amanda by the hair and shoved her face down next to the corpse.

"You will look," he growled, "and you will remember. And you will never, ever try to hide from me again. This was not how I had originally planned on introducing you to death, but I cannot keep wasting time and power hunting you down. You are not strong enough to protect yourself yet, no matter what you might think, and until this is over, your nights belong to me, remember?"

Amanda was dry-heaving too hard to reply. Gabriel shook her until she stopped. "I remember," she finally gasped.

He nodded and dropped her, and smiled when she looked up at him with blazing, hate-filled eyes. "I needed this death, and badly. I'd put it off for way too long. If you ever hide from me again, next time it will be very slow, and very brutal, and I will make sure you get a very, very close view. And you will feed, my protégé, just like you did this time. Do you understand me?"

Shaking with rage and revulsion, Amanda hissed, "Yes."

"Good."

He grinned at her, fangs still bared, covered in drying, smeared blood. Amanda flushed, knowing that blood covered her as well. *I tasted it, reveled in it. Sucked it off his skin.*

"And you enjoyed every minute of it."

She glared at him. *I fucked that woman's murderer before her corpse was even cool!*

But that thought sparked another. *Cool. His power is usually cold, but just now it was so hot it burned me.*

"That's why I can't drink directly from the prey," she breathed. "Drinking a death is what causes the true change."

The vampire clapped mockingly. "Close, very close. It's not death I'm consuming, it's life. The blood is the life. The blood houses the life, just like the brain houses the mind. No one going through the change would be able to stop drinking from that font once they've started. Life force waxes and wanes—take a little, and in time it will heal, be replaced. But to take it all, take a whole life into you, to steal away the very threads that bind body and soul together..." He purred, pressing his hands to his mouth, then slid them down over his body. "That changes you in ways you can't even imagine yet."

Gabriel picked up the corpse, showering Amanda in a tiny rain of blood droplets as he stood over her. "Get dressed," he said. "I'll be back in a few minutes. Wait in the car." Then he strode down the beach and disappeared into the water.

Amanda stared after him, seething with resentment and anger, and still desperate to feed. She caught herself licking a drop of blood from her arm and forced herself to get up. With a growl, she stalked to the water's edge and waded in. The feel of the water on her hypersensitive skin made Amanda start shaking uncontrollably. *Damn him, damn him! If I don't get to bite something soon I'm gonna go crazy!* She tried to wash the blood away, but even the feeling of her own hands touching her made her want to scream in frustrated desire. *I just watched a vicious rape and murder, and all I can think about is getting laid and feeding! What the hell is wrong with me? God, that poor woman...*

She tried to hang onto that thought, tried to use the revulsion to drive back her need. She had lost track of time, though, and Gabriel returned, surfacing just behind her.

"Well, you haven't gotten very far," he murmured, putting his arms around her waist and drawing her to him.

Amanda lost all hope of rational thought as his body pressed against her back, his hands stroking her, washing the blood away. Her legs gave out and the vampire held her up, laughing softly into her ear.

"Your need calls to me," he whispered.

Amanda gave a violent twitch as his lips brushed her skin. Gabriel leaned back, supporting her against his chest, and slid one hand down over her stomach, and lower. His searching fingers caressed the little nub of flesh. Amanda tried to turn, teeth bared, but his other arm still held her tight against him, and he kept his face buried against her neck. She screamed in frustration as she realized she couldn't reach him.

"I cannot resist this," he moaned into her flesh. "Gods below me, no one could resist this." He bit her gently, just enough to break the skin and taste her. Amanda arched against him, like a current of electricity between his mouth at her neck and the hand between her legs. Holding her with his bite freed both hands to caress her, the fingers of one hand sliding into her while the other stroked and rubbed and played with her.

She cried out and pressed his head against her neck, but the vampire refused to bite any harder, merely using his mouth to hold her in place.

No blood, not yet, he breathed into her mind. His questing fingers found that special spot inside her, and Amanda shrieked until she had no air left.

As the euphoria began to fade, Gabriel murmured softly in her inner ear, his thoughts stroking and soothing her into sleep. Exhausted, she had barely time enough to resent it before unconsciousness stole over her.

* * * *

Hidden in a nearby stand of trees, Isolde watched in frustration as Gabriel carried his little toy out of the water. He paused to kick some sand over the worst of the bloodstains before scooping up the girl's discarded clothes and walking to her car.

This was not exactly what Isolde had hoped for.

For one thing, I hate seeing him naked.

For another, having a fledgling always made him notoriously testy and overprotective. Even she—Gabriel's daughter, a Fury sworn to take no fledglings of her own and bound to protect the vampire species—could not be certain that he wouldn't drive her from the city the moment he laid eyes on her.

Dammit, why now? Of all the rotten timing.

A sound from behind her made her whirl, already reaching for the blades in her thigh sheaths.

"Isolde? Is that you?"

Isolde relaxed. Marginally. "Elizabeth?"

She hadn't seen the French vampire in more than fifty years, and that had been on a different continent, but Elizabeth's pouty mouth and her heart-shaped, pixie face were unmistakable. The pout broke into an affectionate grin as Elizabeth approached, holding out her hands for the traditional greeting. Isolde grasped Elizabeth's hands reluctantly, always uneasy when she didn't have a hand near a weapon, but kissed the other woman's cheeks with genuine warmth.

"You look well." Isolde stepped back, looking Elizabeth over as an excuse to let go. "I'm surprised to see you in the States, though, especially here."

Elizabeth's gaze drifted back toward the beach, and the anguished longing on her face made Isolde turn. Gabriel was getting dressed, and Isolde looked quickly away. But Elizabeth wasn't watching Gabriel. She was staring at the car.

"You can't be serious," Isolde said. "You're fixated on his fledgling? You're both ridden at the same time on the same person?"

Elizabeth shook herself, trying to appear nonchalant. "I...I'm not here to claim the girl for myself," she said carefully. "I want to help her. I want to save her from him, if I can."

The sound of a motor turning over made Isolde glance back. Gabriel was behind the wheel, and the car was backing up.

"Doesn't look like the girl is having much luck," Isolde replied sardonically.

Elizabeth sighed, rubbing her eyes. "I know. She thinks she can take Sabiene's path, but from what she's told me I don't think she has Sabiene's self-control..."

"You've talked to her?" Isolde gasped. "Are you insane? Are you *trying* to make him kill you?"

Elizabeth laughed humorlessly. "Somehow I think it would take far less than that."

The car drove away, and Isolde shook herself. "Look, the girl isn't important. You have to be careful, Elizabeth. There is a large group of vampire hunters that have been leading me in circles for the last couple of weeks, but never more than a day's travel from here until two days ago. They must be after Gabriel." *They can't know about Paul,* she told herself for the hundredth time, resisting the urge to feel for his amulet, hidden under her skin. "I have to warn him." *Alone. Dammit.*

"Leading *you* in circles? I find that hard to believe, Fury."

Isolde scowled. "Trust me, so do I, but I think Morales is getting desperate. He's split the group several times, knowing he's the one I'm after. I can't risk the others making an attack while I'm distracted, not without warning Gabriel first."

Elizabeth bit her lip, considering. "I don't think he'll be in much of a mood to listen tonight," she said at last. "It will be dawn soon, and he'll take the girl to ground for the day—that'll leave them both safe enough. Do you have a place to stay?"

"No, not yet," Isolde hedged. She did, in a way—she had several forms that she could use to either hide herself underground or underwater while she slept, but they were perforce smaller creatures—easy prey for larger predators, save for the watchfulness of her crows. But to make it here in one night she'd had to leave the crows behind. It would be days before they caught up.

"Why don't you spend the day with me, and we can try and come up with a better way for you to contact him." The eagerness was plain on Elizabeth's face.

She must be lonely, Isolde thought. *Night knows few enough of the others are willing to talk to her. They fear her as much as they fear the Furies, if for different reasons. Whatever was Gabriel thinking, turning a sorceress?*

"All right," she said aloud, with one last frustrated glance back the way her father had gone. "Maybe you can help me with a little magical problem I've been having as well."

"I can but try," Elizabeth said cheerfully. "Follow me."

* * * *

Amanda woke, groggy and disoriented once again, and near mindless with the burning in her veins. She smelled Gabriel, and water, and sand. Before she had even registered that she was in his apartment, she found herself kneeling on the floor, staring at the bathroom door. She could hear the running water behind it. Totally focused on the sound, she did not notice having crossed the room until her hand touched the doorknob.

She paused. A rational thought tried to surface, but it was drowned out by the roar of her need. She opened the door.

Across the small room was a large shower with sliding glass doors. Gabriel stood with his face turned up to the spray, one hand against the wall, one pressed against the glass. He looked over at her as she paced towards him. Their eyes met, and every ounce of sexual attraction she'd ever felt in her life was but a candle to that heated gaze.

Far away, in the back of her mind, that last rational thought: *Damn come-hither eyes...*

The vampire smiled, knowing and confident. "I thought you might want a shower when you woke up. Of course, there's plenty of room for two."

She went to him eagerly.

* * * *

The bloated dawn was nearly upon them when Gabriel finally allowed Amanda to feed. They'd made it back to the bed some little while before, with, of course, a few stops along the way. As full of life as the vampire was, even he had been starting to feel fatigued as he skillfully maneuvered his protégé from one peak to the next, giving and receiving pleasure and yet always withholding that one thing she craved, which would give her back her sanity. Her growing frenzy was infectious—it was harder and harder to keep himself in check, even with that recent death still fresh on his tongue. Amanda, unsurprisingly, had lost any hint of self-control before they'd even made it out of the shower, but a fledgling like her was no danger to him.

It was the weight of the waking sun on his shoulders that signaled him. Relief warred with anticipation as he released his hold on her. With breathtaking speed she turned on him, throwing him down, her hands and her hips pinning him to the bed.

Gabriel stared up into her face. Her dilated eyes were fixed unwaveringly on the pulse in his neck, her lips curled back in a vicious snarl, the whole expression desperate, hunting, and utterly feral. He had wanted so badly to see her like this, to see her given over to her inner beast, become the predatory animal swooping down on her prey... He arched his back and cried out in triumph as he came.

Amanda struck for his exposed throat, tearing into him, and his cry deepened into a roar. Distantly, he felt her jerk against him as the blood hit her, the life that he had so recently stolen ripping through her, lightning and fire against the acid of her need. She shrieked against his neck, but he had driven her too far and she kept drinking.

The vampire gave himself up to her for a moment, embracing the ecstasy of her mouth at his throat, of her hips against his as they continued to move together. For that brief moment, he let go of everything, lost in the mindless, deadly pleasure of being devoured, before he took hold of her hand and brought her wrist to his mouth.

Amanda cried out as he bit down. He rolled them both over as soon as her lips parted from his flesh, dropped her wrist, and dove for her throat. She was so full of blood that the artery practically burst as his fangs pierced it. She shrieked again and wrapped her legs around his waist.

Her blood burned his tongue, her power crashing into him, her power which was his power, returning, pulling them closer together, then through their skins and into each other. Gabriel reached further with his mind, touching hers, bringing her. She shook underneath him and cried out his name, but it was a command. The vampire obeyed as he obeyed no one save Night Herself, letting Amanda's power take him. He collapsed onto her, screaming his pleasure into her flesh.

The sun crested the horizon, and they fell into darkness.

CHAPTER TWENTY-FOUR

Tuesday, June 1st, 1999

Gabriel grinned down at Amanda's confused face.

"This is a hell of a good way to wake up," he said.

She shoved at him, and he rolled good-naturedly to the side. She winced as he slid out of her, dried blood flaking off his skin and peppering the sheets.

"What do you mean, wake up? It's still…" She caught sight of the clock in the kitchen. "But…"

"I mean wake up," the vampire answered patiently, "because it is once again twilight. Day has come and gone already."

"But…" She looked over at him in confusion. "I didn't sleep."

"Welcome to the day sleep, my dear." The vampire stretched out on his side and propped his head on one hand. He grinned again when he saw her looking, and she blushed.

"But there's no sense of having slept. No break between yesterday and now. It's like the last twelve hours never even happened!"

Gabriel took her hand and laid her fingers against his blood-encrusted neck. "But I am fully healed," he said. "As are you."

She swallowed and pulled her hand away. "I need a shower," she muttered as she climbed off the bed. She shot him a venomous look. "Alone, this time."

"As you will." He rolled over onto his stomach and watched her cross the room. When she reached the bathroom door, he called after her. "Amanda."

She turned to look at him warily.

"The only time you sense that day has passed is if you fight the day sleep. Otherwise the day passes in a blink. It will be this way for you now whenever you drink more of my blood than human blood."

"Only until this is over." She stared at him, musing. "Why did you feel the need to tell me this right now?"

"Because I know you. You'd ponder and wonder and use up all the hot water otherwise, and I want a shower, too." He laughed. "And because I know you think my ass looks good when I lie this way."

For a moment he thought she was going to be angry, but then she smiled wryly. "You look good no matter what position you're in. Damn it all." She stuck her tongue out at him and walked into the bathroom.

Gabriel's smile vanished as Amanda closed the door. Something was wrong. Closing his eyes, the vampire emptied his mind, searching for the source of the imbalance.

His psychic senses were muffled. He could barely sense Amanda in the next room. The bonds to his offspring were often faint, closed away after many centuries of practice, but even the links to his thralls in the city were too tenuous to make use of. The harder he tried to reach out, the more walled-in he felt. His head started to pound, and he gave up.

Time to go.

He picked up Amanda's discarded clothing, shaking the sand out as best he could. He opened the bathroom door, ignoring her indignant squeak, and tossed her clothes onto the counter.

"Hurry up, we're leaving."

A frown crossed her face, but he didn't wait for her reply. Shutting the door behind him, Gabriel crossed to the closet and pulled a small duffel bag from the top shelf. Checking to make sure the stacks of twenties were still there, he started packing. Just a few changes of clothes, enough to hide the cash.

Amanda emerged from the bathroom as he was zipping the duffel shut. "What's wrong?" she asked, furiously toweling her hair.

"How's your telepathy working?" Gabriel asked, brushing past her on the way to the shower.

She gave him a quizzical look that deepened into a perplexed scowl as she tried to reply mind-to-mind. "You're blocking me."

"No, I'm not." He turned the shower on full-blast, not caring about the temperature, his hands a blur of soapy lather. "Can you find Brandy?"

She closed her eyes, concentrating. Gabriel ducked under the spray, cursing the dried blood that made the delay necessary.

"Found her," Amanda said. "No different than before, just farther away."

"It's just me then. I was afraid of that." He turned off the water, snatching a towel off the rack and giving himself a cursory once-over on his way back to the closet. "Get your shoes on. We're leaving." He grabbed more clothing off the hangers.

Amanda pulled her sneakers on, hopping on one foot. "What is going on?"

"If someone is blocking me specifically, then they know I'm here," he snapped, tucking his shirt in. "Blocking me like this isn't easy…" He paused, thoughts racing. "Someone with a blood tie might be able to, but I don't think so…unless…"

He felt his skin go ice cold as all the blood pulled back to the core of his body in response to his sudden panic. Desperate, he reached out with all his strength. *Paulus!*

Nothing. He couldn't penetrate the fog that surrounded him.

Cursing, Gabriel slammed a fist into the wall, sending drywall fragments halfway across the room. If Paul couldn't hear him there was no chance any of the others could, much less his psychically deaf daughter.

I can go check on him, at least… No, if they don't know about him I'll be leading them right to him and Cecelia. Dammit! I don't even know his damn phone number! We've never needed to use it.

Gabriel started to reach for Paul's amulet, but then he glanced at Amanda. She was staring at him with wide, confused eyes. He changed the movement, rubbing the muscle over his heart as if it were a little sore, comforted by the tiny lump that bumped against his rib. *Later. Either he's in trouble already or he's not. I need to get us somewhere safe first, then worry about how I can get some time alone.* He sat down on the floor and pulled on his boots as if nothing had happened.

"Ready to go?" he asked, getting to his feet.

Amanda nodded wordlessly.

Gabriel picked up the duffel and walked over to the security control panel, accessing the two cameras in the outer garage. The stalls were mostly full, but he didn't see any movement, nor any suspicious cargo vans or cars with tinted windows. Just as he was about to turn away, he noticed a scrap of white pinned against the windshield of Amanda's car.

"I had to leave your car out in the public garage last night," Gabriel said. "Looks like someone left us a note. Wait here."

Cautiously Gabriel opened the giant steel door and walked over to Amanda's car, sniffing the air and listening for all he was worth. He lifted the wiper blade and slid the folded piece of newsprint out from under it, returning to the safety of his own garage before examining it. Amanda peered over his shoulder as he spread it open.

The article was clipped from the front page of that morning's State Journal. "Local Woman Feared Dead" ran the headline, with "Car, Blood Found at Marshall Beach" in smaller print beneath. Gabriel skimmed the article, growling curses in every language he knew. "They want to dredge the lake?" he exclaimed. "Over one woman?"

"You just left that mess there for anyone to find?" Amanda asked incredulously.

"Of course not," he growled. "Nicholas was supposed to come by and clean it up." He held the paper to his nose, sniffing. "The paper has Nicholas's scent on it." *And Isolde's. Blesséd Night, she's here.* There was a tiny speck of blood on the corner of the page, just enough to hold her scent and let him know she'd left the note. *Or had Nicholas leave it for her. What the hell happened?*

"Come on, we need to make a pit stop on the way out of town."

Twenty minutes later, Gabriel parked his car in front of Mid Town Pub, just down the street from Marshall Park. He escorted Amanda inside, murmuring into her ear as he found her a seat at the bar. "I'll be right back. Stay here."

She frowned at him, plainly not liking this plan, but she nodded.

I've freaked her out pretty hard, reacting like this, he thought as he walked around behind the bar, pulling the shadows close once he was out of sight of the road. He jogged south, circling around the park and coming at it from the wooded side. *Just when things were starting to go so well.*

The wind was coming in off the lake, which was no help to him. He kept his ears pricked as he picked his way through the underbrush. He made it to the edge of the woods without encountering anyone. Across the parking lot he could see the yellow police tape fluttering in the breeze around the spot where he'd killed Vicki, the sand still stained with blood. Her car was gone—probably towed by now, once they'd been over the scene.

No sign of Isolde or Nicholas.

Frowning, Gabriel whistled softly. He mimicked a few bars of the song thrush, a European bird Isolde had been fond of since her childhood, twisting the notes at the end into a signal she and Paul used to use, but no answering song came back on the wind.

She would be here if she could, he thought, and ghosted back through the trees. *If she wanted to meet somewhere else she would've left a different note. Something is very wrong.*

When he got back to the pub, Amanda was gone.

A drink was still sitting in front of her empty barstool. Gabriel flagged down the bartender. "Where'd she go?" he asked, pointing at Amanda's seat.

The man nodded toward the door. "Friend came by and they stepped outside for a minute. She said she'd be right back. That was only a few minutes ago."

Gabriel took out a twenty dollar bill and passed it to the bartender. "What did her friend look like?"

The bartender shrugged. "Short lady, kinda skinny. Black hair, 'bout down to here." He made a short chopping gesture just below his earlobe.

Not Brandy then. "Keep the change," Gabriel said, and walked outside.

He'd come from behind the building, so he knew she wasn't back there. He scanned the parking lot, but there were no people hanging around.

There was a box next to the driver's door of his car.

Gabriel's step faltered.

Stupid, stupid girl, he fumed, walking slowly toward it, head swiveling in every direction and not caring that he was being entirely obvious about it. *Why can't you listen?*

The box was plain cardboard, roughly a foot square. A dark stain was beginning to show at the bottom. As he got closer the smell drifted to him on the night air.

No. No, no, no.

His gaze fixed on the box, his feet continuing forward as if he were dreaming.

Walk away, he told himself fiercely. *Just walk away. That's what she would tell you to do. Dammit, Avidiacus, you know better than this!*

But he couldn't stop, knew in his heart that there was no way he could leave the box behind. He crouched next to it, ready to spring away, and pulled the top flaps open.

He barely had time to register Isolde's face, tranquil in death, the decay that came to his kind already beginning to set in, when he heard the detonator trip. Making a wild grab for Isolde's hair, Gabriel launched himself from the ground, rolling over the top of his car as the explosives in the bottom of the box ignited. The blast lifted the car, throwing it against the truck in the next stall and shattering the front windows of the pub.

His car's armor plating funneled the blast around the sides, but Gabriel was already gone by the time the two huge gouts of flame met over the roof. He let the car's lift propel him over the neighboring truck, shoving with whatever limbs came in contact with the roof as he rolled.

His right side was caught in the rush of flame, and then he fell onto the hood of the car on the other side. Roaring with pain, Gabriel kept going, hitting the pavement on his shoulder and rolling to his feet, Isolde's head still clutched to his chest. He bolted, faster than a thought, the air behind him crackling with his passage.

He headed west and north, away from the lakes, trusting his speed to be his camouflage. Crossing into one of the city's many growing subdivisions, he ducked into an unfinished house.

There, tucked into a corner of someone's attic, Gabriel let his legs give out. Shaking with reaction, he closed his eyes.

Too close.

His whole right side was seared, the flesh of his arm in particular blackened and split and withered. Gritting his teeth, Gabriel looked down at the burden he had carried away.

There was a slip of paper peeking out between Isolde's lips.

Gabriel drew it forth as the edges of his vision began to darken with a red haze. On the paper was an address, and nothing more. He memorized it and let the paper fall.

With gentle fingers Gabriel traced the leathery skin of Isolde's face and felt the rage wash through him. In that moment he didn't care that she was a Fury, that he himself had seen her trained as an assassin back before her transformation, that she had fought in countless battles before the death of her emperor. All he could think of was that someone had killed his daughter and sent him her head. Someone had carved his amulet from her body and was using it against him.

Someone had stolen Amanda from him.

Rage filled him like life, muting the pain of his injuries. Gabriel reached out with his thoughts, but the paths were still blocked. Snarling, he pulled out his razor and cut into the flesh of his chest. It wasn't a very good tool for such heavy work, and his right hand didn't want to work properly. He reached in with the fingers of his left hand, digging in the muscle over his heart until he found the tiny capsule and drew it forth.

Ancient beaten gold, once part of his son's *bulla*, glinted through the mess of blood. It held Paul's physical essence, blood and hair, flesh and breath, just as the bronze capsule buried in Gabriel's right pec held Isolde's.

Useless now, except perhaps in finding the rest of her corpse. A thought for later. Gabriel set Isolde's head carefully aside and held up the gold amulet.

"Gabrielus Gallus Paulus, I summon you to me."

* * * *

Paul sat up with a gasp, his whole body thrumming.

"Honey?" Cecelia murmured sleepily. "What's wrong?"

"Just a dream," he lied, trying to slow the pounding of his heart. "Go back to sleep. I think I'll get up for a while, maybe go for a drive."

"Mmm." She rolled over as he got out of bed. "Don't be out too late."

"I'll try." Grabbing some clothes, he kissed her cheek on his way out the door.

The thrumming in his blood turned up a notch. Paul winced, leaning against the doorframe.

Gabrielus Gallus Paulus, I summon you to me.

He felt the words more than heard them. Furious, he reached out to his father...and could not find him.

This was a first.

The amulets they'd had made were mostly for Isolde, since her thoughts were as untouchable as any other skinshifter's. His father had the occasional trouble with long distances, but they were in the same city—and distance had never been a barrier for Paul before.

The summons tugged at him, pulling him toward the door. Paul threw on his clothes as fast as he could, knowing once the third summons came he would be completely screwed.

The thrum increased again, nearly unbearable. Paul dashed out the front door in his socks, shoes in one hand, desperately trying to get the lock turned before...

Gabrielus Gallus Paulus, I summon you to me.

You had better have a good reason for this, old man, Paul thought. He managed to jerk the key back out of the lock before the compulsion sent him bolting out into the night.

The call took him all the way across town, to a neighborhood he'd never been to. The house he found himself in front of still showed a skin of blue insulation, the siding yet to be installed. Paul let himself in, drawn unwillingly up the stairs to the attic.

The lack of electric lights did not hinder him any more than it hindered his father. Paul's anger died as he stared at the burns on Gabriel's body, the rage coming off the vampire filling the whole room with its heat.

"Pluto's balls," Paul breathed. "What the hell happened?"

Gabriel pressed a hand against his chest, trying to hold the flesh together long enough for it to seal closed. "We need to plan, and we don't have much time." He winced and swallowed before continuing. "Call Gil. Whatever he wants. I need blood, and I need it now."

CHAPTER TWENTY-FIVE

Amanda woke slowly, fighting her way past an alarming feeling of numbness that somehow had no effect on the pain she was in. Her head was splitting. It was pitch black. It took her a few more seconds to realize that her shoulders hurt because she was hanging by her wrists.

Her knees were bent under her, feet dragging on the floor. Clumsily, she managed to stand, giving herself the few inches she needed to relieve the pressure on her wrists. She rubbed her face against her arm and realized she was blindfolded.

"Mistress?" asked a quavering voice in front of her.

Amanda's head snapped up in surprise, and the movement almost made her black out again. She hadn't felt anyone else in the room. She still couldn't.

She couldn't feel Gabriel at all.

Panic rose up like bile from her knotted stomach, but she forced it away. She took a deep, slow breath, and then another. Her dry throat threatened to start her coughing. "Who are you?" she managed to croak.

"Nicholas," he answered. She heard him move, shifting his weight. Metal clanked above him. "Are you hurt badly, Mistress? They hit you very hard. I think you have a concussion."

"I don't know." It was taking a lot of concentration to stay standing. She swayed, and the clanking noise was repeated above her head. "Why are you calling me that?"

"He's a thrall, not stupid. He knows who and what you are."

Amanda couldn't place the woman's voice at first. She turned her head, carefully, trying to hear more clearly.

"You are close enough to your master now that the boy can feel it even within the circle," the voice continued, sounding exhausted.

Circle? The bone-deep weariness in the voice jogged Amanda's memory, though the sun was still well below the horizon. "He's not my master, Elizabeth." Amanda's voice cracked, and the last word came out as a wheeze. She clenched her teeth against the urge to cough. "I'm so thirsty. I don't suppose you have any water?"

Elizabeth gave a short, clipped laugh. "After observing you last night, water is not what I expected you to be wanting. Perhaps you are not yet lost."

Amanda heard Elizabeth murmur something, but she couldn't make it out. The words grated on her ears like no language she'd ever heard, but maybe that was just her headache. Nicholas shifted uncomfortably in his chains. The repressive numbness eased slightly.

"I can't take that chance, though, for your own sake as well as my own. Gabriel's hold on you is deep. We are going to keep you contained here until this is all over." Elizabeth's voice changed quality, as if she turned her head to speak to someone else. "Give her some water. Do not step on the lines."

Heavy footsteps approached. Rough fingers touched Amanda's face, and she jerked back, then whimpered in pain.

"Easy there," said a male voice. "Here's your water." He had a light Southern accent.

A plastic cup was placed to her mouth, tilted until the liquid washed over her cracked lips. Amanda drank the water eagerly, but it was thin and bitter and did nothing to assuage the dryness in her mouth and throat. Then the cold water hit her stomach and she doubled over, gasping, her belly cramping into a hard knot. The little water that was left spilled over her chin, splattering onto the floor.

"I thought as much," Elizabeth sighed. "Too far changed even for water."

Amanda's knees gave out and she hung dangling from the chains. She heard the man's retreating footsteps, and again Elizabeth muttered something. The sound of it made her skin crawl, though she couldn't say why. The numbness returned. Amanda coughed, then wished she hadn't as stars exploded across her vision. The back of her skull was pure agony. *What the hell did she hit me with, that it hasn't healed yet?*

She remembered that part now—it had been too fuzzy when she first woke up to recall clearly. Only moments after Gabriel had left her, Elizabeth had appeared out of nowhere. *Please, Amanda, you're both in danger.*

I have to speak with you! And like a fool, she had followed her out of the bar and around the corner of the building to get a little privacy. Elizabeth's form had blurred in the way that Gabriel's did at top speed—Amanda hadn't even seen the blow coming.

Nicholas was shouting something. Amanda took a careful breath, and another. Steadying herself, she stood back up. She swayed but managed to stay on her feet.

"Be easy, boy," Elizabeth was saying. "She's all right. We have no intentions of harming either of you."

Amanda grunted, and had to force the words out past the throbbing in her head. "I feel real safe, let me tell you."

"She fed from you," Nicholas said. His voice held both anger and envy. "I watched her do it, when they first brought you here. You were fighting them, so she made you weak."

That bitch! Amanda growled low in her throat. "You said you would help me."

"I am helping you," Elizabeth insisted. "I won't let him destroy you. I won't watch it happen. It's time his evil was ended. Last I checked you still did not want to become a vampire, but after watching you last night, I wonder if you haven't changed your mind." She sounded wounded, as if Amanda had betrayed her.

"I have not changed my mind!" Amanda's voice broke, and she fell into a fit of ragged coughing. When she could breathe again, she whispered, sick with despair and worry, "Don't do this, Elizabeth. He'll kill you. You know he will."

"If it was just her, maybe," the man said, his voice firm and confident. "But between all of us, we'll take him down. Don't you worry."

"Who are you?"

"Enrique Morales, little lady. I kill vampires."

Amanda jerked, setting off another coughing fit. "So you're a murderer just as much as he is," she finally managed to whisper.

Morales laughed. "Self-defense! Well, pre-emptive self-defense."

Amanda tried not to look toward Elizabeth, but failed.

Morales correctly interpreted her movement. "Now, I know all about Miss Elizabeth there. We all do. Couldn't have taken out the Fury without her to lure the bitch in." His voice carried a tone of awe, as if he still couldn't believe it. "Some of us're more comfortable with Elizabeth than others. Me, well, I'd share dinner with old Beelzebub himself if it meant a crack at Gabriel. He's made himself a name, he has." Enrique's voice hardened. "Tain't a pretty one, as I reckon you know. Never heard of anyone as needs killing like he does."

"But what about all the vampires that will come to try and claim Madison?" Amanda's lip curled. "Or is Madison supposed to be Elizabeth's reward?"

"No!" Elizabeth's retort cracked against the walls, reverberating. "Gabriel is by far the most powerful vampire on the continent. Any newcomers will be easy to deal with in comparison. I'm a fairly weak vampire; they'll think nothing of challenging me. The hunters and I can make this city into a giant vampire trap."

And meanwhile, you get to live here unopposed and protected as the cover-story for the hunters. God, it just might work. We'll lose a few people every time a new vampire comes through, but compared to even one baby vampire, that's nothing. Amanda swallowed hard, tried to hide her fear. "What are you going to do?"

"Don't you worry," Morales said again, with an edge of condescension. "We're professionals. We've got it covered."

Amanda swayed again. "Please, can you take the blindfold off?"

"I'm afraid not, Amanda," Elizabeth answered with genuine regret. "The spell I have placed around you is most complex, and though I have studied sorcery for three centuries, I am only so strong." Her words were slow and heavy with weariness. "Isolde's presence forced us to act before all of my set spells were in place. It's possible that, even with the circle containing your telepathy, you might be able to influence someone if you could see their eyes. You'll have to be patient."

"Elizabeth, please…" She ignored her anger, concentrating on the pain, the thirst—more like true thirst than the hunger, was that part of the spell?—making herself feel like prey. Helpless. "I'm so thirsty." She *was* thirsty, desperately so, but not as weak as she pretended. *If I can just get her in here, maybe…or if I can get her to take me out…* "He wouldn't let me feed last night."

Elizabeth sighed. "I am sorry to leave you here in such a state, but I think it will be safer for everyone if you remain weakened. It will be easier to keep you contained, until you are in your right mind again. Once he is dead and his bond to you severed, you'll see this temporary suffering to be worth it."

"Come on, now that she's awake we should get back up front. He could be here at any time." Enrique clumped away to Amanda's left. There was a click and a creak of hinges.

"Don't worry, Amanda. He won't be able to resist the fact that someone took what is his. It will all be over soon." Elizabeth's boot heels clicked across the floor.

This is all happening too fast! Amanda couldn't think of anything to say that might keep them there or give her more information. The door creaked and clicked again, this time with a thunk, probably a bar being dropped in place.

Amanda took a deep breath. "How long was I out, Nicholas?"

"Not long, Mistress. An hour, less."

"Are you blindfolded, too?"

His chains rattled. "No, Mistress, I am not."

"That's one thing," she muttered. "Are we alone?"

"Yes. But I saw two more people outside the door, and there's a video camera in the corner."

"Shit." Amanda tried rubbing her head against her shoulder, but the blindfold was tied too tightly and wouldn't budge. "How far apart are we? I'm assuming we're both chained to the ceiling?"

"Yes, Mistress. About five feet apart." He paused. "It looks like an old freezer. The door is very thick."

Amanda tugged futilely at the wrist shackles and the chain. Even if she were not weakened, she doubted she'd have been able to break free. The physical gifts were not her strong ones. "Is there anything else you can see?"

Again the rattle of chain as the boy looked around. Just from echoes of the sound, Amanda could guess at the size of the room. The ceiling had to be eleven feet high, at least.

"There's a body bag in the corner, and there is paint on the floor," he answered. "A circle around us, and then there are a bunch of symbols, and another circle around that. I don't know what the symbols are." He sounded apologetic. "There is one clear path through the symbols. That's the way the man came and left. Miss Elizabeth was very insistent that no one touch the paint when they brought you in."

Amanda's nose twitched. The thick tang of fear caressed her senses. "The symbols make you afraid?"

Nicholas whispered, "Yes, Mistress."

Please, please let this work. "Why do they frighten you, Nicholas?"

She heard him swallow. "I don't like to look at them."

"I need you to look at them," she told him, her voice cold. "Look at them and tell me why they frighten you."

He drew a shaking breath. Amanda strained toward him, her mouth open, tasting the air. Almost at once the power came to her, like brandy-soaked burrs rolling over her tongue. *Oh, yes!*

"Tell me, Nicholas!" she commanded.

"They hurt my eyes," he whimpered. "It's like they move, but they don't move. It's like they're watching me back." His breathing was harder, almost sobs. "Please let me look away, Mistress."

Her nausea was gone. The headache was still there, but less. She didn't think she'd pass out again. "All right, Nicholas. You can look away."

He did sob this time. "Thank you, Mistress."

She smiled at him. "My brave Nicholas. Why do you call me that?"

"Gabriel is my master." He said this simply, as if it should be obvious. "You are precious to him, his chosen one. We must protect and obey you as we would him."

Amanda was taken aback. "He said so?"

"Not in words, but that is his will."

Queen of mind-slaves. Lovely. Amanda pushed the knowledge aside. She reached up, feeling the chain with her fingertips. It was wide, but she thought she could close her hand around both chains at once. *Here goes.* Amanda held her hands as close together as possible, leapt straight up, and tried to catch the chains. The first two tries she only managed to catch one end, which would make for awkward climbing, but the third time she got it right.

It was slow going at first because her hands didn't have a lot of slack, but the farther she climbed, the more slack there was. "I guess we'll see how closely they're watching, eh? I don't suppose the camera's anywhere near me."

"No, Mistress, it's in the far corner across from the door."

"That would have made things too easy." Her questing fingers found the bend in the chain where it threaded through a thick metal loop. The loop was part of a metal plate, bolted to the ceiling with very large bolts. The ceiling also felt like metal. *Makes sense if this is a freezer.* Taking a firm grip on the chain, Amanda flipped herself upside down. She braced her feet on either side of the metal plate and tried to pull it out of the ceiling.

* * * *

There was only one way to get to the freezer where Amanda and Nicholas were imprisoned. While Morales had kept Isolde chasing him around the state, the other hunters had modified the old slaughterhouse into a series of connected interior rooms, each with fortifications and barricades to hide behind. Remote-controlled cameras scanned the entire length of the channel through which the vampire must pass.

They'd set up the surveillance command center in the last room before the short hall that led to the freezer. Now, Enrique Morales stared at the monitors in disbelief as police squad cars began to fill the street outside.

"What in blazes?" Morales grabbed his headset. "Jefferson, you there?"

"We're in position."

Morales could see the first team of hunters on his monitors, a full dozen pulled in from all over the country, crouching behind their barricades, their weapons locked on the first of the steel doors. The front two ranks sported flamethrowers, while the rest had various automatic weapons. "Hold fire. I repeat, hold fire. We got cops outside."

Motion seen from the corner of his eye caught Morales's attention. He scanned the other monitors, did a double-take, and cursed. "Briggs! Marsters!"

"Here, Boss," came the tinny reply.

"The girl's tryin' to rip out the ceiling in there. Trank her if you have to, but keep those two under wraps 'til the vampire's dead."

"Got it."

The second team, made up of the remaining hunters Morales had taken with him when he ran south, was in the control room with him. The eight hunters took positions at the two doors.

"Keep your eyes peeled," Morales warned them. "He's still gotta come through here if he wants the girl."

He glanced at Elizabeth. She sat motionless in a chair, her hand clenched around something in her fist.

Morales licked his lips, his eyes returning to the monitors. "You're sure he's coming?"

"He's not coming," she replied, her brow furrowing as she concentrated. "He's here."

CHAPTER TWENTY-SIX

Paul crouched with the SWAT team outside the slaughterhouse's front door, cloaked in shadows and projecting for all he was worth.

Don't notice me.

The uniform that the mages had provided him fit well enough, but there was no way the sword strapped to his hip would pass even the most casual inspection. It would be better if the humans didn't see him at all, and the aura would keep them from hearing him or bumping into him accidently.

The industrial park was tucked away on the south-side border between Madison and Fitchburg, sandwiched between the Beltline on one side and half a mile of wetlands on the other. The slaughterhouse itself had stood empty for months, a 1950s rectangle of cinderblock and concrete that squatted cheek-by-jowl with the other one-story concrete-rectangle businesses on the street. All of them were deserted at this late—or rather, early—hour.

There hadn't been a lot of time for recon. One of the mages had been able to scrye some parts of the building, but much of it had been opaque. "Not specifically warded against scrying, I don't think," she'd said as she stared into her silver bowl, "but more like a byproduct of the spells that are there. They feel tight. Meant to contain." She shook herself. "I can't tell you more without alerting the mage who laid them."

"Well, at least we know where Amanda isn't," Gabriel had muttered.

Now Paul tried to touch his father's mind, but the paths were still blocked. His fingers tightened around the gun in his hand.

I hate walking into traps. Especially magical ones.

The warded places all connected, snaking through the interior to a room near the back. They'd seen enough to know that the loading dock doors had been disabled and the dock filled from floor to ceiling with concrete traffic barriers. The room that the back door opened into had been likewise blocked up.

Which left the front door.

The leader of the SWAT team held up three fingers.

Paul's muscles tensed, and he felt that old, familiar, pre-battle adrenaline rush.

Gods, he'd missed this.

Two fingers.

Keep it together, Gallus. This isn't like the old days.

One finger.

In perfect unison, they all let out a deep, slow breath.

Then they flung the door open and burst into the first room.

* * * *

Gabriel stared up at the drain cover. It was convex rather than concave, meant to catch the more solid bits of the slaughtered animals without completely blocking the drain, so the offal didn't end up in the sewer where the vampire now stood. The building itself may have been vacant and clean, but the sewer still stank of old blood. "That's not a lot of space."

"It'll be enough." Martin dropped the welder's mask down over his face and gestured. The two shifters he'd brought with him each bent down, grabbed one leg, and lifted Martin straight up so he didn't have to hold the blow torch over his head.

"Y'see, the floor slopes down a bit so the blood runs down the drain proper, and the drain keeps the metal plate your hunters put over it from bending too much." Sparks and bits of metal rained down as he touched the flame to the edge of the drain. "So all we have to do is make a bigger hole in the drain so's Andrew and Devon can get through."

The slaughtering area had been one of the places they'd been able to see in the bowl, and it hadn't been hard to figure out why there was a big stack of concrete blocks sitting in the middle of it.

"The trick with sneaking into warded places is that most wards usually don't trouble folks who're in-skin, just the ones who're out. So once you're past the wards, you can pretty much do as you please. There we go."

There was a hole a little bigger than a half-dollar in the drain now. Andrew and Devon lowered Martin back to the floor.

"All right, boys. You know the drill." Martin held out his hands.

The other two shifters dissolved into the air without even so much as a glance at the vampire. Gabriel wasn't sure if they were that brave, that trusting, or simply that ignorant. Without their flesh to hide them, the two seemed to him like spider webs of energy, each thread a miniature life waiting to be harvested.

Gabriel resisted the impulse to eat them, which probably would've been too tempting if he hadn't already fed so well. Five mages had been willing to trade their blood for a future favor, more than enough to heal the damage from the hunters' bomb. None had let Gabriel bite them, of course, although one mage had smelled as if he might've if the others hadn't been there. Something to pursue later.

Then again, maybe not. Mage blood is so very addicting.

The formless shifters coalesced into two brown mice, one in each of Martin's hands. Martin lifted them up and they jumped through the hole in the drain.

In a few seconds, Gabriel knew, two vaporous wisps would come ghosting out from under that pile of concrete, one in search of the breaker box, and the other in search of the generator.

* * * *

Amanda, still hanging upside down from the ceiling, heard a scraping sound from outside. The bar across the freezer door was being raised. Amanda let the chain slide through her hands, landing softly on the metal floor as the door swung open. She went limp in her chains, head hanging forward.

A man with an odd-looking gun in his hands stepped into the room. "You need to keep your feet on the floor there, missy." He leveled the barrel at her chest and took a step closer. "Stop playing possum, we know what you—"

He choked on the rest of the sentence as Amanda raised her head. While she hadn't had any luck trying to get the plate out of the ceiling, she had been able to roll back the blindfold. She threw every ounce of power she had left into one look, clawing at the man's mind through the fog that surrounded her.

"Marsters?" came a woman's voice from the hallway.

Amanda tightened her hold, desperation giving her strength. "Shoot her."

The man's body jerked as he tried to fight the compulsion, but he hadn't been expecting the psychic assault and Amanda had caught him off guard. As the woman stepped into the doorway, Marsters turned. The dart thunked into the woman's shoulder. Her mouth formed an "o" of surprise, and then she crumpled to the floor.

Amanda felt her tenuous hold on him start to slip as he looked at his comrade's still form. "Marsters!"

He jerked again, spinning around to face her, hatred in his eyes. Their gazes locked once more.

"Come to me," she commanded, gritting her teeth. He was a hunter, used to fighting her kind, but Amanda knew she would succeed. She had to.

He took a stiff step forward.

"Yes," she hissed, straining against her chains. She reached deep inside herself, pouring everything she had, her very soul, into her attack. "Come!"

He stumbled forward two more steps. Amanda's knees gave out, her heart thudding arrhythmically as she pushed harder. Something snapped somewhere deep in her psyche, but she didn't dare let herself be distracted. *Come on!*

Whimpering, he crossed the painted lines, into the circle.

The spell shattered, and Amanda collapsed.

Marsters shuddered, then he turned and dragged his partner out of the cell.

* * * *

Paul was the last one through the front door, which was just as well.

His gaze swept the room as he entered. The walls were close, a narrow corridor that ran for fifty feet or so before making a sharp turn. The entire length of it—floor, walls, and ceiling—was covered with painted symbols that shimmered like sunlight under the overhead lights.

The glyphs didn't just shine; they *moved*, twisting and writhing until it seemed like the whole room was alive.

Paul winced and raised his hands to block out the sight, stumbling over the flat, even floor.

From down the corridor, a man shouted, "That's the leech!"

"Get down!" someone yelled next to him. A hand grabbed his arm, but Paul was already falling, rolling blindly for cover as a hail of bullets converged on the spot where he'd just been. The thunder of gunfire bounced off the concrete walls, so loud it was almost a weapon by itself.

From just ahead, the comforting thud of rounds hitting a ballistic shield echoed under the clangor.

"Who the fuck are you?" demanded the person next to him.

Shit. He'd stopped bending light when he saw the glyphs.

There was no time for subtleties. If the hunters thought he was his father, they'd press the attack even in the face of well-trained opposition.
Paul tore through the defenses of the officers closest to him, seizing their
minds even as they screamed.

Tear gas grenades. Now!

* * * *

"What do you mean, that's not Gabriel?" Morales pointed at the monitor, as if Elizabeth hadn't been looking at the right one. "The spell hit him
just like you said it would."

The man Elizabeth had dazzled was lost now among the rest of the uni-
formed bodies, who appeared to be regrouping and falling back to the
parking lot. "Do you think I don't know what he looks like?" she snapped
back. "Get your men out of—"

Elizabeth whirled and stared at the monitor covering the freezer. Morales followed her gaze in time to see the door of the freezer close, but
Amanda and Nicholas were secure. Nicholas appeared to be shouting
again, reaching futilely toward Amanda's still form.

Elizabeth touched her headset. "Briggs, Marsters, what happened?"

"The girl's taking a nap," Marsters replied, sounding out of breath. "She
didn't want to go out, so I gave her a tap on the head to help her along."

"Idiot, you broke the containment spell!"

"What's it matter? The vampire's already here and the bitch is out like a
light."

Morales interrupted. "You two just stay out there. And keep another
tranquilizer ready—"

The lights flickered off, and the monitors went dead.

"The hell?" Morales cursed. At least the headsets were on battery. "Jefferson, get out of there. Elizabeth says that's not him."

Silence.

"Jefferson?"

* * * *

Paul kept his eyes squeezed shut and listened to the officers' retreat. It
was a risk, waiting like this. Bending light didn't hide his heat signature; if
any of the hunters had thermal vision goggles they'd see him even through
the dark and the tear gas.

That is, they would if they also had gas masks. Paul doubted they'd
thought that far, but you never knew.

He adjusted his own mask. Once the officers were out the door—he
hoped he hadn't done any permanent damage to the ones he'd broken, but

this would be a lot easier without them underfoot—Paul unsheathed his sword and loped down the hall.

The air sang against the edge of the gladius as he moved, and Paul smiled. He hated guns; if not for them, he'd still be a mercenary. Even he couldn't survive being nearly cut in half by machine gun fire, and the first time he'd seen it happen to one of his mates he'd gone AWOL and never set foot on a battlefield again.

Guns had their uses, just like archers and slingers and spear-throwers, but it was the close combat that Paul missed. The blood and the pain and the rush of the conquest, and the life being spilled into the air so thick you could almost feed just by breathing. *Yes.*

The battlefield had always been the place where his dual natures were most united.

The corner was just ahead. Beyond it, he heard scrambling feet, moaning, coughing.

The men who had killed his sister.

Run for me, you bastards.

* * * *

Gabriel climbed out of the sewer and into a room so dark even he could barely see.

Andrew and Devon stood next to the pile of concrete blocks, which they'd moved off the drain cover once the power was cut and the cameras stopped working.

Martin, who said he didn't have a skin small enough to fit through the hole in the drain, climbed out after Gabriel. "Smells like they used the tear gas already. You'll want this, at least until it starts to clear out." He handed Gabriel a gas mask. "I imagine even your kind gets eye irritation and the like."

Gabriel took the mask from him and slipped it on. "I appreciate your help."

Martin chuckled. "Oh, we'll make you pay for it, I've no doubt. Besides, the quieter and more normal we can keep this, the better. I have a feeling you're not a subtle chap when it comes to taking back what's yours. We don't want another bombing. The one will be hard enough to explain."

"That's a problem for Gil and his lot." The mages had their fingers in civil service and government; the shifters went in more for construction and utilities. "They can always blame it on the students."

"Aye. D'you want us to leave the hole open?" Martin nudged the drain cover with the toe of his boot.

Gabriel was already examining the walls, looking for a way into the rest of the building. "No. We don't want the authorities thinking anyone escaped."

"I doubt they'd notice; this whole section is walled off," Devon said.

Gabriel made a quick circuit of the room. It looked like the hunters had built new interior walls to create their winding corridor trap. He ran a hand over the cinderblocks. This had taken planning. A lot of planning, and a lot of time.

Be on your toes, Paulus.

Devon was right. This area connected to the dock and the utility closet, but the new walls cut it off from the rest of the building. He could break through the walls, but it would take a few minutes even for him, and it wasn't exactly quiet. *Hell, these walls are probably thicker than the exterior ones. But then I'd have to deal with the cops* and *the hunters.*

He scanned the room again, looking for ideas.

Then he looked up.

"Martin," Gabriel said, his eyes following the air duct, "could I borrow that blow torch before you go?"

* * * *

Jefferson stumbled into the second kill zone almost more by luck than by intention. Morales was yelling in his ear through the headset, but Jefferson couldn't stop coughing long enough to answer. Tear gas made his eyes water and his nose run and his lungs burn, and it was damn hard to think through the stinging pain and the choking cough. He recognized where he was only because he was following the wall, and his hand touched the metal door.

Was everyone in? He thought he'd been the last to leave the first choke point, but he couldn't be sure in the dark. No time to wait. If he could get the door bolted it would slow the vampire down, and they didn't need to be able to see in order to shoot through the murder holes. He grabbed the edge of the door and started to swing it shut.

Something hit the door from the other side, throwing Jefferson into the wall. Light blazed across his vision, but it wasn't the kind of light that let you see anything. It was just pain that hadn't caught up to him yet.

The air stirred as something passed him.

From farther in the room came a wet, tearing sound. A second later, Jefferson heard someone scream.

There was a panicked babble of voices, the sounds of feet pounding on the floor, grunts and curses. The thud of bodies hitting concrete.

Jefferson struggled to get up, but his limbs wouldn't move. The attempt made the back of his head explode in an agony of red-hot spikes. He wondered if he'd split it open when he hit the wall.

Someone started shooting. Travis, he guessed, based on the incoherent screaming that went with the barrage of submachine gun fire. *Up and down,* Jefferson thought in exasperation, *not just left and right, you stupid kid.*

Travis made a noise. It was something like "huuh!" with some clicky, groaning vowels on the end.

The gun fire stopped.

"Well, that'll bring the cops back in," a man murmured.

A chill shot through the hunter. The man's voice was unnaturally smooth, almost breathy, like some bad porno actor's. That voice had no place here, with the tear gas and cordite and the warm, wet liquid soaking into Jefferson's pants.

The leech walked past him again.

Jefferson struggled to move his hand, to find a gun, to do something while the creature's back was turned. He heard the metal door boom shut, and the bolts slide into place, but God help him, all Jefferson managed to do was twitch a little. The effort made him wheeze.

The leech was on him in an instant. "I missed one. How careless of me. Father was right, it *has* been a long time."

Jefferson tried to clear his streaming eyes, but it was no good.

His labored breaths turned into gurgles as the sword kissed his throat.

CHAPTER TWENTY-SEVEN

Elizabeth clutched the silver amulet so tightly that she'd squeezed most of the blood from her hand. Gabriel was actively fighting her now, trying to break free of the fetters she'd placed on him.

He is so strong.

But she'd known that. It didn't matter. When Morales had shown her the amulet, she'd realized what it was, and what she had to do. She was literally holding a piece of Gabriel in her hand.

All she had to do was keep holding on.

The hunters were scrambling around the room, piling furniture and equipment into a barricade in front of the door that led to the freezer while Morales barked orders. The gunfire had died out in the corridor, and none of the hunters who'd been in the first team were answering on their headsets.

"Elizabeth, can you slow him down any once he gets in here?"

She stifled a flash of irritation. Did they expect her to do everything? "No. It's taking all I have left to maintain the block on his mind. Besides, my spells take time and preparation. If you want something quick and messy, find yourself a hedge mage."

And I cannot harm him. Not directly. Of course, the one in the corridor isn't him, anyway.

But Gabriel was near.

Isn't it enough that I forced him to choose a fledgling, to make himself vulnerable at a time and place of my design? That I hid your presence— and my own—from him in his own city, and created the spell that would have distracted him long enough for your men to do their jobs? That I led to her death one who counted me as her friend so that we might succeed?

Poor Isolde.

Still, the amulet had come in damn handy.

There was a loud thud from the corridor. The door rattled.

Elizabeth crouched in a corner, away from the line of fire. The hunters gathered behind their barricade. The jet at the end of Morales's flamethrower cast an eerie blue light over their faces.

Behind them, the door that led to the freezer flew open.

Marsters stood in the doorway. With careful deliberation he pointed the barrel of Briggs's machine gun down at the hunters and squeezed the trigger.

Morales and two of the others managed to dive over the barricade while the rest were cut down. Elizabeth shot to her feet, the spell splintering as her concentration shattered.

"It's about time you got here," Marsters said conversationally, sweeping the barrel back and forth with no real attempt to aim. "I thought I was going to have to rescue myself."

There was a laugh from the corridor, and then the door buckled as something hit it.

Morales and the two surviving hunters returned fire from behind the barricade. Bullets tore through Marsters's shoulder, and the rifle fell from hands that suddenly wouldn't work right.

Then the flamethrower caught Marsters full in the chest.

There was a muffled scream from back by the freezer, and Marsters's expression changed from cheerful determination to surprise as more bullets followed. He toppled to the floor. He coughed once, a confused look on his face, and was still.

Even as Marsters started to fall, the door to the corridor gave way. One hunter turned and started firing at the door; Morales and the other man scrambled for cover.

From overhead, the shriek of tortured metal.

Elizabeth looked up in time to see Gabriel launch himself at the hunter who was firing. There was a huge hole torn out of the heating duct that ran along the ceiling.

The man in the corridor burst into the room as Gabriel landed on the hunter. The human went sprawling, and Gabriel snapped the hunter's neck with one savage twist.

Elizabeth didn't wait to see more. Before Gabriel or his ally could cross the room, Elizabeth bolted out the door that led to the freezer.

* * * *

Paul leapt over the barricade, stabbing the hunter with the gun purely because that one was closer to Paul's sword hand. The steeply angled tip burrowed into the soft spot where the man's neck met his shoulder despite the fact that his adversary wore no gorget, no breastplate or cuirass. Old habits.

Gabriel flew past, out the door and after Elizabeth. Paul paid them no mind. His momentum was carrying him past the last hunter so he spun, ripping the blade free and bringing it around to parry the barrel of the flamethrower.

Fire and fuel shot past him, bathing the room with a warm, ruddy glow.

Paul's feet skidded and slipped in the pooling blood as he tried to change direction and avoid the burning corpse of Amanda's puppet, and the hunter was able to disengage his weapon. As the hunter stepped back, Paul lunged forward, his free hand grabbing onto part of the barricade, the gladius sweeping up to knock the flamethrower high. The hunter fired it anyway, but Paul hauled himself forward, and the burning fuel that splashed from the ceiling fell just behind him.

"You're old for a hunter," Paul said as he got his feet under him. He advanced, his blade keeping the nozzle from pointing directly at him. "Are you the ringleader?"

"Enrique Morales," the hunter growled. He moved the tip of the flamethrower in a tight circle, a fencer's move that might have disarmed Paul if he'd allowed it. But that wasn't the hunter's intention. "Perhaps you've heard of me?"

As the nozzle crossed under Paul's guard, Morales fired it again, and only Paul's unnatural speed let him dodge aside. "I have. Was it you, then?"

Morales didn't answer, using the brief reprieve to circle around Paul so that the hunter wasn't backing straight into the wall anymore. His finger still tight on the trigger, Morales tried to bring the gout of flame to bear on his target. Paul jumped over it, tucking his feet close to his chest as his sword once again swept the barrel aside.

"Were you the one who killed my sister?"

Morales backpedaled, trying to disengage before Paul landed, but the sword didn't stop its sweep. It carried the barrel upward again, the gun sliding almost the full length of the blade before Paul's feet touched the concrete and he shot forward. His free hand reached up to grab the barrel, and he brought the sword down and across in a vicious slash.

The metal bit in, but Morales piked backward at the last second and the tip only sliced across the hunter's bullet-proof vest.

Morales let go of the flamethrower, his hands darting for the pistols holstered at his sides.

"Was it you?"

Paul dropped the weapons and charged at Morales, tearing off his gas mask and throwing it at the hunter's face.

Morales ducked instinctively, twisting to one side, pistols free of the holsters, but there was no time to bring them in line. Paul crashed into him, his hands grabbing the hunter's wrists and squeezing until the bones popped and Morales screamed.

The gas mask had helped Paul keep his head. Now, scent assaulted him. The acrid tang of burning fuel and the stink of perforated bowels were nothing compared to the gallons of blood that covered the floor, or the brazen sweetness that pulsed under the hunter's skin.

But under all that, faint as a memory, sharp as the gladius, was the scent of Isolde's death.

With the deadly inevitability of sunrise, Paul raised his eyes to the hunter's.

Morales's screams turned into shrieks.

Paul tore through the man's mind. He needed to know.

He needed to *see.*

His skin felt so tight and hot that he thought it might crack like a dry riverbed. Every line and wrinkle that showed his age burned as if the sun were just behind him, etching time into his flesh. He needed to kill this man. He needed to kill this man *right now*, before the sun withered him down to nothing and his ashes scattered on the scorched wind.

Not yet. I need to see.

When he found Morales's memory of killing Isolde, Paul gave himself up to his need with vengeful joy.

He didn't recall just when he tore the hunter's throat out, but after Morales's heartsblood was only a memory on his tongue and the slow burn of the healing was beginning to fade, Paul regretted not having his father turn the bastard just so he could kill him again.

* * * *

Gabriel saw Elizabeth dash out the door and sprang after her, landing squarely on her back and sending her sprawling.

"Get off of me!" she yelled, and a wave of nausea went through him as she tried desperately to assert her will over his.

He laughed, grabbing her by the hair and driving her head against the concrete floor. Between the potent mage-blood and the long-missed battle euphoria, Gabriel was having a hard time not gleefully tearing her into pieces. But he had things to do first. "You can't command me, Elizabeth. I took care of that already, remember?" He picked her up and body-slammed her into the freezer, pinning her there while he lifted the bar and opened the thick door.

"Took you long enough," Amanda said from inside, her voice echoing in the large room. "Did you bring the key?" She rattled her chains impatiently.

Gabriel smiled at his protégé's imperious tone. "Where is it?" He turned to look for Paul, but his son wasn't there.

"Morales had it. Unfortunately, Marsters didn't make it that far, and I can't wake up Briggs." There was satisfaction and annoyance both in Amanda's reply.

With Elizabeth's spell gone, Gabriel had no difficulty touching Paul's thoughts. The chaotic rage he found there nearly sent him reeling, and he retreated quickly. *Not the best timing, but not exactly surprising, I suppose.* "Paul, see if you can find the keys before you completely dismember Morales, if you'd be so kind?" Gabriel yelled toward the control room, not knowing whether Paul would hear or understand.

"Stupid, fool girl! It would have been over!" Elizabeth shouted at Amanda from where Gabriel held her.

Amanda shook her head. "Not like this. Maybe Gabriel is rubbing off on me, but this whole thing, this whole stupid contest, is just between him and me."

"All the lives he takes after this will be on your head," Elizabeth growled. "Did you think we were doing this just to save you? He has killed hundreds of thousands of people!"

"She's right, you know." Gabriel grinned wryly at Amanda, but never took his eyes off his target. "My dear, sweet Elizabeth. Give me the amulet."

He felt her trying to gather her will, to make one final attempt to use her advantage. He smashed her head against the wall again. "You're only making this harder on yourself." He leaned close to whisper in her ear. "Give. Me. The. Amulet."

She was no longer standing on her own, sagging drunkenly in Gabriel's grip. With a defeated moan, Elizabeth's hand opened, the tiny silver capsule falling out. Gabriel scooped it up before it could even hit the floor. It was still coated with Isolde's dried blood, and that scent soured his triumph and made his head buzz with repressed fury. *My daughter.*

"I wish Isolde hadn't come," Elizabeth said softly. "That wasn't part of the original plan, but there was no way we could kill you both, not fighting together. We had to move the timetable up."

"You had to kill her." His voice was surprisingly even.

She shuddered. "How else do you stop one such as she? How do you trap a skinshifter who is also a vampire? If there is such a spell, I do not know it. Nor could I hold it and have any hope of dealing with you."

"And just how did you plan on dealing with me without Isolde's amulet? How did you get around the binding I laid on you?"

Her laugh was bitter. "You bound me from trying to harm you, but rousing your need to claim a fledgling—how does that harm you?" She twisted around to give him a rictus grin over her shoulder, her eyes already flat and dead. "You of all people should know what I can do with a little sympathetic magic, blood of my blood."

Paul walked out of the control room covered in gore and looking about five years younger than he had the last time Gabriel saw him. *I guess Morales still had some juice left in him.* Paul didn't look at Elizabeth or his father as he passed, but he muttered, "I found the keys," as he entered the freezer.

Elizabeth watched Paul with a bemused wonder. "He's halfblood, isn't he? I thought that was just a legend."

"We like to keep it that way." Gabriel threaded his fingers through her hair almost lovingly, close to the scalp, and gave her a little shake. "Where is Isolde's body?"

"In the freezer. I knew you'd come for it. The girl would have been enough, but I knew you'd come for Isolde."

From inside the freezer, Paul's voice rang with distaste. "I am not walking into that. Catch." The jingle of keys followed, and an annoyed "Hmph!" from Amanda as she caught them.

Gabriel took a knife from his boot and opened a small wound in his forearm, slipping the silver capsule under the skin. There was no safer place for his own physical essence than inside his own body. Unable to hide a sigh of relief, he called out to his son. "Is she there?"

There was a pause. *Yes,* Paul whispered back, with an ache in his voice that Gabriel understood far too well. *They took her heart.*

"Where's her heart?" The words were a clipped, low growl.

"Morales burned it, while I was asleep. That's how they found the amulet." Elizabeth closed her eyes. "He scattered the ashes."

"He knew what he was about, I'll give him that." The fingers in her hair tightened, drawing her head back. "Would you like to make it up to her?"

One last shudder ran through Elizabeth's body. "Just do it."

The blade bit deep into her neck as he drew it across her throat, scraping against the spine.

"Nox, I shed this blood for you, that you may watch over my daughter and yours, Ulpia Isolde, called Constantinus. May this death give her sustenance on her last journey."

He whispered the words in the Latin of his youth, knowing Paul would understand but Amanda would not. From inside the freezer came Paul's murmured, "Let it be so."

Flipping Elizabeth's twitching body onto her back, Gabriel cut out her heart.

* * * *

Amanda fumbled with the keys while the man from the Union House—Paul, she supposed—picked up the black body bag that had been lying in a corner behind her.

"Get yourself out of those," he told her, heading back out the door, "and bring the chain with you."

"What about Nicholas?" she asked, fitting the key into one of the locks.

"He's staying here for the police to find. After all, his abduction is why they were dispatched. At least, as far as they know. Two sets of chains might make them wonder."

Amanda shrugged, pulling the chain through the loop in the ceiling. A moment later, she stepped out of her prison, the long chain doubled up and draped over her shoulders.

Gabriel knelt on the floor beside Briggs. "Shut and bar the door behind you. They're only looking for one prisoner right now, and I'd like to keep it that way." He glanced up at Paul as the bloody man set the body bag down. "Flamethrower?"

"I think it's still in one piece." Paul walked away with a sort of weary, serene calm that didn't look at all healthy.

Not that any of this is particularly sane. Shaking her head, Amanda did as Gabriel had told her, wrapping her blindfold around her fingers just in case they checked for fingerprints. When she looked back, she saw that Gabriel had propped Briggs against the wall. His wrist was at her mouth.

Amanda fought down a surge of illogical jealousy. "What are you doing?"

"Drugs don't work on vampires," he said, his voice a little breathy. "I'm hoping my blood will neutralize the tranquilizer." He looked up at Amanda as she approached. There was respect in his eyes. "You did well."

She didn't know whether to flush at his praise or wince. The memory of taking over Marsters, controlling him like a puppet, was still fresh and disturbingly invigorating. *Although the bullets and the flamethrower hurt like hell.* She settled for a neutral, "I did what I had to do."

Gabriel smiled. "You could have waited to see if they killed me. Their plan was a good one—without Paul's help, rescuing you would have been rather difficult, even with the cops and the shifters."

"And if they killed you, who's to say they wouldn't have offed Elizabeth and me as well?" It would've been a good argument if it had crossed her mind at the time. Instead, her concern had been for Gabriel. "Besides, maybe I didn't like the idea of a vampire turf war."

"That's the biggest reason the others are helping." Briggs was swallowing now, and Gabriel's voice was rough.

"Others?" Amanda asked partly out of curiosity and partly because his eyes were starting to glaze over.

He seemed to appreciate the distraction, blinking and trying to focus on her instead of on Briggs. "The mages are running cover-up and police liaison. The shifters…" He stopped speaking for a moment, teeth clenching as something resembling pain crossed his face. "The shifters got me in here, and they're making sure no one leaves the building that shouldn't."

Briggs made a choking sound and pushed at Gabriel's arm. She tried to scramble away, her eyes wide and wild, but Gabriel pounced, pinning her hands to the wall.

"Hold her," Gabriel said.

Amanda hesitated, then obeyed, crouching behind Gabriel and reaching around him to where he held the woman's wrists against the wall above her head. "What are you doing?"

The vampire let go of the hunter once Amanda had her secured. He stroked Briggs's cheek, his gaze distant as if he were listening to something far away. "She can tell me if there are any more vampire hunters."

"Fuck you," Briggs wheezed, her face wrinkled up with disgust and hate. She kept her gaze turned away from the vampire, but when she saw Amanda, Briggs spared her a venomous glare before looking away from her, too. "Traitorous bitch."

Amanda couldn't really say anything to that. "I'm sure those cops you mentioned will be here any minute. We should go."

"First things first." Gabriel shook himself, settling down to business. "It will take them a little while to break through the barriers in the corridor, and I am not leaving until I know that all of the hunters are accounted for.

I refuse to tolerate however-many vampire hunters running around in my city, especially when they know where my haven is."

He seized the hunter's chin and forced her to face him. Briggs squeezed her eyes shut, gritting her teeth.

"Have it your way." The vampire leaned forward and bit deep. The hunter's eyes flew open in shock, and Amanda instinctively tried to catch her gaze. But the smell, blood and pain and fear, so close, and the soft sounds of Gabriel feeding, all made her lose her concentration, and Briggs closed her eyes again. Amanda groaned and leaned her head against the cool wall.

Amanda.

She looked back at him and Gabriel kissed her, fierce and hard, his mouth full of blood. *The sweetest prey are other hunters. Consider it a present.*

The blood washed over her tongue—hot and thick, and vital. It didn't have the raw power of Gabriel's blood, but unlike his, this was strong with life, bursting with it, even more than Sunny's had been. Amanda pressed against him, forgetting everything but that taste and the feel of Gabriel's mouth under hers. The vampire broke away with a chuckle.

Keep hold of her hands, and watch with me, he told his protégé as he went back to his feast. *We have work to do here yet.* Amanda sat back, breathing hard, and she and Gabriel slipped into the hunter's mind.

Gabriel soothed his prey with an expert touch, forcing her body to relax even as her will fought him. *Show me, Tawny Briggs,* he whispered, sorting through her thoughts. He saw the face of one of the other hunters and caressed the pleasure centers in her mind. *Show me more,* he told her, worming his way from surface thoughts toward memories.

Amanda felt Briggs's hands clench on her own. *What the hell kind of a name is Tawny?* Still buzzing from the hunter's blood, she brought Briggs's left hand to her lips, flicking her tongue over the woman's skin. One swallow was not enough, could never be enough. *Even her pleasure tastes different,* she mused. Her lips traced the knuckles, her fangs tenderly scraping the skin, hardly enough to even tickle... *Would it count if I was just licking the blood off her skin? We could share her.*

I like the way you're thinking, but we don't have that much time. Back to business, little mouse. Pay attention to her thoughts.

Amanda sighed and concentrated. She could see what Gabriel was seeing, but as the vampire chased thoughts of the other hunters, checking them off in his mind against the ones he knew were dead, she also saw what he was ignoring. Briggs was purposefully remembering the horrors she'd seen in her years as a vampire hunter. Corpse after corpse flickered across her mind's eye—young and old, men and women and children, some peaceful, some as violent as Gabriel's kill on the beach. Amanda saw fewer and fewer bodies the longer the vampire worked, but they grew more and more brutal, as if those images were stronger than his touch. The stench of despair filled Amanda's nose. The hunter's hands were growing cold as Gabriel kept feeding.

Make him stop. Briggs spoke directly to Amanda, but Gabriel answered.

I'm not going to stop, little hunter, he purred, his voice vibrating through the woman in a way Amanda knew too well. Briggs whimpered. *I'm killing you, Tawny. You're dying. Let me make it painless.*

There was just one picture now, a little boy. Briggs clung to that mental image, gained strength from it. *Let me go!*

The vampire considered the image. *A little young for my taste, but then, some like them that way. Your brother, I suppose. Is that why you became a vampire hunter? To protect others like him? Tell me, did you ever find his killer? No, don't answer—if you had, your rage would not still be eating you up like a cancer. Delicious. And now here you are, dying to a vampire's hunger, betrayed by the human you were trying to save. Poetic, isn't it?*

In their minds, Briggs howled in denial and rage.

It's over, Tawny Briggs. Stop fighting. It's time to rest.

"Christ, Gabriel, stop torturing her." Amanda dropped the hunter's hands and turned away, utterly sickened. Bad enough she'd betrayed her own species; she didn't need to assist Gabriel's torture of a helpless woman on top of it. *The hunters were trying to protect me, and I helped kill them all. But I couldn't let them kill Gabriel!* Amanda shook her head, angry with herself. *Dammit, why not?*

A loud crash came from the control room, causing both Gabriel and Amanda to jump and stare toward the door. Gabriel frowned when he realized Amanda wasn't holding Briggs. "I told you to...dammit!"

Amanda turned back in time to see Briggs's hand fall away from her mouth. White foam dripped from her lips. She shuddered once, and was still. She was smiling.

"Cyanide." Gabriel dropped the corpse to the floor. "Nobody carries fucking cyanide pills anymore." He turned to Amanda, snarling. "*Now* you get squeamish?"

There was another crash from the control room. Cursing, the vampire looked down at the obvious bite marks in Briggs's dead flesh. He threw the corpse over by Elizabeth's.

"Any luck, Paul?" he called.

"Yeah, just trying to get it untangled."

Paul came out a moment later with the tank in one hand and the barrel in the other. He eyed the extra corpse but didn't comment. Another crash sounded.

"That wasn't you?"

Paul shook his head. "Cops got through the other barrier faster that I would've thought. I piled some equipment behind what's left of the door, but it won't hold them long."

Setting down the pack, he pointed the nozzle and pulled the trigger, dousing both corpses in liquid flame. Elizabeth's body went up like a torch, burning brightly for a moment before collapsing in on itself. Paul set the flamethrower down with a weary sigh and walked back over to the body bag.

"We going out the easy way?" he asked, picking it up with surprising tenderness.

"If you aren't too tired." Gabriel scooped Amanda into his arms.

"I can manage one more round."

They stepped over to the wall and waited. "Pull your thoughts in close again, little mouse," Gabriel whispered as they heard the door give way. Paul appeared to vanish, and Amanda felt Gabriel gathering the shadows close around them. Once the officers stopped pouring into the room, Paul and Gabriel simply walked out.

CHAPTER TWENTY-EIGHT

They parted ways quickly, Paul saying something about needing to get back to his fiancée. Awkwardly, Amanda thanked him for his help, still not sure who or what he was. He'd smiled at her, a kind, sad smile, and left, carrying his burden.

The silence was thick. Gabriel hadn't said a word since he'd brought them back to her car. Amanda sat in the passenger seat, the heavy chain deposited in the trunk, watching streetlights go by.

"I've never heard of a vampire calling the police before," she said finally.

Gabriel gave a quiet laugh.

"What will happen to Nicholas?"

"He'll be dazed and vague, and between the diagram on the floor and a few choice things he 'overheard,' I'm sure they'll figure he was kidnapped by devil-worshipers or something similar. Very traumatic for someone so young. His 'suicide' will have to be sooner than I had planned," Gabriel mused. "They're sure to send him to therapy."

"Afraid they'll break your hold on him?" Amanda could not quite hide her disdain.

He barked a laugh. "No, of course not. But the devil-worshipers didn't have him long enough to instill that kind of conditioning, and while he's a very sweet boy, his lack of free will becomes very obvious very quickly if he has to talk for any length of time."

"I see." She had gotten rather perversely fond of Nicholas over the course of the evening, but the only thing that came to mind was *Aww, can't we keep him?* Instead, although she really wasn't, she said, "I'm sorry about Briggs."

Gabriel sighed. "I don't think there are any more of them. I didn't see anyone in Tawny's mind that wasn't already accounted for. Would've been pretty dumb to split their numbers, anyway. Although I think they had the majority of the experienced vampire hunters in the country hiding out in that slaughterhouse—I'm rather flattered."

"Who is Paul?"

His face closed down until she couldn't read it at all. "If you want to know, ask him. They're his secrets to tell, not mine." He pulled into the parking lot of her apartment.

"And Isolde?"

Gabriel shut his eyes, and for the first time since she'd known him he looked almost human with weariness. "My adopted daughter."

"Oh." Amanda didn't know what else to say, so she gave him the only comfort she could think of. She kissed him.

* * * *

Cecelia blinked and raised her head, certain that she'd just heard the back door. She rolled over to look at the clock and was not surprised to find Paul's half of the bed empty, but the time made her sit up with a frown. It was after 4 a.m.; the sky was already beginning to glow with the first hints of dawn.

Paul was not exactly a morning person.

More sounds, muffled movements. Cecelia climbed out of bed, wincing at her stiff back and trying to stretch the ache away as she threw on her robe and went out into the hall. She didn't bother with the light until she came to the kitchen and saw the dark footprints scattered on the linoleum, some near the cabinets and some in the hall, but most clustered around the basement door. An odd sort of ripping sound drifted up the stairs.

She turned on the light to get a better look and caught her breath. *That is definitely blood.*

"Paul?" she called down the stairs, her voice quavering, half wanting to run down and see if he was hurt, and half afraid it wasn't him at all. The sound stopped. "Are...are you all right?"

There was a pause so long Cecelia thought her heart might burst with anxiety, but then he spoke. "I'm not injured."

His voice was heavy, dull and lifeless, and she darted down the stairs before he could try and forbid her. That would just make her angry, and she didn't want to be angry right now; she wanted to help, if she could. She'd never heard him sound so hopeless.

Cecelia came to the bottom of the stairs and followed the tacky stains into the unfinished laundry room. Paul knelt on the floor beside a sheet-covered shape that could only be a body. She'd seen enough TV shows to know what one looked like, but the shock of seeing one in her basement made her stop short, her breath catching in her throat. She'd been to a few funerals and wakes, but this was different. You expected dead bodies at funerals.

With an effort, she wrenched her gaze upward, and the gasp got caught on the breath already stuck in her throat so that she nearly gagged. His shirt, his arms, his pants, and his face, dear God, his face...all caked with sticky, drying blood, so thick his moustache and beard were stiff with it.

She'd let him bite her before, of course, since he'd told her about being half vampire last December, but that had been just a little blood while they made love, nothing like...no one could have lost that much blood and...Cecelia squeezed her eyes shut and forced herself to breathe while she counted to ten.

When she opened her eyes again, Paul was trying to wipe off his face with an old towel, dipping a corner of it into a punch bowl full of murky water. The sheet covering the body on the floor had been one of the ones she kept for the bed in the guest room, the one with the little pink flowers. It had scarlet handprints on it now.

"You hated those sheets," Paul said, dropping the towel next to him. There was absolutely no emotion in his voice, and his eyes were, if not dead, the next thing to it.

"No." She spoke without thinking. "Don't you use that tone of voice. Not with me, Paul."

His lips curled upwards at the corners, just a little, but it was a sad smile, full of regrets. Streaks of blood ran like wounds across his face, but... Her eyes were playing tricks on her. She knuckled them roughly and blinked hard, but the illusion remained.

"You look younger," Cecelia said slowly, with a weak half-laugh. "But I must be imagining things." *It's the shock, and just having woken up. And the lighting. And the blood.*

"I am younger." His tone hadn't changed. "I ate someone, Cici."

Hearing him use her pet name in that deadpan voice was like a punch in the gut, almost worse than what he actually said. "Is...is that..." She pointed at the sheet, and swallowed hard.

"No." He looked down at it, and for the first time she heard a hint of emotion. "This is my sister. Isolde."

Paul's voice broke as he said the name; his face was the same frozen mask. Cecelia was only a little sensitive, but she tried to reach out, tried to get past the barrier he'd put between them. Even that light brush made her knees give out, grief and anguish and rage slamming her like a Mack truck.

And then it was gone. Paul's head was bowed, his hands clenched into fists. "I'm sorry." He picked up a bundle of cloth and ripped a long, ragged strip from it. Cecelia recognized the bottom sheet from the set, and she thought absurdly that even in his extremity, he wouldn't ruin her good sheets. *He's always been thoughtful like that.*

"Tell me," was all she could think to say. "Please?" *Please stop shutting me out. Please stop acting like I've already lost you.*

Paul glanced at her, hesitating, and hope rose in her chest, but he shook his head. "There's no time." He tore off another strip. "I have to have her somewhere safe by sunrise. Somewhere she can burn without bringing too much attention." He reached for the sheet covering the body, and hesitated again. "You might want to go upstairs."

I won't run from this. For better or worse, Paul. I told you that. But she couldn't get the words out. She shook her head.

Paul peeled the sheet back as if the form underneath was only asleep and he was afraid to wake her. Cecelia stifled a cry of disgust. The corpse was definitely that of a woman, but human? No. The skin was wrinkled and leathery like a rotten plum, dark with age and shriveled like a dying balloon. The head rested at an odd angle, and the lips had pulled back from the teeth to expose the long, white fangs. Half of her chest was nothing but a gaping hole, broken ribs jutting up like fractured girders, with something dark shoved down at the bottom. Cecelia didn't look to see what it was.

Paul was stripping what looked like bandoliers of knives from around wrists and waist and thighs, pulling more knives out from the supple leather boots, and more still from who knew where. She wasn't sure where he was finding them all.

He kept hold of the last one and carefully cut away the shirt covering the corpse's—*Isolde, he said her name was Isolde*—Isolde's chest, or what was left of it. His lips tightened, but he didn't look at Cecelia. He sliced into the muscle just above the breast while Cecelia covered her mouth, trying not to be sick. A moment later, he teased out something small and oblong, about the size and shape of a vitamin pill. A glimmer of gold shone through the dark fluid that covered it.

Paul stared at the little golden thing. "You still had it," he whispered. "Damn you, Isolde, you could've summoned me. Even if you were afraid of leading Father into a trap, you could've summoned *me*." His hand closed into a fist.

His pain was so palpable Cecelia could feel it like pressure on her skin. She tried to reach out to him, to touch his arm, but he moved away. He shoved the thing into his pocket, picking up his torn sheet. Stung by his rejection, Cecelia turned her head away, blinking back sudden tears.

"Cici."

There was a hint of pleading in the name. She took a deep breath and met his gaze.

His gray eyes were lifeless as stone. "I can't yet," he said. "Not yet. Will you help me?"

She tried to look brave. "What do you need me to do?"

"Will you hold her head still while I put the bandages on?"

Her skin crawled with the thought of touching the dead woman, but she took another breath and nodded.

She hadn't realized the head was severed, and watching Paul line up the stumps was nearly enough to make her vomit. But she kept it down, and when Paul indicated she should hold the head in place, she did so with hardly any hesitation. Isolde's hair was thick and loose, and Paul swept it back before wrapping the torn strips under Isolde's arms and up around her head and under her chin, binding the head to the body. Soon it was secure enough that Cecelia could scamper back, trying not to wipe her hands on her bathrobe.

When he was satisfied with his work, Paul arranged Isolde's hair so it gathered to one side, the long strands half hiding the damage to her chest. Then he wrapped her in the top sheet and picked her up, cradling her against his chest with one hand holding her head to his shoulder.

"Will you get the door for me?" he asked without looking at Cecelia.

God, she couldn't stand this coldness, this distance. This was not her gentle Roman, her tender, loving fiancé. "Only if you promise you'll come back," she said desperately. "Promise me you'll come back when you're done and tell me what happened."

He looked at her then, but his storm-gray eyes were too cloudy for her to read. "I promise."

* * * *

Amanda stood in the entryway of her apartment. Gabriel had left for the night a short time ago. It hadn't been hard to keep him distracted.

He had sympathized when she told him how Elizabeth had weakened her, and while they sported in her bed he had refused to drink from her. She was glad of his consideration, whatever his motives were—without the true sharing of blood their thoughts did not intertwine, and she was afraid he would have sensed some of her intention if they had.

She had drunk from him, though. She could still almost feel his hands where they had cradled her head, holding her close as she drank from his neck, or his wrist. At first he had been gentle, almost tender in his uncharacteristic melancholy, but after a while he had made it a game, showing her the best places from which to feed.

"This will be good practice for you."

"I don't need to practice."

"So you say. Indulge me."

"If I indulge you much more, you'll go blind."

"Very funny. Now, the bend of the elbow…where are you going?"

"This one looks more fun."

"That's the femo…" His eyes had closed. "Oh, yes. That one's good, too. That one's *very* good…"

Amanda shook the memory away. It was the only time she could think of when she had drunk from him without him drinking from her. It had felt wonderful. She had taken him again, and again, and again, shamelessly giving him pleasure because it served her needs, fed her, made her strong. She wondered if that was what feeding was like for him. She rather thought it was.

Imagine living your whole life like that—taking what you want, giving only what you want to give. Using people up and throwing them away, because it really is just all about you. Your needs. Your desires.

I want that. What girl doesn't want the world at her feet?

The sun rose, and the vampire faded from her consciousness. Amanda staggered under the weight of the dawn, fighting the day sleep. The light seared her eyes as she forced herself out into the parking lot.

But whatever I want, it will be on my terms, dammit. This has gone too far. I killed people last night. The gun wasn't in my hand, but it was my will that pulled the trigger.

Amanda made it to her car and fumbled the key into the lock of the trunk.

They were trying to help me, and I killed them. She should feel something about that, she was sure, but the thought rang hollow. It was the numbness that scared her, not her actions.

She slammed the trunk lid closed, the chain dragging behind her as she struggled back to the building. It was easier going out of the day than in. At least the buildings kept her in shadow.

It wasn't much better inside. Weeping, she crawled to her apartment door, pushed it open. Forgot about the chain, tried to shut the door. Cursing, she pulled the chain through, locked the door. The hallway to the bedroom had never seemed so long.

No one else was ever supposed to get hurt. This has to end, she whispered to herself as she made her slow, painful way to the bedroom. *I won't play this game anymore. I refuse.*

The sight of the bed gave her strength. Amanda shoved the rumpled sheets aside and hoisted the chain onto the mattress. She grinned maniacally as she wove the length of it through the bars of her wrought-iron headboard.

When the shackles hung with the right amount of slack—just enough so that she could touch her hands together—Amanda dug the key out of her pocket. She popped the plastic back off of her alarm clock, tucked the key in amongst the electronics, and put the clock back together. Back in its usual spot on her nightstand it was out of reach of her hands, but not her feet.

"I doubt he'll look there," she whispered as she lay down. "And if he does, well, I'll just have to not let him use it."

She closed the shackles around her wrists, and surrendered to sleep.

* * * *

The hole in the ground looked big enough to swallow a cathedral. Paul stood at the edge of the surface mine, well back from his sister's body. The sun seethed just below the horizon, ready to boil over at any moment.

He'd swept a section of stone free of the sand and gravel they produced here, and Isolde lay with her hands folded over her abdomen, a penny under her tongue. There'd been no time to find a more suitable coin, and copper was traditional. He'd opened and closed her eyes, called her name the proscribed three times, given her the last kiss.

"It's all out of order," he told her now, as they waited, "but it's the best I could do."

He'd left her one blade, clasped between her hands. The blade was spellforged and he knew it wouldn't burn, but he couldn't send her on without one. Even as a street urchin, he'd never known her not to have at least one.

Father did his part, Paul thought as the sun crested the horizon. *This duty is my charge.*

The sun's rays scourged him, but he was his mother's son as well as his father's. Just as Night would not claim him, neither could Day call forth the fire from his blood.

Isolde's fire was gone, but she burned all the same.

When it was done, he gathered what little remained and took it home.

Cecelia was waiting for him, perched on the edge of the couch like a bird waiting for the cage door to open. She'd scrubbed down the floors. The house reeked of bleach.

His heart shuddered, looking at her. He didn't think he could survive losing them both, and he didn't see how she would want him to stay. It was too soon; she hadn't even known his nature for six months. How could he expect her to accept the fact he'd murdered a man?

But she took his hand, dried blood and ash and all, and drew him down next to her.

"Tell me, Paul, please. I have to know. Who was she?"

He could deny her nothing, not today. "I have always been between two worlds, since the day I was born." He took a deep breath. "Isolde was the only one who was between worlds with me, even if we were between different worlds. The only one."

And he told her how Isolde had tried to steal his father's purse, back in the days when she'd just been a skinshifter, before Paul's Liberalia. He told how her desperate desire to be a Roman had tied her to them, how they'd trained together, how Isolde had taught him to pick pockets, and he'd taught her to use a sword. How she'd risked her own life to save his father's. How she'd lost that life later, trying to save them both, and how his father had brought her over at such terrible, terrible cost. The years they'd spent together, brother and sister, a matched set of assassins, mercenaries for hire. And that final, brutal battle at Constantinople, when she turned her back on him because he would not let her die.

And when the telling was done—hours or days later, it was all the same to him—he touched Cecelia's cheek with one finger, tracing the line of her tears. *She is crying for me.* His own tears had been beaten out of him centuries ago.

"I wanted to hold on," he told her, silently begging her to understand. "I wanted to be human for you, but I can't. I'm not strong enough. I've never been strong enough." He shook his head as Cecelia tried to speak. "It was good, being older than you. I age so much more slowly. We could've had those years together openly, but now I'll be too much younger than you to be your husband that much sooner." He hung his head. "I tried but I couldn't...even if this hadn't happened, I couldn't..."

She laid a finger over his lips. "You told me you're not human, Paul. I knew that when I agreed to marry you, even if it was the man I fell in love with, and not the monster." She hesitated, and the tinfoil and sweat taste of her nervousness belied her calm words. "So the killing makes you younger?"

He nodded, spellbound, too weary to hope.

"And the one who killed Isolde. Is that the one you...ate?" She swallowed.

"Yes." He couldn't keep his voice level, the word coming out as a fierce hiss.

Cecelia only nodded. "Good." She stood, and pulled him to his feet. "If you shave off your beard people will think that's why you look different. And maybe we can bleach your temples a bit, give you some gray." She looked him up and down while he gaped at her. "Let's get you cleaned up, and then we'll go to bed and deal with it later. I think we can both use some sleep, don't you?"

CHAPTER TWENTY-NINE

Monday, June 7th, 1999

Amanda thrashed mindlessly on the mattress, her body still trying to get away from the pain that was eating her up from inside. For a time she had fought the pain, fought to remain still, but now was satisfied with just staying silent. She was barely aware of the manacles binding her to the iron headboard anymore. How long had it been since she had cuffed herself to the bed? One night? Two? She longed for the oblivion that daylight brought, when the weight of the sun pressed her down into unconsciousness and she could no longer feel her own blood trying to consume her. She had acid in her veins now, burning her, etching her insides, and yet she was so cold. So very cold. She needed warmth, heat. She needed life...*no, I must not think that!* She tried to separate herself from the pain, tried to focus on what had become her mantra. *I will not scream, I will not scream, I will not...*

Gabriel was at her side. She did not remember him arriving. His cool presence made her shiver harder. *So cold. So cold.*

"Tell me where you hid the key and I will bring you blood."

His voice caressed her ears, cajoling, but held no power over her. She knew the haze of pain around her kept him out of her head, and she was pathetically grateful for it now—she could not have resisted him if he could've touched her mind. She ignored his words—she barely recognized them as having meaning—and kept her eyes tight shut. He had brought a hacksaw once—was it just once? She couldn't remember—but she had kicked at him and shrieked with her thoughts and grabbed at the blade where he tried to saw through the links. The pain had been no worse than what she went through now. At least it had been an honest pain of serrated flesh, not this unholy consumption. Maybe he'd brought another hacksaw? The thought cheered her. *I will not scream, I will not scream...*

Gabriel had been so angry that first night, when he'd come bursting in. She'd still been full of his blood then, the hunger at bay. What an odd thought, that such a short time ago she had not spent every waking moment trying not to scream, trying not to reach out to those who lived around her, to bring them to her, to fill her up with their rich, dark blood...

She screamed soundlessly, because it felt better than just lying there. *I should not have kicked the pillows off the bed,* she told herself quite seriously. *I should have kept one to smother my screams. I will remember that, should I ever find myself in this position again.* She giggled, and could not stop.

Angry, yes. Gabriel had been very angry. Now he was trying to bribe her. As if a little blood would make her give up, after all this. He had threatened her but that hadn't worked either, because she had simply reminded him that he had promised not to hurt her. He could not call the police, as he had with the vampire hunters, because Amanda was perfectly willing to tell them everything—and she could make them believe it.

She could smell blood now. Had Gabriel come back? Had he left? She was unsure. Her fangs had extended some time ago, but her ravaged lips refused to bleed anymore. Now her teeth trembled in their sockets as her gums tightened. Oh, that smell. Not quite fresh, no, not dripping from the body, not running in rivulets from a still-beating heart, no, but it would do. Almost fresh. Almost life. She needed life. The smell was warm in her nostrils. Warm. *So cold.* Her bones were icicles.

The mattress creaked under the vampire's weight. A gentle hand lifted her head. A cup was placed at her tattered lips. Sounds reached her ears, but made no sense. Bloodsmell like a truck running her over. Liquid touched her lips, and the broken flesh soaked it up, healing, before it could pass into her mouth. Then ambrosia on her tongue, coating her throat. Warmth flooded her, melting her bones, soothing the pain. The balm of the blood brought life back to her limbs, and she realized she hadn't been able to feel her fingers for...for a long time. The joints creaked as she flexed them.

As the pain receded, the vampire moved in. His mind caressed hers and she welcomed it. Sounds resolved themselves into words, feelings tugged at her that weren't hers. *Come back to me, little mouse. Come back to me. Open your eyes...*

Her eyes cracked open before she could think better of it. It had been a while since she'd had to think and she was a little slow. Gabriel's face swam into focus, expressionless as always. She licked her lips slowly, trying to form the words in her mind. Her throat felt too thick and full for speech.

When? she asked once she remembered the sound. *What day?*

"Four days left, little mouse," he murmured. "Four days remain."

She closed her eyes. *Then leave me be.*

"I will not!" Hands gripped her shoulders, shaking her. She let him. No pain compared with what she had already been through. "Six days you lay here before you became weak enough for me to cut you free. Six nights since you have fed. By all the gods, there's almost nothing left of you." The last words were hissed. He continued in a more controlled tone, low and growling. "But you are not free of me yet, do you understand? You are still mine, Amanda."

She laughed softly. *Never yours.*

The apartment's buzzer sounded harsh in the quiet. The bed bounced as Gabriel got up. There was a gleam in his eye she did not like.

Leave it, she called after him, but he didn't answer.

Amanda lifted her hand from where it lay on her stomach. A few links of chain still dangled from the cuff. He had cut her free. She stretched, coming more awake. Voices in the living room, footsteps drawing near. A shrill, angry, and all-too-familiar voice was coming toward the bedroom. Amanda tried to roll over and had marginal success. *Don't let her come in here, Gabriel!*

Tell her yourself.

Brandy stormed into the room in a cloud of angry perfume. She gasped when she saw Amanda, her anger instantly becoming worry. The taste of the emotions made Amanda giddy, but she scuttled away from her friend as Brandy rushed to her. Brandy's heart was racing, bloodsmell flowing from pulse points near the skin. Amanda tried not to snarl. Life. Life and blood and heat...the cupful had not been enough. Of course it hadn't, how could it be? Brandy would make her strong... Amanda shook her head.

"You need to leave, Brandy." Was that her voice? That thick, inhuman growl? Well, what did she expect, she hadn't used her voice in days.

"What happened to you? Did he do this? If you've harmed her—" Brandy rounded on the vampire, and Gabriel pounced. Too fast for even Amanda to follow, Gabriel pulled Brandy to him, one hand on the back of her neck, the other at her waist.

"Gabriel, no!"

Amanda caught his eye for a moment, but he only snarled at her. Brandy saw his fangs and screamed, and Gabriel buried them in her throat.

Amanda's breath caught as the wave of fear and pain rolled over her. Brandy continued to scream, more hoarsely now, and the sound rang sweetly in Amanda's ears. Life…

Death, the vampire hissed to her. *She is sweet and strong. Her death on my tongue…or yours…she would fill you, little mouse.* Gabriel pulled away, blood dripping from his mouth, running over his chin. His gaze caught hers and held it as easily as he had the first time. She was so weak…

You have almost destroyed yourself in trying to escape me, and where has it gotten you? Your friend dying at my hands and you too weak to fight me. Can you resist her blood even now?

Brandy's screams had died off into pathetic croaks. Amanda bit her lip hard, tasted blood as her fangs tore the skin. Trembling with weakness, she pushed herself up to her hands and knees. She burned with hunger. She needed strength and had none, no reserves left.

Gabriel shoved Brandy toward the bed. "You chose to do this to yourself," he hissed. The girl stumbled to her knees, the bleeding wound face level with where Amanda crouched on the mattress. "Let's see if you can handle the consequences."

The smell of Brandy's blood literally hurt her, clawing at her senses. *Not Brandy! Please, anything but this!*

There is power in sacrifice, and self-sacrifice.

The memory of those words was like a lifeline. Amanda flung open the doors of her soul, felt herself standing at the edge of a great dark ocean, and the dark was looking at her. Desperately, Amanda offered up everything she was save one all-consuming desire. *Please. Anything but this.*

The ocean rose up, a great wave crashing into her, through her. It was cold, so cold it hurt as much as fire, but it swept away the hunger and the burning in her veins. It scoured Amanda's insides of fear, of worry for Brandy, of the emotional ties that weighed her down, until she was cleansed and empty of everything except the choice she was about to make.

Amanda gave herself up to it, snatching at Brandy and pressing her still-bleeding lips to the wound in her friend's throat.

Gabriel closed his eyes, snarling, every muscle tight with the rush of her surrender.

Amanda shoved Brandy aside, her own potent blood smeared across her friend's skin, and launched herself at the vampire.

I won't murder her, and I won't let you, either! she shrieked as she collided with him. She fastened her teeth on his throat, tearing into him even as he slammed into the wall behind him. *I'll kill you, you son of a bitch!*

The vampire roared, tearing at her arms where she clung to him, but she would not let go. Blood poured from him, stolen blood, stolen life, but as precious to him as it was to her. *I'll drain you dry! I'll squeeze you like a sponge!* Amanda screamed, the words ripping at his mind. He slumped-ed against the wall with a cry of anguish, clutching at his head.

But then the icy tide receded, and her strength failed. Amanda's assault faltered as her energy fled. Gabriel's hands clamped onto her face. He forced her head back, her fangs slipping out of his flesh with a slick *pop*. He kicked her feet out from under her and she fell, pulling him down. He landed on top of her, and then he had her hands held down against the floor.

She watched the bleeding in his neck slow, and knew she had not weakened him enough. *I'm sorry, Brandy.* "Well? Kill me, then!"

"Are you so eager to die?" Gabriel hissed.

"I will not be forced into this! I won't do it, Gabriel!"

The blazing fury in his eyes flickered and went cold. "You would truly rather die than become a vampire?"

"Yes! I will not submit to you, Gabriel. It's my choice, and I'd rather die." She spat the words at him, glaring. "Release me, Gabriel. One way or another, let me go!"

He looked down at her for a moment before answering. She thought she heard regret in his voice, but then it might have been admiration. "As you will."

She turned her head to the side so she wouldn't see him strike. Tearing pain as Gabriel bit deep. She let him sweep her away, until darkness came to claim her for its own.

CHAPTER THIRTY

Thursday, June 10th, 1999

Amanda woke. This was so unexpected that at first she thought she must be dead. Her brain was fuzzy, though not as bad as it had been after the six days of starvation. The light was dim, but as she gathered her wits and looked around, she recognized Gabriel's apartment.

This led to her second thought, that he had made her into a vampire after all, in spite of everything. She was able to dismiss this quickly enough, but the initial spike of fear that lanced through her heart alerted the vampire.

You should be sleeping, he chided her from somewhere in the city. *You need your strength. Tomorrow will be time enough to talk.*

Still somewhat disoriented, Amanda tried to argue.

Getting back to your normal self, I see. He was clearly amused. *Obey me just this once more. Sleep.*

She had no strength to fight him, and no will to do so. Amanda closed her eyes and slept.

* * * *

Amanda woke to a brief jolt of pain. She opened her eyes to see Gabriel bending over her.

"Sorry," he said, pressing a wad of gauze against her arm. "I haven't had much practice." He put a piece of surgical tape over the gauze to hold it in place. He picked up the discarded IV and moved into the kitchen. He threw the bag, tubing, and needle into the trash, then came back around the counter and sat down on one of the stools.

Amanda sat up and looked around. There was a metal stand next to the bed, the kind you saw in hospitals holding bags like the one he had just thrown away. She looked down at her taped arm. She was even wearing pajamas. She met the vampire's neutral gaze quizzically.

"How do you feel?" he asked.

She had to think about it. "Other than confused? Groggy, mostly. Thirsty." She swallowed. "How come I'm not dead?"

Gabriel finally cracked a smile, albeit a small one. "Let's see how you handle some water." Without answering the important question, he got a glass from the cupboard and filled it at the sink.

Amanda rather expected him to sit down on the bed when he brought it to her, but he retreated to the stool. She looked at the glass doubtfully, remembering the last time she had drunk water. She took a small sip.

It tasted like water this time, anyway. It was cold going down. At first her stomach wasn't quite sure what to do with it, but after a moment, it subsided. When she was sure it was going to stay down, Amanda started in on the rest of the glass.

"Easy," cautioned Gabriel. "Your stomach will have shrunk some in the past few weeks. Don't overdo it."

She nodded reluctantly. She held the glass in both hands and looked at him. He stared back, face unreadable, eyes hooded, their bond tightly shielded.

"Gabriel, why am I not dead?" she asked again, gently.

He considered her, picking his words with care. "You gave me your life," he said. "I choose to give it back to you."

I gave you my death, she thought to herself. *But who am I to complain?* Out loud, she said gravely, "Thank you. Why?"

He paused, and she wasn't sure he was going to answer. "I think Isolde would've liked you very much," he said at last. "You're too stubborn for me to bully."

Amanda, listening to his words, thought she should feel something, but she didn't know what. She was empty, dissociated, and too tired to try and make him stop dancing around her question. "What happened to Brandy?"

Again the tiny smile. "That was clever, healing her like that. You saved her life. I certainly wasn't thinking about her. I made her forget and sent her home. She was probably sick for a day or two."

Amanda's smile echoed his. "Again, thank you."

His gaze wandered to the metal stand. "I wasn't sure if it would work," he told her. "This could not have been done when last I had a fledgling."

She rubbed her arm. "You gave me a transfusion?"

"Three of them."

She gave a start at that, and he met her eyes for a moment, before his gaze slid lower. His voice was distant, and a little rough. "I nearly killed you on Monday night, I took so much. There was very little human left in you by then, though. Do you realize that you would've turned if I'd drained you that night? You were so contaminated that the first transfusion didn't take. The blood became tainted."

Amanda couldn't quite repress a little shiver at how close she'd come, but she couldn't pinpoint what had prompted the response at first. It wasn't fear… *No, for a minute I thought I felt that ocean watching me again. Whatever that was.*

Gabriel either ignored her reaction or didn't notice. "On Tuesday night, I did it all again. The second transfusion worked better; I could taste the difference on Wednesday when I took you one last time. You were much more human." His gazed passed over her in cool, impersonal appraisal. "The third transfusion seems to have done the trick. My blood's too thin now to affect you. You even woke up for a little while last night, while I was out for supplies."

"I remember," she murmured. "Is today Friday, then?"

"It is. The last day of the fourth week."

Amanda looked down at the glass in her hands. "So now what?"

"Well, do you have any intention of changing your mind, now that your life is yours again?"

Her head jerked up. She glared at him. "No!"

This time he grinned at her, a broad, playful grin that for once held no edge of malice or mockery. She glared at him for a little longer, but when she felt the corners of her mouth start to turn up, she gave in and grinned back at him.

"Then you're free of me, Amanda," he said. "Congratulations."

"Um, thanks." She wasn't sure what to say, and covered by drinking the rest of the water. "What happens now?" she finally asked.

"I could make you some soup if you like," he offered with a straight face.

She threw the empty glass at his head, knowing he would catch it. He did.

"Seriously, though," he continued, setting the glass on the island, "what happens is you go back to your life. I go back to mine. You will see me, or not, precisely as much as you wish. Just like I said."

"And if I never wanted to see you again, I would not?"

"You would not." He hesitated. "I do want you to know, though. Once I give my protection to someone, that doesn't go away. If you should ever need my help, you have only to let me know."

"Did you give your protection to Elizabeth?" Amanda asked, her voice just as neutral as his had been.

"No. Elizabeth was a special case." He grimaced. "I never should've turned her. I did it as a punishment."

"For putting the spell on you?"

"She told you that?" he asked, then shrugged. "Yes. She didn't realize what I was, and nearly killed me in her ignorance."

"She said you were a demon."

Gabriel smiled. "I am. All vampires are. But not demons in the way you mean it."

"So not damned souls, or whatever?"

"No." He laughed, a wry twist to his lips. "I'm not damned. Quite the opposite, really. Elizabeth never understood that part." He shook his head. "I should have just killed her, but breaking her was so very satisfying."

"I tried to kill you, you know."

"Elizabeth actually had a chance of succeeding," he replied, a gleam of humor in his eye. "A not-quite-vampire after a six-day fast had no chance." He poked a finger in her direction. "And don't look a gift horse in the mouth. You never know when I might come in handy."

Amanda had to laugh. "I think...I think I would like to see you again, at some point. But I'm going to need some time..."

"It's the height of summer," he replied dismissively. "Spend time with your friends, soak up some sun. Hang out at the beach." He grinned as she wrinkled her nose. "Or maybe the pool."

"Definitely the pool," she muttered. She didn't think she'd be up for a trip to the beach again for a long, long time.

CHAPTER THIRTY-ONE

Saturday, September 4th, 1999
Three months later

The sun beat down on Amanda's face. Her eyes were closed, and her head tipped back where she slouched in the wooden deck chair. The heat and humidity didn't bother her like they used to. Not much did. *Not even the sun.* Sweat trickled down her spine, just as it ran down the sides of her iced tea glass. She didn't drink alcohol much, anymore. Couldn't stand the loss of control.

Robbie sat in the chair next to hers, his presence a pressure against her shields. His defenses had improved since Memorial Day, but that seemed to be because he was less nervous, more guarded, more wary, than he had been then. Chi hadn't told him yet, she was almost sure. *I'd like to be a fly on the wall for that conversation. "Hey, Robbie, guess what? You're psychic. But that's okay, 'cause I am too."*

She cracked an eyelid and looked over at Chi. He was seated at the table with Penny, both of them shaded by a giant umbrella, safe from the ravages of the great carcinogen in the sky. Chi was explaining something to Penny which involved lots of hand gestures and diagrams sketched on cocktail napkins. Penny had her brave face on, but she was nodding and at least pretending interest.

Amanda's gaze flicked over to her father. He was manning the grill, as usual, and ignoring them all, as usual, but it was the relaxed ignoring of a master craftsman at work. The Zen of Charcoal radiated from him, bathing the others in a calm, mellow mood. *Well, except maybe Chi.* The aura lapped at her shields like wavelets against the lakeshore on a calm day, but she politely declined to be influenced.

"Thanks for organizing all this," Robbie said out of the corner of his mouth.

She tipped her glass toward him. Beads of cool water shivered over her fingers. "No problem."

"No, really." He took a swig from his beer bottle, but otherwise didn't move, basking in the sun. "I really appreciate it."

Amanda closed her eyes again. The relaxing, lethargic heat soaked into her muscles, but couldn't quite penetrate to the core of her. That part of her was always cool and dark. "It was nothing."

It hadn't been nothing, and they both knew it, but Robbie had no idea how many long, agonizing phone conversations Amanda had sat through, or just how hard she'd had to push before Penny had finally "decided" to see a therapist. Amanda figured it would take better if Penny thought it was her own idea. *God, Mom can be stubborn.* She'd had to implant the suggestion five or six times, which meant she was coming home nearly every other weekend.

I should've done it before I got human again. It would've been so much easier.

But it had finally stuck, and Robbie had been able to get leave, and was willing to get leave, and here they were. Nearly four hours and no one had even raised their voice. A new Bairns record. They weren't talking about The Big Issue, but hey, she wasn't a miracle worker.

"How did you ever convince Mom to see a shrink?" Robbie's already low voice was barely above a whisper.

"It was her idea."

"No, really, tell me."

Amanda opened one eye, just a brief flicker, and closed it again. "Ask Chi."

Robbie made a soft, annoyed huffing sound. "He's not fond of you."

That's okay, I don't like him, either. "As long as he makes you happy, bro."

There was a ceramic clatter that Amanda knew well, the sound of her father picking up the serving plate from the prep table. The tongs made a metallic click as he snapped them once before beginning to transfer the meat off the grill. Chicken this time, the skin seared crispy and then basted with generous brushfuls of Open Pit barbeque sauce. Amanda's stomach rumbled.

"Dinner's about ready," Daniel called over his shoulder.

She'd had exactly one conversation with her father about the whole psychic thing. Once, while Penny was out of the room, Amanda had asked if he believed in ESP. "Your Uncle Stu bought into that nonsense," he'd replied after a moment. "Do you know, he used to swear we used to talk to each other in our heads after lights out, me in my room and him in his?" Her father snorted. "He dreamed it, but he sure was insistent."

"So you never heard him?"

"No." There was too much emphasis. He swallowed, and gave a weak smile. "No, I never did." He paused, and then, almost as if he couldn't help saying it, he added, "You'd think, if there was anything to all that, he'd've known that car was coming."

There was a touch of sick bitterness in Daniel's voice. Amanda remembered then that it was her father who had always found her when she was hiding in the woods, who'd always known where to look for her. And she also remembered the comments—some teasing, some chiding—from her dad's family about how, though Stu was the one who knew who was at the door before they knocked, it was Daniel who so often picked up the phone before it rang, and knew when not to take his cycle out even though it wasn't supposed to rain.

She'd let the subject drop and never brought it up again.

Penny's chair scraped back from the table and interrupted her daughter's reverie. "Amanda, help me bring out the side dishes."

Amanda hid a smile. *Not Mandy.* That was another thing she'd fixed. It was only fair. "Sure, Mom."

The kitchen was dark after staring at the sun through her eyelids, and Amanda's vision was slow to adjust. Penny had half disappeared into the fridge. One arm stuck out, waving a Tupperware bowl. Amanda grabbed it and set it on the counter.

"Thanks, dear." Penny's head poked back out, and she handed over the container of potato salad that Amanda had brought. "I'm glad the food's ready," Penny continued in a stage whisper. "Chi was trying to explain the whole Y2K thing to me, and I thought I was going to have a seizure trying to follow him." She shook her head and ducked back behind the fridge door.

"It's all totally overblown anyway." Amanda set down the potato salad, and then a container of baked beans and bacon. "The world is not going to come crashing to a halt when the millennium changes."

"That's what he said. I think."

They ate outside at the table, enjoying the quiet of an early afternoon. The Bairnses were not much for conversation at the best of times, and eating gave them all a great excuse not to talk. Amanda bit into a chicken leg with gusto, savoring the tang of the sauce and the way the crisp skin crackled just a little under her teeth. Hot juice ran down her chin, tasting of chicken fat and her dad's dry rub seasoning. *Bliss.* To think how close she'd come to never tasting this again.

Amanda brushed a gentle thought over each of her family members in turn. It was...nice, being here. They were all happy. That was good. She wanted them to be happy. She couldn't exactly say why, but she did. There was debt between all of them. History. They were her people, and she took care of her own.

Chi was watching her out of the corner of his eye. She could tell by the way he held his head, and the sidelong glances he stole every so many seconds. She wondered how he'd managed to keep anything from Robbie, much less the brass, when he was so bad at subterfuge. Did he notice the change in her? Had he suspected her condition when they'd met three months ago, and now was wondering how she could eat? *Or does he just think I'm unstable?* She couldn't smell emotion anymore, but nervous energy rolled off of him like mosquitoes from a marsh.

She reached out with a thought. *When are you going to tell Robbie?*

Chi jumped, slapping at his arm half a second too late for it to truly have been a bug bite. *When he's ready,* came the cautious and controlled reply.

Amanda continued eating, showing no outer sign of their silent conversation. *Is that like saying you'll have kids when you can afford it?*

He frowned at her before taking another bite of chicken. *He's got a lot to deal with right now.*

He might deal better if he wasn't fighting off everyone else's thoughts all the time. Amanda set down the bare leg bone and beamed at her father. "Fantastic chicken, Dad." *Do you want me to tell him?*

No! Chi glared at her so hard that Robbie noticed. Amanda pretended not to see her brother's frown, but she let the corners of her mouth turn up just a little when Chi ducked his head in embarrassment.

"Did you hear something?" Daniel was looking around the backyard, his brow furrowed.

"I thought I heard a dog bark," Amanda replied blithely.

As Daniel shrugged and turned back to his plate, Chi shot back with a thought so narrow and pointed it might've stung if Amanda had let it through. *There's something wrong with you. I don't know what it is, but you're dangerous.*

You have no idea how right you are. She didn't let that thought past her shields. Instead, Amanda dabbed her lips with a napkin to hide her smile from Robbie. She so wanted to threaten Chi, to say that she'd gut him like a fish if he ever came against her or let her brother down. She wanted to rip into his shields and show him just how pathetic he was. Not because she was angry or anything; just to make a point. *And because it would be fun.* The smile was all she allowed herself, though. She didn't need to fabricate enemies, especially psychic ones.

Setting down the napkin, she picked up a wing from the platter. *Do you love my brother?*

Chi was obviously taken aback. His shoulders relaxed as his anger wavered. *Yes.*

She looked up and caught his eye, but didn't dare do anything with that advantage. Fascination didn't work quite the way it used to for her, and he was good enough that he'd probably notice if she tried the human version she'd used on Penny. Still, Amanda put all the solemnity she could muster into that look. *Then you watch his back, and keep him safe, and you and I will never have to worry about which one of us is more dangerous. Yes?*

Chi hesitated, then nodded. *Yes.*

Amanda broke the wing in half. Setting the drummy aside, she sucked the meat from between the two small bones and gave Chi her most winning smile. *Good.*

* * * *

The Inferno was as boisterous as it ever got, filled with students cramming in one last Leather and Lace before the start of the fall semester. Amanda had made the drive home from Point in plenty of time to get ready, since L&L didn't usually get momentum until after ten p.m. She'd once again fobbed off her parents' requests to stay the weekend, or at least the night. There were limits to her benevolence, after all, and filial affection only went so far.

She let her mental fingers brush through the minds around her as she danced, savoring the desperate abandon of people bound and determined to have a good time. She itched to burrow deeper, to dig down to the core of them, to their nightmares and worries and guilty pleasures. It would be harder now that she was just a human again, but wouldn't the challenge make it that much more rewarding?

Brandy tugged at her arm, and Amanda reluctantly pulled her feelers back in. She didn't have time for a pet, anyway. "What's up?"

"What about that one?" Brandy pointed back toward the bar.

Amanda groaned. "I really don't—"

"No, this one's perfect. He just transferred here from out east; you totally have to hear his accent, it's so cute!"

Why couldn't Brandy stop trying to set her up? Despite herself, Amanda glanced back to see just who her friend had picked this time. Deep brown eyes met hers squarely from across the room. It took Amanda less than ten seconds to break into his mind, and she didn't bother sticking around. "No."

"Aw, c'mon, you haven't even talked to him." Brandy tugged at her arm again. "I swear, you haven't been interested in men at all since you and Gabriel broke up. Was he really that good?"

"Brandy!"

"What? It's true."

Amanda shook her head. "Let it go, Brandy."

There was a mage sitting next to Mr. East Coast, and he was giving her the stink-eye. Amanda spread her hands, cast her eyes to the side, and bowed slightly from the waist, but she kept a polite, untroubled smile on her face. *Sorry, didn't realize he was with you, no offense meant,* the gestures said, but the smile indicated a lack of deference. The mage eyed her warily, then gave a short nod and turned back to his friend. She was learning the etiquette, even if Madison's mages would have nothing to do with her.

Brandy was not to be deterred. "Well, what about—"

"If I take someone home, will you lay off?" Amanda snapped.

Brandy's head jerked back as if Amanda had slapped her. Amanda sighed. She didn't want to hurt Brandy. Brandy was hers, and Amanda needed to take care of her.

"Sorry, hun," Amanda said as contritely as she could. "You know how visiting my folks puts me on edge."

Brandy's expression cleared. "Well, that's over. The family obligation is fulfilled, right? Get in the now, girl. There are *boys* to be had!" Brandy put an arm around Amanda's shoulders and pointed at the door. "Like that one."

The guy who had just come in was alone, his dark hair gelled into haphazard spikes, studded leather adorning his wrists and waist in a throwback to the punk fashions of the early part of the decade. He looked around furtively as he waited to show his ID to the doorman. Amanda reached out and touched his thoughts. He was new in town, a freshman using his older brother's driver's license, nervous about getting caught, excited for his first experience in this den of iniquity. Amanda bit back a laugh.

"If it'll make you happy." She kissed Brandy's cheek, fighting the urge to linger just a little too long. Her blood was in Brandy now, and even if the vampireness was gone, there was still a sense of...not exactly owner-ship, but obligation at least. *I saved you. That's something, isn't it? The one thing I did right.*

Brandy called after her as Amanda headed for the door, but it was easy enough to let the music swallow the words. A plan was forming in the back of Amanda's head. She reached out to the crowd as she made her way through them, gathered their passion and excitement in her mental grip. This much she could still do. She walked up to the boy where he stood in line and metaphysically clubbed him over the head.

"Hey," she said, smiling so that her teeth showed and her eyes sparkled and crinkled up at the corners. "This place won't liven up for an hour or two. Do you want to get a coffee?"

His eyes had flicked down to the low neckline of her stretchy shirt, and as soon as they flicked back up again she dropped all that energy on him like an Acme safe. He blinked and staggered, and was following her out the door before he even finished blinking.

They took his car, but she drove. As the miles slipped by, through downtown and out the other side, the boy began to get a little uneasy. Amanda deflected him with conversation and more subtle mental nudges. His name was Zeke, and he'd just moved in, barely knew anybody, grew up in Crivitz of all places, wanted out, wanted more, was going to be some-body. Amanda listened really hard, but the words just washed over her, knowledge with no meaning.

He was confused when she pulled into the parking lot for Marshall Park.

"C'mon," she urged when he hesitated. "You have to see this."

She drew him down to the water's edge, their feet sinking into the sand, then wrapped her arms around his waist. "Isn't it pretty? Your first view of the city."

"I thought we were getting coffee?" he asked with a little creak in his voice and an uncertain smile.

"There's coffee," Amanda purred, pulling him close, "and then there's coffee."

She kissed him. He was stiff at first, but as she pressed up against him, he slowly responded. His mouth opened, and his arms tightened around her, and he took a little more of her weight so she could lean into him even more. *He's done this before,* she thought, but she still wasn't feeling it. She kissed him harder, coaxing his response, but only when she actually dug into his mind did she find any satisfaction of her own.

She broke off the kiss with a sigh of disappointment. Zeke's eyes were glazed, his breath coming in heaving gasps. Amanda stroked his cheek with the back of one hand.

"Nope," she said. "It's just not working."

"What?" Zeke blinked, trying to focus, but she still had hold of his thoughts.

"It was worth a shot." Amanda frowned at him, pushing her lower lip out at one corner as she considered. "See, the problem is me, not you. It's like there's this distance between me and everyone else. I'm separated. Disconnected. I thought it was going to go away. I mean, I'd basically died, right? Agreed to die, anyway. That'll mess you up for a while, you know what I mean?"

Zeke was trying to follow, but Amanda wasn't really talking to him anyway, and her grip on his mind made it hard for him to think. "What?"

"Exactly. That's exactly how I feel. What? What the hell is wrong with me?" She traced his lips with her fingers. "I won. I get to go back to my old life. That was the agreement." Her brows drew down. "But you're all such...such *sheep.*"

Zeke blinked, frowned, tried to formulate a response, but Amanda just kept talking. "I mean, I seriously just can't relate. And the mages all look at me like I've got the plague. Elitist bastards. Did you know they think psychics are low class?" Anger crept into her tone, and the heat of it made Zeke whimper. "As if anything done without using their stupid ley lines is hick magic, or parlor tricks. If their shields weren't so damn good, I'd show them a thing or two."

He was struggling now, his eyes rolled back a little in his head, sweat breaking out on his skin.

"And just look at you. I would have *owned* you before. But the human version of fascination has to be subtle. You have to tease and suggest and plant and nurture. That's so much *work.*"

Her hand slipped into her pocket and pulled out her little folding knife. "The worst part is that your death won't bring me any power. But I have to *know.* You understand, right? It's nothing personal, but I have to know just

258

how much I gave up. If I can hug my brother, who I loved better than damn near anyone in the world, and feel nothing more than mild affection, did I lose whatever it was that made me not want to kill people in the first place? Was Elizabeth right after all?"

Zeke's eyes widened, and he tried to pull away despite her hold on him, so she dug her fingers into the muscle on the side of his neck until his knees gave out.

"Please don't!" he choked as she thumbed the blade open. "Don't hurt me!"

"See, I like that," she murmured. "That feels good. Power. Control. I like that a lot." Her eyes found the pulse jumping on the exposed side of his throat. "But I already knew that."

Her hand darted forward, and the blade slipped through skin and muscle, piercing the carotid artery like a steel fang. She twisted the knife as she pulled it free, stepping back and to the side. Blood fountained out as his heart raced, Zeke's eyes screaming denial, and as the spray made abstract patterns on the sand Amanda felt...nothing.

"Dammit," she sighed.

CHAPTER THIRTY-TWO

The blur of motion was not entirely unexpected. Zeke was wrenched from her grasp, and then Gabriel was there, his mouth covering the spurting wound, his arms wrapped around the boy, holding him up. Zeke shuddered and arched, his expression twisting from shock and pain to obscene bliss.

Amanda wiped her knife on Zeke's shirt, then closed the blade and put it back in her pocket.

A moment later Zeke went limp, and Gabriel lifted his head. Blood still smeared Zeke's skin, but the wound was gone. Gabriel let the boy fall. Zeke landed in a boneless heap and didn't move, silent except for the almost soundless breathing of deep sleep.

"Raising Madison's murder rate is not likely to elevate you in the mages' esteem," Gabriel said.

This was the first time she'd seen him since let her go. He looked exactly the same—same color-changing eyes, same tight jeans, same expressionless expression. It was to be expected, of course, but somehow it made her feel dislocated all over again, especially because he still made her feel *safe*. "I would've taken him out of the city."

He shook his head, a smile playing at the corners of his mouth. "You have a lot to learn about hiding bodies. Best leave that to me." He glanced down at Zeke. "I might keep this one. He reminds me a little of Nicholas."

"You and your pets." She cocked her head to one side. "You've been watching me."

"Of course. I'm responsible for you." He spread his hands, somehow indicating the mages and shifters without saying anything. "Thank you for not killing anyone during the day."

Amanda looked up at the night sky and frowned. "It wouldn't be the same, during the day."

The sky was a deep, deep black out beyond the light pollution, like a dark sea whose surface shimmered with stars. She could get lost in that sea if she looked too long. That had happened a few times already, mostly when she was unable to sleep and made the mistake of going out for a walk. She could still *feel* the night somehow, like a cool, refreshing breeze on her soul. It made her feel the same way that the woods used to, that she was part of something bigger, tiny but no less important than any leaf or tree or bird or squirrel.

Not that her old tree meditation seemed to work anymore. She'd tried, even in Schmeeckle a few times, but it was no different than relaxing in the sun with her brother. It was kinda nice, but nothing special. The connection was broken, superseded by this nocturnal fascination that even now threatened to distract her, soothing her frustration and confusion. She shook the comforting influence away.

Gabriel watched her with eyes that shone like stars. He said nothing.

"I haven't felt you." Amanda could've reached out with a thought, but she didn't. "I thought you said the bond was forever."

"It is." His voice was soft. Was that pity in his tone? "I've kept it blocked. I thought you might prefer some time to readjust to humanity without my presence in your head."

"I thought that, too. That's why I haven't contacted you." She looked down at her sandy shoes without seeing them. "It hasn't worked out that way though."

"Was it worth it?"

The question startled her into meeting his gaze. "I…" Sudden nervousness made her gut tighten. Did she truly want to know? She swallowed, and tried again. "It's not going to come back, is it? I mean, I used to feel stuff for people. I used to cry at sad movies and get all warm and fuzzy when I heard about random acts of kindness and feel guilty when I hurt someone. And now?" She shook her head. "I remember that it happened, but I don't remember *why*."

He raised an eyebrow. "You wouldn't feel guilty if your killing this boy made a load of trouble for me?"

Amanda pursed her lips. "Sort of. I mean, that's a respect thing. I wouldn't beat myself up about it, but I'd go out of my way to avoid putting you on the spot if I could."

"I've missed you," Gabriel said.

That made her feel better. In precisely what way, she couldn't quite grasp. The statement had none of the tenderness one might expect; it was just a fact, and spoken as such. But she had missed him too, in the same simple way.

Amanda reached out a hand and touched Gabriel's cheek. Her fingers slid down his jawbone to his chin, but his expression never changed. There was no zing, no spark, no picking up of the pulse. There was something, though. Almost like recognition. Like homecoming.

"I don't love you," she murmured, examining his face as if it would give her some clue to the questions that plagued her.

"Nor I you." He raised his hand, copying her caress, except his fingers brushed over her lips instead of her chin. "Do you remember what I said before?"

There is power in sacrifice. "No love. No compassion. No empathy."

"But there is affection. Protectiveness. Loyalty. Duty." He cupped her face with both hands, the starlight of his eyes igniting into bonfire. His lips quirked up at one corner, revealing the tip of a fang. "And desire."

He kissed her, his fangs pricking at her lips and her tongue as she kissed him back. He tasted of blood and venom and sex. Gabriel stopped shielding their bond, and awareness of him flowed into her mind like hot molasses. The sense of recognition was stronger. Here was one who understood her, who felt and failed to feel just as she did, who had power he was willing to share. Who could teach her how to conquer the world.

Amanda pulled away. Her breath came hard, and her heart pounded, and her whole body ached at his nearness, but she forced herself to stop. "So there's no fixing me?"

"If you could go back to being prey, you probably would've by now. But I can't know for sure. I'm not a god, Amanda, just a *daemon*."

She nodded. "I thought as much."

"Was it worth it?"

That question again. "If I knew then what I know now, if you'd asked me then, I probably would say it wasn't." Yes, that felt right. She'd prized her humanity so highly back then. Nor had she expected to live long enough to find out about the repercussions of her choice. "But now?" She shrugged. "I can't remember why it was so important. Looking back, all that emotion seems like such a waste of energy. I don't miss it. I just feel like I should."

He nodded, and she thought that she'd answered more for him than just the question he'd asked. "The feeling passes. It's easier once you stop trying to remember."

"So what now?"

"What do you want?"

She blinked at him. She'd been so focused on trying to recover that she hadn't considered what would happen if she couldn't. What did she want? A normal life, like the sheep? Her lip curled. *No. I want power. I want the world at my feet.*

"I don't want to be a vampire, but I want…I want to be part of that world again. And I want you." The night teased the edges of her awareness. "I wish I could be your fledgling forever."

Gabriel closed his eyes, and through their bond she felt him reaching out. Suddenly she realized that not only was the night all around her, it was teasing her through him as well. He was just another leaf in Night's forest, like she was. Gabriel let out a long, slow breath, and when he opened his eyes again, his gaze was filled with peace and calm and purpose.

"You could be my guardian."

The words rang in her ears like bells. "What does that mean?"

"You would live with me and guard me during the day. You would be my eyes and ears, my hands and mouth. My blood would sustain you as it did before, but the bond between us would tie us even tighter. Just as you could borrow my strength, I could take some of your hunger, allow you to feed through me."

Amanda swallowed hard. "And this would be permanent?"

"No. It must be maintained. There is a ritual to the blood sharing. Sympathetic magic. Abandon the ritual, and you become like any other fledgling; you can be human, or vampire, as you choose." Gabriel paused, then added, "Although, if you die with that much of my blood in you, you'll turn whether you want to or not. Assuming you aren't killed in a way that would kill a vampire, of course."

It sounded too good to be true. "Why don't you have a guardian now?"

"I rarely do. They don't tend to last long. It's a very hazardous occupation. My first guardians all died in a fire, and it…bothered me." His gaze was distant, and echoes of his disquiet rippled through Amanda's stomach. "They were mine, and I couldn't protect them. If they hadn't bought the time for Paul and Isolde to get me out, none of us would've survived."

Protectiveness. Loyalty. Duty. She understood that.

He refocused on her, as if her resolve called him out of his memories. "I am a monster, Amanda, as well you know. I kill, torture, corrupt, and destroy. As my guardian, you would also do these things."

"I know." She gave him a tiny, almost apologetic smile. "I think we've established that human morality isn't a problem for me anymore."

He returned her smile, without the apology. "Would you be willing to follow my lead without question when there is danger, and hold fast to the rules I set down when there is not? I won't coerce you, but I won't suffer insubordination either. I have two millennia of experience on you; will you trust me to know what's best?"

That was harder to agree to. Crazy, that she should agree readily to murder and torture, but balk at taking orders. *If that's the price of power...* "I'm willing."

"Thank you. Remember, my life will be in your hands as much as yours will be in mine. There will be times where you have to make decisions for both of us."

Now *that* she liked the sound of. "So what's this ritual?"

"Come."

He led her along the water's edge, leaving Zeke sprawled on the sand behind them. Gabriel picked his way along the rocky shore until he found a thicket of trees that hid them from view. "This is best done outside," he said as he guided Amanda into the dark grove.

Damn, but she missed the vampire-vision. She stumbled over roots and had to lean on Gabriel's arm to keep her feet. Slow excitement was building in her chest. She was going to do this. She was going to have that sweet, heady power she'd lost when she went human.

She was going to be strong enough that no one would be able to make her helpless ever again. *Except one. The one I choose to follow.*

My choice.

She was going to become a monster.

Gabriel turned to face her. A stray bit of moonlight caught the edge of his razor.

Amanda thought of Zeke, and her own sharp blade. *I already am a monster.*

The thought filled her with elation.

"Give me your hand," Gabriel said.

Amanda held out her right hand. The blade sliced across her wrist. Then Gabriel's wrist pressed against hers, warm blood running down his arm. She laced her fingers through his.

"We have shared blood, and flesh, and breath," he whispered, with a fierce reverence that sent shivers coursing down Amanda's spine. "We have shared thought, and life, and death."

He squeezed her hand, and she repeated the words back to him.

His grip tightened, and he spoke so softly her ears could barely catch it, but the sound echoed in her head, clear and strong. "I, Gabrielus Avidiacus, would have us be one flesh, one blood, one life. I vow to uphold you in strength, to carry the burden of your hunger, to honor and reward your service. With Night's blessing, let it be so."

She heard the capital letter this time, felt the pregnant darkness listening, as if the air around them were holding its breath. Amanda wondered if there were specific words she should say. She didn't think so. This felt like something that had to come from inside.

"I, Amanda Marie Bairns, would have us be one flesh, one blood, one life. I vow to defend your life above my own, to hold sacred your trust, and to serve you faithfully." The darkness wasn't just listening; something was building out there, an energy unlike anything she'd felt except...yes, just like the night she'd saved Brandy. An ocean of power hovering over her head. "With Night's blessing, let it be so."

The ocean swept through them, ripping wide the bond that connected them until it engulfed them, drowning them in each other, in the night that embraced them.

She tasted blood. His wrist at her mouth. Her wrist at his lips.

One blood.

Yes.

Amanda drank until the night ran thick in her veins. This was a union deeper than sex, even more primal. It wasn't just that they'd spoken vows, made promises, but that their very lives intertwined. A thousand tiny conduits formed, until she felt his breath expanding his lungs, felt his heart match itself to hers, felt her own presence inside him just as his settled into her, part of her and yet not, separate and yet part of some larger whole.

Their joining was hardly equal, however. It was as if every cell in her body, every molecule of air in her lungs, every scrap of emotion left in her head all reoriented on Gabriel, but his compass was already fixed, like a magnet that continues to point north regardless of the metal filings it attracts. Exactly what guided him was unclear to her; it was hard to think beyond him, his presence too bright to allow her to see past it.

And then that brightness folded around her like great wings, and she forgot that anything else existed.

Mine. It wasn't even a thought. It had more power than that, more resonance. She felt his blood take hold then, all at once instead of gradually. Hot and cold convulsions swept over her. Her muscles trembled and twisted and then went limp. There was pain, but it was sharp and brief, and overwashed with the sense of awakening, recognition, release. She hadn't realized how much of her still carried the infection. It had just lacked the proper catalyst.

His blood.

Our blood. One blood, one flesh, one life.

She found herself wrapped in his arms, cuddled protectively to his chest, while her limbs slowly came back under her control. The grove was no longer so dark, and she could hear the cars passing on Allen Boulevard and University Avenue, and Zeke's soft breathing from farther down the shore.

Relief flooded her, threatened to make her wobbly knees buckle completely. God, but she'd missed this. She could literally feel her muscles getting stronger, her mind expanding, the reservoir of her blood filling with power born from Night herself.

With Gabriel at her side, there was nothing they could not do.

"Careful," the vampire teased, stroking her hair. "Hubris is the leading cause of death in vampires over the age of seventy."

Amanda laughed, and the sound shivered among the leaves before echoing out over the water. "Good thing I'm not a vampire."

His tone didn't change. "Guardians usually last half that long."

"I'll keep it in mind." She raised a hand to his lips, tracing their outline with her fingers, and looked deep into his steel-gray eyes. He looked back, a silent mirror. There was emotion there; she felt it, too, something more than the pull of like calling to like. It didn't have the selflessness of love, was more mischievous than simple affection, lacked the warmth of sympathy.

Co-conspiracy, she finally realized. *Partners in crime. Maybe not equal partners, but partners, nonetheless. United by our desire to take the world by the throat and strip it of whatever we want.*

A slow grin spread across her face. She could live with that.

He leaned forward and kissed her, and even that simple touch made her belly burn with lust. Damn, she'd missed that, too.

"We should deal with Zeke first," she gasped, breaking away with a pang of regret. Her bones ached with the desire to see just how deep these new connections went, but safety and secrecy were more important. "He's just lying there for anyone to find."

"Thinking like a guardian already." Gabriel's smile was full of pride, and for once it didn't piss her off. "Come, then."

"Besides," Amanda added, picking her way over the tree roots as she followed him out of the grove, "there's plenty of time for nookie later."

Gabriel glanced back. His expression plainly said that she still had a lot to learn. "Never as much as you think, little mouse. Dawn will come." He turned and led her back toward the beach. "Dawn always comes."

ABOUT THE AUTHOR

Mercy Loomis grew up in a haunted house, and has had quite enough of ghosts for one lifetime, thank you. Though she now lives in a 150-year-old house, it is remarkably ghost-free. (That, or they're staying on the down-low. She doesn't care which.)

She finished writing her first vampire novel when she was in middle school, and hasn't stopped writing about them since. She loves stories about the paranormal because monsters are scary, but less scary than real people. Or at least less depressing.

Mercy graduated from the University of Wisconsin-Madison one class short of an accidental certificate in Folklore. She credits her love of mythology to her mom reading Greek myths as bedtime stories, and her love of fantastical adventure stories to watching cheesy movies with her dad. Her love of history (and coffee!) is completely her husband's fault, but she doesn't know who's to blame for the fascination with physics.

She guesses that hanging out with Dad while he butchered deer also had an effect on her character, but exactly what effect, she leaves up to the reader.

See what Mercy's up to and find links to her other work at her website, www.mercyloomis.com.

www.ingramcontent.com/pod-product-compliance
Lightning Source LLC
Chambersburg PA
CBHW031610240626
47153CB00002B/703